THE HISTORY OF HISTORY

THE HISTORY OF HISTORY

A Novel of Berlin

Ida Hattemer-Higgins

faber and faber

First published in the UK by Faber and Faber, 2011

First published in the US by Alfred A. Knopf, 2011

© Ida Hattemer-Higgins, 2011

The right of Ida Hattemer-Higgins to be identified as author
of this work has been asserted in accordance with Section 77
of the Copyright, Designs and Patents Act 1988

A CIP record for this book
is available from the British Library

ISBN 978 0 571 25050 9

The paper this book is printed on is certified independently in
accordance with the rules of the FSC. It is ancient-forest friendly.
The printer holds chain of custody

FSC
Mixed Sources
Product group from well-managed
forests and recycled wood or fiber
Cert no. SGS-COC-004311
www.fsc.org
© 1996 Forest Stewardship Council

2 4 6 8 10 9 7 5 3 1

Dedication to come

CONTENTS

CONTENTS

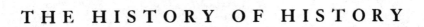

THE HISTORY OF HISTORY

PART I

Flesh

*The coming awakening stands like the Greeks' wooden horse
in the Troy of dream.*

—WALTER BENJAMIN

ONE · The Persistence of Documents

The oceans rose and the clouds washed over the sky; the tide of humanity came revolving in love and betrayal, in skyscrapers and ruins, through walls breached and children conjured, and soon it was the year 2002. On an early morning in September of that year, in a forest outside Berlin, a young woman woke from a short sleep not knowing where she was. Several months of her life had gone missing from her mind, and she was as fresh as a child.

She sat upright. Her hair was long, her clothes made for a man: stiff trousers, a slouch hat, and a long woolen overcoat, although underneath she wore a pair of high-heeled boots.

South of her chin was the body of a harem girl—a luxurious body moving lithely, ripe with the knowledge of its strength, youth, and loping good health. Her face, on the other hand, was the face of a mandarin, overcome with sensitivity and perpetual nervous fatigue. The dirty postcards of the French fin de siècle sometimes show women of this kind: even while offering their bodies with abandon, such females wear faces charged with the pathos of intellect, growing kittenish with leery, fragile, world-weary grins. All in all, Margaret looked like someone who would find trouble, or in any case already had.

The night hung low. Margaret cast her eyes about and saw the birches. She reached for her bag—a leather briefcase lying slack beside the tree she leaned against—and noticed in the movement that her hand ached. Both her hands hurt, and she did not know why.

For want of a better idea, she stood up and began to walk. Twigs cracked under her high-heeled boots. The sound startled her.

She came to a brook and put the bag on her shoulder and her hands down on the stones and picked her way across on all fours. The woolen overcoat dragged in the water. She saw by the aging moonlight that came through a break in the young pines that her palms and fingers were rubbed deeply with dirt, so deeply it looked as though they were tattooed with it, although the skin of her wrists was clean and shining.

Margaret found the edge of the forest as the day came, as the air turned grey and smoky. The slash of birdcall was shrill; it blotted out her thoughts for a while, and she stopped wondering what had happened in the night.

She found a dirt road, and then asphalt, villas, green awnings, slate roofs, wheelbarrows and hibernating rosebushes, and finally Grunewald Station.

By the time she was riding the train homeward into the city, Margaret was becoming afraid again, but after a new style. No longer did the threat sit at her throat. Now it lay in the marrow of things. She saw a perfectly miniaturized beech leaf pasted with wetness on her sleeve, and it seemed a souvenir of bad and mysterious things. She looked at her dirt-printed palms and did not know why the dirt. She shifted her body on the plastic seat and felt the drag of wet fabric, pulled aside the overcoat and heavy red scarf. She saw her clothes patched with bluish pine needles sticking to the wetness, and on the hem a displaced ladybug made its slow way, and she did not know why there was evidence of so much nature, of so much disorder.

The roofers, the chimney sweeps, the deliverymen on the early morning train—they looked at Margaret's windswept face and saw an expression rarely seen. There she was in her heavy wool, her face with its broken parts even heavier, and you could almost see it: she was crushing under the strain, trying to modernize herself to match the day. Some fine imperative had gone missing.

The S-Bahn train pulled into Zoo Station and paused. The cold air rushed through the open doors. With a heave of strength and puffed screech, an intercity train came to a halt on the neighboring track, and a platform clock struck six with an audible spasm of the minute hand. There was a chime over the loudspeaker: the announcement of departures to Lyon, to Trieste, even to Amsterdam, and the crowd on the platform shifted like a hive.

The doors shut and the train slipped into motion. Margaret looked out through the milky graffiti scratched in the window. There was the glory of the morning city, and soon, intermittent through the trees, the gilded angel in the park caught the light. A woman walked under the bridge in the Tiergarten, on cobblestones the same color as the automatic pigeons picking between them. She wore a narrow white scarf and pushed a pram, and her hair blew up toward the sky with the wind.

Margaret looked away. She looked down at her knee. She saw the red and black insect crawling there. She frowned. Her lips turned under. She felt a fury and an envy and a sense of starvation. She reached down, and with two fingers, she lifted the checkered insect and held it in her hand.

She closed her eyes, but there was no escape.

She hauled her eyes open again. Sleep frightened her as well. She looked out the window through smarting eyes, her right hand cradling the crawling beetle, and then she saw, but now in the far distance, the woman with the white scarf, and again the wind lifted the woman's hair toward the sky, and it was like a scream.

All it took was a tightening—the red and black beetle became a streak of syrup on her hand.

She could not help it: Margaret slept, sinking deeper toward the window, her knees nudging the knees of the woman opposite, the membranes of her eyelids so pale they were translucent to the shock of the sun. She dreamt terrible dreams.

She woke up at the end of the line at Ahrensfelde, in the grasses and trees again, but the morning was no longer in its early tooth, and she was on the eastern edge of Berlin instead of the west. She had slept through her transfer at Friedrichstrasse. It was a train employee who woke her. He asked to see her ticket. Margaret jerked her head up. She reached into the breast pocket of her heavy man's overcoat and found an American passport, soaked through and reeking. She fingered the pocket on the other side and found a laminated student ID with its semester train ticket.

When she got home to her apartment in Schöneberg, she was so light that, moving toward the bedroom, she hardly had to walk, lifted by a wave and thrown against the surf.

One Margaret, then, a more solid one, pulled herself under the covers and slept hungrily, and another one, a shadow of the sleeping girl, went into the wardrobe and took everything out. She carried it all down to the courtyard and heaved the clumps of clothing indiscriminately into the trash. She came back up to the bedroom, where she slipped in with the sleeping Margaret again, and they were one.

When the reunified Margaret awoke from the third sleep, it was a new planet. On this new planet, she went back to her old life.

TWO · The Glass Globe

Margaret Taub was her name, and she worked at Hello, Berlin! as a walking-tour guide. Every day she marched a gaggle of tourists across the length of Berlin—around Hackescher Markt and over the Museum Island, in single file down Unter den Linden, through the Brandenburg Gate, south beyond the dust-white construction sites, and along the path of the disappeared Wall. Later they cut through vacant lots to the remains of the Nazi ministries, and ended finally sometimes at the buried bunker of Adolf Hitler, sometimes at Checkpoint Charlie. It all depended on the tour's theme.

Along the way, Margaret told the customers about the comedies and tragedies of Berlin: the erstwhile cabarets on the Friedrichstrasse and the tirades of Honecker; the night in 1989 when the Wall fell and the night in 1938 when the synagogues burned; the afternoon in 1967 when the students came out for the Shah's visit; the night in 1919 when Freikorps soldiers clubbed Rosa Luxemburg with rifle butts and threw her into the canal to die.

In the weeks after her emergence from the Grunewald forest, Margaret gave the tours as she always had, and in some ways it was like old times. But the days grew colder, the trees wept their leaves, and—who could say why—she grew strange. She no longer made eye contact with her customers. And whereas before, if she had avoided their gaze, it was because she was either cocky or the reverse of cocky, something like a child frightened of its own precocity, now the inner mechanism had changed. When Margaret's eyes slid off toward the far horizon these days, it was without a trace of flirtation.

The fact was this—she was entering a kind of trance. Walking the city, she encouraged the events she spoke of to crowd up against her eyes, and everything glimmered. Flames blackened the Reichstag when she looked over to it; on Friedrichstrasse there were nothing but dancing girls in nude tableaux; at the Pergamon, day after day, Peter

Weiss was creeping in on his way to clandestine meetings with his fellow socialists, and it was all vivid, and it was all a balm.

Even the so-called present was unnaturally animated. On the street once called Hermann-Göring-Strasse, they were clearing a site for a giant memorial during the months of her "convalescence," and every time she went by it with the tourists, the site had changed a little and seemed to be growing like a garden. All the pictures of the stages of its growth came together as she walked along its flank, and played before her eyes with the whirring breeze of a flip book.

As for her customers—not looking at them, it became possible not to notice a single one. Sometimes a bolder of their number, usually a gregarious Australian, would trot beside Margaret from site to site, and ask what she, Margaret, an American, was doing in Berlin. It was not that Margaret failed to answer, but these days she replied by rote, almost as if it were part of the official tour script. She had moved to Berlin six years ago to study history at the Freie Universität, she would say. No, she never went back to her native New York. To which the customer would show surprise. She was so young, never going home—what about her family? Didn't they miss her?

At this, a strange transaction would occur. Margaret would fix the customer with a gaze of the profoundest curiosity and pity, as if the customer had not asked a question but rather confessed to some rare and grotesque character trait. A moment later, her face would change very abruptly again, and it would become apparent that the look of curiosity had been an act. Although there was no hint of malignance or mockery in the deception, the piece of theater would strike the customer, who had merely been trying to be friendly, as somehow cruel. This was the only sort of unkindness that Margaret ever served up, but it was something she did more and more.

And the customer, downright uncomfortable then, because after the disappearance of all expression from Margaret's face, her gaze was likely traveling—with a bird as it crossed the sky, or flipping back and forth together with a flag at the top of a ministry as it rattled in an oceanic wind—the customer might continue to chatter, voluble and embarrassed, still banging on the same pot. But oh, were her parents still in New York? Didn't she go home for the holidays at least? No, she would reply, somewhat dreamily. She never went "home" (you could hear the quotation marks in her voice); she did not get along with her mother. And her brothers and sisters? She did not have any.

At which point, if it had reached such a point, Margaret would turn and pull back, her face white, and make a quick head count before leading the group further on to the next site, or beginning to lecture in her large, artificial voice.

If there had ever been a time when the customers might have made another type of miscalculation and assumed Margaret was one of those alert and artistic young expatriates of the kind that showed up in such numbers in Berlin in the 1990s—to open galleries in bombed-out ruins, found clubs under manhole covers, form neo-glam bands and squat in abandoned apartment houses as the ill-used city rose caper—some, a recovered invalid, from its long stay in the hospital bed of the twentieth century—there was something about the smell of Margaret Taub, something sour and somnolent and quieted out, that suggested that she, no—this one had never belonged to that happy swelling. And she knew it, and they knew it, and maybe she even knew that they knew it.

Should Margaret have tried to discover what sinister chain had wrapped her life?

Perhaps she should have, but she did not.

The night in the forest and everything around it was an elementary blank. If pressed (of course, she was never pressed), she might have simply said: "Lately, I'm a little uneasy." With no one did she mention how the city's past was dancing before her eyes, nor any of her more alarming symptoms, which had begun to pop up, one after the other.

Margaret returned to her classes at the university in these weeks, but there she did not speak to anyone either. She rode the U-Bahn down to the dying meadows of the Freie Universität and sat by herself in the library. She wore an assortment of men's dress clothing: moth-eaten woolen trousers and broadcloth shirts grown stiff with age, and always a particular grease-smeared topcoat that looked to be several decades older than the rest. And she wore a felt hat—perhaps to disguise that she was not in the habit of washing her hair. The effect belonged to no subculture anyone knew of, and gradually rebuffed the other students.

Margaret did not mind. During lectures she sat well away from them, deep in her own thoughts, taking methodical notes from her perch at the back of the hall—notes which, not long after having been made, their blue, reptilian ink already fading, seemed foreign to her, not of her own hand. She memorized dates, causes and effects, uprisings and assassinations, theories and countertheories—this was for the sake of the tours in the city, where, if the customers quizzed her, it was distasteful to be caught out.

But she did not register for examinations that might propel her toward a degree, nor make any other frantic efforts on behalf of semester deadlines. She ignored the early notes she had made for her master's thesis, which had been on the topic of Karl Liebknecht and the Spartacists.

Margaret was leaving something behind. She no longer suffered from ambition. Information was fodder for the tours, nothing more. She studied avidly but always remaining in place, and the university was large and remote as an unjealous god, and took no notice of her treadmill existence.

And though the calendar appeared to be continuing its slow plod whenever she checked it, Margaret was dogged by a peculiar sensation. She felt that somehow, somewhere along the way when she had not been paying careful attention (and how could she have been so heedless?), time had come to an end. Now it was only a matter of a short interval before the world faded out entirely. Sometimes she was even gripped by a strange suspicion, unlikely as it seemed, that every last thing was already gone. All that now met her ears and eyes was a vestigial flare or after-impression, like the shape of the sun burnt on the retina.

So in that case, the logical (and yet also illogical) conclusion was this: the more she looked, the less there was left to see. To observe was to eat. She had to ration.

This was difficult, as everything burned terribly brightly. The Berlin street came shining to her, whore for attention that it was, offering up this face, that reference, and it was all a magic lantern show, cheap and profligate. She began to feel, in a hallucinatory kind of way, that brightness and time were competing siblings, tugging resentfully at one another's realms. Brightness was winning. The brighter the city burned, the more time as a linear ray exhausted its last dregs and died. And conversely, the more time narrowed and dropped off for reasons of its own, the brighter everything became.

It all filled Margaret with dread. She tried to control the terror of the conquering brightness. First with the tours in the mornings, in this period of convalescence, the twinkling past was an opiate. But afterward, in the afternoons, the dread returned, and she was forced to distract herself.

Distract herself she did. She bought flowers for the side table in the long hallway of her cavernous, echoing apartment in Schöneberg. She cooked lentils. She went for a beer now and then, sat outside during the last of the lukewarm days, and as it grew colder, in smoky corners of pubs. Sundays, she walked around the Berliner flea markets, buying this or that or anything at all—a chalky pot for the kitchen, a flower box for the sill.

After that strange and terrible night in the Grunewald forest, the weeks went by and became months. And then the months flew by and became *two years*. Time will pass very quickly, if you are convinced it is already over. Two years rolled away, never to be seen again.

By the time autumn of 2004 pulled around, Margaret was so solitary, she was an almost unrecognizable version of herself.

She had used the purgatory well, however. The dread that had been her constant companion—it was close to gone. At the end of two years, the terror was swaddled and buried; it hardly had a heartbeat. A mirror to the lips of the sleeper clouded so slightly, it might be thought nothing at all.

And this is where the real story begins.

THREE · Time, Flowers

In November 2004, there was an event, and it is best to describe precisely how it happened. Right from the start, it was a ruinous development. Margaret came home from the university one afternoon when the final leaves were yellow, and found a letter in her mailbox, standing like a flag of surrender.

It had been a long time since Margaret last received a letter. The upstart scrap of intimacy—for she saw it as an intimacy from the beginning—surged at her, a gust of wind. Merely the sight of the handwritten address, and she felt herself begin to tilt.

When she looked at the letter more closely, however, she found that, no, in fact it was not addressed to her. She was Margaret Taub, but this was for a Margaret Täubner. And then she checked the return address, and it too was unfamiliar. The letter must have come to her in error. Perhaps someone searched out an address on the Internet and tangled the rows of names.

But even though it was not addressed to her, Margaret opened the letter. For some reason she could not name, she was excited. On this yellow autumn day, Margaret Taub became more excited than she had been in a very long time.

The letter turned out to be nothing but a formality—a medical doctor summoning this other Margaret T. to an appointment. Margaret's face fell, although only the *Hausmeister* raking leaves in the courtyard garden was there to observe the plunge.

The wording, however, struck Margaret as unique and it is worth reproducing it here in full.

Very honored Frau Margaret Täubner,

Belatedly I have scheduled an appointment for you on Tuesday afternoon, November 16, 2004, at 15:00. Please come to my office in the Schwäbische Strasse and bring your insurance card.

I would also like to add, in case you are concerned: let it be known that, although you and I have not always seen eye to eye, I remain interested in your fate.

With friendly greetings,
Dr. Gudrun Arabscheilis

Margaret glanced over it, and then over it once again. The strange show of familiarity in the second paragraph puzzled her. "You and I have not always seen eye to eye." More perhaps than a medical doctor was in the habit of expressing to a patient.

Margaret took the letter up into her apartment.

She went to make tea, but waiting for the water to boil, pushed by an unseen hand, she came back almost instantly to the whispering letter. She reread it, tracing its grain with her fingertip. The letter gave off a gentle warmth, an oddly bright iridescence. She noticed too, in the letterhead, a telephone number. She took up the phone and dialed.

The answering voice was brittle, feminine.

"I'm afraid I received a letter from your office in error," Margaret began. "A letter meant for a Margaret Täubner. But I'm Margaret Taub."

The woman commanded Margaret to hold. Footfalls went clapping—heels against wooden floors, echoes against high ceilings, slamming doors. There was a swish and the phone was taken up again. Margaret found she had been holding her breath.

"Doctor Arabscheilis has instructed me to tell you—if you are the Margaret who lives at Grunewaldstrasse 88—" The woman cleared her throat: "Are you Margaret at Grunewaldstrasse 88?"

"Yes, I am," Margaret said.

"In that case, she said to tell you expressly that your family name is of no interest to her. She'll expect you on Tuesday the ninth."

Margaret was astonished.

"I don't know the doctor," she said.

"Better you come here and work it out with her yourself." The woman was businesslike in the usual way.

"No, but thank you, I—" Margaret felt the muscles of her back tightening.

"You'll discuss it with the Frau Doktor when you're here," the woman cut her off. *"Auf Wiederhören."* The line went dead.

Margaret did not call back. She sat with the lifeless receiver in her hand for a good ten minutes, maybe more.

By Tuesday the sixteenth, Margaret had in fact decided to appear at the appointment. Since the call to the doctor's office, the flowers of time had been blossoming, cracking open slowly instead of racing toward death. The key, she thought, was that it had been such a long time since anyone had paid any attention to her, even mistaken attention, and, truly, it must be admitted that despite everything, Margaret was lonely. Now here was this doctor: "interested in" her "fate." She did not yet suspect nor wish for anything more than companionship.

FOUR • The Speculum

When she arrived at the doctor's address on Tuesday, she found she already knew the place by sight. Outside, a small gold plaque screwed to the entryway shone in the sun, and Margaret recognized it. Often when the day was bright and she rode her bicycle north to Wittenbergplatz, the gold of that plaque caught her eye.

The building itself was patrician *Gründerzeit,* with balconies heavily filigreed, and a cool, damp, white façade.

Margaret came into the courtyard and looked about. The walls were close around the quiet garden, looming and corpulent. But as for an entrance to a doctor's practice, there was none to be seen. Margaret wandered about the instantly claustrophobic courtyard, her feet sinking into the mossy ground.

At the last moment before she turned about in frustration and went home, she spied a small green door, only as high as her shoulder and almost disappearing in the ivy that climbed the southern wall. Beside it was a sign, also caught in the ivy:

DR. GUDRUN ARABSCHEILIS
Gynaekologie und Geburtshilfe, 3.OG
Sprechzeiten ganztäglich

Dr. Gudrun Arabscheilis
Gynecology and Obstetrics, 3rd Floor
Doctor's hours all day

Margaret's eyes glided over the specialties. Funny, she thought. These had not been included on the letterhead. Her eyes flitted over the sign a second time. She thought of running away.

But then—there was something about the wax on the surface of the ivy, something about the damp moss catching its green against her shoes, something about the smell of the wet stucco (it had recently rained) that made Margaret press the buzzer after all, made her even a little light-headed.

The door chimed, and the lock sprang open with no comment from the intercom. Margaret ducked low to get through. She began to climb the stairs leading to the office.

In the stairwell, a familiar aroma overcame her, a smell she could not describe but which she knew well. At first she thought the smell came from the polished wood of the banister. It smelled of long-ago hardened varnish and dirt, like the smell of human skin after a day outside in the summer city. She heard her feet plodding beneath her and dipped her nose down toward the banister. All in a rush it came upon her: no, the scent did not come from the stairs, nor from the stairwell, nor even from the banister. It came from something within Margaret. It came from the experience of climbing the stairs. It wasn't the emotion that was triggered by the smell, but the smell running out of the emotion within her. For a moment she forgot the doctor entirely and had a rampant euphoria.

At the top of the stairs she came into an empty waiting room. There was a rubber plant in the corner. The plastic chairs were bright, and white paneling lined the walls. A nurse-receptionist with hair drawn tightly back from her brow sat behind a counter so high, Margaret could not see her face.

"Name, please," the nurse said.

Margaret had not yet caught her breath. "Margaret," she said.

"*Family* name," the woman corrected.

"Taub," Margaret said. She went close on tiptoe and peered over the counter.

"Taub?" The woman looked up from her paperwork. Her irritated eyes were ringed by green and golden shadow.

"Yes, Taub." The practice had a hospital style and Margaret felt a shock of cool.

"I'm going to enter you into the logbook as Margaret Täubner," the receptionist said.

"But that's not my name," Margaret said. Her euphoria of only a few moments before was quickly ebbing.

The receptionist, for her part, thought little of the disagreement. Her head disappeared again. Margaret went higher on tiptoe. The nurse filled out a form with a calm left arm, not even asking to see Margaret's insurance card. Margaret tried to see which name the woman had chosen but even tall Margaret could only see the top third of the woman's body. The woman's tightly drawn hair pulled ever more taut as she concentrated.

Margaret took a seat in one of the plastic chairs. She waited a long time.

At last another voice, a very loud, warbling voice, called out Margaret's name, or rather Margaret Täubner's name, from all the way down the hall.

"The doctor will see you now," the nurse said. "Fourth door, all the way at the end."

As she walked the long hallway, Margaret felt an old fear returning. By the time she came into the doctor's room, however, it had vanished.

All at once in this spacious back room, gone, too, was the feeling of hospital. Here, the ceiling loomed three times her height over her head, and there was nothing fluorescent or sterile about the place, but rather a dark and golden, leathery atmosphere of Wilhelmine brass. Bookshelves nicely laden covered half the walls, and the windows were all but obscured by rich, chestnut-colored velvet curtains with frayed golden tassels. Over the wide, creaking floorboards, well-worn Persian carpets crept. There was a massive oak desk at the center of the room, and only off to one side was the padded doctor's table with the much-despised metal stirrups. A low steel counter ran along another wall and held two microscopes, several jars of sterilized tongue depressors, boxes of rubber gloves and antiseptic agents in tall, white plastic bottles. On the wall above the oak desk, an antique medical drawing of the human musculature—a male and female figure side by side—was yellowing and curling at the edges. Next to it was a rather fine, large, and dark-toned portrait in oils of a middle-aged man with a watch chain, holding a good-looking infant in white laces to his breast.

Behind the desk sat a woman with an enormous head, so large, in fact, that Margaret stepped carefully farther into the room without being called, trying to see it more closely. The woman's hair was thick and grey, piled in glistening layers. Her forehead was massive and also glistening with what might have been sweat or might have been extremely healthy skin, Margaret wasn't sure. Her cheekbones pushed up into the area just beneath her eyes, so that her thickly lensed bifocals rested very high on her face.

She looked up as Margaret entered. Her glasses magnified her eyes out of all proportion to her head—Margaret was faced with eyes as big as golf balls, of a grey-green color, peering out of lashless lids.

The doctor nodded knowingly and seemed to coo ever so quietly under her breath—the airy tones of a pigeon. The woman was old, improbably old.

Margaret also realized, as the woman's utterances began to amplify, that what had seemed to be cooings were in fact the raspings of a pulmonary disease, emphysema perhaps.

The doctor spoke to Margaret in a voice that was both croaked and purred: "My dear, if you'll undress—we'll get started. Let's begin with a general exam. I imagine you haven't had a Pap smear in a very long time."

Margaret stepped back in alarm. The doctor seemed to be focusing on a point in the middle distance and did not look at Margaret at all. Margaret spoke up. "I'm not here for an examination," she said. She looked at the woman. "I should introduce myself. I'm—"

"Of course you are, my dear. I have been concerned for you."

Now it must be said: these words should have puzzled Margaret, and in any case should almost certainly have been corrected. Instead, Margaret accepted them like a gift. *I have been concerned for you.* Margaret, in her strange state, was so soothed, her loneliness so instantly assuaged, that she was almost willing to go along with the doctor unconditionally from that moment on.

Still, she tried. "I got your note in the mail." She cleared her throat in an involuntary expression of sympathy with the doctor's wheeze. "I believe there has been a mistake. I'm not the intended recipient."

"What if I were to tell you that you are free to be anyone you like?" The old woman moved her hands in the air. She was not looking at Margaret.

"Oh." Margaret studied her. Secretly, she felt a kind of vindication. Again, it was the choice of phrase: "free to be anyone you like," that pealed in her ears. She decided she would play as if she were Margaret Täubner for the time being at least. She did not see the harm, except perhaps to the real Margaret Täubner, if that woman could be presumed to desire an appointment with the strange Dr. Arabscheilis.

"Where shall I undress?" Margaret asked.

So they would start with the yearly exam, she thought; so be it.

The sun fell through the muslin curtains inside the heavy, velvet drapes, and lit up the dust motes in the air.

"You can undress right where you are," the doctor said.

"Right here?"

"You don't want to?"

"Well—" Margaret began.

"Gymnophobia! I remember now. You were always so coy. There is that same screen you used to use, there against the wall. You can unfold it and mask yourself just as before, leave your clothes behind. Then come over here and lie on the table."

Now it was true that Margaret had decided to go along with the misunderstanding, and that was all well and good. But by this time, surely, the woman should have sniffed out her mistake. Margaret was not Margaret Täubner. This was plain as a pikestaff, even to a very old woman. "I remain interested in your fate," the doctor had written, but now any imposter was welcomed greedily. And because Margaret did not know the meaning of the word the doctor had used, *gymnophobia,* she began to thrust on that term all her fantasies of what was going wrong. *Gymnophobia*—perhaps it was a fear of self-revelation. She even began to develop an image of this other Margaret T. in her mind. She would have very short hair, she decided, and a habit when she was sitting of holding her handbag on her lap, rather than letting it rest at her ankles.

Behind the screen, Margaret pulled off her trousers. She looked down at the floor and saw that the deep burgundy and intricate pattern of the Oriental carpet disguised years of grime. She was disgusted. She came out from behind the screen, nude from the waist down, and the doctor gestured toward the leather table with its swathe of white paper and stainless steel.

And now Margaret's nakedness made her even more wretched; her misgivings ducked from her mind to her stomach.

The doctor hurtled to the table and began to adjust the stirrups to their full length. "Legs spread! Feet in!" she commanded. She turned around and went to the cabinets below the long counter, rooted about, searching for something with both hands. Margaret climbed up on the table. She watched the doctor more closely than ever.

The doctor returned and gripped Margaret's knees to steady herself, sighing melancholically. She screwed the instrument tight. She seemed not to glance at the thing as she did so, her hands working automatically. "I know you're uncomfortable, my dear, but practically," she said in a low voice, "you're very lucky." Her golf-ball eyes seemed to mist over again and she gazed into some middle distance that seemed to be her eyes' preferred resting point. Her hands went still, and she again gripped Margaret's knees. "The speculum of the nineteenth century presented a challenge to the nervous system of much greater consequence than the one you are enduring. It had a system of mirrors and lenses, and the light source, my dear girl, was a lamp flame. These early specula burned a mixture of alcohol and turpentine, and I shudder at the thought of the burns that were occasionally the sad drawback to their use. Knowledge of the inner in exchange for the beauty of the outer, I'm afraid."

"My goodness," Margaret said.

"You might well say." The doctor sighed, her head falling forward as though gone overripe. "Tell me," she said, "have you become *afraid* of doctors in the meantime?"

Margaret looked at her. She twitched. "I'm uncomfortable with gynecologists," she said, having come to the realization only at that moment.

The woman gave a wheeze of satisfaction. "And what might this discomfort be?" she asked sharply, shrugging off her rasping illness. "Young comrade, there are two categories of people who are afraid of visiting the doctor. Their fear may seem at first glance identical, but in fact has neither the same cause nor the same effect. In the first case, the individual never goes to see the doctor at all—he suffers from a generalized atelophobia—fear of imperfection, that is—which masks a dark and disastrous thanatophobia. He thinks if he ducks out of sight of his personal emissary of malignant mortality," she chuckled, "he might possibly escape the reaper.

"The second type of fear is much more complex," the doctor went on, "and because it lacerates in waves, rising and abating," she drew up her hand in a trembling arc, "the sufferer sees the doctor on occasion and can even develop a hippocratophile's hypochondria which brings him to the doctor regularly. It is not easy to categorize, but seems to be an unhappy conjoining of gymnophobia, algophobia, and myxophobia: the fears of nudity, pain, and slime respectively. May I call you comrade, my child? You're a grown woman."

Margaret nodded in surprise, pleased at least to learn the meaning of gymnophobia. The doctor went on, "Comrade, you were willing to see me today. Thus, I deduce your fear is of the latter kind."

"But—" Margaret hesitated. She looked at the doctor again. She was still convinced that the woman would recognize her as *not* Frau Täubner at any moment. But the doctor, her eyes drawn into slits almost closed, seemed self-satisfied as a cat. Margaret tried her hand at a declaration. "I am only uncomfortable with gynecologists," she said carefully, "not with doctors generally."

"I do not change my case," the doctor said without slowing down. "A fear of nudity may only be associated with genital nudity in your case, and a fear of slime only with those moist feminine organs which remain mystical and disgusting to you." The doctor's head and eyes were strangely fixed.

The old woman started coughing very violently then, and when she finally stopped, a new light had entered her face. Margaret tried to speak, but the doctor raised her hand and silenced her. She sat down on a little stool between Margaret's spread legs. She rattled the speculum clamped inside Margaret's underbody as if she were about to go on with the exam, but her hand stopped and dropped. She breathed deeply in and out, more and more slowly, until, with her rasping breath, she sounded almost as if she were asleep.

Margaret waited. The doctor finally lifted her head. An expression of unbelievable discomfort began to twist the woman's face, as if she were choking. With difficulty, she asked:

"How is your little boy?"

"What?" Margaret craned her neck up, peering over the hillocks of her body.

"Oh," the doctor let out. "Oh, dear me," she said woodenly, and it was as though she were reciting a line in a play. Margaret had a sensation—she had opened a drawer not in her own house, and stumbled onto a treasure not her own, a treasure whose revelation was as awkward for her as it was for its owner. The doctor lifted her head toward the left corner of the room. "Perhaps I was mistaken," she said. "You don't have a child?"

"No—" Margaret began.

She should not have come here. A feeling crept up. She was surrounded by barking dogs. She closed her eyes and held still. She had blundered into other people's lives, and this was a musty place, smelled of bodies not her own. She said: "I am not Margaret Täubner."

The doctor snapped her hand away from Margaret's thigh as if she had touched a snake. "You're not Margaret Täubner?"

"No."

"Who are you then?"

"I'm Margaret Taub."

But at this, the doctor surprised Margaret. She gave an exaggerated snort. She stood up, and there was a twitch around her eyes. "Comrade!" she said. "As for names—you can use Arabscheilis when you speak to me. As address I will accept both 'doctor' and 'comrade.' This question I leave up to you to decide. But don't expect me to call you *Taub.*" The doctor spoke fluidly, but Margaret could see by her twitching checks that she was upset and unsure how to proceed.

The woman turned around as if to return to the counter, but she was not fated to reach it. She walked head-on into the screen that Margaret had propped up to indulge her alleged gymnophobia. The screen fell with a clatter, and the doctor stumbled heavily, groaned, and bounced into the side of an armchair. From there, she ricocheted into Margaret's shoulder. At the impact, Margaret felt as if she had been deliberately attacked. The cold clamp of the speculum in her nether regions prevented her from alighting to fight or flee, nor did she know how to remove it. She was certain only that if she would hold still, nothing would hurt her, while any movement would mean certain internal crunching—of what, she knew not.

"Is there a problem, Doctor?" Margaret asked from her spot on the table, losing control of her voice.

"I'll admit: I'm legally blind," the doctor said, and Margaret made a sound like a mishandled guinea pig, "and in no position to act as a gynecologist any longer, not to you, and not to anyone else either. But you, my dear—it doesn't need to matter to you that I am blind, I recognize your voice. Perhaps it was irresponsible of me to try to give you an exam today in light of my eyesight or lack thereof, but let's be honest, shall we? You have problems of your own."

"That's true," Margaret said almost automatically, "but—"

"I should never have let you out of my sight." The doctor cried out, almost wailing. "I knew you were distraught." And the doctor was in fact wringing her knuckly hands, her gigantic head swinging back and forth.

Her voice, when it came, sounded like river rocks knocking together. "Something terrible has happened." She breathed with difficulty.

"You've got the wrong person," Margaret said.

"Is that so?" the doctor said. "Where do you live?"

"Grunewaldstrasse 88."

"How many American women by the first name of Margaret live at Grunewaldstrasse 88?"

Margaret's fingers were cold, her head was beginning to swim. "I don't know," she said. "Only me, I suppose."

"The wrong person." The doctor gave a dry laugh. "Don't delude yourself. I *know* you, Margaret. You're the girl that left her family behind in America." The doctor pointed her finger.

"Not exactly," Margaret said. "My father was a German."

"What?"

"I said, my father was a German."

"That may be. Whoever he was," the doctor said, contempt in her voice. She was silent. When she spoke again, her voice was even more hoarse, but the contempt was gone. "What have you been doing these last years? I would assume that for some time now you have been pursuing novelty, am I right? Those lost in a fugue seek novelty automatically; they can do little else."

It was unaccountable, Margaret thought, that the woman immediately made such insinuations. Margaret wanted to get out of the room, but the contraption was still clamped in her. "Doctor—"

"We must do something. *I* must do something," the doctor said. "But what am I to do?" The question was not directed at Margaret. The doctor craned her head upward toward the left window.

"You don't need to do anything," Margaret said. "There's been a mistake. Please explain to me the circumstances of your—your falling-out with this Margaret Täubner." Margaret thought perhaps this was the best way to clear up the misunderstanding. Find out what had happened, and then explain in a step-by-step manner why none of it could possibly be in accordance with her own identity.

But the doctor would have none of it. "Do not lure me into rekindling the flames of your punishing wrath!"

Let us pause and say that in the very broadest sense, the doctor caught Margaret off guard. Margaret Taub was a young woman who had been living for a very long time without certainties. Trying to establish one now, even in the privacy of her own mind, was almost entirely beyond Margaret's capabilities, like trying to switch into the tongue of a long-deposed tyrant. Her attempts to counter the woman were sclerotic, if not to say completely lame.

The doctor, meanwhile, was still rising to her full vigor. "Listen to me," she was saying. "The role I am going to play is neither that of gynecologist nor actually that of mentor. I will act as memory surgeon. I think that is better than going to the police."

Margaret's face went cold. She lay her head back on the table and took several deep breaths. A madwoman. A "memory surgeon" the doctor called herself. Colors swam at Margaret's eyes. At last she ventured, using her most accent-free German—and it was true that in this moment she did something peculiar: she adopted the problems of someone else, carried the whole situation over onto herself with an aptitude at which she later wondered. "I do not *mind,*" she said, slamming the last word into the room, "that I can't remember."

And the doctor pounced. "So it's true that you can't remember?"

Margaret was breathing with difficulty. So she was going to be "cured," she thought, just as if she were Margaret Täubner. "I've had problems with my memory. I admit that," Margaret said. "But that—that doesn't mean I'm Margaret Täubner."

The doctor was barely listening. "My dear, a patient of your type—the type, that is, I'm assuming you are, since it seems you are clinging to your illness invidiously—is infatuated with the nonexistence of the past. Recovery is like falling out of love."

"No," Margaret said, shaking her head. "That's not right."

"Does this not frighten you," the doctor said, "to think of your life passing and leaving you with nothing in exchange for the years you've forfeited toward death?"

Margaret breathed in and out through her nose. She tried to calm herself.

A tall clock ticked in the corner. The doctor seemed to gaze at Margaret sadly from behind her blind eyes. She had managed to set herself up behind the desk again.

"Let us begin your therapy," the doctor said, and Margaret saw that she was to be held captive. A blind woman was not going to release her until she had done everything for the recovery of a collection of memories that belonged to someone else. Margaret could feel the now warm stainless steel of the speculum; its temperature had risen to match her body's.

Something occurred to Margaret with which she might make one final effort.

"How is it that you suppose an American like myself has the last name Täubner?" she asked. "We don't even have the letter *ä* in my country."

"Of course, comrade, your father is German, just as you say. *Just* as you say. Or at least, the man who gave you his name—Täubner."

Margaret did not know what to reply. She thought: another American at Grunewaldstrasse 88, also Margaret T., whose father was also German? It did in fact seem very unlikely, and she felt alone.

"My dear," the doctor said gently, as if having sensed this, "I am not a blind woman passing as a doctor. I am a doctor who has passed into blindness." The doctor swiveled about in her chair.

She opened two cabinet doors that climbed the length of the wall behind her. She began feeling about in the darkness. Margaret looked into the grotto where the doctor's hands played and saw what appeared to be, if she was not mistaken, a film projector. The doctor held her head at an odd angle. She was performing all her intricacies by feel. "It has been many years since I've treated a case of your type," she said. "Immediately after the war, I saw violations against memory more egregious than yours. Sometimes I had success with a cure—not always, but when, then mostly through what we would today call guided imagery therapy, although at the time it had no name, it was merely something I thought up spontaneously, thanks to my practical genius." The doctor smiled.

She went on. "Let's begin, shall we? You seem to be highly lucid, I will assume for the time being that yours is a case of psychogenic amnesia. If it is organic, there is little I can do in any case, so let us assume it is psychogenic."

Margaret did not try to understand. She was thinking of other things.

"It happens there is a film I have right here in the office," the doctor went on. Her fingers were busy, and her voice caught for a moment in distraction. "If this film has the effect it occasionally has had on others, we might see—*dramatic* changes in you." The doctor fumbled with the projector. Finally it began to tick. It started and it stopped. Once it was responding without fail, the doctor turned it off again and sat facing Margaret.

She began to speak slowly, the stresses of her words falling like a clock's hands. "As you watch this film," she said, "here is what I would like you to consider, my girl," and the doctor's voice glided up, becoming ever more incantatory and commanding. "In its entire history," she said, "the Western world has produced nothing more meaningful than what you are about to see. Nothing has ever surpassed it for density of significance. Can you believe that?" the doctor asked, with real curiosity.

Margaret looked at the woman. "Not really," she said. The speculum was not painful, but the denatured steel in the bottom of her was worse than pain.

"A work of perfect meaning, that is, of perfect pregnancy," the doctor went on, "is the opposite of oblivion. It is the linking node between fantasy and reason, at which point all is remembered and correlated. If you imbibe an expression—whether it be symphony, poem, or sky-scraper—whose creator has endowed it by intention or accident with perfect pregnancy, you will attain perfect consciousness."

"But—" Margaret began.

"Wait," the doctor said. "You *will* understand. After experiencing a work of perfect pregnancy, or, otherwise put: an artwork of perfect meaningfulness. The mind will enjoy a season of pulchritude, finding the grace to read all metaphors as they ride in: the symbols hidden in the clouds, the analogical proxies buried in the faces of dogs and clocks, the eyes and ears of subway trains will open, the slightest corner of a footprint will summarize the Avesta, the threading of an oak stump will tell whence came Jupiter, and every poor crescent finger-nail will be a prophecy of the future history of the human earth. You will admit—this sort of miracle has the capacity to become the greatest therapeutic tool of all, my darling.

At this last term of endearment, the doctor turned away from Margaret toward the projector, and at that moment, Margaret did not think about perfect pregnancy or perfect meaningfulness or anything of the kind. She was struck by something else—it must have been latent all along, but she only recognized it now. She was sure: the doctor did not like her. Or she did not like, at least, the person she believed Margaret to be. She spoke to Margaret kindly and with many loving names, but only as a self-discipline and camouflage. There was a movement in her neck, a slide of the gullet as she spoke, that Margaret saw now to be the jerky passage of pride being swallowed. Margaret considered again what the doctor had written in the letter: "You and I have not always seen eye to eye." All at once, the phrase seemed ominous. Coolness licked her; she was bathed in a new flush of sweat.

The film projector began to tick, and the doctor was now circling the perimeter of the room, running her hands against the walls to find each window in turn and pull the tall brown drapes closed, until she and Margaret sat in a chiaroscuro world. Margaret, from her vantage point on the examination table, where she was still coldly exposed, was compliant. She turned her attention to the wall across from the doctor's desk. A small black-and-white film began to play there, its light glowing yellow.

It is fair to say that Margaret both watched the film and went to sleep. She saw the film in the same sort of trance in which she gave tours of the city, where all that is perceived is blown up so large that it crowds out other elements of consciousness. The darkened room, the buzzing light of the projector, her sudden freedom from the obligation to speak—all came together and allowed her to swim away.

The little film was poor-quality 8mm, in black and white, at least fifty years old. The air in the room seemed to become thinner as it played.

It began in the woods. From the top of what seemed to be a narrow rock outcropping, the camera looked down on a lake nestled in the forest. Trees sprang up around the lake like scaffolding. The water was inky, black, and cold.

Gradually, however, there came a dance of light on the water, and soon it burned. More and more, and then the surface of the lake was all ablaze, the fire so bright the woods around it went dark.

And then a black shape, a smudge like a thumbprint, formed in the center of the lake amidst the flames, a shadow rising at the crux of the water. It was a figure—a man—who was rising from the flames, and the way he rose was not with volition or muscular energy. He rose sideways like a doll on a string, jouncing along the slope.

But then he straightened, and when he did, he glided through the air, flew through it, amazingly!, and landed perfectly straight on his feet at the top of the cliff, next to the camera. And there he was, standing with wide stance, quivering and proud, leonine head held high.

But the figure was more distinct now, and it was not a man. It was only a boy, fourteen or fifteen, in costume—a medieval huntsman. Long, waving black hair, and his broad, well-shaped forehead caught the light as he turned it to the side, a forehead that was square and flat and fine, a vein like an *M* pushing from it, and he had as much beauty in that moment as the young Gary Cooper coming toward the camera out of the Moroccan desert.

The boy took a sword from a sheath hung on a carnival belt slung low around his narrow hips. He held the sword aloft, his face earnest, his arm extended and utterly convinced. Then, with a helpless, backward gesture, he brought it back down.

And the lake below continued to burn ever brighter, until abruptly it went black. At the same moment there was a flicker of movement, a neat parabola on the right edge of the frame, and the forest came back into focus and went still.

For a few seconds the projector continued to tick, and the forest persisted—only a slight rustle of branch now and then; a lonely bird alighting on a twig. And then gracelessly, and yet still with a kind of charm, like a cat lifting its paws out of water, the boy moved out of the frame.

The film ticked off.

For a while, Margaret and the doctor sat still: Margaret in one of her trances, and the doctor asleep.

The doctor finally woke herself with a snort. She said, as though time had not passed, "Treat your memories gently when they return, my dear."

Margaret did not reply. The doctor sat for a while longer.

"Can I trust you will come back to the office?" she asked. "When your memories return, I mean? Your treatment isn't finished, you know." There was something much gentler about the doctor now.

Margaret said she would come, but she spoke in a flat voice.

"I'll wager," the doctor said, "that you believe you'll never set foot in my office again. Perhaps you have judged me insane, or perhaps you are not as mentally disturbed as you pretend, and even now you are planning your escape to Brazil, or to some other country that has no extradition treaty with Germany." She sat very still, drumming her fingers against the desk. She sighed. "In any case, I'm willing to take the risk."

She felt her way across the room to Margaret, and at last removed the speculum from Margaret's unfortunate abdomen.

At the prompt, Margaret rubbed her eyes and sprang off the table. She dressed and went as fast as she could back down to the courtyard and out into the street.

On the way home, the buildings on the Grunewaldstrasse grew farther into the sky. Margaret's heart pounded and her cheeks flushed. She felt mysteriously unwell. Not as though the doctor had any right to her insinuations, but as though Margaret had somehow been complicit in the accusation.

Another strange thing: the film, for its part, was the very opposite of what the doctor had promised. It offered nothing in the way of pulchritude, pregnant or not. On the contrary. After the viewing, Margaret felt much worse than before. The gentle breathing terror was wending back to life.

Poor Margaret! That evening, she went to the phone booth on Gleditschstrasse and looked in the Berlin telephone book, and then on the Internet. She found no Margaret Täubners listed in all of Germany, nor Margarethe Täubners, nor Margaretes, nor Margaritas nor Grits nor Gretchens nor Marguerites nor Maggies. She looked over the world, she looked in the U.S. telephone directories online. She tried various alternate spellings of Täubner. She found a record of a Margarethe who married a Taubner (without an *ä*) once in Missouri, but that woman had been dead more than fifty years now. She even did something she could not quite explain to herself. She looked for other Margaret Taubs. But Margaret Taub, too, was a lonely name.

Why was it Margaret did not chalk the whole thing up to a misunderstanding? Why did she let the doctor trouble her? After all, Margaret was neither crazy nor imbecile. Surely, once in the safety of her own home, she could have shrugged the whole thing off.

The answer is twofold. One, there was the rushing silence of the missing time, the time up until and including the night in the forest, which she could not remember. This effectively rendered her without alibi. The complete knowledge required in order for her to stand straight and declare herself a stranger to the doctor, once and for all— it was not there, she could not defend herself. She could not say for certain she had never been acquainted with this doctor, and she knew it.

There was another problem, however, something far less concrete, and therefore more dangerous. It was a matter of an ineffable distortion in Margaret's mental landscape. Just as a man of chronically injured pride believes a bank error in his favor to be a matter of celestial justice, Margaret's anxiety framed her vision, and she was incapable of understanding the doctor's interest as fully accidental.

The result was this: after the doctor's visit, Margaret no longer stood straight. She went about crookedly.

On that very first night, she dreamt she was leading a walking tour, but all the city's buildings were infected. It seemed there was a kind of mold. It was in the walls, even in the stone, and she did not know where the trouble lay. Was it in the atmosphere or was it in the soil, was it growing from within the city, or was it blowing in from the outside—a cancer or a virus?

The next day she again went to the computer. She clicked farther and farther back in her e-mail account, trying to reach the e-mails from two years before. She was swimming beyond the buoys marking the shallow sea. She found a few pieces of mail from her boss at the tour company dating from March 2003. She clicked backward. The dates jumped. The next set of e-mails was from August 2002. There was a six-month gap.

She called her boss a wonderfully correct Englishman, at home. At first he did not understand what she was asking. "Well, Margaret," he finally said, "that was when you went traveling, wasn't it?"

"Was it?"

"I can look it up in our finances." He went from the phone and came back. "Yes," he said. "We did not make any payments to your account from August 2002 to February 2003. I'm remembering now, you went traveling in the East. Something about Odessa, or Yalta, wasn't it? You told us at the time."

"Right," said Margaret hoarsely.

"Is that why you called?"

"I'm trying to straighten things out in my mind."

"Is everything all right?" He paused. "I see you are scheduled to give a tour already tomorrow morning. Shall we find you a replacement? You don't sound well, Margaret."

"No, no," Margaret said. She reflected. She thought she would try something craftier. "I hope I haven't inconvenienced the company over the years with my—absences," she said.

"Absences?"

"Back then, you know . . ." She let her voice trail off, hoping he would fill in.

"Margaret, you've always been very reliable. We've appreciated that. Freelancers are not always of your kind."

"I see. I couldn't recall whether I had . . ." She allowed her voice to trail off again, but her boss too was silent, and the moment became awkward. "Well thank you anyway." She rang off.

She had never taken a trip to Odessa or Yalta. She was sure of it.

In the bookshelf she had thirty-seven chronological notebooks in which she copied passages from historical documents and kept records of her lectures and seminars. Again, she began sifting through the dates. Again, she found a hole. The period from August to February had left behind no notes.

She sat back down in the chair. She thought of the time she had lost. The record stopped, the colors ceased, the numbers jumped and skidded and went dark. To think of the gap was to stick her tongue into the soft, itching place where a tooth has been lost. The effort to remember life experience is a strange kind of effort.

And then that night as Margaret looked out her window and saw the rhythmic streetlamps getting smaller in the distance beat by beat an image did arise in her after all, vaguely. It was so weak, so soft. A poorly sketched little dream. A woman in a blue dress came wavering before her imagination. Margaret closed her eyes. The way she saw her, the woman was walking up a red staircase. She was climbing around an oval spiral that circled a central shaft. At the top of the stairwell was a skylight made of convex glass. The woman climbed up and up around the brilliantly curving banister, and as she did, the milky light from the central shaft played on her face.

But Margaret could only feel the woman visually, she could not see her, and this sensation—of visual knowledge without vision—made her think it was not a memory at all, but something she had once seen in a film. Right away, she tried to think of something else, frightened by the triviality of it. In things one knows to be critically important, triviality is a kind of horror.

Finally, later that night, the phone rang, and although Margaret did not manage to get it in time—when she spoke into the receiver there was no one on the other end—still, it jounced her down from the high wire. She stared into the mirror in the hallway by the telephone.

She began to laugh: What a fool I've been, she said to herself. Of course she was not Margaret Täubner. Of course she did not know the strange doctor. She would not have forgotten such a huge and bulbous head! And she laughed and wondered at how the doctor had rattled her. She thought of the doctor's office, which now seemed very far away: its mustiness, dark drapes, the shadows, the film projector hidden in the cupboard. It was absurd; it belonged to another dream, a missing country. It was not hers.

FIVE • The Slur of Vision

The next day, something occurred which might tax the reader's imagination to believe, but no more than Margaret's own faith in perception was stretched to the limit. But this thing that happened—it *must* be believed. Without belief, Margaret's story will quickly blanch for us, and the reality—that the world morphed and contorted and slurred around still and unchanging Margaret as cataclysmically as the body grows and ages and dies around its antique polymer codes—this will be misunderstood as nothing more than a fable. That is also a kind of tragedy: crisis fixed and framed too early.

Specifically, then, it was the city of Berlin. It rolled into a new phase all on its own, while everyone slept except the taxi drivers loose on the sun-smeared boulevards. By eight o'clock, it was already done.

The city transformed into flesh. When Margaret awoke, there was no stucco or timber any longer, only human flesh and bone. Pygmalion's Galatea as Berolina, though the name of the lover who craved the city and wished her living flesh, no one knew.

Emerging from Number 88, Margaret turned her head up to the sky, and there before her eyes were the city apartment houses, all of them made flesh. And how severely the sun cut through the windows! What an effect of blush and glow, the sun purpling through the skin webbing, as through diaphanous alabaster in late afternoon church windows. The external walls of the buildings swelled and contracted, so heavy with life that the skin stretching over the façades seemed to veil a giant fetus or a set of opulent organs: hushed, lush, and enormous. Or was it not a single set of organs, but many millions of individual, quivering muscles?

There on the sidewalk, Margaret gave a cry of the most injured surprise. She put her hand out to touch the wall of Number 88 and found the house soft, like a woman's cheek.

There was a spectacular quiet. All the natural sounds: the rumble of trucks, crosswalks clicking for the blind, had gone mute. Instead, out of the silence rose a sound like distant thunder: wide, echoing sighs, breeding themselves up from over the crest of the horizon in the west, symphonic as fireworks going off on every New Year's street corner, but soft enough to be nothing but the shivering anguish of six-story houses. The city was softening; it was pulped; it was breathing.

Margaret touched the building a second time, sure even now that the change would undo itself. But at the stroke, the contrary: the shuddering of the flesh rushed to the core of her; all her emotions flashed into a loop with the dreaming sleep of the building—flesh of her flesh, body of her body, and she drew her hand away in reflexive pain.

Margaret looked off down the street, her eyes unsteady. This street, the Grunewaldstrasse, was a commercial paradeway, assembled during the hustle and razzmatazz of the 1890s; for years now, nothing but an old dog waiting to die. The shops once grand sold junk furniture, chop suey, and lottery tickets. Pigeons nestled undisturbed on the decayed moldings.

Margaret looked hard westward, down the ray of the street, toward what had once been called Jewish Switzerland, and there she could see the spires, high roofs, and art-nouveau windows glinting and winking: the architecture of lost wealth. The endless view was wonderful—it had a trick of simultaneously revealing and concealing the splendor of times lost, a hologram somewhere between a vision and a memory.

Just then she was startled by a sound very close to her. It was Okhan from the *Döner* bistro, emerging from Number 89 to tend his little restaurant. He began heaving rusty café tables onto the sidewalk for the day's customers. Margaret breathed hard, waiting for him to lift his head. But Okhan, when he finally did look up, gave only a distracted nod. He appeared convinced he would catch the last of the sun revelers, putting out first tables, then chairs, then plastic flowers, although it was so late in the season. A wind blew dead leaves into spirals, and even with the crush of sun, there was a chill now and again washing across town, leaving goose bumps on the walls of flesh.

Yes, the wind blew, and the buildings exhaled. Margaret looked back into her own apartment house through the carriage entryway and saw Erich, the *Hausmeister,* delivering in-house mail to the tenants under the arch. He too was going about his business as if nothing were awry.

Margaret began then, with a quiver of uneasiness, to suspect she was alone. The city had changed, but only for her.

She strapped her bike lock onto the rear rack of the bike with a bungee cord; she blinked back loneliness, and a feeling—what was it?—a feeling of having been betrayed.

She was scheduled to give a tour, a three-hour walking tour of Third Reich sites. What made her head feel strange and heavy was this: if the city center were made of flesh as here, then she would have to look at the horrific transformation all through the tour. And even if it were not real, still, it was real *to her*—how would she behave as if she did not see it?

She mounted her racing bike. She had never missed a tour, and she would not now.

She rode down the Grunewaldstrasse eastward. The Universität der Künste was covered with a light down of hair. The BVG head-quarters, a Nazi-era curving giant of a building, had flesh with skin so dry that she recoiled as the wind sprinkled her with dandruff. She curved sparrow-like through the almost empty streets to the S-Bahn station.

At the station, her mind cleared. It was a whiff of sweat suspended in the air—the oily, purring, homely smell of bodies—that led Margaret to connect the change in Berlin to the visit to Dr. Arabscheilis. The sense of some inevitable kinship pressed itself on her. The doctor had shown her a film of "perfect pregnancy," and in passing had men-tioned the possibility of inanimate things awakening—"the eyes and ears of subway trains will open," and now, as Margaret gazed around her, she felt with a perspiration of intuition that there could not but be a connection. Something had been tampered with, some crucial mech-anism's fine joists thrown out of alignment, and every possible horror was now a latent possibility now. She whispered to herself: *There is more madness in me than I knew.*

Arriving on Wilhelmstrasse to give the tour of Berlin's Third Reich sites, Margaret found the city center too presented as node after node of humanoid giants, just as it had in Schöneberg.

In the east, in the distance, the spires of majestic Gendarmen-markt, usually with their twin, gold-plated domes, were today breasts crowned with pinkish-brown nipples—as though a woman lay with back spread over the kilometers of city space, hair streaming into the morning traffic. The recessed balconies of the apartment houses running up and down Wilhelmstrasse appeared moist and pink-shadowed, mouths, ear canals, nostrils, less sightly orifices as well, all quaking with secrets. The bricks of flesh and the stucco walls of flesh, crowned first by gutters, then by shingles, and finally by chimneys of flesh—brown-, rose-, and parchment-colored, some glowing with health, the older buildings covered in the wrinkled and loose skin of age—rose up into the heavens.

Here in town, Margaret also spotted carcasses—buildings already dead and rotting, or even older ones that were nothing but skeletal remains.

She was late. The customers were already congregated at the meeting point on the corner of Mohrenstrasse and Wilhelmstrasse, in shorts and white cross-trainers, all with sunglasses. British, Brazilian, American, Australian, and Finnish, and an Icelander in the back, dressed in black, peering reed-like out of pessimistic eyes.

And now already Margaret was changing her mind. With the city laid out before her and the suspicious eyes of the people in front of her, how could she believe it was the doctor and her film of perfect pregnancy that had caused the change? What was more believable—the trace memory of the blind doctor of yesterday with her fantastic claims, or the buildings quaking and echoing with breath under Margaret's very touch? Faced with the testimony of her senses, it was a very thin filament of rationalism that suggested it could all be traceable to Margaret's mind rather than to the soil and beams of the city itself.

She looked at the tourists, her customers. Didn't they mind the smell? Of course they did *not,* she muttered into her own ear. It was only she who minded.

But in the end, Margaret had to stop breathing through her nose. She could not stand to take in the scent of life flowing out of the architecture around her.

"Ladies and gentlemen," she began the tour. Selling tickets was a trial. Twice she dropped change on the ground, even dropping the same change more than once from a certain sweaty palm. Straightening up, she saw that an elderly gentleman from Florida had lost faith in her already, just for that.

She rushed forward with the tour, gradually coming into the safety of her usual recitation.

It will be better to set down exactly what she said, for these seemingly vacant recitations concerning the city of Berlin later became the weed—or perhaps it was the flower—that matured to greatness and suppressed other forms of life.

"Although these streets of 1980s Communist blocks," she began, "dreadful in their uniformity, and the seventies-era Czech Embassy here at my right—" Margaret gestured at what today appeared to be a muscular flesh lump—"might suggest that we have gone far afield of our topic, in fact we are standing where once the heart of the Nazi government pulsed. Bombings and Communist-era refurbishments have delivered this place from the accusations of the eye, but I'm sure you still feel its desolate rhythm. Over there, where today you see a Chinese restaurant, its life seeping away for lack of patronage, once stood Hitler's mortal monument to immortal glory: the new Reich Chancellery."

No one in the group showed any reaction to this announcement. Everyone's eyes were hidden behind sunglasses, and the sunglasses held steady. Margaret reddened. She turned and hurried to the next stop of note—the Propaganda Ministry of Joseph Goebbels. The flesh of this ministry shuddered slightly when Margaret arrived, as if its sleep had become restive. She scanned the faces of the group again as they came abreast of her, but still they were placid and remote.

"In the Berlin of the Nazi era, the street we're standing on was non-existent," she said. "On this site stood a baroque palace, made over in the classical style in the 1820s, and commandeered by the Nazis in 1933 after Hitler's election. The young Dr. Joseph Goebbels, vicious, club-footed, and intelligent, was at the helm of this new Ministry of People's Enlightenment and Propaganda'. Dr. Goebbels expanded the role of propaganda to the point where nothing in the nation breathed entirely free of it. The ministry building, by 1935, had mushroomed, a steroid-fed monster, with addition after addition spreading cancer-like over the central city. The original palace was ultimately destroyed by an incendiary bomb, but these Nazi-era additions live on," Margaret rattled off by rote.

The Floridian stepped forward, his hand pressed into the air.

"Yes?" Margaret said. She stopped breathing. She knew what was coming—she had ignored the transformation at her own peril.

But no. All he said was: "What sort of a 'doctor' was this Dr. Goebbels?"

"Ah!" Margaret cried. "Goebbels received his doctorate in literature in 1921. He even wrote a novel. Extremely long, ranting, autobiographical. Never published."

"He killed his children, didn't he, Goebbels?"

"No, that was Göring," said his wife scornfully.

"Marian, God damn it, it was Goebbels."

"You're ahead of me," Margaret said, relief swelling her. "Yes, the short answer is—yes, it was Goebbels, the propaganda minister, who killed his children at the end, together with his wife, Magda."

"What kind of a lady was she?" asked a young Scotsman.

"Oh," said Margaret, blushing at the question. "Oh. Goebbels's wife." And then all at once Margaret felt the sweet old trance returning, just as if the city had not transformed. "She was—" Margaret paused, her eyes light, "a highly intelligent woman. She was an only child, the apple of her Jewish stepfather's eye. As a young woman, before she met Goebbels, she was first devoted to Buddhism, then to Zionism. She married a wealthy industrialist at the tender age of nineteen, one of the Quandts—do you know them? A family that still controls Germany. Unhappy and drowning, headstrong, she became the zealous lover of the Zionist leader Vitaly Arlosoroff, does anyone know of him?"

The groups' eyebrows were raised. No one replied.

"An important man as well." Margaret went on. "Goebbels's diaries indicate without any doubt that Magda continued to sleep with her revered Jewish lover long after she started with Goebbels. Goebbels, the wag, adored her wild ways, her perversity; he wrote"—and here Margaret made a show of speaking in a buffoonish, Nazi-style German—" 'Magda ist von bestrickender Wildheit. Sie liebt, wie nur eine grosse Frau lieben kann,' which means, friends, in English, 'Magda is of a mesmerizing wildness! She loves as only a great woman can love!'

"Goebbels was insecure, jealous, romantic, and cruel. Insecurity-driven romantic jealousy will make you sick, maybe some of you know this," Margaret looked at the crowd before her. "It made him sick anyway, and he lamented, justifying his cruelty to all his other little tarts. What a fool he was!" Margaret crowed. She could feel herself getting carried away. Her heart was beating, and she could barely decide what to tell them, there was so much that occurred to her. "He was obsessed with the power of his 'eros,' as he called it, and his imperative to conquer and master the love force within him! He was grandiose, self-aggrandizing. Strangle and conquer your love, he always said—and what an agony when he couldn't! He champed at the women who stayed distant, those in particular. The early, great love of his life, whom he lusted after, limping, following her from university to university, and by whom he was ultimately jilted, was also a Jewish intellectual, like Magda's Arlosoroff." Margaret's mouth was full of water at the thought, as if it were a sweet and pungent apple fermenting against her tongue. "Can you believe it?" she asked. Her audience said nothing, but appeared to follow her gossip carefully. It was especially well-tolerated by a short, apparently wealthy Brazilian businessman. His tall and beautiful wife, however, seemed to be coming undone from boredom, as were their two teenage daughters, who wore makeup so heavy it appeared intended for the stage.

Margaret gave a great laugh. She was trying to drive up interest. "What a fanatic Magda was! What a waste of herself, always donating herself to some cause—"

But at that moment Margaret happened to glance backward at the building behind her. She caught a glimpse of movement there.

"Magda, Magda," she went on desperately, looking back at the group, trying hard to ignore the sensation of movement behind her. "Magda was constant only in her fanaticism toward one cause or another. She married Goebbels in the end, telling her friend Leni Riefenstahl that her love for Hitler was much stronger than her love for the propaganda minister. Goebbels had a—what's it called?" Margaret asked. She was distracted. The feeling continued. Something or someone was moving behind her. "What's it called?" She was flustered; the hair on the back of her neck stood up. "You know, when one leg's shorter than the other, and twisted?"

"A peg leg?" an American woman suggested.

"No, no," Margaret was getting out of breath. "That's not it." She left off. "Anyway, he was, well, handicapped, and Magda told Leni that she was marrying Joseph even though she didn't love him, in hopes of a closer union with her Führer—whom she wanted very much to marry, but whom she couldn't have! Couldn't have, you see, because Hitler's great love was for his dead niece, you know, little what's-her-name who shot herself in Hitler's rooms down in Munich back in '31, apparently a suicide in response to Hitler's withdrawn love. Magda adopted the feminine duties of state within the Third Reich, however, always to be found at Hitler's side on grand occasions, and yes, giving birth, too. What a tool, what a weapon it was! But why, does anyone have a guess, why was it all her babies turned out to be girls, all but one, and the little boy that did come was *slow* in the head? The award, you see, the state decoration, the *Mutterkreuz,* the Mother Cross, something like the Iron Cross, that Hitler and Goebbels, her own husband, thought up; its highest grade went to those women who had eight children, so she was continually pregnant through those years, giving birth to her six *H*-named children, Hitler's loving het-aera—ha-ha!" Margaret laughed. "It was little Helga, Hilde, Helmut, Holde, Hedda, and Heide.

Margaret turned her head upward then—upward and to the side in a faux-contemplative gesture. Stealing the moment, she twisted back to see finally what it was that was moving behind her. She couldn't quite make it out. She wanted badly to turn around all the way, but the sound of her own voice dragged her on. "This building, the onetime Ministry of People's Enlightenment and Propaganda, is today the Ministry of Health for the state of Germany."

Still breathing with the performer's excitement, she gave in to her impulse and turned around all the way. She saw—more than the cancer, more than the lump of living construction—she saw a woman, moving at one of the second-floor windows of the ministry. The woman drew back gauzy curtains, her face electrically familiar, shining sharply in the illumination of Margaret's upturned gaze. The smooth, blond, wig-like hair, carefully set in marcel waves, glistened over a beaked face, her prominent brow bone so low that her little black, unblinking eyes were in heavy shadow. The hair on her tiny skull, with its cultivation, and the beautifully tailored dress—black gabardine, high-waisted—almost managed to obscure the woman's body; the woman was hunchbacked, but uniquely, peculiarly—inhumanly. The woman leaned out the window. There was a sense of dirty feathers, of sickening, phosphorescent droppings, a strong suggestion of violence, as if at any minute she might coast down from her window perch and fall on Margaret with the talons of an all-knowing, all-destroying intelligence. She smiled at Margaret with such a tight, familiar grin. Margaret drew back. The woman smiled again and nodded her head.

Margaret turned around toward the group, but her eyes dragged along the ground, and among her tourists there was an uncomfortable silence. They regarded her expectantly. Margaret stuttered, making sounds as if she would begin to speak, but her mouth was dry. It was the Floridian who saved her.

"Who was the architect of this building? I guess you haven't told us the most basic information."

"Oh," Margaret said quickly, pulling her eyes up, "an excellent question. The building may indeed appear to be in the archetypical Nazi style, so-called Nazi Monumentalism, which, in turn, would seem to imply the signature of none other than the famed technocrat himself, Albert Speer. But in fact this building is the work of Karl Reichle, an architect whose name is no longer remembered. Reichle's architectural innovation was the subterranean garage with overhead lighting." Margaret smiled, her head cocked. "The first of the modern kind."

She glanced behind her again. Now the woman in gabardine was no longer in the window. Margaret smiled more brightly still.

Too soon. There was someone coming out the side entrance of the building near them, in sunny waved hair and heavy grey feathers, and a face Margaret now recognized without any doubt. In one hand this person carried a leather cosmetics case, in the other, an ax. She nodded at Margaret meaningfully.

Just a few meters away, the hawk-woman walked up to the flesh of the propaganda ministry, and putting the case down on the ground beside her, she raised the ax over her head and made a broad down-ward arc. She chopped. With its soft flesh, the building façade gave way instantly, the skin rolling back from the muscle beneath it like sea-water contracting from the shore. Floods of blood gushed into the street. Some of the group was spattered with it. Tufts of muscle, ripped by the dull blade, budded into the perpendicular.

Margaret felt as if she'd been hit. Her mouth pulled into a closed-lipped, cheerful yet cheerless grin, and she could feel her eyes losing focus. She wheeled about and looked at the group of tourists. They looked back at her, the undazed souls, some chatting quietly, others taking snapshots. Margaret gazed at their blood-daubed traveling clothes. The man from Florida who had asked the question about the building's architect even seemed satisfied. His arms were folded across his chest and his legs cast wide. Margaret rubbed her brow. She blushed. In her stomach, an ache spread quickly through her middle.

She led the group away. From a safe distance, her heart still speed-ing like a rabbit's, Margaret turned back and caught a last glimpse of the sensational wound on the side of the building. The hawk-woman, for her part, was gone. A quarried gouge of missing flesh was apparent, and the streets ran with blood as though water up from the sewers.

Margaret steered the group southward at a clip. They went to the looming air ministry of Hermann Göring—the elephant to the mice-like buildings around it. In its fleshly state, it exuded the stink of obesity: sweat trapped in fold upon fold. Margaret hurried by without stopping; the customers followed. Later they went by the sites of the SS and the Gestapo. These reassured, as no human dwellings were left to remember or incarnate. The trace remains of the foundations of the buildings appeared to Margaret not of flesh but of bone, and discoursing on them was easier.

They neared the Anhalter Bahnhof to look at the ruins of the once-palatial train station, and on this longer walk, Margaret finally had time to reflect. She saw that she could not possibly go on giving the tour. She was wrapped in a nightmare. The hawk-woman and the strange smell had made of Berlin a changeling desert, and in this desert she was ailed by the inverse of claustrophobia; she was trapped in a space so large, so endless, so ever-broadening, that it was without nook or shelter; she was trapped in a cloudless sky.

But she still had an hour to fill.

It occurred to her that if the buildings' transformation had something to do with her own mind, perhaps she could outmaneuver this mind. Couldn't she escape the hallucinations if she left the path of the scripted tour? She reasoned she might easily go somewhere she had never been, thus to a place upon which she would be incapable of overlaying imaginative visions. In fact, breathlessly, she realized that not far away was just such a place. A 1937 post office stood empty and abandoned on Möckernstrasse, and she had read about it often—she could easily improvise a tour-like commentary.

Margaret hummed to herself to keep her mind at rest. She led the tourists a bit farther down wide Stresemannstrasse than she had ever been before, and turned into Möckernstrasse. One side of this street was empty. Bombs had knocked out all the old buildings, one winter day.

In the distance, Margaret caught sight of the abandoned post office; the L-shaped building reared up on the corner. The building was bony, shuttered and prehistoric, as if the street were the hall of a forgotten and half-empty museum, and the building was the skeleton of a

Pleistocene beast in a shadowed corner, dusty and massive. Its façade was punched out in looming vertical lines—ribs of massive bones.

No, Margaret saw, leaving the route of the tour, she had not escaped. This building too was a carcass; the smell was enough to throw you down—a mass of bone drawn over with flesh decaying; blackened and bruised, rigid and retracted, a mutilated corpse.

The main entrance on the corner loomed. The opaque glass doors were shattered and covered in graffiti. Looking closely, Margaret could see a tattoo in the rotted flesh—a globe traversed by a banner emblazoned with the word *post*—that had been partially eaten away. She turned her back to the building and faced the group. "This was once a post office," she began unevenly.

The group drew up around. They seemed to sense her uncertainty. Margaret went on in a more brassy tone. "The entire district of Northern Kreuzberg was flattened in a single daytime raid on February 3, 1945. The raid was meant to decommission the train station. It also killed three thousand people. Almost everything was destroyed; only one building in fifteen survived. This building had the most miraculous of escapes: it wasn't hit, but the land in the crook of its L-shape was. If you look through the window here, clear through to the other side of the building, you'll see a bomb crater filled with water; it's as big as a lake." The tourists craned and peeked, but the windows were opaque as though the smoke of a long-ago fire had left them murky, and there were mutters of dissatisfaction. Margaret beckoned, and they followed her down the road to the far end of one of the arms of the L. On the opposite side of the street there was a mess of heavy trees on the bombed-out land, with a jungle depth to its green—the crush of foliage cast a shadow like a stain.

Here, on this side, beyond the end of the post office, wasteland stretched farther, fenced off with falling-down sections of carelessly erected barbed-wire fencing. The Queen Anne's lace was overgrown; nothing had happened here for years. Through the metal grill, the back of the building could be seen. It was an unadorned pink lump of rotting flesh.

And just as Margaret had promised, a bomb crater filled with water, a great pond, sat in the crook of the L, like a welt of saliva before receding gums.

"What does this building have to do with Nazis?" It was the man from Florida.

Margaret grabbed the wire lattice of the fence with both hands, peering through to the back entrance of the building. The door of the back entrance to the post office was missing. The empty hole was alluring to Margaret, like the entrance to a cave: a windy, unprotected void, unbelievably dark. Why did it appear as if wind were blowing from it? A memory came to Margaret of a cave she had once visited in South Dakota as a girl. In that place, there is a vast underground cave, with many miles of subterranean tunnels, but on the surface of the earth, almost no trace: only one tiny hole, no bigger than a rabbit's burrow. Margaret stared at the dark entrance to the building, where the weeds outside were bobbing, laden with air, bowing and swaying in the artificial wind. Margaret was quiet.

"What does this have to do with anything?"

That was the Floridian again.

"In the basement of this post office was the central bureau of the Berliner pneumatic dispatch," Margaret said. "Before the war, there was a total of three thousand kilometers of vacuum tunnels connecting every post office in Berlin. A dispatch could be sent through the vacuum tubes from Ruhleben in the south to Hiddensee in the north in twelve minutes."

"Does it still work?"

Margaret made a descending whistle: a bomb falling. "Almost everything was destroyed," she said. "But the bureau was connected by a tunnel to the New Reich Chancellery and the Führer's bunker. If Hitler had made an escape at the end of the war instead of killing himself, as some people believe he did, then he would have come here, to the basement of this post office. There was even a bowling alley down there."

The tourists nodded, and Margaret turned away sharply. She began to lead the group back toward Potsdamer Platz.

She did not turn around and speak to them the entire way. When they got to the S-Bahn station, she told them simply the tour was over. Some of them muttered within earshot that it had been a disappointment of a tour. No one tipped her.

Later that same day, Margaret went back to Schwäbische Strasse. She went into the courtyard. When she got to the little door in the back leading up to the doctor's office, there was a note pinned to it. "The practice of Dr. Gudrun Arabscheilis will be closed for the holiday, from 11-11-04 to 11-20-04."

Today was only the eleventh. And then Margaret thought of something else. There was no holiday to speak of. She ripped the note off the door. And now that she considered, what sort of practice could the old woman possibly have, blind as she was?

SIX · Magda's Face

The next day it rained. Margaret did not set foot outside. Several times, however, she went to her window and looked down the Grunewaldstrasse, and each time there were the buildings, softly puckered, pink and tan and breathing under the raindrops. She threw open the window as the sun went down; she looked for the cool shadow. The chill, wet, autumn air blew into the apartment. She gazed off down the Grunewaldstrasse. Winter was coming. Some of the younger buildings had become pinker with edges chapped; older buildings—that was the majority—looked red in harsher tones, as if they were bursting into flame. The vague, soft scent of flesh, stronger than the smell of coal dust, had already become easily recognizable.

Yesterday was repeating in a flashing loop in her mind. It was drawing her into a repetitive circle. Instead of swaddling her memory in sleep and slipping it away as was her custom, she was sifting through the day before with both hands.

The hawk-woman with the ax. Margaret knew very well who the woman was. It was Magda Goebbels. Magda Goebbels—Joseph's wife.

That evening, she began to read a biography of Magda Goebbels. She had read this particular biography once before, but she was reading it now with new eyes.

And it was that evening as well that she had the first of what she would later call simply an *episode*.

It began about thirty pages into the book. She had a sensation as if a bright light had been switched on, or as though she were drunk on red wine and a searchlight were coming in through the window. And whereas she usually read with systematic attention, tonight her interest was untamed and frantic, full of desire, like the need to scratch an itch that has already been scratched to blood. She was making some unsteady attempts at note-taking as she read, but again and again she stood up from her chair, went out of the room, brought herself back, and just as soon was ready to run out of the room again. There came a horrible pleasure, a pleasure that was laced with a kind of shame—her heart was overflowing. Even her handwriting changed: it was crabbed, controlled only by its extreme miniaturization and intense pressure of the pen. She came to a description of Magda Goebbels's corpse when the Russians found it after her suicide, and the thing struck her so—she felt the need to copy the entire passage into her notebook. Each time she tried, however, the gremlin of her gaze went wild: she mangled sentences, unable to concentrate for the time it took to move her eyes from book to notebook. But still she would not, indeed could not, leave off and let well enough alone, and so five times—each time more desperately than the time before—she began to copy the following:

Berlin, May 3, 1945

On May 2, 1945, in the center of Berlin, on the premises of the bunker of the German Reich Chancellery, several meters from the entry door to said bunker, Lieutenant Colonel Klimenko and the Majors Bystrov and Chasin (in the presence of Berlin residents—the German Lange, Wilhelm, cook of the Reich Chancellery, and Schneider, Karl, garage superintendent of the Reich Chancellery) at 17:00 hours found the charred bodies of a man and woman; the body of the man was of short stature, the foot of the right leg was in a half-twisted position (club-foot) in a charred metal prosthesis; on it lay the remains of a burnt party uniform of the NSDAP and a singed party badge; near the burnt body of the woman was discovered a singed golden cigarette etui, on the body a golden party badge of the NSDAP and a singed golden broach. Near the heads of the two bodies lay two Walther pistols Nr. 1 (damaged by fire).

On the third of May 1945 Platoon Leader of the Russian Defense Department SMERSH of the 207th Protection Division, Lieutenant Colonel Iljin, found in the bunker of the Reich Chancellery in a separate room on several beds the corpses of children (five girls and a boy) from the ages of three to fourteen. They were dressed in light night-gowns and showed signs of poisoning.

As she finally finished the copying, Margaret grabbed her head in her hands.

Achtung! (Margaret wrote to herself in the notebook.)
Regarding the children:

Their ages, at the time of their deaths, were between four and twelve, not three and fourteen as the Soviets say here.

They were taken by SMERSH to the prison of Plötzensee, where the bodies were viewed by more Germans, for the sake of identification. And by more Russians, for the sake of the press, and the lurid sight of the enemy's surrender of even its children.

Regarding the photographs:

Margaret held the pictures up to the light and considered whether or not she could sketch what she saw on the page, but she felt nauseous. Instead, she wrote,

The children look fresh in death. They can be seen in the photographs—mortuary pictures from Plötzensee— still in the clean, white cotton nightgowns they wore to bed, blond hair still in braids, color in their cheeks, the apotheosis of everything the National Socialists meant by the word Heimat. Their heads are turned toward the camera, each in turn, held erect by a young Russian coroner in a butcher's apron, round tortoiseshell glasses, and long, black rubber gloves.

A few moments later, Margaret was still on red alert. She recalled that once, she had read a letter Magda Goebbels wrote with her own hand. It was reproduced in its entirety in a book that she knew was very likely still somewhere in the flat. It quickly became shining and irresistible. She went to the shelf and began to page through several books. She couldn't remember exactly where she had read it, that was the trouble. She went into the hall and knocked over two piles of books and rummaged.

The passage was nowhere to be found.

Back at the desk, she grabbed her forehead in her hand again. Her mind pulsed. All at once, like a word on the tip of the tongue bubbling up after sleep, she knew after all which book it was. She plunged her hand to the shelf and withdrew a dust-covered book: *The Death of Adolf Hitler.* She paged through it, and there indeed was the facsimile.

She could feel hives blooming on her neck. She was so excited—it was as if someone else's body were moving under her head. Her heart beat, and it was hardly her own heart.

> *My beloved son! Now we have been here in the Führerbunker for six days—Papa, your six little siblings and I—in order to give our National Socialist lives the only possible honorable finish. Whether you will receive this letter I don't know . . . You must know that against his wishes I have stayed by Papa's side, that even last Sunday the Führer wanted to help me to get out of here. You know your mother—we have the same blood, for me there was no question of it. Our heavenly idea is going to pieces—and with it everything beautiful, awe-inspiring, noble and good that I have known in my life. The world that will come after the Führer and National Socialism is no longer worth living in, and therefore I have brought the children here with me. They are too good for the life that will come after us, and the merciful Lord will understand me when I give them salvation myself. You will live on, and I have one request of you: Don't forget that you're a German, never do anything that is against your honor, and take care that through your life our death was not in vain.*
>
> *The children are wonderful. Without any assistance they help each other in these more than primitive conditions. Whether they sleep on the floor, whether or not they can wash, whether they have something to eat or not, never a word of complaint or tears. The bombardments shake the bunker. The older ones protect the younger ones, and their presence here is already a blessing in that every now and then they manage to bring a smile to the Führer.*
>
> *Be true! True to yourself, true to humanity, and true to your country. In each and every regard! . . . Be proud of us and try to hold us in proud and joyous memory. Everyone has to die sometime, and isn't it more beautiful, honorable, and brave to die young than to live a long life under shameful conditions? The letter must go out—Hanna Reitsch is taking it with her. She's flying out again! I embrace you in closest, warmest, motherly love! My beloved son, live for Germany! Yours, Mother*

By the time Margaret finished, her hands were shaking and her eyes were wet; she thought they were bleeding, but it was only a few tears. Magda's strange idea gripped her—this choosing of death over shame.

Margaret made herself ready and went to bed. For a long time she lay still under the covers. It was raining out and there came a tapping. The panes shook.

Margaret could not sleep. She began to read a second time, now with heavier eyes. She read about Magda Goebbels's high marks in *Gymnasium;* about the details of her relationship with the Zionist Arlosoroff; about Magda's own efforts on behalf of the Zionist movement as a young woman. Regarding the Soviet inquest, she learned that Magda killed her children with the help of a doctor, that none of the children had struggled, except the oldest girl, who, according to the coroner's report, had bruises on her body and so apparently had been held down. No one was sure exactly what the poison was, as the Russian coroner had not been able to ascertain, but it left the tips of the children's fingers yellow. When Margaret read this, she was very quiet inside, her thoughts slowing and then stopping altogether, her head pulsing.

It was almost morning. Margaret got out of bed. She had a thick twist of energy in her chest.

She took a gesso board out of the closet. She flipped through the biography of Magda, to its glossy centerfold pictures. She propped the book up on the desk. Over the gesso board, her hands moved. She was surprised at herself, and frightened. Her fingers were of steel, and she applied so much pressure to the stick of charcoal that twice she broke it. Finally she drew with only a nub. She watched as Magda Goebbels's face bloomed in black lines. Magda Goebbels's face rose up, in the form of a glamour shot taken in Magda's youth. It was a young face, from the time before she had given birth to any of her six children with Goebbels.

The image of the face held Margaret and mesmerized her. It had traces of all the later forms of ugliness that came to dominate—the low, heavy brow bone; the snideness of the lines between the wing of the nose and outer corner of the lip; the thin mouth; the priggish tilt of the forehead. And yet—and here is where Margaret dragged her charcoal back and forth, craving the curve: something, something in the young face was still bleeding, still searching for metaphysics, and Margaret carefully traced every softness and hardness. She felt her disgust stretching, becoming a concentration that was almost tenderness.

Later she took out oils. She brought in color. One corner of the face became so vivid, it seemed ready to move. Margaret, possessed by some devil, produced a large, cold face, with silver-blond, salon-waved hair—a face glaring out at her with civilized eyes and callousness. Margaret brought in the squeezed-out bits of light and dark, setting the woman's hair to gleaming, the shadows of her nostrils to deepening. And finally, Magda Goebbels stared out at Margaret Taub, pert and quizzical.

As dawn broke, Margaret was in bed. The last thing she remembered before falling asleep was that she could feel the heat of a bird at the window, the slash of its wings against the glass—although it may have been nothing more than the rain grown violent.

SEVEN • Privacy and Devotion

The Grunewaldstrasse was an old West Berliner street, too far behind the front lines to have been rocked by the fall of the Wall or any other terror of the metropolis, so the street did not want for eyes, the kind of eyes that grow like lichen if a street knows no heavy winds.

Even an abbreviated inventory must include the eyes of the old lady from Armenia with bottle-black hair, who leaned permanently from the window of a half-height flat that was squeezed under the airy *bel-étage* at Number 89. She folded her arms across the cobwebbed ledge and watched, especially at night. Although it was not unheard of that a pedestrian's eyes wandered up and met the old lady's by accident, something about the way her eyelids squared with her brow seemed to suggest a lack of involvement: "have no fear" they seemed to say—"we will not tell a soul if we see you hot-wire a 1986 Mercedes." Meanwhile, across the street, two glossy dogs were on standby behind the door at the Internet café. They had eyes as blue as forget-me-nots, with the same yellow center, and roused themselves for the man in a neon orange traffic cop's uniform, who passed several times each day, bicycling up and down the Grunewaldstrasse without once touching the handlebars, yelling his head off. Everyone called him Loud Guy, or sometimes only the Loud One.

So if Erich, the *Hausmeister* at Number 88, where Margaret Taub lived, was watching everyone and everything, who could blame him? He told himself it was a defensive stance—he lived in a neighborhood of ghouls.

Erich was the hero of his own story. In the courtyard of Margaret's building he lived, in a little ivy-covered house. He was unusually flesh-less, his skull easily visible through the skin of his face, and already the night when Margaret returned from the Grunewald Forest, he had seen her while she was heaving clumps of clothing into the trash. And he had observed her long before that as well.

Erich was old. He seemed stern but in fact he was kindly; he was blindingly efficient, and he was knowledgeable about all matters literal and very few matters figurative. He was one of those men who think simply but are politically resolute, much like the plain-spoken Georg Elser, the carpenter who built cabinets and clocks, kept his own council, and in 1938 almost managed to assassinate Hitler single-handedly.

Erich was an *Autonomer,* an old one—he had been part of the '68 generation before there was a '68 generation to be a part of, one of those West Berliner anti-warriors who use the informal *du* to one and all, even to plumbers and bank tellers, and the plumbers and bank tellers almost fall to the floor with a heart attack at the audacity if they are new to the quarter and he hasn't broken them in yet, although around here, almost everyone was broken in long ago.

Now it happens that Erich's story must be told as well, for through no fault of his own (almost no fault of his own, that is), he was destined to betray Margaret Taub.

The very same morning the city turned to flesh, Erich was wearing his black leather pants and matching vest, busying himself eagerly, delivering mail from the co-op management to the tenants. This was a practice he had thought up himself, officially so that the management could save the cost of postage, but he was also (although he would deny it if accused) using the opportunity to peek at the contents of each letter box—no real reason and it was certainly not mean-spirited, but he was interested. To see who had letters from the tax office, who had letters from collection agencies, and by Jove, if he saw a letter from abroad, perhaps from a lover! These were his great pleasures. Erich, who as a young man had been an anarchist, was, in his old age, something he would never have expected. His anarchism had taken a turn for the officious, his native kindness had twisted into rodent-like curiosity.

After the letters, he would check the trash. Here too, he had been active: Erich had introduced a new system of trash sorting which would save the building co-op forty euros each month. It meant the recycling was far stricter than in other living communities. A relatively low rate of compliance concerned him. Certain tenants insisted on throwing trash into improper receptacles, and thus he found himself required to sort through the trash thoroughly every week, reorganizing, rescuing treasures here and there. Today he pulled various letters and even a couple of books out of the slimy heat of the decomposing biodegradables, also a glass jar full of pickles! The letters, at least—he could easily see the names of the addressees. He would have a look at them, and then take the matter up with those individuals later.

He heard the main door to the apartment house open. Sunlight broke through from the carriage entryway. He poked forth his head. Ah, it was the American. He rustled through the trash again, watching her out of the corner of his eye.

The foreign girl was a difficult case. She always seemed to be sunken, her eyelids heavy. Erich had theories on this. In the past he had played with the idea that she slept fifteen hours a night. He knew when she came in (as he knew when everyone came in) and he knew when she went out (he could see these things from his garden house in the courtyard), and he also had a good view of when her lights were on and when they were off. Unless she was reading with a flash-light, there was no way around it: the girl slept extremely long hours. This was one of the benedictions of the winter for Erich, when the sun in Berlin rises so late and sets so early—he had an unusually profound insight into the sleeping habits of the building's tenants.

Still, he considered the possibility that the American, this Margaret, had found some way to fool him. It seemed like her, somehow. Maybe she was awake in some invisible corner of the flat. He had had certain outrageous experiences with her in the past that would support this. On one occasion when her lights were *on,* Erich went and rang her bell in order to discuss with her the new basement allotments, and she did not come to the door. Even after repeated ringing of the bell. He went back downstairs and looked up at her windows again and saw the lights were certainly on and a shadow was moving behind the curtains. He went up and rang the bell more forcefully. Still, she did not come to the door. He watched from his house in the courtyard as her bathroom window went from open to shut, and he fumed. Erich would not have minded helping the girl, back at the beginning. She was not unsympa-thetic. But she had been so morose toward the community for several years now, he had lost his goodwill.

After the incident with the door, Erich even considered not saying *Guten Tag* to her. If he wanted, he could certainly pull this off. When angered with another fellow who lived in the building, he had done exactly this—for twenty-five years. Even after repeated pleas from third parties to relent. But Erich believed in an apology. When, after twenty-six years and three months, the man did apologize, Erich had been more than willing to drink a beer with him, and from then on, all was well. But he did like to hear that someone was sorry. It was worth the wait.

His general aggravation with the girl had led him to do something he would normally *never* do: he had read the contents of some of her discarded mail. He learned that she worked as a guide, gave historical walking tours, and although she considered herself an intellectual and read a great deal (or made a great deal of photocopies) of Foucault and Stephen Greenblatt, and for a while took a close interest in Rosa Luxemburg, otherwise, for the most part, she was merely interested in the Third Reich. You know: who was guilty here, and who was guilty there; the Auschwitz trials; how many died here, how many died there. To judge by the papers that went into the recycling, she seemed to make all sorts of photocopies related to gossip about whores like Magda Goebbels, Geli Raubal, and Eva Braun, and he had once peeked through her door as she went in and seen a bookshelf with the complete diaries of Joseph Goebbels, with their distinctive spines. Erich thought it was a most unpleasant business—foreigners who sensationalize or even think they can call Germany to task. Where had she been when he had taken a stand against his own father, the old Nazi who didn't like his (Erich's) leather pants (that was a laugh!), been partially disowned and had to make a new life for himself? Not even a glimmer in her *grandfather's* eye, that's where.

That Margaret Taub!—she was so sympathetic at first glance, such a soft-looking girl, almost clownish, as if she were ready to be touched, ready to feel pain over anything. After a while, though, you saw that she was soft enough, but so dreamy as to be almost criminally oblivious. All in all, Erich thought, the impression was of a poisonous cobra that believes itself, very genuinely, to be a small dog.

But Erich kept saying *Guten Tag.* The trouble was this: although she never seemed surprised at his presence in the courtyard, she never seemed to recognize him either, even after six years in the flat. Yes, she didn't seem to know him, and although she never withdrew that half-smile, she also never looked at him. Her eyes always found something to rest on off to the side. Perhaps it was for this reason that he continued to say hello: there would be no satisfaction in withholding his friendliness if she wouldn't notice him doing it.

Today he watched her. There was something more distressing about her as she locked up her bicycle, more wild-eyed. (Recall: this was the very day the city turned to flesh.)

Erich said *Guten Tag* and Margaret gave a kind of cry, as though she had been about to scream but quickly suppressed the noise before it escaped. She turned her head and took a few swaying steps toward her stairwell, paused as if to regain confidence, and then darted away like an animal into its burrow.

Erich took off his gloves and went in his own ivy-covered house. He opened the file cabinet in the downstairs room that was almost black with weeks-old cigarette smoke. Without much trouble, he found the heavy notebook he was looking for, thick with several paper clips holding in loose pieces of paper.

It was a diary. He had found it once in the trash, along with a number of Margaret's other belongings. He had held on to it only as evidence, should it ever come to that: evidence of the outrage! *Some* people in this building, they threw reams of paper matter thoughtlessly together with the general trash!

(The irony—that Margaret with her obsessive privacy, her self-isolating ways wanton in their thoroughness, would be hounded by precisely such a busybody as this. She had thrown the journal in the general trash expressly because the paper receptacle was dry-looking and odorless—it seemed a comfortable place to dig through and steal from. The general trash, the foul-smelling option, appeared to be a roiling abyss that swallowed up far more conclusively. Little had she known!)

Erich thought, now, that he would read the diary. The English would be a struggle. It was the English that had stopped him from perusing it before. There had been, however, reasons to learn English once, reasons having to do with international anarchism. And, Erich told himself consolingly, he liked a challenge.

And then it happened that Erich the *Hausmeister* read several long passages Margaret Taub had once written. He became quite interested; he encountered a Margaret very different from the Margaret he knew. The American, it seemed, had not always been as she was now.

February 18, 1999
(Ah!—Erich thought—an old diary then, from when she first moved in. Not a bad thing at all.)

My dearest diary,
   Why do I write to you? Why do I write!!! I'm in love, you see. And I'm too proud to really talk to anybody about it (not that I

know anyone here anyway) because honestly, I'm afraid I'm in love in the most terrible way—the way of taking oneself and one's situation too seriously, of the mind brushing over the same sad fibers of conversation one had with the beloved with such loving repetition that if it were alcohol, I'd have passed out long ago.

It's Amadeus. I'm in love in the way I thought only thirteen-year-olds could be and I haven't felt anything close to it for such a long time and the terrible thing is that I don't think he loves me back. It's ridiculous, this kind of full-blown sweet torture, that the poets know so well and is so utterly ridiculous, where one vacillates between intense ecstasy and intense agony throughout the day, because one feels as if one were walking a tightrope where falling one way will mean waves of joy unknown to humankind and falling the other way will mean the darkest hell. Your mood simply depends on which possibility you take most seriously at the time. Meanwhile, you attempt to stay on the tightrope, because that way at least you preserve a chance at the ultimate beauty. For instance, you would never attempt to force the beloved with an ultimatum even though that is obviously the quickest escape from this terrible state. It's the best idea nevertheless, because that way, if he says "no chance, not now, not ever," then you could at least start grieving and move on. But no, you don't have the courage. You would rather stay on the hideous tightrope.

Amadeus is his name, and he was a good friend of my father's. I had the sense to look him up after I got to Berlin. Dad used to get dreamy when he talked about him, as though just because Amadeus was behind the Wall, he was dead. I think he talked that way because Amadeus couldn't travel and Dad felt guilty for being free.

Here's what I know so far: Amadeus Vilnius is his full name (no middle) from Magdeburg in Brandenburg. His parents are both of Russian-German stock—ethnic Germans who lived for centuries in Russia and were driven out by Stalin during the war. He's forty-four, a professor of Russian history. He teaches mostly theory, speaks perfect Russian, also English and French. Needless to say, he's brilliant. He is not particularly good-looking, although he has china blue eyes with black lashes around them that are wonderful. Christina says that he looks and moves like a snail that has lost its shell, and that's entirely true. He keeps his shoulders pulled up for the most part, and he is all around slightly higher on one side. He smokes continually, Gauloises Légères. He's about six feet tall, and his hair is graying rather severely, and he's very unhappy about that. He laughs frequently and amicably, puts people at ease the way he laughs. He has a wife. He's been married to her for two and a half years—her name is Asja and she's as pretty as a picture. I saw her at the library once. Very skinny, with bird-like bones and high color in her cheeks, dark hair that stands up, and lovely clothing—brown and auburn clothing that suits her perfectly, and matches him, actually. In other words, I can't compete with her physically. Beyond that, he has a girlfriend of a year and a half whom he was with last year when he was on sabbatical. She is nineteen years old (like me— hardly a coincidence?), Russian, from a musical Jewish family; she lives in Petersburg. She is starting to rebel, Amadeus says, and having a rough time of it. He took her virginity. He says that she lied to him and said she had had many experiences before. I don't know whether I believe him on that count. Supposedly, although her dependence on him has become a burden, he doesn't have the heart to call her in Petersburg and break it off, because of her precarious position trying to establish some kind of independence from her parents. Many of her childhood friends have stopped talking to her completely and her sister as well, because she quit the orchestra. But Amadeus says, being young, she has to believe in something, and she has made him her new god. So he thinks it would be devastating to her for him to for- sake her. Asja (the pretty wife) does not know about Yulia (the Russian girl), or about me. Yulia knows about Asja, but not about me. Obviously I know about Asja and Yulia. Hopefully there are no others.

So I am the idiot. And you know, I suspect that I am the least cherished of the three of us, and not only because I'm the newest addition.

It's awful. You can see what an idiot I am. If it weren't for the all-consuming love I have for him, I would never in a million years stand for this kind of degradation. Oh Margaret, Margaret, Margaret! You will read this later and say to yourself, Look at what the loneliness did. I have always said in these pages that it is only the emotionally vulnerable who fall in love. And look at me. I should have taken precautions, knowing that these first months in Germany would be difficult. And I tried my best. I got plenty of books (well, maybe not enough truly stimulating books), and I traveled. I tried. I feel as though falling in love were catching a disease. Because I don't know how to finish this.

Well, maybe I should help you understand what I do see in Amadeus. The above description makes him sound awful. It's this: he's lovely in every way. We recognized each other's intelligence almost immediately because it's the same type of intelligence (and believe me, not everyone recognizes my intelligence). What he is doing with all these women is the same thing I do with my multiple men, you know so well: trying to gain a secret power that won't have any risk, trying to put a wall up against disappointment—the dominating pleasure of the juggler, the clandestine thrill, the sense of quiet self-congratulation. And oh, the way he responds differently to me every time I talk to him is so suspenseful; the way his personality changes. His obvious vulnerability and cravenness, but also his endless sweetness. The way he loves his books. After only a very brief time I felt like I knew him extremely well, also the bad things about him—what trouble it would be if I were his beloved. But also what joy, to be with someone who is so similar, so familiar. We can't lie to each other because we are too much alike—we both lie about the same things and for the same reasons. For example, once during an intimate moment, when he was above me, I said, "If there's anyone who deserves a harem, it's you." And he said, "If there's anyone who deserves to be queen of my harem, it's you." We were lying through our teeth, both of us. He knew I thought he was rotten, and I knew he had a great ability to crown a new woman queen of his harem every single night. The momentary truce, though, *that* was glorious.

Oh, this is horrible. If only I could quickly fall in love with someone else. I pray that it's a product of my loneliness and as soon as I start classes at the university it will dissipate. (I've transferred to the history department!) Please let it be so. That much is clear at least, that even my endless joy at his nearness would not be if I could actually possess him, because he would never stay faithful to me, so it would be an endless torture. Oh please let this infatuation pass quickly.

Erich leafed further through the book. The entries were not regular, altogether just twenty or thirty pages for a three-year period. He skipped forward to 2001.

June 20, 2002

I must tell you, poor journal, about my extraordinary good fortune. I have no one else to tell! Of course it is regarding my happiness about Amadeus. And somehow, maybe—don't jinx me!—I'm actually having an effect on him and he seems to be starting to love me. (Oh God, let it be so!) When we were in bed and had both had something to drink, I said, "Well, if I can't be your girlfriend, can I at least be your *Schatz*?" and he hugged me and said, "How about my sister?" and I objected on the grounds that then we couldn't sleep together. So he said I could be his *Schatz* but that I already was his *Schatz* anyway, and that I was a *Tier* and he liked *Tiere,* and that he liked me even if I weren't a *Tier.* Then the next day he dawdled at breakfast, and said he felt relieved that he wasn't having affairs with multiple women anymore and pulled me onto his lap and kissed me and told me he liked me and said I had a right to be jealous, that I could call him anytime I wanted because he didn't mind if I behaved as if he belonged to me, and that his wife still thought I was just an overzealous student and wasn't suspicious. Then the next day we went to bookstores together, and we had lunch and he talked further about the possibility of making a trip to Prague together, and he seemed slightly hurt when I acted like I would go somewhere alone in August instead. If you only knew Amadeus, you would see what progress this is.

Let it go, let it go. If there is anything I've learned at this point in life it is not to ask for everything immediately and at once. Getting things from Life, and from people, is like trying to catch an animal: if you run after it, it will flee; if you are still, it will come to you. If only I can be completely still!

———

Erich flipped through the book. He came to a very short entry over six months later.

January 22, 2001

I don't know what to think, but I am certain that for all the travails, the heartache, the intimate acquaintanceship with Amadeus's worst qualities, how he and the passion he arouses in me bring out my worst qualities, for all of that—I do want to try. I rejoice in him endlessly, when we're together the smell of him drives me crazy with pure love, just like in the very beginning. I I've always known that Amadeus will bring me pain—and maybe it's for later years to examine why even the pain attracts me. And yet, I don't think it's to be condemned, my love for him, because in the end, I have won. My life is not so much a happy one as one that gets zapped full of bliss over and over. Amadeus is the zapper, whether I like it or not. I've gotten more from him than he has from me, although I would give him everything I have.

EIGHT · Don Quixote of the SS

The days since the city's transformation—they passed Margaret by. When she emerged from Number 88, the city was burlesque and untamed.

Margaret was jaded now. She was not surprised that the city appeared fleshy, and she walked past it all, half blind. Let the city's bosoms spill out over the top of its dress—what did she care!

But while the sight did not disturb, the sounds still sometimes exhausted. When she heard the doors and windows drawing in breath all at once, making a reverse hissing sound up and down the avenues, she braced herself. The groaning and symphonic sighs sure to follow, as thunder follows lightning, rattled her still. The city meant it vindictively, she thought, knew she was its wind instrument with a reed calibrated just to its melodizing breath.

It had a message, too.

Something would breathe at her, whisper in her ear: *Magda was not the only one,* it would say at first, more on the quiet side. But then louder, with a slight sneer: *And what about the stupid ones?*

For reasons Margaret could not quite understand, her mind would run with this instantly. When she heard the question she would begin to ask herself again and again: but what *about* the stupid ones?

And inexplicably, the question would expand in her mind in the following manner: should stupid people, she would ask herself bitingly, be called innocent? And then she always thought of Hitler's consort, Eva Braun, as exhibit A. It was Eva Braun and her almost successful suicide attempts at the altar of her desperation for Hitler that suggested themselves to Margaret as the purest idiocy. And then the little matter of her mania, her wild love.

Was Eva Braun, Hitler's mincing little girlfriend, innocent or guilty?

The stupid could not be called incontrovertibly guilty, so Margaret's ratiocinations went. In the case of Eva Braun and Hitler's other concubines, their womanliness held them aloof from activity, like the fatness of larvae. Eva Braun's three suicide attempts during the years of her affair with Hitler might even be interpreted as resistance, albeit of an exclusively self-referential kind. By no means, however, could these plump larvae be called innocent either. Their coarse minds were complicit by default in any crime offered to them. Margaret had a picture in her head of Eva Braun with her broad, girlish face and swelling hips, her chamois underwear, driving her Volkwagen Beetle, that chubby little car.

The question of how to judge Eva Braun seemed terribly important.

More than once, Margaret read over the few surviving diary entries of Hitler's mistress.

March 11, 1935

There is only one thing I want. I would like to be seriously ill, and to hear nothing more about him for at least a week. Why doesn't something happen to me? Why do I have to go through all this? If only I had never set eyes on him! I am utterly miserable. I shall go out and buy some more sleeping powder and go into a half-dreamlike state, and then won't think about it so much.

Why doesn't that devil take me with him? It would be much better with him than it is here.

I waited for three hours in front of the Carlton, and had to watch him buying flowers for Ondra and inviting her to dinner. (That was just my mad imagination. March 16.)

He only needs me for certain purposes, otherwise it is not possible. This is idiocy. When he says he loves me, it only means he loves me at that particular instant. Like his promises, which he never keeps. Why does he torment me like this, when he could finish it off at once?

February 18, 1935

Yesterday he came quite unexpectedly, and we had a delightful evening. The nicest thing is that he is thinking of taking me from the shop and—but I had better not get excited about it yet—he may give me a little house. I simply must not let myself think about it. It would be marvelous. I wouldn't have to open the door to our "beloved customers," and go on being a shopgirl. Dear

God, grant that this may really happen not in some far-off time, but soon.

. . .

I am so infinitely happy that he loves me so much, and I pray that it will always be like this. It won't be my fault if he ever stops loving me. . . .

Miss Braun's submission to fate, her longing, and the dependency of her desire! It was monstrous.

And then, by chance, in these weeks, another person appeared. A man in a polyester golf coat it was; he walked into Margaret's life, and it was the reality, rather than the unreality, that threw down the gauntlet this time. Berlin had yet another trick up its sleeve.

It began when Margaret was giving a tour of general sites to a group of middle-aged Irish and Australians. The group was standing at Hitler's bunker, when a heckler accosted them.

Margaret had positioned the tourists on the parking lot that covers the eastern edge of the Führer's final cubbyhole, at the end of the flat expanse opening onto the Wilhelmstrasse, beyond the shuddering apartment buildings. She faced them, and in the distance, behind the backs of the tourists, she caught a glimpse of a gangly, bobbing figure coming through the arcade.

On most tours, even through her trance, Margaret maintained a monitor of all people nearby not part of the tour. Passersby might always cause her trouble. Precisely because her trances were so precious, she knew how to deflect, without even stopping to think, all of the following: Italians and Americans who joined the tour surreptitiously without paying, Germans who didn't appreciate foreign interest in the Third Reich, drunken Brits visiting Berlin on stag weekends, beggar women who weaved in and out of the group asking for money and unsettling the tourists, jeering teenagers of every nationality, and the mentally disturbed. She protected her tourists like a lioness from these intrusions.

And on this day, the man in the distance wasn't moving with intention, but was rather making circles, coming slowly closer to the group, and this set Margaret's alarm bells ringing. Finally the man was mingling with her customers, and sure enough, he began to crow at them.

He prattled. He spoke German to an Australian, one of Margaret's customers, a man who had walked off on his own to take a few snapshots, and the other tourists saw what was happening. They gave Margaret questioning glances. Margaret stopped the tour. She fixed the man with a glare, as public embarrassment of the intruder was always the first step.

The heckler was an octogenarian. He was thick-shouldered, horse-faced, and comically tall. He wore a polyester leisure suit of the East German kind. Because he was behaving impolitely, when Margaret spoke, she too was coarse. She said, *"Was wollen Sie mit uns? Dies hier ist eine Privattour—die Leute können auch nicht mal Deutsch."*

"Ich war dabei," he crowed, with saucy pride.

"Ach so?" said Margaret, with disbelief.

The man's elderly voice sounded cottony, as if the tip of his tongue were wrapped in duct tape, and his timbre warbled like a pubescent teenage boy's.

"Ja, ich gehörte dazu, damals."

"Wozu?"

"Na, zu den Hitlerleuten in dem Bunker."

Margaret did not want to be drawn in, but she did notice that a quick shot of adrenaline flushed her veins. She thanked him with a caustic twinge, told him that these people didn't understand him and he'd better save his stories for more sympathetic ears, but inside, she was excited. She turned back to her charges and said, by way of explanation for the interruption, "This man here says he was in the bunker with Hitler." The faces turned back to the man. He was not insensible to her ironic stance, and cried out again, *"Sie glauben's mir nicht! Aber ich bin der Prell! Ich war dabei! Das können Sie nachgucken."*

"Ich bin es mir sicher," Margaret said with conciliatory warmth.

"Ja, ja! Glauben Sie es nicht? Dabei war ich aber."

Ignoring him, Margaret turned toward the group. "Perhaps we should be moving on now?" and they returned her raised eyebrows and set off to the south.

Behind her, the old man was still crowing, this time at a group of children wearing in-line skates: *"He! Kinder! Erkennt ihr mich? Ich bin der Prell! Ich war dabei!"*

So his name was Prell. She would look it up. Maybe he was crazy, but maybe he was not. The people on the tour tumbled after her, everyone eager to discuss.

When she got home she took out her books on the topic of Hitler's last days, and it was not long before she found that there had indeed been a Prell, a certain Arthur Prell, who worked as bodyguard and radio operator in the bunker. She looked for a picture on the Internet and saw a photograph of this Arthur Prell, taken in 1942. He was very different but also very much the same: the long, horse-like face, the exceptionally broad shoulders. Her fingers shook with excitement. She swallowed. Having stumbled upon something entirely real was as good as a draught of air. She breathed deeply, and for a few moments, she felt herself a soldier called to a just war.

NINE · The Whale Ducks

A bird of prey traces a certain kind of line in the sky because it need not flap its wings, and every time Margaret glanced out the window, so this line came into her peripheral vision.

On Saturday afternoon, Margaret opened one of the windows and put her head out. She looked up into the sky. It was a blue sky, shocked out of all clouds, making the slow sound of an airplane. After a squinting perusal, she concluded there were no birds; her peripheral vision must have been mistaken. She drew back and began to pull the window closed. One final glance at the shuddering flesh of the buildings, however, an almost admiring glance at their vivacity, and she saw something move on the balcony of the building catty-corner.

Something flashed in her eyes. She squinted, and saw: the grey-feathered, hunchbacked woman in black gabardine, standing at attention. Not only that: the hawk-woman held a pair of binoculars, and her long eyes were trained on Margaret's windows. Her perch was one of those ornamental balconies from the 1890s, the kind that are convex from the house, so the woman, with her hair molded in its immaculate water waves and the lenses of her voyeur's binoculars glinting in the light, caught the full gift of the sun, and the reflection from her telescope eyes blinked into Margaret's apartment like Morse code signals.

Quickly, Margaret closed the window and drew the curtains. It was the middle of the day, but she climbed into bed.

Under the covers, she whispered to herself violently. She muttered, tossing this way and that. She told herself in a grave voice to pull herself together. She told herself in a grave voice that she was sane, but a fool. She told herself to buck up, to strike down her gullibility. She closed her eyes.

She tried to sleep but then, striking her down, came that old jangling vision she had had once before—of the curving, oval staircase with its red runner. It rose from deep in her skull, bearing its blunt weapon, and pressed against her eyes. She could smell the flaxen runner, taste the chalk of disappointment; she could touch the shadowed walls, flinch at the cold.

She slept, but when she woke up, she was not refreshed. And her heart beat again, and never had it beat faster. She thought of the sight of that feathered woman in gabardine, a feathered woman who she believed was a figment of her imagination and yet who made her stomach dive and flip.

If she could not return to the doctor right away, she decided, she would have to talk to someone else.

But Margaret didn't know anyone. She had managed that—she really had.

She decided to ride her bicycle over to Akazienstrasse and buy a guidebook to European birds.

When she got home from the bookstore she parted the curtain a crack to see if the bird was still there. Indeed. Present and alert. When the nasty beast saw the curtain move, it flew right at her window in full bird form and landed on the wide outer sill. It cocked a topaz eye at her, Margaret the helpless zoo animal, the bird gawking.

Margaret reached for the book. She compared several pictures. The bird had long tail feathers with banded stripes and yellow eyes; this bird must be an enormous version of the *Sperber,* the sparrow hawk— *Accipiter nisus.*

The *Sperber,* according to the book, was "a bird of prey with long, pointed talons that nourishes itself on smaller birds. These it hunts with lightning-quick loops and dives, knowing how to rip them out of the air in mid-flight with its beak."

At this description, a sharp and bracing sort of panic took hold of the room, and Margaret had to shut her eyes.

That evening, as she sat over her books, the memory of a friend crossed her mind after all. Or perhaps he should be called an acquaintance; in any case, she remembered someone. It was a certain Benjamin, a fellow expatriate, a music critic, with whom she had once spent a good deal of time. She had never known him well, but she had liked him; he let her sit in his kitchen for hours with a newspaper while he went about his other business, entertaining women in the living room and making loud international calls to magazine editors.

He claimed having a silent and strange woman in the house put everyone on edge, and he was eccentric enough to like the idea of putting
his guests on edge. As for Margaret, she was permitted to eat his
canned bratwurst and sauerkraut, and so for her part she had never
complained.

It was not until ten in the evening that she finally made up her mind
to go to him. It had been years since she last saw him, she did not even
have his telephone number any longer. Late at night, too, there was a
risk he would not be at home—he had been in the habit, she recalled,
of spending every night at some sleek club or other. She would have to
take her chances.

She traveled half an hour on the U2 line, all the way up to Prenzlauer Berg. She went through a concrete courtyard to a rear building where Benjamin's dark apartment house decayed. All this, she
remembered well. She rang the bell, and praise be—her heart skipped
a beat with gladness—Benjamin himself came to the door.

He was a portly man, almost forty. He had the air of a ringmaster
or a butcher, his cheeks a deep pink, his muttonchop whiskers thick
and black. His eyes were white like hard-boiled eggs, the irises
friendly and burlesque. Now he narrowed these eyes at the young
woman in his doorway.

There might have been some question as to whether he recognized
her. Before the night in the forest, Margaret knew, her features had
been soft, as though one were seeing her through a grease-smeared
lens. Now she had become sharp—the bones of her face had floated up
to the surface, and her oversized men's clothing too moved about her
in harsher shapes. After a long glance, however, Benjamin's eyes
relaxed, and he opened the door.

"Margaret Taub," he said. He was in his pajamas and a tattered
smoking jacket, reeking of garlic.

"Benjamin."

"Do you wish to visit me now, Margaret?"

"Yes, Benjamin." She tried to take him in her arms, but he stiffened.

"It's been a long time, Margaret." He looked down the stairwell to
see if anyone was with her. "After three years, all of a sudden Margaret
Taub shows up."

Margaret, relieved and excited, headed straight for her old spot in
the kitchen. Benjamin followed. His eyes widened, the whites waxing
larger. "You know what, Margaret? You're in luck, I was about to eat
a can of sauerkraut."

"Oh, yes." Margaret breathed a sigh of happiness, although she was speechless for lack of socialization. She sat down at the table in the kitchen and looked around her.

Just a moment before, standing in the hallway ringing his bell, she had had no image of his apartment; the door to his flat seemed as if it would open onto nothing at all, as though part of a stage set. But now that she found herself inside, she discovered she knew the place in every detail, was sure that almost nothing had been moved since she was last here. The same dusty, poolside furniture in orange-and-white plastic was scattered here and there, the same album covers were thumbtacked to the walls featuring lounge lizard girls in blue lipstick; the electric organ; several lamps made out of coconuts; tall piles of CDs and LPs, white-and-green-striped wallpaper falling off the walls for the moisture. Benjamin took an open can of sauerkraut out of the refrigerator and brought it to the table.

"To be honest, Margaret, I didn't think I'd ever see you again," Benjamin began.

"Neither did I," Margaret replied aimlessly and at once.

"I won't say I wasn't fine with that."

"Benjamin—" Margaret longed to touch him. But everything about the way he stood, about his rigid expression, suggested he did not trust her.

"Are you still living in Schöneberg?" he asked.

"Same place," Margaret smiled up at him.

"That's a surprise."

"It's not so easy to change," Margaret said.

"No?" He raised his eyebrows in his burlesque grimace. "Well," he said, in a falsetto. He brought two beers over to the table and sat down. "Margaret Taub," he said, still in the falsetto, opening his beer. "To what do I owe the pleasure?"

"Well," she hesitated. She swept the dust off the unused end of the table. "I wanted to talk to you about something in particular."

"Oh yeah? I wanted to talk to you about something in particular too," he said.

Margaret sensed this was not good.

"Do you want to know if I ever went to Gau-Algesheim?" he asked.

"To where?"

"The dumb monkey, eh?"

"What?" Margaret looked at him.

"It was scummy of you, Margaret."

"Benjamin—"

"Don't try to Benjamin me. The answer is no. I didn't go. You said you'd interpret for me, I was on the platform, the train came. No Margaret. No one came. Margaret cut out. Now the old man is dead."

"The old man?"

"I guess you knew we had to go down there before the asshole died. Now my father won't ever get the house back."

"Benjamin, Benjamin," she said plaintively, trying to buy time. What was he talking about? "Benjamin," she stuttered. "The thing is, I never leave Berlin. I haven't gone outside the city limits in years." She said that, and realized with a start that, except for Sachsenhausen, which was still part of the Berliner public transport network and so hardly an exception, it was true.

"*Now* I know that. I found out the hard way. You could have told me before I bought both the tickets. Three hundred and seventy five euros each, nonrefundable. My father's sure not coming over to Germany, I can tell you that. You were our chance."

Margaret tried to mask her confusion. "But you always behave so badly, Benjamin," she said. It was the only honest statement that occurred to her.

"They did not give me German citizenship for my charm, Margaret, they gave it to me because they killed half my family."

"Okay," Margaret said. "Okay." She swallowed. Something jogged her. She remembered a time—waiting in line with Benjamin at the ticket office at Zoo Station. He was smoking a cigar; she was worried about the smoke, then an altercation with the station police. Of course, she must have been preparing to make a trip with him. A trip to the south, it seemed to her, fuzzily. Why hadn't she made the trip?

"Do you still want to go?" she asked. "I'll go," she said. She wanted terribly to befriend him.

"*Now* you want to? Well—" He looked at the calendar on the wall next to them. It displayed June 2001; it too was covered in dust. "The bastard is dead now anyway," he said. "There's no point. We'd have to sue the state. The fun part would have been tearing it away from the anti-Semite." He took a bite of sauerkraut. "What did you want to talk to me about, Margaret?"

Margaret drank her beer. The single bulb on the ceiling cast a light that fatigued the eyes. "Benjamin—" she began, but stopped.

The fact was that in this location—with the old, precariously tilting stacks of records around her, the smell of curry and mildew, Benjamin's kind, impossibly familiar face—the events of the last weeks seemed remote. She wondered if she had really seen any hawk-woman. She wondered if she had not perhaps been inwardly exaggerating about the flesh, the transformation, the bird. Now, picturing everything in her mind, it all seemed extremely unlikely.

But that had been the entire reason for coming—so that Benjamin could bring her back to reality. So Margaret spoke up. "Do you have any idea what I was doing, say, about two or three years ago?" she asked. "Any idea at all?"

"What? You want me to tell you about your own life?"

"Well—" she said, her face starting to itch, "there's this time I can't remember. I know it's odd, but—that's how it is." Margaret caught her breath.

"What do you want me to tell you?"

"Well, back when we were friends, for example. After that, there's a foggy time. It's like when you think back on your childhood. Sometimes you can remember when you were six years old, but weirdly, not very much from when you were seven."

Benjamin pulled on his mustache. "Okay," he said.

Margaret leaned over the table and kissed his cheek, trying to solidify any goodwill he might have toward her. Benjamin put his hands on the table and licked his lips.

"You lived down in Schöneberg," he said. "What about that guy? You were in love with the German guy, right? Not with me, that's for sure."

"A German?"

"You've got to remember that guy. Even I remember him."

"Benjamin, I told you, I don't remember anything."

"What, not even the German? You were crazy about him."

"Really?"

Benjamin looked at her and became still for a fraction of an instant. Then he began to chew the side of his cheek. "Are you sure you're okay, Margaret?"

"I think so," she said, but her eyes stung. This seemed to mortify Benjamin, and he pulled on his whiskers.

"Well, all I can tell you is what I know, Margaret. The thing is, you were always secretive. You never introduced me. I thought you were embarrassed of him. I only saw the two of you once, on Wein-bergsweg, and it was dark, and you didn't see me. He was older, I remember that. And then after you didn't show up to go to Gau-Algesheim, it was like you'd dropped off the face of the earth. You never called, your phone number went out of service. I figured you'd left Germany."

"You were angry at me." Margaret rubbed her face. So there had been a man. She looked at the beer in front of her, picked it up, and drank almost the entire thing down in one go, wincing. Her eyes began to water in earnest.

"True enough," Benjamin said. "Let's see. You always wore those girly little dresses back then, didn't you. Not like now," and he gestured at her oversized man's trousers, whose cuffs had lately been dragging behind her in the sod, their hems unraveling, and the broad-cloth shirt. "But okay. What happens when *you* try to remember?"

"I told you, Benny. There's nothing. Nothing comes to mind at all."

Benjamin poured her a shot of Unicum.

"I don't want that," Margaret said.

"Don't drink it if you don't want it."

Margaret picked up the shot glass and drank it down. Then she began to laugh. "It's all ridiculous!"

"It's ridiculous all right."

Margaret laughed on and on. The laughter kept coming even after she was ready for it to stop. Benjamin sat with his arms crossed, looking at her with an uncertain smile.

Finally she took a breath. "There's one thing," she said, swallowing. "I often see one thing. But it's not a memory. It's more of a picture. Maybe even more like a smell than a picture. I think I dreamt it or saw it on TV. It comes to me sometimes when I try."

"That's good, Margaret. That's a clue. What is it?"

Margaret gave a last hysterical peal of laughter. The sound was shrill. "It's a staircase in an apartment house," she said, choking on saliva.

"Where?" Benjamin asked.

"I don't know where. Nowhere I've ever been. But I can see it perfectly. The staircase curves in an oval spiral upward around an oval shaft in the middle. At the top there's a skylight with wedged panes. I can see it all really well. The window is like a wheel with spokes. But oval-shaped, to match the shape of the stairwell. And because of the skylight, the stairwell is bright at the center and shadowy around the edges."

"Okay," Benjamin said.

"And the stairs are covered in red flaxen runners, the kind that smell like straw."

"So it's probably Berlin."

"What?"

"Red flaxen runners are mostly a Berlin thing."

"Oh," Margaret said. She had not thought of this.

"What else?" Benjamin asked.

"At the bottom, there's a girl, about my age, walking up the stairs."

"Bingo, Margaret," Benjamin said. "That must be you."

"No, no. Not me at all. She's wearing a bluish dress. I don't have a blue dress." Margaret felt herself sinking in—seeing in her mind the narrow blue stripes of the faded fabric, the brown plastic belt made to look like leather. She let out her breath. "The girl is looking up, and she can see there's a man up at the top of the stairs. The man doesn't see her. He's leaning both arms on the banister way up there under the skylight, he's smoking a cigarette, almost at the top of the house, maybe four or five stories up, pretty far away from her. She can see the smoke from his cigarette, it's curling grey against the skylight, and even sometimes next to her, she notices ash fluttering down. She calls up to him, but he doesn't call back. She's walking up the stairs, holding on to the banister, and calling. But every time she puts her head over the edge and looks up into the white light in the shaft, he's never any closer, and she gets blinded by the brightness. When she looks back down at the stairs, the ovals are burnt on her eyes, and she can see the shape of the skylight on the stairs, black spots like silverfish."

"Like silverfish?"

"Yeah."

"Okay, that's good. I should be taking notes on all this." Benjamin poured himself another shot of Unicum, and then one for Margaret. She drank it down. "What else?" he said.

"Actually, there *is* something else." Margaret swallowed. "Maybe it's a different dream. Sometimes I think it's a different dream, totally unconnected. Or maybe it's later. It's probably a different dream. But in any case, on the same stairs, while the girl is still climbing, something actually crashes through the skylight. It crashes a hole in the glass up there in the roof and it drops down. Down past the fifth- and fourth-floor landings, all the way down to the bottom. Once it's down on the floor in the cellar, the girl knows something. *Nothing will ever be the same.* And the reason: she's lost the fight."

"What fight?"

"I don't know. That's just what's going on. I don't even know if it's in her mind. Maybe it's a narrator saying it in the background, or some music playing which has those lyrics."

"Okay."

"Well, anyway, the thing, whatever it is, it falls all the way down to the bottom floor, way down below, onto this blue-and-white-checkered floor down there. There's a mosaic on the underground level, and it falls onto those tiles. But it doesn't make a crashing sound. It lands silently. And the girl looks over the banister, looks down, and sees whatever it is, maybe something the size of a fist, a little red and grey on the blue-and-white tiles."

All of this Margaret had remembered that very afternoon, while she was fretful in bed.

"You have no idea where this came from?" Benjamin asked.

Margaret considered. "I think I probably made it up." Her eyes were closed, she felt like sleeping now. Benjamin spoke again, but his tone had changed.

"Margaret," he said, "there's someone I want you to meet."

Margaret opened her eyes. There was a movement at the doorway. She roused herself to standing, feeling much more drunk than she had known. She held on to the chair for support. She peered. A young woman at the entrance to the kitchen. The newcomer was barefoot and wore only a T-shirt and underwear. Her hair was in disarray, her cheeks pink with sleep. And the funny and terrible thing was that Margaret was looking at herself. The woman had the same wide-set eyes, the same long bones, the same skin dotted with moles. Her legs had the same sparse hair, the same narrow kneecaps, her veins the same streaking presence through her freckles. Her hair was like Margaret's, long and fine and curly.

"Hello," Margaret said.

"Hello," the woman said.

Looking at her, Margaret felt a change. Warm curtains closed around her eyes. Through the diaphanous fabric she could see alternating shadows, a correspondence between prisms. She heard a radio far away playing a tin melody she already knew.

There was something else, Margaret thought, something else she was meant to remember. What was it? Margaret put her hands over her eyes, and sat down at the table again.

The young woman went over to the refrigerator, took out a bottle of water, and slammed the door. She left the kitchen.

Benjamin turned to Margaret and said with embarrassment that could still not mask his excitement. "What do you think of her?"

"She looks exactly like me," Margaret said.

Benjamin looked at Margaret a long time. "Not really," he finally said. "I found her at the King Kong Klub last night."

"Is she German?"

"She's Czech," Benjamin said.

Margaret gave a cry and tried to get up to leave. She did not know what was coming over her, but again, as after meeting the doctor, she felt a creeping sensation of rot, as of having found by chance some terrible thing for which she was partly at fault. She stumbled and caught herself on the table, but in the process she knocked Benjamin's beer onto the floor. He went to get a rag, she poured herself another glass of Unicum and drank it down.

In the end she was so drunk he had to carry her into the bedroom. She felt like a sea creature with arms gushed on the currents. She fought back a little: she told him she did not want to stay; she told him sleepily that she would go home. Benjamin said not to worry. He said he and Lenka, as the girl was called, were going out anyway, the bed was free. He took her shoes off, covered her, and went out. Margaret heard him talking quietly to the young woman in the other room, and the plink-plank of her own voice. It was angry.

Margaret slept

When she woke up it was still night and she did not know where she was. She was alone and she could smell that she was not in her own bed. She raised herself on her elbows, her heart beating.

Then she saw the Jägermeister Christmas lights.

She could hear Benjamin clomping around hastily in the kitchen, his footsteps deliberate. Margaret decided he must be getting ready to leave. She listened for the girl, too, but did not hear a second pair of footsteps. Finally the door to the apartment sounded. It opened and closed with a bang. After that, all was still.

The room where Margaret lay was narrow. It dead-ended into a grotto balcony. The Jägermeister Christmas lights were wound around its balustrade.

Margaret remembered this room from before. She had always thought it had a quality of fungus, or fungal nearness, as if it were in the shade of a giant mushroom.

She couldn't sleep. Why, she didn't know—she had drunk enough. But her heart was pounding awfully. She closed her eyes and lay back into the pillow. By some dark trick of the imagination she thought she could hear a magpie out on the balcony, scratching at the cement floor.

She listened. She lay very still. She turned on a little lamp by the pillow. There was a book lying on the floor next to the bed. She picked it up. The title was *Die Wal-Enten* (The Whale Ducks). The author was one Olaf Therild, the book was in German, published in West Berlin, 1975. She opened it and began to read the first page. Right away, she found herself sliding in.

The Whale Ducks

Millennia to come, the world was overwhelmed by floods whose causes even then were in dispute. Berlin was buried at the bottom of a great sea. Above this sea over Berlin, only the tops of the tallest buildings still protruded from under the water.

A new animal reigned, a species that called itself the whale duck. The whale ducks were large, robust creatures. They fed on the old human buildings under the water. These had become soggy and nutritious during the centuries of inundation.

One of these whale ducks was one day vanquishing her hunger, diving down under the surface of the water to take bites out of architectural glories of the past, when she came up having unknowingly bitten off the top of a church steeple (the whale ducks were very large indeed), and developed a stomachache not long after. An operation was necessary. When the whale-duck surgeon looked inside, she found that while the steeple itself had been digested, there was something else, the entire skeleton of a human being in the stomach of the duck, and this was the source of the problem. The skeleton clutched a bottle of scent in one claw-like hand and in the other, a glass jar which at first appeared stuffed with cotton. Closer inspection revealed that the vial contained a sheaf of paper, rancid and pulpy and covered in the symbols once used for communication by the humans.

The skeletal remains met a fate not entirely atypical. It happened that the whale duck who had swallowed the skeleton, by the name of Botuun, was a great lover of the theater. She had mated in her youth, had been the wife of a great monster of a duck, so large in fact that he had not been long for this world. But she had been left a fortune (and some very large ducklings): meadowlands, swamps, and several factories that derived extracts from the swamp which were then used in making dye, in turn used to make paints.

Botuun saw to it that the skeleton became part of her own theater—her own house of shadows, as such it was known. Shadowing was a theatrical form, an entrenched part of the "ancient" culture of the ducks—a theater of the dead. The remains of dead things, usually skeletal, sometimes mummified, were painted in bright colors, and bits of putty were used to round the edges, so that the skeletons appeared as they would have in life. Or at least, as the ducks supposed they would have looked. Humans, for example, had been extinct for so long, and their records submerged and dissolving under water for so many eons, that no one knew exactly what they had looked like, what color their skin had been, or even whether they had had fur. It was possible to imagine that they had been green creatures, an adaptation designed to camouflage them against the green of grass and trees, as some archeologists held, or that they had been blackish like the bats of today, the only non-water mammal to have survived the floods and often kept as pets by the whale ducks. In the traditional shadow theater, however, the views of archeologists were predated and later ignored—the impulses that had given rise to a theater of the dead were much older and more ingenuous than would allow for scientific influence. So the puttied skeletons were painted in many colors, exactly as the whale ducks in their earliest powwows had imagined that humans, the chief recipient of the ducks' tireless fascination, might have appeared. They were given false hair, not only on their heads but protruding from points all down their spines. The hair was traditionally black or white, although villains were sometimes blazing green.

Because the humans were tiny by the standards of the ducks, their remains were also easy to maneuver. In the shadow theater, the joints of the humans—every finger, every vertebra—were articulated by white threads that hung from the ceiling. The skeletons became something very similar to marionettes.

The stories that the ducks made the humans tell were often

tragedies of the distant humans' lives, and usually in lyrical, exaggerated motion, projected into much larger sizes with light and magnifying lenses so that the audience would not be forced to strain its eyes. The ducks were wont to enjoy shadow theater while sitting in semidarkness, under the influence of an herb that made them more susceptible to extremes of emotion.

The ducks liked best that which was farthest away but which was capable of seeming the nearest.

The skeleton that had been discovered in Botuun's venerable stomach was a narrow, dainty piece, and gloriously, blindingly intact. There was a symmetry to its godly rib cage, a swoop of the cheekbones, a set of teeth that gleamed with pearly winks of light. It was clear from the moment it was removed from Botuun by the surgeon that it would one day be a celebrated shadow piece, perhaps famous throughout the nation of the whale ducks. After her convalescence, Botuun saw to it that the skeleton was taken to the workshop of a master shadowist, and made into an object of great beauty, and with pride she turned the skeleton over to her theater.

The first piece that the new skeleton was made to perform was an old standby, an opera, *The Magistrate of Naragir.* All the whale ducks were familiar with the story.

It begins in a time of relative peace, in the country of Lon. The intermittent wars with the enemy country to the north are in abeyance. The eponymous magistrate begins not as any kind of magistrate at all, but as the ninth of thirteen impoverished children—a family so poor they live in a clay cave they have hollowed out of the side of a cliff. To add insult to the situation, the young man who would become magistrate, by the name of Hans, is born with a deformity: his arms are short and twisted: his hands join directly with his elbows. At his birth his mother weeps; she believes he will be useless as a laborer. He will starve or live off the charity of relations for the rest of his life.

But the boy grows, and slowly he proves himself: he is goodhearted. He is loving to his sisters and brothers. He is constant, reliable. But above all, he is tenacious: he has an extraordinarily tenacious temperament. He is so stubborn that we see him as a youth of thirteen or fourteen, working tirelessly for only his dinner as a hireling at one of the farms in the valley. He has been leading a bull, when a wasp bites it in the rump! And the boy refuses to let go of the tether around the neck of the bull, even as the animal bounds through a rocky field. Two of his sisters shout and scream at him to let go of the rope. They think he will die; they scream in fear. But he holds on to the rope with his left hand and his teeth, and his sisters will always remember the gleam in his face as he is pulled by the bull—his eyes rolled up into his head, only the white showing. And then he shuts his eyes, and his face is red, and the blood is everywhere. Hans breaks two ribs and his left ankle, and for the rest of his life he will bear scars on his face and chest where large pieces of skin were scraped away.

Not long after this incident, young Hans, still hardly more than a boy, sees that his only chance in life is to work with his mind. He ties his few belongings in a kerchief on the end of a stick, bids his family goodbye, and begins the several days' journey by foot to the capital.

Many years pass. Through sheer determination and constancy, he manages to work his way into the civil service and eventually rises high. He also becomes talented at placing bets on the market. The first gold coin he earns, he bids a barber plait it into the coarse hair of his beard, and the gold stays there. The weight of it tugs at the tender skin of his face every minute of every day, as if it would pull the hair out at the roots, reminding him of his early toil.

In time he is appointed magistrate to the provincial town of Nara-gir. The peasants there, enraged to learn they have been appointed a magistrate who is both a cripple and from their own class, decide to drive him out of town. Before his arrival, they take apart the manse that is reserved for the magistrate, and carry it onto swampland, brick by brick, where they rebuild it. When the magistrate alights from his carriage, the new home smells of rotten eggs and is already sinking into the ground. The magistrate, however, doesn't make a complaint to the capital. He never says a word. Instead, he sets about taking apart the house again on his own and carries the bricks on his back, load by load, and then every floorboard, every glass window he carries to a new spot far from the reeking swamp, to a high overlook—a spot even more well-chosen than the original location of the manse.

Again, time passes. He plays the markets in the capital. His coffers are enriched further. He manages to earn the aloof respect of the townspeople.

The one and only reward that eludes his grasp, finally, is a wife. The people of this country are a superstitious people who feel sure that the good and hardworking man will pass on his deformity to any issue he might have, and his scarred body and his gaze as intense as an iron tong do nothing to increase his appeal. The magistrate suffers many long years of loneliness and self-hatred, but he does not think to look far away for a wife. He is stubborn, and knows he will win the people only with a wife from among them. So he continues to labor and widen his influence, proving himself a faithful and wise friend to all comers.

Every year, the magistrate gives a small velvet bag containing two small rubies to each and every father who is willing to give his daughter the choice of marrying him—and in return the father must respect the girl's choice, whatever it might be. The magistrate does not care whether they all laugh at him as a fool. He gives out the jewels nonetheless. In the first year, all the girls say no. In the second year, all the girls say no likewise, and so it goes. But finally, in the magistrate's fifty-third year, a woman, a widow, thirty-two years of age, agrees to marry him. Her name is Minnebie, and she is very beautiful. Her first husband was cruel to her; no one knows how he died. She moves into the magistrate's home with what appears to be relief, and, praise God, over the course of the next seventeen years, they have six children together and are very happy. And so it is that the Magistrate of Naragir is able to wake those fine mornings in his seventh decade, and greet his wife directing the servants preparing breakfast in the kitchen on the first floor of his mansion, or teaching the children (none of whom was malformed in the end) in the library on the second floor, singing in the conservatory on the third, or cultivating ferns and orchids in the glass winter garden at the top of the house. It is an unprecedented happiness he can hardly believe.

But the years go on and war breaks out. The country of Lon is again fighting with the enemy to the north. It is a war of great pomp and saber-rattling. The magistrate, the good citizen, invests heavily, and right away sends his oldest youthful son away to fight, and his daughter, by the name of Lonie, only sixteen, runs away to volunteer as a nurse at one of the army hospitals in the capital. What can he do? The magistrate does the only thing he can—he makes a profit off the new industries that spring up around the enlarged military.

When the war has been going on for several years, it happens that the country begins to lose. The news coming over the radio is more and more chilling. Finally, distraught, the magistrate becomes sick; it's the smallpox. It seems he will not be long for this world. Several tormented weeks pass.

But finally his fever breaks, and among his doctors there is much rejoicing. The magistrate will live. With his new, clear eyes—and it is a wonder he did not go blind!—the magistrate asks that each of his children be led in to see him. He breathes and is flooded with the joy of returning health.

But his children do not come in to see him. No, his children will never come in. It is his wife and the stout housekeeper who enter the room. Minnebie's face is swollen almost beyond recognition.

"What has happened?" the magistrate asks, sensing immediately that nothing is right.

Minnebie turns her back. There's something about her movements that has all the lost grace of an elephant. The stout housekeeper puts her arms across her wide chest. "I think it's best if I do the talking, sir," she says.

"All right," the magistrate says helplessly.

"You see, sir, the enemy reached the capital."

"I see."

"In the battle for the city, your boy fell."

The magistrate does not speak. He closes his eyes.

"At the time the young master was killed, the enemy had only just managed to surround the city, but it hadn't fallen yet. He died valiantly in the effort to save it." The housekeeper stands with her head bowed and her hands clasped behind her. For a moment she is silent. "I'm sorry, sir. He was a good boy."

"Yes, he was a good boy," the magistrate manages to say.

"Well, there's more, sir. By chance there was Lonie working in the lazaret at the same time; she was at the sickbeds when they brought her brother in. He was alive for a few minutes at first, but his body was trampled and his intestines spilled out like snakes. She said they moved as if they were living reptiles. The boy's skull was smashed. After, they let her come home.

"But she wasn't well, sir. How shall I describe it? She complained of headaches. She said she couldn't get the sight of her brother out of her eyes. She was awake at all hours, we couldn't get her to stay in bed. She said she was looking for a place to hide. She was terribly sleep-deprived, and if you ask me, she began to hallucinate because of it. But no one asked me." She glared at her mistress. Then she whipped around and went on. "We did our best with her, but you see, we found her one day in the morning, up in the top of the house, she had cut her eyes out of her head. Her eyes were out, sir, by her own hand."

"She cut them out herself?" asks the magistrate.

"Yes, that's right," says the housekeeper.

The magistrate swallows.

The thought crosses the magistrate's mind that all along he had thought he was an angel, where in reality he must have been a devil.

The worst thing is that his wife, at the window, still seems unable to move or speak, and he senses there must be more. He waits.

"As you know, the . . ." the housekeeper goes on, stammering. "The war is lost."

"Yes," said the magistrate, "but perhaps . . . perhaps, not entirely lost—"

"No, truly lost," she cuts him off, "and the money, your money, even this house . . . I'll stay on until your health is better, sir, but then I'm afraid I'll have to leave. Wages are wages."

"Of course they are," says the magistrate, beginning to have trouble catching his breath.

"I'll try to keep this brief, sir, I don't want to be cruel." The housekeeper pauses, then speaks. "Jasper—you know he always got in such trouble—he tried to climb up through the big chimney, but he got stuck in the middle. Lonie was nearby and heard him crying. She herself was too large to climb into the chimney after him. She seems to have run for help, but the little children and the mistress and I were out picking blackberries in the valley, and blind and wounded as she was, she didn't find us in time."

"When the doctor told us Jasper was dead"—the magistrate's wife, Minnebie, whirls her face from the window; her voice is queer and unexpected—"I went to the upstairs lavatory to cry, at the top of the house, and there I found the eyes of Lonie were still in the wash-basin—"

The magistrate thinks he will be sick. "Where are the babies? Where are my little ones?" he asks, with a terrible fear in his voice.

"Can you imagine my disgust?" his wife goes on. "I learned at that moment: *we are an unlucky people.* I do not wish to give my children to this defeated land, nor to this defeated house. I shall save my gifts for the victorious kingdom of heaven."

"Don't get abstract on me now. Where are the little ones?"

"Smallpox."

"What?"

"All three boys, one by one; after Jasper died. Within a week of one another."

The magistrate draws a long breath. He pulls the covers up further under his chin. His face glows like a moon rising from a green ocean.

There is a long silence in the room. In the performance for the whale ducks, the entire theater sits in silence for fourteen minutes. Then the music begins to rise, and the magistrate throws off the bed-clothes.

"My wife," says the magistrate slowly. "Minnebie. Do you know? There is a way. We will bring back the children."

Minnebie looks at him in hatred.

The magistrate begins his beautiful aria.

"We will journey far away from here to the valley of oblivion," he sings. "Forget the defeat and all the lost children. We will forget and start again from the beginning. Do you know how much like a dream all this misfortune seems to me now? Imagine how much more like a dream it will be when the trees have lost their leaves and regained them. How much more like a dream when the earth has passed into shadow again and again and the stars have grown colder and colder! When the birds have laid eggs until, with the generations taken together, they have laid more eggs than would cover the ocean floor?"

(At this, the whale ducks exchanged meaningful glances, touched to the quick—"It's our time, he's speaking of the time of the whale ducks!")

The magistrate pauses. Minnebie says nothing, and a great silence again envelopes the stage. The magistrate seems to go just a little red in his white face, but only ever so slightly, so that, looking at him, it isn't clear whether it is blood rising with shame into the net of capillaries over his facial muscles or whether it is because he has raised his head from the pillow and taken a bit more of the rays from the vanishing sun. (The whale ducks insist on only the best lighting for a production of *Naragir.*)

"How much more like a dream will it be then!" he shouts into the darkness. "I'll tell you how much more! Much more like a dream. Dreams are lovely things. I am an old man, but still, even in what's left of my life, I have time. There is always time. And listen, my darling— we will be blessed with new money, made through new industrious-ness, and God will bless us with new children, different children will be born to us. And although you'd never believe it, having forgotten the ones that came before, the new ones will be better than what we've lost. The songs the first ones used to sing won't be sung, but other chil-dren can sing other songs, and the richness of their lives . . . will outdo any richness—" and the magistrate begins to cry.

Meanwhile, Minnebie's fury is gradually reaching the breaking point. "I have no children in me," she screams, "not now, nor ever

again. The children I had are the children of the country that was shattered and I shall never forget—*I shall never forget the shattering.* Would
you have me go on? Would you have me walk away from death as if it
were less than life?" Minnebie says, and with that, in the way the story
would have continued if the opera had not been interrupted on the
night of Botuun's skeleton's debut, Minnebie kills herself; she uses
the magistrate's own revolver from the commode next to his bed, and
the bullet goes straight to her brain, for she puts the barrel against the
roof of her mouth.

The magistrate rises from the bed and his expression travels from
pain to stillness. With stony face he walks by the dying Minnebie. He
never looks backward. He tears the gold coin out of his beard. He uses
the money to travel to the capital, and there he haggles for a pack of
cigarettes, some ladies' silk stockings, and a sausage. He trades these
on the black market, and soon has enough business to live well, and,
his integrity unbroken to the end, he lives out his days with a new
young wife, and a second set of children. And also his blind daughter,
Lonie. She cannot see, and in later years she chooses not to speak
either.

However, the opera that night was to be interrupted and the story did
not come to an end. It happened that Botuun's fine, donated skeleton
was playing the role of Minnebie. The audience was much taken by
the new puppet, and they watched in amazement as the fine motions
of the treasure put the other "actors" to shame. But an extraordinary
thing happened. When the skeleton mimed the final words of the play,
which happened to be set to music in a long and exquisite aria, with
much repetition, the skeleton slowly began to turn to powder. The
process was so slow at the beginning (although quickly accelerating)
that none of the ducks was sure that the skeleton hadn't been disinte-
grating since the first act. By the time the song was ended, half the
skeleton lay in dust on the floor of the stage, having fallen away from
its crystal suspension strands. The other half of the skeleton, the top
portion, widened its jaws and seemed to be laughing at the crowds
of whale ducks, those curious, hungry birds with their long necks
craned toward the extinct species' remains, watching them enact their
grotesque failures to thrive. The skeleton that was turning to dust,
with a twinkling eye, seemed to be asking how much longer she would
be made to reenact her humiliation—when would she be released into
nonexistence? The whale ducks craned their necks ever further for-

ward, cooing and crying, waiting for catharsis as the infant awaits birth.

Margaret stopped reading. She let the book slide to the floor. Some of the parched and rustling pages of the book fell out—the spine was broken. She could still hear the magpie scratching at the ground out on the balcony. She thought: Minnebie! She didn't pay heed to the rest, she fell in love with the insane wife, Minnebie. There was more than a strand of nobility in the madwoman's actions. Would not anyone have felt vindicated—refusing to forgive, refusing to forget, refusing to create in this turpentine world? How much finer than the old soul who clutches at the gold in his beard, grabbing at a life gone squalid. Then she heard a small voice coming from outside on the balcony. The voice was avian, squawking.

"Don't you want to know about the sheaf of paper?" it said. "The one the skeleton was clutching in the steeple, in the beginning. Do you want to know what was on it?"

Margaret raised her head in surprise. "Who's there?"

"The question is: don't you want to know?" the bird said. Margaret laid her head back on the pillow, the Unicum she had drunk taming her alarm. She considered. Now she remembered the pages referred to.

"But I thought the whale ducks were not able to read human script," she said. "They wouldn't know."

"But I know what was on it," said the voice.

"All right," said Margaret. "What then?"

"It only had two words written on it, but two words written over and over."

"Which two?"

"The two of her name."

"I see."

"Her name, because she did not want to be forgotten after her death."

"Ah," said Margaret. She thought of this and laid her head back. She breathed deeply. She slept and woke, and slept again. Then she woke herself with a start.

"Why did Minnebie want her name to be remembered, if she chose to die?"

It was as if the bird had been waiting for her to ask just this question. "The dead do not wish to be forgotten. It is only their suffering they wish to erase. 'Remember me, but ah, forget my fate.' That is the creed of the destroyed."

"I see."

"But why do you assume the skeleton was Minnebie's?" the bird asked.

And Margaret saw that she had made a mistake. "Whose was it then?"

"I can't tell you."

"Why not?"

"The skeleton was that of someone yet to die."

The magpie on the balcony laughed a screeching, birdy laugh. And then it scratched at the ground twice, rustled its wide wings, flapped frantically, and was gone.

Margaret drifted back into sleep. When she woke up the next morning, Benjamin was still out. Margaret found the story of the whale ducks fresh in her mind, even fresher than when she had read it.

She reached down beside the bed. She thought she would read the story again straight through from the start.

She searched, but she didn't find the book about the whale ducks.

And it was only after she could not find it that she thought how strange it was that Benjamin owned *The Whale Ducks,* a book in German, a language Benjamin did not speak or understand.

Margaret stayed in Benjamin's bed for most of the day. She was hungover and ailing. In the kitchen she found that Benjamin had left her a note with his telephone number written on it in oversized digits, as if she were a child. She waited for him, but he never appeared. Finally she went home when the sun was going down.

For a while after she got back to Schöneberg she sat very still in a chair at the kitchen table. She looked out the window, down into the courtyard as the last of the light disappeared over the orange roofs. She sat, and the silence of the apartment became thicker. "Remember me, but ah, forget my fate."

The story of the whale ducks wrapped tentacles around her mind. There were two models there for how to behave if you were tried like

Job. Two models, each one so evangelical that Margaret would have a hard time not making a decisive choice between the two. There was only one trouble: Margaret herself had never been tried like Job. Why did she assume that she had been, with hardly any hesitation? Why did she assume it as a matter of course, that it was for her, too, to make such a choice, between the way of Minnebie and the way of her stubborn husband, the magistrate?

At the edges of everything, Margaret thought, there came a whitening, as if some glassy being had drawn a circle in dust around her feet, curbing her thoughts and her world to here and here, but never *here.*

She was cooperating. If there was an invisible fence that had stunned her once, she only circled the perimeter now, avoiding the shock.

Now Margaret decided to act out. She went into the bedroom. She stood for a while. Then she began to take all of her clothing out of the wardrobe. She laid each piece on the bed, mustered it with her eyes. She fingered the seams; she checked the pockets. She methodically emptied two wooden trunks that sat on top of the wardrobe, also filled with old clothes, books, tennis rackets, and broken this and that, and there too, she looked at every item carefully. She was not looking for anything in particular, no, she was particularly looking for nothing. To prove to herself there was nothing to find—this was her purpose. Every box opened and found to be empty of significance was a little triumph, every half hour that passed in which she saw nothing unsettling was a half hour closer to victory. She went to the desk and reorganized the drawers. She piled and repiled the stacks of books in the hallway, shaking each one to see what loose paper would fall out. She went through the closet: old shoes, a basketball, a Frisbee, screwdrivers of different sizes, an old bag of planting soil. She began to weary, but still, she went through the pantry; she looked at all the canned goods. It occurred to her to look in the bathroom, too. The night drew on; she searched. The dawn broke; she was losing energy.

Finally, about to take apart the commode in the bathroom, jiggling the drawer whose key she had lost but which could easily be broken into, she was stopped by a powerful itch at her temples. She rubbed and rubbed the sides of her face. She felt light-headed. The room rocked back and forth. She went into the bedroom and sat down on the bed.

There, as the itching sensation diminished, dreams began to fly behind her eyes. She saw herself as a child—holding fireflies in a mayonnaise jar with holes for oxygen punched in the tin lid. Another time, on a ferryboat with a wide paddle wheel hauling up the waters of a beef-fed river, and once too, sitting in a darkened theater touching the horsehair seat that lifted her toward the bright, warm beauty of the stage.

Oh, she had felt things, and smelled things, and lived things—all things that had a different feel, a different smell, a different organization, than this cold and forsaken life she was leading here.

The morning sun was burning brightly in the room. Margaret was still sitting on the bed, motionless. In the moments she had been there, her mind had wound around, considering every angle. And now—

She had made a decision.

She would fold.

She did not want to find out anything at all. Job was an innocent—an innocent trapped between God and the devil. But she, Margaret—she did not know how or why, but she was guilty.

She must fold. The stakes were too high. Uncertainty was preferable to certainty, and although the peace she would win would be a shallow one, she need not play the dangerous game.

Yes, she would fold her hand. Let the others go on playing without her. Now she wanted to be still.

Because whether or not she found evidence, it did not matter. She could smell it on herself and on the wind, in how her heart raced every day, how her mind craved an escape: she was guilty. The wind came in the open window. The smell of it was nothing but threat.

TEN • The Concubine's Mind

How to describe what happened next? The historical ones—Magda, but not only Magda—were rising around Margaret like ocean waters filling in cavities. They flowed according to the justifications already written in the land, deep where deep, curved where curved. Margaret's self-examination was finished now, and the era of the dead Nazis had begun.

Yes, when Margaret awoke the next morning, she went to the window, and the hawk-woman was standing at attention on the balcony across the way, even larger now, hulking and frivolous. The lady pulled a compact out of her kit and made up her face under its heavy, brilliantine waves, her attention directed languidly at Margaret's three windows, and the sight burned Margaret's eyes and could not be fled.

Margaret was looking at the hawk-woman through a single rotated slat of the venetian blind. She kept the blinds closed all day and checked after the monster only surreptitiously. The woman perched with a live mouse in her beak sometimes, and in those cases her face was all bird, her head cocking jerkily around, and around, and around, until she seemed to be looking at Margaret from behind. Sometimes she winked at Margaret conspiratorially.

And then, as the days went by, Margaret did not always close the blinds. As she fell asleep, she began to be not frightened but preoccupied—with the question of whether she would find the hawk-woman at her perch on the following morning. She began to develop methods of prediction, ideas halfway between superstition and science: when it rained and the street was empty, the bird was likely to be in attendance (but not always). When it was sunny and the street was full of traffic, the bird was likely missing (but not always).

And then Margaret found herself not afraid—not at all. Instead, when the hawk-woman was not there, she longed for her. She came home in the afternoon and if she did not find the enormous bird preening her feathers on the terra-cotta balcony cattycorner right away, she ran back to the window again and again, to see if the bird had finally come.

She did not like it. She did not like that she was broken in. She said to herself that only a corrupt person could become a friend to a vision at the window of the deceased Magda Goebbels.

Yes. This was patently so.

But for the life of her, she could not arrest her fascination.

And so, as if seeking to justify herself, she began to study the life of the woman with great seriousness. She was looking to find something. Margaret wanted to find an element in Magda Goebbels's biography that would make the hawk-woman's presence outside the window proud and fine, not shameful, not wrong.

And who knows why, but it did not take her very long. Only a few days into her focused studies, Margaret made a crucial discovery regarding Magda Goebbels.

Margaret read what the woman allegedly said to a friend a few months before she killed her children.

For me there are only two possibilities: if we win the war, then Joseph will be so high and mighty that I, an aging, used-up woman, will be finished. And if we lose the war, then my life will be at an end anyway.

Margaret jerked her head up from the book.

The Magda Goebbels of this quote was not the woman who so bombastically wrote to her son in North Africa. This was someone else. This was someone in an advanced stage of self-loathing. Margaret was sitting at the desk, but the book before her seemed suddenly lashed to the room around it, a beetle caught in an almost invisible web. And later, Magda Goebbels wrote to the same friend:

Don't forget, Ello, what has gone on! Do you still recall . . . I told you about it hysterically back then . . . how the Führer in Café Anast in Munich, when he saw the little Jewish boy, said he would prefer to flatten him into the floor like a bug? Do you remember that? I couldn't believe it, I took it as nothing but provocative talk. But much later he really did it. Unspeakably cruel things have happened, done by a system that I too have represented. So much vengefulness has been collected in the world . . . I can do nothing else, I have to take the chil-

*dren with me, I must! Only my Harald will be left behind. He is not
Goebbels's son, and luckily he is in English captivity.*

Margaret glanced sharply around the room, almost blushing,
embarrassed at the enormity of it. She stood up and began to pace.

But she was too moved to walk. She took hold of her woolen
trousers lying on the floor whose hems had come undone. She backed
into the Biedermeier sofa. Straw butted out of its red velvet where the
cushion had ripped, but she sat down hard. She grabbed the shoebox of
thread and needles from beneath it. Her mind was clacking at high
speed.

If Magda knew what the Nazi government was guilty of—it would
mean everything.

Magda Goebbels wrote to her son stationed in North Africa that it
was because her children with Goebbels were too good for the later
world that they must die. But to her friend, she said it was because they
were too soiled for it.

Margaret's eyes narrowed onto the sewing before her. She felt something hardening in her throat.

She threaded her needle. Perhaps in a good and just world, children
are not murdered for their parents' crimes.

Margaret plunged the needle into the wool that was stiff, stiff as
sycamore bark, where the hems had dragged in slush and dried. Perhaps in a good and just world, children do not die as payment.

Perhaps, so Margaret thought, but it is not Nazi justice. The Nazis
saw humans as carrying political guilt in their blood, with their birth,
before their naming. This was the very axiom of the Nazi crime.

Here is what Margaret knew: at Joseph Goebbels's incitement,
ninety percent of Jewish children—Jews under the age of twelve—
who were alive in Europe in 1938 were dead in 1945. Ninety percent of
the Jewish children of Europe were tortured to death. These tortured
and murdered children will never have children, and these children
will never have children. With every generation, there will be a new
wave of the unborn.

Margaret began to stitch, her throat stricken, her eyes shaking,
pushing the needle in and out guttingly.

And the world after the war—it left the children of Nazis alone.
Only last week, she had read a firsthand account in Niklas Frank's
memoir, carrying the following bitter cheer:

There really were advantages to growing up in the Federal Republic [of Germany] as the son of a major Nazi war criminal. [The] help was especially beneficial when it came to hitchhiking. . . . From the moment somebody stopped to pick me up, my path to success was assured. All I had to say after a couple of kilometers was, "Do you happen to realize that I am the son of the Minister of the Reich without Portfolio and Governor General of Poland, executed at Nuremburg as a major war criminal?" . . . It wasn't long before the driver indulged himself in glorious reminiscence (omitting all mention of his somewhat lesser crimes); for as a soldier, either on the march to the East or on the way back, he had crossed through [Poland]. Then came the inevitable moment I would be waiting for, the moment when his emotions would be touched, when he lamented the unjust sentence that ended [my father's] life, and said it was so obvious that I, skinny little fellow, was now so bereft and impoverished, and when you think how the English had bombed Dresden, and that he himself had seen how two SS men had dragged a wounded American GI out of the line of fire at Monte Cassino and taken him to a German doctor, and that really the Jews were to blame for what happened to them because it was true that everything had been in the hands of the Jews, and just take a look at this marvelous autobahn we're driving on, my friend— may I call you that? In memory of your father?—the Führer built this autobahn, and now I have to get some gas and you're going to get a fine lunch on me. Only one person . . . , only one solitary postwar German automobile driver in all those years of hitchhiking (it was in 1953, near Osnabrück), turned onto the shoulder of the highway and without saying a single word, in silent disdain, let me out of the car. The memory of that still makes my ears burn. I wonder if he is still alive. Democrats usually die so young.

The very opposite of Magda's fears! (Margaret took out a thimble, her finger already bleeding with rage and frustration.) Nazi children lived on, under the impression that it was democrats who died young. And young Frank's experience was paralleled in the lives of the Bormann children; in the life of the medical technician, Edda Göring, in the life of the architect whose name is Albert Speer Jr., who even now, Margaret knew, was in the process of designing a stadium for the Beijing 2008 Olympics. Even the daughter of Heinrich Himmler—she, too, was smuggled, effortlessly snuggled, into everyday life. The actual retribution against the Nazis' children, the penalty that would have been meted out to Goebbels's offspring had their mother and father not murdered them, was a pair of shamed ears once a decade or so, and this was assuming they ever developed a sense of shame, which was not a given by any means. Margaret's stitches picked up the exterior fabric, her eyes shaking.

If the second version of Magda's motivation were to be believed, then Magda was the only Nazi parent, indeed, the only tribunal in the world, to understand and confirm the Nazi crime—*as a Nazi,* for she was the only one to inflict upon her own family the Nazi penalty: death for the crime of evil-in-the-blood.

And now Margaret already knew what she thought. She threw down the heavy wool. She stood up. *Magda was right.*

It was right the Goebbels children died. Margaret wanted it by any means at all. She wanted it—not for the sake of vengeance, she told herself, her footsteps watery as she walked back toward the bedroom. She wanted it for the sake of equity. For the sake of the generations who will be born one day empty of all of us: who will have, from their ancestors, all genes and no memory.

If Magda knew what the Nazi government was guilty of—it would mean everything. The monster loose on the streets of Berlin would no longer be a symbol of fanatical evil, but a symbol of fanatical shame.

On the mattress on the floor of the bedroom, Margaret sat down. All she had to do was verify that Ello Quandt was a reliable source. It didn't matter whether Magda's action was out of fear or out of repentance; all that mattered was that she *knew.* Margaret only needed to verify that Magda killed her children thinking of the evil that ran in their bloodline, and Margaret would change the categorization of Magda's crime for good. She would call the crime consistent. And consistency, after all, feels exactly like justice.

The verification was going to be difficult. According to the notes in the end pages of the Anja Klabunde biography, Ello's testimony came not from an interview with Ello Quandt herself, but from another, earlier, biography of Magda Goebbels. This earlier biography was written by a contemporary of Joseph Goebbels who worked at the Propaganda Ministry, a certain Hans-Otto Meissner. When Margaret searched the Internet, she found the Meissner biography was available in France, America, and the UK, but not in Germany. This was not what she had been expecting. There was something wrong about it. Right then, she had a prick of uncertainty.

But she did not lose heart.

The flea market at Ostbahnhof occurred to her. At Ostbahnhof, the blustering men with their long mustaches, the military history buffs, selling books about bunker engineering, FlaK guns, and Werner Heisenberg, would certainly have the Klabunde biography. They had everything that was difficult to find.

Margaret went to bed hopeful. Her speculations would perhaps be confirmed. She would read the testimony of this Ello Quandt the very next day, and perhaps make of Magda Goebbels a heroine of consistency—the hawk-woman at the window a fine and permanently reennobled sort of Lucifer.

Of course, Margaret still couldn't sleep. She lay in bed not unhappily, however, going over the details of Magda Goebbels's life, becoming more and more entranced by the idea of the woman as a self-entrapped intellectual initiating and carrying out her own form of justice. The bedroom, as Margaret had these thoughts, was lifting; the bedroom was lifting and flying.

In the morning she rode her bicycle a long time to reach the Eastern flea market.

A great swoosh of upward feeling buoyed her when she was there. The flea market ran in a trough of flesh behind the looming S-Bahn station, parallel to the tracks. The station hovered over it like a giant with wide-open throat. When Margaret emerged into the light and saw the stands crackling with people, she began to buzz happily. It was easy to filter out the buildings all around when she focused on the tables and their hypnotizing wares.

A souvenir collection of ten high-gloss photographs of the town of Kleine Scheidegg in Switzerland; a series of 1930s brochure books, showing large pictures of the Tyrolean alps: *Du Mein Tirol,* one was called; an aluminum cigarette etui from the Ukraine, emblazoned with the slogan *"Slava Oktyabryu"* and a rendering of the October Revolution in formalist strokes; a brown leather GDR pencil case decorated with golden fleurs-de-lys; a Berlin guidebook from 1902 with four-color map—Margaret bought all of this, in a burst of something like affection.

Then she got down to the work of finding the Meissner biography.

She went to each bookstall in turn. All the booksellers with their beards and gruff ways, heavy books encased in plastic, had indeed heard of it; no one had it for sale. Each one said he was sure another one did, but no sooner was the next man found than he referred her away again. She went down a grapevine of rebuff through the market, all the way to the end. The biography was nowhere to be found.

Now Margaret felt a bit of fever, the kind that had come once when she couldn't find Magda Goebbels's letter. She felt as though everything were riding on not just the content, but the tone of this biography she was seeking, as if it would reveal some shining, heretofore unimagined subtlety to Magda's friend Ello Quandt, or even suggest some soulful depth to Magda Goebbels's own character.

Beyond the lines of tables, around the corner on a cobblestone side street, the market continued unofficially. In this impromptu aisle, the wares were on card tables brought from home. It was a sad-looking market. A young man with red face was shouting with another man farther on. *"Leck mich am Arsch, du Arschloch."* His Berlin accent was heavy. The other man became sullen and silent, his gaze fixed ahead. Margaret glanced over their tables, without any particular hope.

The table before her, for instance, was almost entirely empty. There were only two heavy books lying on it. These were sitting wide apart from each other, carefully placed. Margaret glanced at them and thought they were ornamental Bibles. The books were very thick, bound in leather with gilt pages, Gothic type on the spine. Margaret put her hand out to examine one of them.

She had approached casually, but the young man with the red face whipped around and fixed her with fury. She regretted going near, but she was already in motion—she could not stop herself; she went ahead and opened the book and began to fumble with the tissue-thin paper as if to see the title, although after she saw the man's face—it was funny, but she already knew: she was holding Hitler's diatribe, *Mein Kampf*.

The book was illegal in this country. She had never seen it for sale; she had in fact never seen an unabridged German edition with her own eyes anywhere at all. Two generations after the war, and the book that had once been in every house was nowhere to be found. She did not know whether the man could be arrested for selling it, or whether she could be arrested for buying it.

It is impossible to overstate how much it meant to Margaret in her present mood—precisely this book.

She asked: "How much?" in a low voice. The man snapped up the other copy and packed it away. At first she thought he would not answer.

Finally he said: "That one is two hundred euros. This one here is two hundred fifty."

Margaret was shocked. "That's far too much."

"Don't buy it then." He turned his back on her.

Margaret had *Mein Kampf* in an English translation at home, but the German edition looked nothing like it. What struck her was how carefully the book she held had been designed to look like a religious text. That would be Goebbels's work. She noticed a tiny embossed gold swastika on the leather cover where a cross would usually be. Margaret had a Bible at home that felt just like this, the same weight and leather flop in the hands. The pages in both books were like onionskin, and the smell was also the same.

She was holding the book under her nose. And right then, to her surprise, just as Goebbels had meant her to, she saw Nazism as a religion. In a flash, she felt the scope of it, bigger than ever before. It was a religion because it steeped everything in Germany in meaning. Fascism had made the world's fluttering sights and frothy sounds, buoyant wares and technicolored sensations full of weight and pith and awesome death for those who could manage to live with its cruelty. Even now: inversely, here was Margaret herself, borne up on the tide and design of it, all her landmarks came out of it, her compass was calibrated to those lodestones. How could it not excite her? Margaret's own identity, blank as it had become—her own sense of herself as redeemable—was dependent on it as on the devil; what a role it had to play, if you would let it!

Could she grow out of its soil? What could this moral system teach her, inversely, about how to live and how to discriminate?

Could she manage to reject its songs, its films? Yes, that easily.

But could she reject its ideas, its only slowly dying people, its correlations, its loose ends? What was one to do with the truckloads of lost meaning? The correlations sat now in a garbage dump. Margaret put the heavy book down, her cheeks flushed with shame. She wandered away, so deep in herself she could not see.

Maybe it was the intense of the blue sky over Holzmarktstrasse, or maybe she was tired from the nights of insomnia—but all at once she broke through a membrane and thought: I have nothing. None of these things once offered by fascism are things I have in my own life. Nothing means anything to me at all. How could it, without memory?

She walked a few steps farther. She realized with a kind of surprise that her own life had no meaning at all, and with this she was not saying that it had no larger meaning—although it did not—but rather that there were no small correspondences either. Buoyant, frothy, wispy little life.

She was drawn back toward the book. She took a few steps toward the table.

Margaret's mother's family had been loud, her father's family silent. When things happened in her father's family (she remembered her grandfather), they disappeared forever, whether they be double-jointedness or stock market gains, failed marriages or stillbirths, they remained unnoted and uncorrelated with other incidents in the same life. By contrast, in her mother's family, events and characteristics were repeated endlessly, told to laughs or made into a refrain, until everything you did or had done to you was part of the pounding myth, a link in the chain, part of history, part of television. Margaret had not been able to stand it, she had gone the way of her father's family, in silence.

The city had turned to flesh. What if soon she had no choice but to decipher every sign, just as the doctor seemed to want when she showed her that forest film?

Margaret spun around. The young man with the red face looked at her. She said, before she had even made up her mind, so that the words surprised even her: "I'll take it."

"You don't have the cash," the man said quietly. If he was surprised at her, he did not show it.

"Yes, I do." It happened that Margaret was carrying her work wallet with her, the one with the money from selling tickets for her tours. She decided that she would borrow from this wallet. It would make her month very tight. When she handed him the cash, the man did not even look at her; he took the money and made it disappear like a magician pressing it into his palm. Clearly he thought she might grab it back. And perhaps Margaret would have, too. But now it was too late. The man turned his back.

Margaret gripped the book and put it in her backpack furtively, hoping no one had seen her. And just as quickly as the money was gone, her stomach churned. She was trembling, but she could not bring herself to ask for the money back. It was already done.

She walked a few steps. She did not want her own life to signify. But she did want a certain amount of meaning—that sweet sensation of sphericity. The meaning of something else. The meaning of Magda Goebbels's life—the meaning of the *lost world*.

She would make good on her connection to the hawk-woman. Even if Magda Goebbels had not seen the irony linking her husband's crimes and her children's deaths, even if she had never recognized her guilt, Margaret would begin to know Magda Goebbels's side of it: the primrose labyrinth leading her to justify a social movement of murder, maybe how the philosophy of the madman in his own words makes it all smooth and fine. Margaret thought this would be the single richest trick of her amnesiac's brain. She would allow meaning—but only the meaning of someone else.

Riding home on Linienstrasse, she passed a quiet entrance to an industrial courtyard. As she sped past the dark entryway on her bicycle, she caught sight of a sun-filled courtyard beyond a tunneling entryway. All she saw was instantly gone: the glinting windows, exposed pipes, the ivy and the smoky sunlight. The flashing pace of the view into the courtyard felt like nostalgia. To think of nostalgia, even without nostalgia itself, was painful and searing.

She bicycled home. She sped down Friedrichstrasse. She flew through Potsdamer Platz. Slowly, she began to smile. She had Adolf Hitler's book in her backpack. When she got home she would draw the curtains, shutting out even the hawk-woman, in order to read, and it would take the time out of time: not freeing her from her burden of guilt, not releasing her, no, even weighing her down all the further, but at least now with her cloudy burden no longer unpaired—no longer without an understanding of its kinship, as a small-time evil, with historical evil, which is large, large enough to rest on. For the great arduousness of guilt is its loneliness.

In the next days, Margaret finished the portrait in oils of Magda Goebbels. It was a beautiful piece, and when it dried, she put it on the pillow next to her own. They slept, the flesh woman and the painted woman, one with eyes closed, the other with eyes open.

She read *Mein Kampf* according to plan. At every turn, she looked for places where Hitler's sensibility overlapped with her own. On page 65, Hitler asks:

Have we an objective right to struggle for our self-preservation, or is this justified only subjectively within ourselves?

And although Margaret knew that Hitler's idea of "self-preservation" was built on a persecution complex, she was elated. In the year 1925, he acknowledged, even if later rejecting, the possibility that his right to act on that persecution complex was perhaps only subjectively reasonable. It seemed akin to her own constant inner quizzing. And it suggested to fervid Margaret that there might be something flaccid and forgiving—not in Hitler's life, but in his character.

Finally, she came to exactly what she had been looking for. She found it in a passage of no particular significance: Hitler's description of himself as a soldier, on a transport train during the First World War.

I saw the Rhine for the first time thus: as we rode westward along its quiet waters to defend it, the German stream of streams, from the greed of the old enemy. When through the tender veil of the early morning mist the Niederwald Monument gleamed down upon us in the gentle first rays of the sun, the old Watch on the Rhine roared out of the endless transport train into the morning sky, and I felt as though my chest became too narrow for my heart.

At this, Margaret's own chest narrowed. Perhaps there was nothing in the quotation that justified it, but for one moment, Margaret saw Hitler as young and soft and grasping and sentimental. And she did the arithmetic and figured that Hitler must have been twenty-five when he was on that train. This year, Margaret was also twenty-five.

So she saw herself there. And although to be like him was the opposite of goodness, and even the smell of it made her walk around the house weak and bleary-eyed, without blood in her veins, not remembering to open the curtains in the morning or at any other time, afraid of all things light and springing, what could she do? The Nazi past was her encampment now, her nest, her burrow.

ELEVEN · Sachsenhausen

In mid-December, a cold fell over the city. Much to everyone's surprise—for it was uncommon in this part of the country and at this time of year—Berlin fell under a thick layer of ice. Temperatures dropped to twenty below zero, and people, streets, trees, and buildings shriveled into muted silhouettes of themselves. It was so freezing that Margaret didn't know whether her flesh city was still living; the buildings had frozen, had become one with the sandy ground, indistinguishable from stone.

On the coldest of these cold days, Margaret was assigned to give a tour of the concentration camp memorial of Sachsenhausen. Surprisingly, given the weather, eighteen people booked places for the excursion. In the regional express train shuttling north of the city to the little town of Oranienburg where Sachsenhausen spreads its sad cloud, Margaret looked out the window, her eyes slack over the dead plains around Berlin. The open expanses of winter fields were punctuated by bails of hay tightly wrapped in plastic. In the morning light, their frost-covered surfaces smoked like glass, dull with the secret of cold.

She thought of Magda, and then of Minnebie, whom she had pictured in her mind as looking something like herself. The collapse of Magda into Minnebie into Margaret was not an unpleasant sensation. The sense of camaraderie since the hawk-woman had come and Margaret had begun to read *Mein Kampf* was familiar to her: a sense of sure-footedness, of buttressing, of walking with a phalanx.

Whence did she know it? She racked her mind. Then she realized. She knew it from early childhood. To be dependent on others without resentment—what a sweet time.

She thought back on her earliest years. The time before her father became sick. She did not have very much of it. She remembered that he sometimes played "Du Bist Verrückt, mein Kind" on the harmonica, and then sang the refrain in a language that, in those years, she did not know. And once, she remembered, he had pulled the Great Dane up on its hind legs and danced with it. How she had laughed! The man who danced with a dog was the man she had loved. This was before he shut himself in his office and before they got rid of the dog.

So the feeling of walking with a phalanx, she decided, also had something to do with the sunshine of the psyche before it is hacked apart.

Around the train car wafted bits and pieces of the sort of conversation that always preceded a visit to the concentration camp memorial.

"Why did Hitler hate the Jews?"

"We'll never know. Terrible."

"One of them bullied him as a child maybe. You know, innocent kids' stuff, but he took it the wrong way."

"Do you think so?"

"Really, he was a weird man, wasn't he."

"What we'd call today a sociopath—"

"Like Pinochet."

"Yes, like Pinochet."

"But the Jews did have all the money, they never minded making a pretty penny off the Germans—"

"But I've heard that his own mother was Jewish—"

"Never mind that, I saw a documentary on BBC2 where you could see plain as day he was a homosexual."

"Bah! He wasn't any different than the rest of us. Anyone might do the same thing for power. Power corrupts and absolute power corrupts absolutely. Say what you will, he was a sort of genius."

"The Germans were anti-Semites from the ground up, going back a thousand years," said another voice. "No sense looking at Hitler out of context."

The quick rattling off of chestnuts never ceased to amaze Margaret. It was several British, Australians, and Americans who sat in a group of eight seats facing one another from across the aisle, while a Norwegian couple of middle age sat farther off, outside of the anglophone gathering. A group of Argentine students sat farther away still.

Margaret herself sat with her back to the anglophone group, in a seat where she could hear them but not see them. She was seething with dislike for a particular English businessman. It was because he wore a trench coat—an inadequate coat, given the extreme cold. Margaret knew who would suffer, whose eyes would glaze over with dilettante misery. She knew it in advance. These people would be displeased with her tour no matter what she said, make her feel useless and inadequate, the tour into an endless plodding. And likely as not, she would attempt doggedly, with mounting sensationalism, to entertain them. And because she disliked the Englishman guiltily, for nothing but his coat, she felt the need to charm them all now, impress them, while still on the warm train.

So she popped up from behind her seat and addressed the sitting customers. "Hitler didn't come from an anti-Semitic family," she said loudly. "Here," she said, and reached into her backpack. She pulled out *Mein Kampf*. She waved it for them to see, and it was as if she had drawn a lizard out of her pocket: most drew away in disgust, but her despised English businessman leaned forward with a grim smirk that seemed to say, Finally we are getting down to business.

She found the passage she wanted with little delay.

She read to them:

Today it is difficult, if not impossible, for me to say when the word "Jew" first gave me ground for special thoughts. At home I do not remember having heard the word during my father's lifetime. I believe that the old gentleman would have regarded any special emphasis on this term as cultural backwardness. In the course of his life he had arrived at more or less cosmopolitan views, which, despite his pronounced national sentiments, not only remained intact, but also affected me to some extent.

"You see?" Margaret said. "He didn't learn anti-Semitism at home."

"He learned it when he saw what the Jews were up to in Vienna," said the businessman, smugly.

"And what was that?" asked Margaret.

"What was what?" he asked.

"What were the Jews up to in Vienna?" Surely this little man could hear the poison in her voice.

"Well, they had all the money, didn't they now," he said.

Margaret noticed with discomfort that when he spoke she was aware of his social class; she disliked British English for its blatancy; she didn't want the information, saw it as a premature intimacy. Far better, she thought, to preserve, between strangers, a veneer of sameness.

"They didn't have 'all the money,'" Margaret said. "The idea is ridiculous. Why do people still believe the garbage spread by the Nazis?" Margaret jerked her head. "If you look at the facts, neither German nor Austrian wealth was concentrated in the hands of the Jewish people; it is horrible how Nazi ideas persist even today." Everyone looked at the ground and there was a heavy silence.

Margaret relented. She said, "But more important: how can you be sure Hitler hated the Jews?"

"Ha," the man scoffed. "Oh, I think he must have. Eccentric guide we have here!" he said to the Australian couple across from him. "Isn't she? Imagine Hitler, wanting to have tea with his Jewish friends? Is that what you'll argue?"

"Hitler didn't have to hate in order to destroy," Margaret said. "He was evil—but evil doesn't need any motivation." She looked out the window of the train. "And people without hatred—are doing evil things everywhere."

It struck Margaret very hard—that it was possible to be evil without being motivated. It ground into her. She applied it to herself very broadly.

But then she looked around, and all in a rush she seemed to see the faces of the customers before her as if for the first time. She told them brightly, as an addendum, that Hitler was a vegetarian. This was greeted with general disbelief. Theories of evil came and went. The train clacked northward.

When they got up to the little town of Oranienburg, the wind whistled around the train as it left them behind, making a shriek that the businessman said sounded like an incendiary bomb blowing down from a plane. The remark was met with appreciation.

Margaret marched them down the main street, past the gun shop and the florist, avoiding the proprietress of the sausage and beer house, who trailed Margaret in hopes of convincing her to bring the group back to her establishment for lunch.

They walked the same route along which prisoners were once force-marched, all the way down the main road, then out of the center of town. Many of the buildings along the street were abandoned, with vacant lots overgrown.

All around was a winter silence. The cold was so thick it was difficult to breathe. No one spoke, and the silence became tighter. They walked in an involuntary single file down the sidewalk covered with ice, and turned into the last street before the camp. The houses were small. Each one had a tiny garden, enclosed, still, and frost-covered, laden with ornaments; a sundial here and a gnome there. A small dog came and pressed its bugging eyes to a parlor's picture window. When he began to bark machine-gun-like at them, everyone jumped, even though the sound was muffled through the glass. The trees on the street were old and much taller than the one-story houses, these houses both neat and run-down, in the East German way, the windows made into proscenia with plastic lace curtains.

A chorus of cries began to echo in the distance then. No one knew exactly what it was. The sound was horrible. The sounds became louder. As they neared one of the oldest trees, a tree whose roots had piled up the sidewalk, the cries were all around them, and Margaret and the customers looked up. A colony of crows was gathered in the frozen tree, branches spread in the skeleton of a canopy. Between them, the birds were fighting over the carcass of a large white bird. Some of the black birds had bloody beaks, and the snowy white bird's feathers, as it was dismembered, became pinker. Margaret felt a drop of moisture on her face, and touched it. On her finger was a spot of blood, fallen from the tree above her. The group of tourists shuddered and skittered toward the camp hastily, like game pieces being slid into a box.

Inside the camp the coniferous trees were low, and the sky tilted in an arch. The natural world made way for an open dreamscape, a geometry of cryogenics. Sachsenhausen, built by the SS in the childish shape of an isosceles triangle, with long walls rushing off to pine and guard-tower vanishing points, was a pedagogical place, giving lessons in sharp draftsmanship. The few barracks still standing smelled of paint, mildew, and ammonia; they called to the visitor for inspection, these lone seashells on the beach of weeds. This day, at Sachsenhausen, the great open space was shining with melted snow that had, in the extreme cold, refrozen, giving the open tundra a glassy surface reflecting the blue of the broad sky. Just inside the walls, Margaret noticed that underneath the snow there were mouse tunnels. That is to say, the snow was several inches thick under the ice, and the mice had tunneled inside it, although the tunnels could only be seen when a mouse ran through, its black form tracing a vaporous line under the ice.

The first stop was the roll-call square. Here, Margaret told the tourists, thousands of prisoners had assembled every morning and every evening. The coarse, sandy earth of the Brandenburg mark was stretched flat, stamped down ten thousand years ago by receding glaciers and sixty years ago by a cement wheel rolled about by prisoners. Today it was a shining mirror in its cloak of ice. The beech trees inside the camp were large, and their black branches stark in the cold. Margaret spoke of many things—margarine rations, suicide rates among the prisoners.

Jakob Zhugashvili walked into the electric fence around the perimeter of the camp just here, in order to end his life. Margaret's head, as she spoke, seemed weighted. It dropped toward the ground. Looking at her feet, her eyes grew hotter despite the freezing cold, and her vision buzzed. All of a sudden, here at the camp, everything seemed dreadful. But why was her head so hot? Her eyes were itching. When she looked up, the sky was white.

She looked down again. Under her boots, a woman's face glowed in the ice. The reflection of the skeleton trees flashed, and the woman down inside appeared bound; it was as though the trees had dug their claws into her. The woman's hair was chalk-like and her eyes dark.

Margaret reached under her coat and gripped the flesh of her stomach. She pinched hard. She could not afford to lose her sanity here, not while trying to give the tour. She must not. She looked up into the sky.

She led the group to the old infirmary buildings. The customers straggled along behind her in silence. The wind rose, and it sounded like ocean waves drawing back from the shore.

This tour had never been an easy one for Margaret. Early on, she had become accustomed to lying at several points along the way. Or, not lying exactly—omitting, underemphasizing, and sometimes overemphasizing. She was conscious that she did it, but that is not to say she did it deliberately. She had never planned the disinformation in advance. The "lies" had developed over time of their own accord. In each case, it happened like this: one day she looked at the group, looked into their faces, and instead of her saying what she had planned to say, something new came out of her mouth, something more pleasing. Because we are creatures of routine and the lie usually went over well (she had only gone over the limit of her customers' credulity once or twice), on the next occasion it came out reflexively again. She had a guilty conscience about it, but at a certain point it became physically difficult to say anything else—as difficult as doing a backbend after years of stiffness. Then too, it hadn't started as artlessly as she made herself believe. It had begun because she couldn't bear the discomfort of trying to tell things in an unshaped way. How much better to make a good tour of it.

Today she started out well enough. She talked about the Jewish children who were deliberately infected with hepatitis. She talked about the SS doctor, Aribert Heim, who pumped gasolines into the veins of inmates to see how quickly they would die, the same Aribert Heim who was sighted not long ago on a Spanish beach, allegedly having lived out his postwar years in South America. She showed the customers where there had been forced sterilizations; she took them to the mortuary and told them that it was here that doctors gave lethal injections to healthy young men who happened to have a complete set of white teeth, so that their flesh could be stripped away and skeletons sold to the universities, the universities who desired perfect specimens; the living humans murdered for the sake of an academic model. Had there ever been—before this—such a motive for murder? She asked this question out loud. She talked about how the prisoners helped one another—when a new arrival came to the camp, a young man who perhaps had a complete set of teeth in his mouth, the old boys knocked out a few incisors, so the man would have a better chance.

All this was true.

But then the next part: "And there was also—" she would start to say. "At the infirmary, there was also—" she would begin. She had tried sometimes like that, early on.

It was not such a big thing. There had been a brothel here. That was all. There was a brothel in the infirmary for the prisoners' use. She had seen the photographs of the women in narrow beds.

But who would want to know about Himmler's incentive plan? About the stamps received for efficient labor—the point system— these points that could be traded for the use of a body. Who would like to hear about the young women from Ravensbrück held here in captivity as sex slaves?

Yes, there were some who would. Some had come to learn the truth about the concentration camp. The picture it would have made, however, as far as Margaret was concerned, both for her tour and for her own sake, would be impossible, and that was the central point. What kind of unity would the tour have, what were the people to think? If concentration camp victims raped their fellow victims under the point system, what was that for a story? The women were given a lethal injection after a few months of "service" or whenever they showed signs of venereal disease, and the male prisoners who made use of them knew that.

How was Margaret to continue the tour? Instead of giving Margaret their pious, sympathetic glances, the customers would look about the camp cockeyed. She herself, formerly priestess, would become a rogue. The camp was a temple. Certain things were a desecration. The only thing that belonged here was piety.

She had learned early on: too many tales of horror and she began to think that her piety sounded propagandistic, like a tabloid television show. On the other hand, it clearly would not do to talk excessively of the camaraderie among the Communist inmates, the evenings of "Bella Ciao," and the radio hidden in the laundry that picked up the BBC; of the "kindness" of certain SS men who had shared whiskey with the prisoners, helped others escape. All in all, then, Margaret was also guilty of omitting "happy" stories, of how, for some, it had not been so bad at Sachsenhausen, because these, too, went against the grain.

And Margaret had noticed something: the ratio between the uplifting stories and dystopian stories became the basis for the customers' conclusions about the camp, later their conclusions about the concentration camp system in general, and finally the conclusions they reached (usually while on the train back to Berlin) about the Holocaust. Margaret had heard all of them. And because of this, she could not help but become manipulative.

Theoretically at least, she would have liked to give a realistic picture and leave it at that. But there was a problem: there was no realistic picture to return to, because no one knew how it had really been. No one could ever know that. Even the survivors who had lived to tell the tale did not entirely know how it had been; the experience was too large for that. There are magnitudes of suffering that cannot be held in the mind. So there was a camp, and there was a "tour," and one was bigger than the other and would always be bigger.

Often she imagined saying out loud what she so often thought:

You want to understand? But here's what there is to understand: there's nothing for knowing minds to glean. The more you learn about the camps, the less you know. The more you see this place, the farther away it is. The human social brain wasn't designed to understand the human social terror, and the more it tries, the more it dies. There are people who notice the unwillingness of this place to curve toward comprehension, and so they deny the camps ever existed. These are people who have no tolerance for guilt and especially no tolerance for the things that guilt demands. So instead they mistake the emptiness they find here for an absence of content. They are wrong; there is something here. There's more content here than in universities and museums and churches taken together, but you won't see any of it. All I can show you today is a mirage. This tour is a virtual tour.

But Margaret didn't say that. She would never say it. It wasn't in her. She was a social animal with a social brain, and she did not want to begin to try to communicate what little she knew of the deformity, the chemical structure of which would suffocate, slowly, the brain's chance at happiness—she knew it even from a distance—if it were ever ingested.

As they were on the way to the Jewish barracks the sun came out. Margaret struck up a conversation with the Norwegian couple. The man was a high school history teacher, he was older, and he taught about the concentration camps to the kids. That was why he was here, he said. It also happened that his father's brother had been sent to Sachsenhausen. The uncle survived, but he came home to Trondheim without arms or legs.

Margaret felt dizzy. The white sky seemed immortal. That's how she said it to herself: the sky was immortal. She glanced away from the man to the open field. Her eyes lost focus. She saw, on the other side, between two trees, a great basket swaying from enormous ropes strung high above from the top limbs. The basket, swinging, held a heap of appendages, a head with long grey, mouse-colored hair, a curled human being. Before she had time to blink, Margaret looked back at the Norwegian. When she glanced over again to the field, the basket swinging between the trees was gone. Reflexively, Margaret remembered a few lines—"the sibyl, in her basket swaying, tells the children: I want to die."

Now she looked back at the group, and they were looking at her inquisitively, for they had arrived outside the Jewish barracks. But when she glanced at the trees again, the sibyl was swaying there.

It seemed the thing could blink into existence. Margaret's ears were ringing, her eyes aglow, and her throat stiff. The group looked at her, waiting.

Unexpectedly, Margaret became angry—angry at their expectant eyes. When the Argentines began to whisper to one another, their sibilant sounds searing her ears, she thought she could feel they all hated her, hated her for not speaking; hated her silence. And all eyes were on her again, the eyes of the seekers, who had come to the camp for the exotic suffering. Looking back at the sibyl in the high basket, she thought she heard yet more whispering and saw a face whose eyes had been removed, who blamed her for her lies, for her tour-shaping. She rubbed her face, convinced of her idiocy, inadequacy, inability to navigate between her visions and poor pandering to the worst of the interested eyes around her.

She drew a breath. She would spare them nothing, she decided, *nothing*.

"Jewish prisoners," she began, "were brought here late. They were always a minority at this camp, most others were Slavs and politicals. The arrival of the first permanent group was heralded at the end of August 1939, when all the air vents of blocks 37, 38, and 39—these you see before you—were sealed, and the same thing was done to the windows and the walls, so that no air or sound came out or in. These little barracks were emptied of bunks and tables, and then over a thousand Jewish men were sealed in; only with severe beatings allowed out to the toilets. Soon the rooms were running with moisture and human filth. Sometimes the SS guards came in and told the men to lie down and then ran back and forth over their bodies, apparently for the 'fun' of it. One morning a month later, after over a third of the men had died from asphyxiation and starvation, three were found lying outside the barracks. We know from the memoir of a prisoner who wrote about it later: one of the men's faces was completely destroyed. An eye hung out of his skull, resting on his cheek." Margaret blinked before she went on. "The *Blockälteste* reported that in the night the Jews suddenly all said they had to use the toilet at once, and then fell upon the capos and the SS, who 'defended' themselves.

"The surviving men, however, told a different story. In the night, SS men arrived armed with legs of chairs, they said, and began to beat them, killing and injuring indiscriminately. In the confusion, some ran out of the barracks, and they were beaten to death."

Margaret stopped. She blinked again. The twelve closest huddled around, bodies rigid with attention. Margaret's tension disappeared all at once. She took a deep breath.

"Do you know which version of the story is true?" she asked.

They shook their heads. "No," came the replies. "No, which one?"

"Maybe there was a revolt of the Jewish prisoners against the SS," Margaret said. "That would be some kind of consolation, wouldn't it? To think of a revolt. Or maybe the prisoners were entirely innocent, that's possible too. That would be some kind of consolation in another way, wouldn't it?" Margaret's voice had grown raw.

"Which one is it?" she asked. A slight note of cruelty.

The problem was what to do with truth in matters of the spirit.

"No one knows," she finally said. "No one has any idea."

Margaret whirled and entered the Jewish barracks, breathing hard. The tourists had a struggle to keep up with her. Margaret had become reckless in her upset; her movements were quick and lurching. She told them they would have twenty minutes to look around on their own. The group spread apart.

Now, Margaret thought, she would have time to make a plan, to bring herself under control.

At one end of the barracks were the bunks, and the rusty, lidless toilets once used by the prisoners, at the other was a multimedia exhibit. The group trod quickly through the dormitory, that dirty old lumber-yard, but soon headed back into the heated exhibition. The charred rooms in the front were even colder than the outdoors; they still smelled of cinders from the arson attack a decade before. Margaret stayed by herself, watching her breath puff out of her mouth. She leaned against one of the primitive bunk beds.

The floor creaked. The bunks creaked. Margaret closed her eyes. She heard—what did she hear?—a tiny scratching sound coming from the corner.

A second scratching sound began soon after the first, as though in canon, this time from a portion of the wall behind the bunks, a little distance away. One mouse in the wall, now two. And then a scratching, scuttling, tunneling—just under Margaret's feet.

Margaret caught a glimpse of red in her peripheral vision, and turned quickly—it was the English businessman returned. "Aha!" Margaret cried out. She was embarrassed at her upset. "I was just noticing the mice in the walls."

"Mice? Of course, this place built like a cracker tin as it is, there would be no place for a mouse to make a home. No, no insulation here!" He laughed. "Now I have a book in my collection, maybe you would know it, *The Death of Adolf Hitler,* it's called, would you know of that one?"

"No, I'm afraid I don't."

"A pity really; fascinating book. Hitler had a phobia of cats, it outlines that in detail. And the book also has some interesting words to say about Stalin. The man was *in love* with Hitler. He used Hitler's bones—the ones that Zhukov brought back to Moscow—to make combs for his hair, for his moustache, you know. High style, if you ask me." He gave Margaret a wink. Then quickly, as though to cover himself, he let out a guffaw.

"Really?"

"I've always been interested in history. One of my chief interests, I would say."

Margaret smiled, colored. Without any warning, she darted for the door. She left the man so abruptly he didn't have time to follow her.

Margaret looked up and down the camp. The man from Norway was outside, smoking a cigarette some distance away. Margaret pretended not to see him. Whether or not Hitler liked cats was the topic in her mind. She had never heard he didn't. But it made sense to her that he would not. She decided it must be true.

She wandered farther, this thought of cats dangling, distracting, even as she felt a long rope in her head begin to tighten, everything tightening and filling, becoming denser, a feeling of her large body flipping up into her tight, claustrophobic brain like a gymnast on the parallel bars folding into the above.

She focused her eyes with difficulty. Between the trees in the distance was the sibyl swaying in her basket. Her long, dying hair flowed down below her curled body. As Margaret came nearer she could hear the whisper of the sibyl.

Margaret backed away from the trees. But another sound, the rushing sound of scratching, tunneling, running, miniature nails began again below Margaret, only now out here on the great plain.

She walked toward the old laundry building. She saw a forlorn entrance to a tunnel by the door.

A second great, fanning group of barracks had once stood out here on the field. These were all gone now. Margaret could see shadows of movement under the ice-covered snow. Mouse tunnels, invisible when empty, became dark when the mice ran through them, their bodies like smoke.

By the camp prison compound and over at the gallows, the tunnels in the ground were running with darkness. A kaleidoscope of movement began to trickle into her eyes from every direction.

A vast network of mouse tunnels—legions of beasts running just beneath the surface of the sandy, ice-covered, tumbledown, slipshod ruin of a camp—the network was vast, oh, but not nearly vast enough, for each tunnel branched, and then branched again, exponentially expanding into an enormous city of scamperers, yes—but then, just as at the edge of the world, or the edge of life itself—every tunnel dead-ended at the demarcation line of the triangle that was the universe and the humiliation: the tunnels did not run outside the camp. The work of the mice—the suspected rats, the parasitical beasts—their work was dirty, abject, senseless—and the mice, they were filled with motivation as they ferried scraps here, carried a message there—they ran hither and thither full of assurance of reward. Their scampering was wonderfully glittering, the scuttling speed through the tunnels reminded one of vacuum tubes, the mice drawn rocket-like by the sucking emptiness beyond the end walls.

Margaret tried to calm herself. It was the burden of secrets that was making her crazy, she thought. To have all the pictures playing simultaneously in her head, but trying to follow one single string of speech, it would drive anyone mad.

When she got home to the Grunewaldstrasse, the hawk-woman was waiting for her on the balcony above her apartment, standing in the cold, still and glassy-eyed like a piece of taxidermy. Margaret was afraid, more than she had been before.

And she thought, then, that the alliance was crumbling.

She shut all the curtains and covered herself in the bed. There was no way to visit a place like Sachsenhausen and try to be a Nazi at the same time.

It can hardly be a coincidence that later that very night, unable to sleep despite her exhaustion, Margaret found another quotation from Ello Quandt.

In March of 1942, Ello said that Magda complained to her of what Joseph told her. *"It's horrifying, all the things he tells me. I can't bear it anymore. You can't imagine the terrible things he burdens me with, and there's no one to whom I can open my heart."*

And what immediately followed stopped Margaret short. It seemed that not long after she complained to Ello, the right side of Magda's face became paralyzed. This was verifiable, and not exclusively based on Ello's testimony. Trigeminal neuralgia, said the doctors. Margaret looked up the diagnosis in the encyclopedia. *"The condition can bring about a paralysis of the facial muscles, and stabbing, mind-numbing, electric-shock-like pain from just a finger's glance to the cheek. Believed to be the most severe type of pain known to human beings . . ."* And then in May of 1943, a full year later, after Goebbels declared total war and the Wannsee decision went into effect, Magda was operated on, but the operation was unsuccessful: the right side of her face remained paralyzed, the muscles gone slack. Her beauty was gone. Her friends said she looked unwell, her enemies said she looked like a corpse.

Margaret lay in bed for a long time. The minutes passed slowly, and she could not stop her galloping mind.

Shortly after three in the morning, despite exhaustion, Margaret was awake. A light came into the bedroom from the courtyard. The room was quiet and the light was sharp. Margaret could hear the bang of the trash lid and the thud-whisper of falling papers—someone had turned on the timed lights and was unloading newspapers. Then footsteps moved away. All went quiet.

Without warning a flicker came. Margaret jerked up. A shadow was on the wall, on the right side of the room. At first Margaret thought it was the hawk-woman—maybe she had come nearer, outside the window. Margaret's heart began to pound. But soon she saw that the shadow was not the shadow of a bird.

It was the shadow of a pair of hands, dexterous and sinister. The hands were moving: they made figures—a duck and a dog. Then one changed, now it was a dog and a stork. Bowing and twittering, miming, putting on a show in the path of the light, a restless pair of hands unable to sleep. The shapes of the animals were vivid and animal-like—adept at the pageant, while at the same time remaining human fingers, as if human flesh could mirror any creation under the sun.

Margaret huddled under the covers, watching the movement of the hands on the wall. Her fear froze her for a moment, but then suddenly it was gone. In each thing, she thought, all things are to be found, and this is innocence—the world bundled into the head of a pin, in the fist of a hand, in the brain of a human, in the sun and in its microcosmic imitation of the universe; all patterns existing potentially in all other patterns, the world full of the energy of things it does not yet know, in its insides and in how it projects itself to the out. Design flows into design, every thing perceives and mirrors every other thing, and becomes more like it.

And then Margaret thought of Magda Goebbels, and of how that woman had been still while patterns moved and changed around her. Magda Goebbels could never be called innocent, no matter what she might have said to Ello Quandt. No matter what she might have said.

After sleeping, Margaret thought, she would have likely forgotten this, as she so often forgot the illumination moments that came to her during the night.

She heaved herself up from the bed and went to her desk. She thought she would write down what she had learned about innocence—it was that important to her.

But instead of beginning to write, she was still and unmoving, and then her hands began to wander on their own, and she found herself opening a book and looking again at the Russian mortuary pictures of Magda's children at Plötzensee. She looked at their waxen faces. Their nightgowns were white, their faces were still. Margaret pushed her fingers against her head. She thought: Magda Goebbels drank it in. Magda Goebbels knew everything and absorbed it and became stiller and stiller.

Margaret touched her own face. The skin of her forehead felt scaly, unanimated.

Woe to the unthinking, woe to the empty-headed, woe to the unre-membering, she thought. For they are the static, the blanketed, the uniformed, the shrouded, the dead in spirit.

TWELVE • The History of History

Margaret went back to the doctor. Three days after Sachsenhausen, and there were still dark circles under her eyes and she was dizzy from lack of sleep. That hanging, greyheaded sibyl: she had not been able to pull away from it, nor from the scampering mice.

The small green door in the ivy was unlocked, and before long Margaret was sitting by the tall plastic plant in the waiting room, her body taut and ready. She had a handkerchief in her hands; she wound it around her fingers.

After a while, the doctor's voice warbled from down the hallway. "Margaret Täubner."

Margaret rose and walked down the length of the flat. As she neared the doctor's door, music flowed loud from inside the chamber, a stereo playing at high volume—harpsichord, violin, cello, and soprano.

Somehow—and mark well, it was merely by chance—Margaret had an impulse to open only one panel of the French doors. She turned her shoulders and slipped into the room, and she caught a glimpse of the old woman behind her desk, upright, her giant head wobbling on her narrow neck. The music blared: something seventeenth-century, pure, operatic, without vibrato. What was it? Margaret thought she knew the melody. Yes, it was *Dido and Aeneas*.

Just at the moment of recognition, a very quick and confusing series of stimuli bore down on her. The music reached a height of emotion— the words "in my breast" were sung, full of pain. A dim, silver light passed at high speed across her left shoulder by her ear, from fore to aft, and the air was displaced; a flicker of a breeze puffed her hair. In a fraction of an instant, there was the sound of a *thunk* at the French doors behind her, loud enough to be heard over the ballooning music, followed by a vibrating *twang*. She spun around in the direction of the shuddering.

A small knife quivered in the wood—the panel of the French door that Margaret had left closed—in a target made of cork attached at eye level, a red- and yellow-striped bull's-eye. There were two other small steak knives also standing in the target perpendicular. At the sight of the knives, Margaret cried out. She ducked her head in a belated reflex. There was a sense of the room coming apart, as if it had been thrown, the entire box, into black space. The doctor, for her part, held her head rigidly, facing the door. Margaret yelled to the doctor, "Did you just throw a knife?"

"What?"

The music blared painfully beautiful harmonics, shaking the room in a tumbling stretto. And then Margaret could make out the words *remember,* and *fate* plummeting over each other in polyphony.

"Did you throw a knife at the door?" Margaret yelled.

"Comrade! I'm going to have to turn down the music. I can't hear you." The doctor trailed her hand against the wall, leading herself to the stereo in the cupboard, where she finally managed to turn off the CD.

In the silence that followed, the rogue knife, long since home in its target, still quivered like a tuning fork. The doctor's rasping breath marked the time.

"I turned on the music when I heard you were here because I thought you'd help me with the lyrics. I can't make out what's being said. You're a native speaker of English."

"Ah, yes," Margaret said, breathing heavily. "I suppose I can."

"All the music is in English these days. In exchange, now that I'm your mentor, I would help you with the Wagner librettos."

"I don't need any help with the Wagner librettos," Margaret said.

"Oh." There was a quiet. "The part I'm wondering about is in the beginning of Dido's lament. It sounds as though she's saying"—and here the doctor spoke in an English so heavily accented Margaret almost did not recognize it as English—" 'May my ahms create no trouble in my breast.' "

" 'May my *arms,*' " Margaret corrected. "Is that what you said?"

"Yes. Ahms."

"But that doesn't make any sense."

"I know," the doctor agreed. "What are ahms?"

"*Arrrrrms,*" Margaret said, emphasizing the American *r.* And then in German: *"Arme."*

"Oh!" the doctor said with excitement. "Comrade, you're very clever."

"But still it doesn't make sense," Margaret said. " 'May my arms create no trouble in my breast'?" The doctor was now busily scanning the CD. She played the section of track again, and Margaret listened. "May my *wrongs* create no trouble in my breast," Margaret said, when she realized what it was.

"You're lovely, my dear. Very efficient." The doctor sat down.

But Margaret remained standing, still trembling like the knife. "Did you throw a knife at the door just now?" she asked.

The room around her was dusty and lush. The only light was from the windows, which, with their thick curtains on either side, and their inner blinds of parchment muslin, let through only a dusky light. Margaret noticed that now, in contrast with last time, there was a potted orange tree with lush foliage taking up much of the free space to the left of the examination table, growing halfway to the ceiling. Its leaves seemed to rustle now and then.

"I was practicing my aim," said the doctor.

"I thought you were blind?"

"Yes, my dear, blind as a badger, which is to say, not entirely blind, but mostly. My dear child, I have to have regular practice sessions for myself: challenges, obstacle courses, tests, and self-maintenance drills. I'm keeping myself sensitive to the world. For example, the knife throwing. I put up the target; I feel its location very carefully with my fingertips. Then I back away from it, counting the steps and feeling the floor with my toetips as I go. Finally, I install myself behind the desk, and *wham*! I always hit it. I can hear the blade entering the cork. A wonderful sound!"

Margaret looked back at the French doors. It was true that there were three knives in the target now, but she also saw around it, on both sides of the door, many gashes in the wood, most of them in the vicinity of the bull's-eye—but not all. Margaret's stomach turned. Funny, she had not noticed this on her last visit.

"So, comrade," the doctor began, her voice becoming more rasping, "have you remembered? Are you ready to talk?"

"No," said Margaret, irritated, despite her best hopes for the visit. The business with the knife, the lyrics—the doctor was getting her rattled in record time.

"Really? Nothing at all?" asked the doctor.

"That's precisely what I wanted to talk to you about. That's why I'm here."

"About what?"

"The treatment is not what you said it would be," said Margaret. "Not at all."

"What is it then?" asked the doctor.

"Nothing."

"Nothing?" the doctor asked.

"Well," Margaret began. Although she would have liked to speak frankly, she found something rising in her, a column of secretive smoke, that forced her to speak in only vague and encrypted terms. "I haven't remembered anything, but—there have been changes. In fact, everything has changed. But none of the things I remember are my own life." Margaret said this and shuddered, thinking of the sibyl in her basket. Come to think of it, the swinging, grey-headed sibyl had borne a striking resemblance to Dr. Arabscheilis.

"But that's quite fine, my dear, quite fine!" The doctor, for her part, seemed encouraged. "What is it that's changed?"

Margaret swallowed. "Well, for starters, the buildings," she said.

"The buildings?" The doctor stopped her in surprise.

"Yes, the buildings," Margaret said. "They've turned into flesh. They've turned into flesh and they're made of that now, instead of brick and stucco . . ." Her voice trailed off in embarrassment. "Flesh."

"Flesh!" the doctor said. "Fascinating!"

Margaret was enlivened by the woman's apparent ready belief. "Yes, they turned into flesh. So I think—in any case, there's been a— malfunction of some kind. I'm not remembering my own life," she repeated again, dumbly. And then very forcefully: "I want you to reverse the treatment."

"If I remember correctly, my pet," the doctor said, "when I saw you before, you didn't have any desire to undergo treatment for what was a startlingly acute case of retrograde amnesia, if I may say so. So if you truly have not remembered, what are you complaining about? Isn't this just how you wanted it?"

Margaret was surprised. She had assumed the doctor had not listened to her at all during the last visit. She cleared her throat. "Yes, that's right. I was happy as I was."

"And now you say nothing has changed, and that makes you upset?"

"Well, no. *Something* has changed! The city is made of *fat*. My life is poisoned." This was truly how she felt in the days since the Sachsenhausen tour and the skittering mice.

"Aha!" the doctor cried, a cat after a dangling string. "So! It worked after all! Tell me, why is your life 'poisoned' as you say?"

"I'm doing the things I usually do—"

"Quite right," the doctor said.

"But I can't sleep anymore. I feel guilty."

"You feel guilty?"

"Yes," Margaret said. "Yes, I would say that. But I didn't do anything wrong," she said quickly, her voice rising involuntarily.

"Then why do you feel guilty?"

"Because the residue comes off on me. My job has become horrible. I feel sick." Margaret was not willing, even now, to mention the hawk-woman.

The doctor was quiet for a moment, seeming to consider. "It's history you work with as a guide, and history you study at the university?" she finally asked.

"Yes."

"Have you considered that might be the trouble?"

"No," Margaret said.

"But of course that's the trouble!" And again the doctor became excited. "Let me explain it to you this way. History, for an amnesiac—comrade, my pet—is a shill, a stool pigeon, a decoy, a trap. All these years, you've been charming yourself with the dry bone, not the bloody flesh. For the sake of the bone, you have danced and been entertained. You've been reading history so that it will be easier to shed your own flesh. That is the history of history—the violence against the body for the sake of the skeleton."

Margaret drew her head back as if she'd been struck. Oddly, the doctor's words made instant sense to her. And she was defensive. "You don't know anything," she said. The presumptuous doctor didn't know her. She thought of her apartment, the hallway of which was like a rope bridge over a great gorge of knowledge, with its many piles of books on either side—biographies, histories, sociologies, old telephone and address directories stacked so high it could only cunningly be traversed—used books bought over the Internet from dealer-collectors, new books from the fair in Frankfurt, books from the *Antiquariat* on the corner. And then she thought of her painting of Magda Goebbels. No one could say she, Margaret, of all people, had been gesturing frivolously at the past.

But the doctor went on. "You want to drain the elderly fluids so you can march hypnotized into the future!" she said. "Your living, breathing, fleshy Berlin—ha-ha! I'll tell you what that is!" the doctor laughed. "A step back from disingenuousness! For nothing living can ever be completely misunderstood. If you have to see the buildings alive, then it will put a stay of execution on your murder of time." The doctor beamed. "Everything is going according to plan, comrade— your defenses are breaking down. My way, " she said, "is winning you over!"

Margaret was dizzy with anger. "You're most certainly *not* winning me over, doctor. I'm here to say it's not working!" She stood up. "This was supposed to be a cure for amnesia. But my amnesia is not cured."

The doctor's voice lowered to a purr hardly louder than the sound of her rasping breath. "I know you feel guilty, my dear, I know it hurts you. Regardless of whether you remember what you've done, you will still feel guilty, for guilt is not a matter of history but a matter of character, and therefore a contagion. It is very difficult to become connected to someone else's crime, but never difficult to become connected to someone else's heart. You can always stop seeking the truth of life, but you can never stop seeking the truth of character! You can never stop worrying over the shadows of your own, riddling heart!"

The doctor waved her hands in the air. "Bid the history of history adieu, comrade! The living apartment houses are eager to have their way. A new sun is rising, the time of the anesthetized past is drawing to a close."

Margaret clutched the lip of the desk. "Doctor, I have *never* tried to *anesthetize* the past. On the contrary."

"Oh, I've been on your 'tours of Berlin,' " the doctor said.

Margaret cried out. No she hadn't! She would have certainly remembered an ancient, goggle-eyed German woman.

Or would she have? Recently she had been so distracted . . . But the doctor cut her off. "If you are not in the habit of anesthetizing the past, then how do you explain that you don't remember one bit of your *own* past?" She wrapped her knuckles against the desk.

Margaret pulled at the bottom of her sweater. "I have nothing to remember." Her cheeks burned.

"Yes, you do."

"In that case, why don't I remember it? Why don't I find it? It doesn't make sense! I am fully tuned in. I can memorize anything I choose."

"My dear, let me answer that question with another question: what is the difference between having a knife thrown at your head and reading a story about having a knife thrown at your head?"

Margaret hid her face. She wanted to get up, but her whole body was leaden; she suspected that she was rooted to the floor as a rabbit freezes in hopes of camouflage. So many animals believe predators cannot see them when they are still. She didn't say anything, her nostrils sick with the task of breathing. The clock ticked in the corner. With little warning, the heavy handle of one of the knives in the door won out against the blade, and it fell to the ground with a clatter.

"Dr. Arabscheilis," Margaret said. "Did you throw a knife at me?"

"I did not throw a knife at you," the doctor said. "But come, come, that won't do. What's the difference?"

"Any number of differences," said Margaret, breathing heavily.

"No, there are two."

"There are more than two," Margaret said.

"No, there are precisely two differences," the doctor said. "The first is this: in the story, there is a *multiplicity* of things—the door opening, the doctor in her white coat, the doctor launching her weapon, the knife flying, the sound of the knife lodging in the corkboard, the cowering girl—I am merely assuming you cowered. Did you cower? Well, never mind. But in the experience, by contrast, there are only *two* things. There is *confusion,* and there is *fear.*"

Margaret shifted in her chair.

"And then there is the second difference," the doctor went on. "Can you guess what it is?"

"No," said Margaret.

"Really? Not a single guess?"

"No," Margaret said. She was nauseous.

"Did you guess *Dido and Aeneas,* comrade? *Dido and Aeneas* is the correct answer. In the story, the sound of Dido's aria flowing through the room changed the style and tone of *everything.* But in real life, the music made no difference."

Margaret was silent, shielding her head.

"If you read some scrap of history," the doctor said, "you are doing nothing but replaying your own life, only in heavy makeup. The world is pregnant with your own face, and it will never give birth to anything else, because you know nothing but this life of yours, which is plain and pure emotion, stripped of all gratification of meaning—just a whimper in the dark. A story, by contrast, is a symphony blooming in the sunlight, trying to draw you away from chaos. Anyone who doesn't know this has been nursing herself with lies plugged into her consciousness, as the symphonic sound track is plugged into the films in the dark of the movie theater, trying to make us believe that all experience carries an emotion familiar and long since invented, making a case for religion, trying to prove—foolishly, comrade, so foolishly!—that we all know the same beauty."

Margaret held her head tightly in her hands, trying not to open her mouth and scream. Her mind was going black and white and black and white again, as if there were a strobe light pulsing the room.

She sat for a while so, but then with sudden brightness something suggested itself to her, and she lunged across the desk at the doctor. "That's not true," she broke out. "It's not true about *Dido and Aeneas.* It's not incidental at all. When I came into the room and the knife went by my head, Dido sang, 'in my breast.' And that's all I remember about the knife now. Just those three words. And if I were to remember what happened later, I might think the knife went into my breast instead of the door!"

"Only because you'd already be remembering it, which is to say mythologizing it. It has nothing to do with the actual event." The doctor was not necessarily reasonable, but she was quick.

Song lyrics—thinking of them, Margaret's thoughts jerked over to the moment on the train on the way to Sachsenhausen, when she had remembered her father and the song he used to sing. "Du Bist Verrückt, mein Kind." He had sung to her in German, a language she did not know as a child. He sang, and the German words sounded in the child's ears like radio static. But sitting here now, she could remember it, she could remember his voice and his song, and to her mind now it was full of meaning. The German words could be dropped like coins into the new slots cut into her mind in the years since, and there decoded by their very grooves. He had sung:

> *Du bist verrückt, mein Kind,*—and now she knew it meant: You
>   are crazy, my child,
> *du musst nach Berlin,*—you must go to Berlin,
> *wo die Verrückten sind,*—where the crazies are,
> *da gehörst du hin*—that's where you belong.
> *Du musst nach Plötzensee*—you must go off to Plötzensee,
> *wo die Verrückten sind*—where the crazies are,
> *am grünen Strand der Spree.*—on the green banks of the Spree.

The meaning of the lines touched icy fingers to Margaret's back.

She remembered more: he had sung it at a party. She was wild with delight, he was drunk. She was running in loops with the other children; he plucked her out of circulation, took her in his arms and held her up above his head, and she looked into his light eyes, which were small behind his glasses, and he sang to her.

However, the doctor was right in a certain way. Her memory was foreign to the experience of the child, who did not understand German, who did not know how to recognize drunkenness, who did not know where she was, or whether her father would one day disappear into a mental hospital, where he would make thinking of the time before he had gone away from home into an act of nostalgia.

The doctor seemed to regard Margaret very closely, but with her ears rather than her eyes—her head was cocked. "Writing history, reading history, my dear, a person will always try to stage a symphony in a cave where nothing but a whimper dwells," she said, "but at the end of your life, perhaps even sooner, you'll realize that there's nothing to chronicle, nothing to remember, or even to know, that bears any relationship to experience at all. Eventually there will be no more pantomimes, only the acute attunement to the whimper."

"But if there's nothing to chronicle, then why do you care whether or not I remember?"

"Comrade! I am not opposed to the ideal—the ideal of the remembering human mind! I'm only opposed to false expansions of same. Meaning is private, puny, and constructed artificially. If you recognize that fact once and for all, the meaning you will eventually have no choice but to construct will be proportionate. That is to say, it will be very small. You will know it to be essentially provisional, even fraudulent!—and then, as a result, it will be powerless, and remembering all things unbearable will become bearable to you."

"Will it?"

"Yes."

"And is that good?"

"What?" asked the doctor.

"To remember unbearable things."

"Of course it is," said the doctor. "Truth is a worthy cause, even if it is wildly limited in scope. From all your copper mine, you'll get only one penny."

Margaret took a step toward the door. She saw that the doctor was not going to help her escape; on the contrary, the doctor was part of the nightmare. Margaret opened the door. One of the knives was still stuck in it.

"Comrade!" the doctor cried out when she heard the door opening. "You have to go nearer before you can get farther away from it! Ascribe significance to everything, but only personal significance!"

The cry of advice sounded in the room, the doctor's voice had grown hoarse and exalted.

At home, Margaret again heard the first bars of "Du Bist Verrückt, mein Kind" playing in her mind—an earworm of the most insistent kind. It wasn't long before she began to feel the song around her like flames, licking at her feet, polluting the air, and there was a terrible moment. Because of a sense of rising chaos, she thought the fire would shatter the panes of the glass globe that had been around her head for so long.

She went over to the bookshelf. In the inferno of the earworm's heat, a book flew at her eyes. It was a book that was fat with letters from her mother, some opened and others not, all left so long untouched that it was blurred into something almost imperceptible.

She wanted to escape the song. The song suggested damning things about her free will. She longed to pin down the specifics of her mother's modest handwriting. It seemed that in comforting herself thus, she would draw something monstrous out of the sky.

She pulled the book out of the shelf—it was a Russian novel called *Moscow-Petushki,* and all at once a wave of bad feeling came over her again. *Tick-tock, this is the end.* Her hands shook. The veins in them had risen. She tidied the letters.

You are crazy, my child. You belong in Berlin. Her father had sung that to her when she was only a girl. He had danced with Alphi, his beloved Great Dane.

She could not go on. She put the letters back into the book, and the book back onto the shelf, all the while staring at her hands. Another wave of bad feeling pushed her back, with a mighty shove to her solar plexus.

So she did not read the letters from her mother. And it shall be noted, much to the frustration of anyone who might be wishing to tether her tale to a rational mast, she also did not bother to look and see that one of the letters, written in a cribbed hand, contained all the lyrics of "Du Bist Verrückt, mein Kind." It was postmarked October 2002—that is, it came from the period that Margaret herself was in the habit of designating as "lost time."

THIRTEEN • Face Tattoos

There was a day in January that began in the yellow phone booth outside the supermarket on Gleditschstrasse. Margaret pulled open its heavy door. She needed a phone book.

Margaret was turning to the man who had claimed to have once been Hitler's bodyguard.

She opened the city phonebook in the sweaty little box, and when her finger hit his name, it jumped. There was Arthur Prell, Hitler's own bodyguard, woven into modern Berlin by the good offices of the telephone book. In 2005, his name stood in blameless black letters. Beside it, an equally modest number stood, only five digits. She dialed. The phone rang. It rang until the possibility of an answering machine was eliminated.

A faraway voice sounded—the cottony, warbling voice Margaret remembered, the voice of a very old man.

"Hallo?" said the distant voice.

"Yes, hello." Margaret invented herself on the spot. "I'm Margarethe Taub, journalist."

"Yeah?" the voice said, sounding childish and confused.

"Yes. I write for—*Smithsonian* magazine," Margaret said, haltingly. She wondered if the publication still existed. "I'd like to know if you'd be willing to give an interview."

"Give a what?"

"Give an interview."

"Why?"

"My understanding is that you were one of Adolf Hitler's bodyguards," Margaret said.

"Oh, yes. That's true. So you want an interview. They all come to me for that. Well, I don't have much time. But I can fit you in I guess, I can probably fit you in." He sounded resigned and proud. His words, even more than when she had heard him at the bunker, were soggy and mucous-filled.

"Would you like to meet at the bunker?" Margaret asked.

"What?"

"Whether you'd like to meet at the bunker," Margaret said loudly into the receiver. "I've seen you there before."

"No." He paused, and seemed to swallow thickly. He badly needed to clear his throat. "No, no. My knees, you see." Margaret didn't tell him that she had seen him there, hopping about on spry feet.

"Where would you like to meet for the interview, Herr Prell?"

"Well, I guess we can meet here at my place."

And they set up a time to meet at his house, in Rudow.

Margaret went home triumphant. She discovered, online, that Prell was selling a CD: *Songs from the Berghof,* to raise money for his cause— the support of old SS officers who were "denied a pension" by the German government.

She reread several detailed accounts of Hitler's last days in the bunker.

Later, she went to an electronics store down on the Kurfürstendamm and bought a cheap microcassette recorder.

After that, still feeling incomplete, she went to a brilliantly lit department store and walked around the candy department. She should bring Prell some small token, she thought. She decided on chocolates, but couldn't decide what size box. There were small ones, and then there were large ones that cost a pretty penny. She spent a long time making up her mind. She chose a small one in the end. Waiting in line at the cash register, however, she looked at it and thought it appeared trifling, insulting even. She darted back to the glass wall and got an impressive tin of individually wrapped truffles.

The day of the interview arrived. Margaret spent a long time deciding what to wear. The skirt she eventually chose was short, but at the same time, very becoming.

A long and oppressive subway ride followed. Prell lived all the way at the far eastern end of the U7 line.

In Rudow, Margaret hauled her racing bike off the train. She peddled through the settlement of little homes, the gabled houses, the towering pine trees. The streets were named for flowers. She turned in at Eucalyptus, found the house number on the gate, and there it was, Prell's little house. It had plastic white lace curtains, the wont of the elderly East, and a low wall around a little garden, with a gate that opened and closed on a remotely controlled lock. Margaret pressed the buzzer.

All was quiet.

She pressed again.

A door on the side of the house sprang open, and Prell appeared. He took the stairs sideways, apparently with a bad knee after all, but still he lunged toward her quickly, on spry, stilt legs, and opened the gate. They shook hands. Margaret blushed. She followed him inside. He took her coat.

She looked about the living room—artificial flowers in abundance, the smell of gumdrops and potpourri, paintings of spring bouquets and clowns dotting the walls in sloughs of stale color.

At the table, Margaret fumbled to get out her tape recorder. Prell's eyes gleamed hungrily at the sight of it.

She took a deep breath. She asked a question, and they began.

It should have been interesting, the things he said. But the old man began to drone. He recited empty things, things that sounded as though they were memorized from books—freezer-burned, senseless chatter, and, most troubling of all, his answers did not correspond in any way to her questions. She asked about his life before the war—he talked about the bunker. She asked about the bunker—he talked about his life before the war. He pulled out a shoebox that at first appeared to be full of photographs but was actually piles of laminated photocopies of photographs—of himself, at Berchtesgaden, with the Hitler-Braun dogs, in front of the door to the Berlin bunker, and at the Wolf's Lair, in East Prussia. The only point of interest to Margaret was this: it was easy to recognize the face of the old man in the face of the young one at Berchtesgaden.

He was a drone, but he was not an imposter.

Through great effort, Margaret managed to finally steer the conversation to the Goebbels family. Prell began to speak of them, and at long last, Margaret became interested, for it must be said: ever and again, she was the yo-yo and Magda Goebbels was the hand holding the string. Margaret sometimes flew away, but always she zinged back into that woman's tight palm.

"Well, let me see," said the old man, moving his lips thickly. "Goebbels and the kids arrived suddenly, about fourteen days before the end. Then Hitler's doctor, Dr. Morell, had to move out so that Dr. Goebbels could move in, and his wife lived one story higher in the connecting bunker, with the children. But the children came down to play all the time, you know? When they were too loud we sent them back up."

He laughed.

"Usually they were up in the New Chancellery; there were people around up there and they had freedom to move about. Anyway, I went up there too, shortly before the end, because the big kitchen was there. Goebbels sat down at a long table with the children. A young man played the harmonica. And Goebbels was saying goodbye to the civilians with the children; there were so many people there up in the New Chancellery, people looking to take shelter there. And it occurred to me for the first time that maybe I should say goodbye, too. That was the moment it became clear to me that Hitler and Goebbels would stay. And Eva Braun and Frau Goebbels had agreed they wouldn't abandon their men either. They would stay to the end too. And then plans were made for the children. The other women in the bunker all offered—Frau Rindell for example, from the office, she said, 'Frau Goebbels, if you want to stay here, that's your business, but the children can't possibly stay here—' and Frau Graf said, 'I'll take them to Darmstadt to my sister, she can't have children—she would be happy. Please!' and she cried.

"You know, we, the service people, we all knew that the children were meant to stay, and what would happen. They would stay and they would die."

Prell spoke so loudly Margaret had to draw her head back.

"Oh, and then of course the aviator, Hanna Reitsch, offered to fly them out. She said even if she had to fly back and forth twenty times, she would fly them out. Of course, that's not what happened." He paused.

"Frau Goebbels, she had to come down to my room to get the children ready."

"What do you mean?" Margaret interrupted. Her eyes dropped. She felt a glass hand on her shoulder.

"Well, she was going to give them a soft finish."

"In your room?"

"Oh yeah."

"Why there?" Margaret's voice came out as a purr. It was not how she meant it at all.

"Up above there were so many people around, but down in our rooms there was no one. We ourselves weren't even down there. We only slept there. So she could take care of them on her own. I went out of the room and waited outside. After a little while Dr. Naumann came out of the room. He said to me—he whispered in my ear—that if it had been up to *him,* Dr. Goebbels he meant, then the children wouldn't still be in the bunker, they would be evacuated. And I had seen Naumann talking with Goebbels up above before, and he was probably right. I took him as a trustworthy representative. Goebbels didn't want it. It was Frau Goebbels who wanted it. One must stick with the truth. That's how it was!" Prell yelled, as though Margaret had challenged him.

Margaret breathed out. She looked at him. She saw his flashing eyes; she saw that he thought he was on trial.

But he was making it too easy for her. Because she wasn't putting him on trial. He was waiting for her to rise up against him, but she— she didn't know what she was doing at all. She looked at him.

When Margaret thought about the interview afterward, it was that moment, with Prell yelling, "That's how it was!" which she would always remember as the point at which a blue sky went yellow-black, like a character in a crime novel pulling a previously friendly upper lip into a sneer. Because as far as Margaret was concerned, it was at that moment when it began to be *not Prell* who was on trial. Not Prell, but Margaret herself.

And Magda Goebbels, suddenly, was everywhere in the room. She was hovering against the walls and in the jars of potpourri; she was a black fume around the curtains and darkening the craft-fair paintings on the walls.

If Margaret were going to take a stand against Magda Goebbels, it must be right now.

Margaret stuttered, buying time. "Did you—?" she began, un-certainly.

Again, however, Prell did not wait to hear the rest. He cried out as though she had already accused him outright: "It wasn't for me! I did as I was told."

He was helping her along.

Margaret was quiet, her palms burning. Her muscles locked.

Prell gambled: "But sure, it was a shame." Margaret sat with her head down.

Prell began again. "Next to the site of the bunker they're putting up the big memorial for the Jews right now. Two thousand seven hun-dred concrete blocks—they're allowed that. But I say, how would it be if over there around the corner by the bunker, we put in *six* blocks, just six? The children of Goebbels were *murdered,* killed, deliberately murdered. Couldn't they be honored, the children? It won't do them any good now, but at least we could honor them, put up a sign that says, 'Here died six murdered children.' Two thousand seven hundred blocks for the Jews, but six children can't be honored?"

"What about the neo-Nazis who would make it into a shrine?" Margaret's voice came out in a squeak. She began to dash lines on her notepad. She drew a lighthouse with a black stripe twisting around it.

Oh, if Margaret were going to grab the demon and pull it where she wanted it to go, it must be *now*.

"Ach, 'neo-Nazi.' No such thing," said Prell. "What does neo-Nazi mean? New Nazi, right? There aren't any. That's just a buzzword. What you have are nationally conscious people, people who say, 'my fatherland,' right or wrong. 'My fatherland,' nothing more, am I right? You Americans say it, the Swiss say it, the Israelis say it—'My country,' they say. 'And I'll fight for it.' The Israelis are nationalistic people, they defend their region, they defend their people. They have as much right as anyone."

He looked at Margaret over the tin of chocolates she had brought him. Then he tilted his head toward her conspiratorially.

"I've got an idea for what the memorial for the kids could look like. A sort of design. I do some of that on the side."

Margaret's face was red. She was breathing hard. She didn't look at him.

"I'm thinking there would be six blocks and each one would be the height of the respective kid when it died. So one meter thirty, one meter ten, and so on. Pretty good, I think."

Margaret started to cough. The air in the room was very dry.

Prell was on a roll. "You can't talk about guilt, you know." (But she had not.) "All these things they write about Hitler nowadays. If he had really done all the terrible things they say he did, how could he have been our Führer?"

Margaret coughed harder. Prell ignored her. "Let's think about it. I'm telling you, one way or another, the war would have come, the war would have come ONE WAY OR ANOTHER, it didn't take Hitler to make the war, the Jews now, they declared war on Germany in the 1920s, and then again at the end of the 1930s, The war right now in Iraq isn't about Saddam Hussein, it's about Israel! That Israel, it can't exist on avocadoes and oranges, a nation lives from business, they have to have money, and the Americans always pay in, don't they? This is just my opinion, but why did they occupy Iraq? Supposedly because of atomic bombs!" He laughed straight from the belly. "In my opinion Iraq is a wealthy oil region, and with this money they can support Israel; they can't keep pumping in their own money forever. There's something I'll tell you about Israel . . ."

And on and on he talked. Margaret looked at the tin of chocolates she had brought him. These sat next to the artificial roses, petals adorned in drops of plastic dew. I bought him expensive chocolates, she thought to herself. It was a tough bludgeon and knocked his voice right out of her mind. And foggily, it seemed the blood and dust that rose in the cloud afterward dampened her will to fight. The chocolates—bought before she ever arrived at this house—were a pivotal battle already lost days before, on some distant front, news of it coming back to the capital over the radio only now.

She lifted her head. He was still moving his jaw muscles, his thick tongue flickering in and out of his mouth.

She watched him, but his voice was whitening out, a volume dial had been rotated down, and now not only could she not hear him, but even his physical form grew blurry in her eyes. When she strained to bring him back into focus, bulging her eyes out of her head, she saw him before her again, but this time his clothes had begun to drip off his body in scales. He was molting. Finally, the hulking, chanting body sat before her in its slate-white skin.

As Margaret looked on, tattoos began to appear in this skin, rising to the surface like water mammals fountaining up for breath. Intricate tattoos they were—high-contrast black-and-white photographs. All over his body, the photographs began to nose up. Photographs of faces, almost mug shots, laid out like a map. A woman's high cheekbones here and a child's large cranium there.

Margaret squeezed her eyes shut.

She breathed in and out of her nose. Finally she felt herself coming down. She opened her eyes again and there he was before her in his polyester golf coat and cardigan. He reminded her of her grandfather. She smiled brightly and he smiled back.

By the time she got home to the Grunewaldstrasse, she only had one question. Why had she given him chocolates?

Margaret had not been able to stand up to him. Her spaniel fidelity meekly fed the tortoise-man chocolates!

She had *not* asked the key questions, she had *not* begged for the key answers. The next day, she would go to the university, continuing her search for the Meissner biography, bumptiously searching for Magda Goebbels's "true" character; yes, this she knew she would do, but none of it would have anything in the balance. She had given Arthur Prell chocolates, and the results were already in.

It was the chocolates, in the end, that wore the yoke of her shame.

FOURTEEN · Sweet Vitaly

The doctor was not Margaret's ally, to Prell she had brought chocolates, and Magda Goebbels—who somehow for a moment she had borrowed to play for a finer spiritual division—was becoming a more threatening type of ghost by the day.

At the university, her worst fears regarding Magda Goebbels were catastrophically confirmed.

It happened at the Rostlaube: the central building of the Freie Universität, a metropolis of a structure. Previous to the change in Berlin, it had looked like a massive collection of junked cars piled into a glinting mountain. Stretched over acres, it was dissected by narrow hallways. All the hallways looked exactly alike; inside it quickly became labyrinthine in the modernist way: every path and room was exactly the same as every other, so there were no locations at all.

Since it had turned into human flesh, however, the building had taken on personality. It was pulsing—the most active building Margaret had yet seen since the change, and it seemed the great size of the structure made the difference. In contrast with other architecture, which tended to be only bodies abbreviated, one could make out, in this instance, what sort of identity the flesh carried. It was a giant red-headed adolescent boy—the roof sprouting with orangeish hair—a boy of enormous virility despite bad health. Where there had been rust on the old Rostlaube, today there was acne, and an atmosphere of melancholy strength and hope wrapped in mourning for the recently lost happiness of childhood—these were recognizable in the walls. This building, Margaret saw, was a node of power.

On her way to class, Margaret entered N street, with its bright orange carpeting and ramps zipping up to low balconies and rubber floors, bright with the white light of sky from the windows in the roof. Students were everywhere, students of the German kind: men and women no longer in their first youth. They were clustered in the smoking area, or marching along the low corridors, or sloping themselves up the ramps. They moved quickly and their faces were closed,

so beautiful and unknowable they looked like goblins. They flowed
with certainty—no, it was more than certainty: with style. They had
so much style that they were alarming to Margaret, who thought—
looking at them now as though she herself were an inert rubber doll in
their midst—that the purpose of style was to release reference into its
natural habitat, that good style had a jubilant, horrifying freedom to it,
at once attractive and repellent, like a jungle cat liberated from a concrete zoo loping back toward the forest, returning to itself; style was as
monolithic as character.

Margaret was afraid she would see the wizard of the students, the
king of the Berliner panther style: Vitaly Velminski. Vitaly had been
studying philosophy and history at the university for ten years. It was
known that if Vitaly ever finished his *Magister*—he was a dawdler in
the intellectual bath like everyone else—since he was both a brilliant
mind and an adequate politician, he would become the heir to Meitler,
Wolfgang Meitler, founder of Meitlerian metaphysics, center of a
buzzing hive. Vitaly had achieved a closeness with all his professors,
but with Meitler in particular, that was reflected in Vitaly's ancient
leather shoes, his dark three-piece suits, his cat-like eyes, his cutting,
staccato voice that he barely raised above a whisper of precision when
he spoke in class. There was excellent loose tobacco in his breast pocket
along with rolling paper, and this he feinted into cigarettes when standing outside talking with one of his friends in intimate, casual tones.

For that was the point about Vitaly—he had many friends. He was
a friend to anyone of any stylistic note; his human aesthetic was impec-
cable. He knew, and sometimes flung an arm around, the long-haired
professor of philosophy who swept in on the wings of a great black
cape and streaming green scarves; he was friends with the stiff man
from the south, the one with curling, fleshy red lips and fiercely enunciated accent, whose trench coat was starchily belted and whose
knowledge of Hegel seemed to be in his bones. Vitaly was friends with
the icy and diminutive Frau Beitsch, who wore nothing but black lace
and looked to weigh no more than ninety pounds, painting her skin
white and her lips scarlet, but who had the broadest and deepest familiarity with Deleuze this side of the Rhine. Yes, Vitaly knew and
inclined his tall head toward all of them. And yet he was also at ease
with the run-of-the-mill boys of certainty, who were not noticeable,
but who would still go far, because knowledge gave them no trouble—
no trouble at all.

Vitaly—there he was: she had spotted him a level above her, outside the doorway to Koerfer's classroom, standing in conversation with a man who looked like a rabbinical student. Margaret felt hungry when she came into Vitaly's orbit. But she felt this hunger as though she were also on morphine. The students, Vitaly included, seemed so distant from her that if she were ever to open her mouth and speak to them, they would disappear. And in point of fact, whenever someone in class asked Margaret if she had an extra pen, say—or if she had the time, or the handout—her voice always became so hoarse, her German so stilted, that it was assumed she was on an Erasmus exchange and did not know the language. Over time, Margaret thought, her aura had become clear even to the naïve, and they had left off trying to speak to her.

The class was on media and assassinations in Weimar Germany, and after they were all sitting down—Koerfer was a celebrity, so the "seminar" had over ninety people smashed into a room meant for no more than fifty—Koerfer began to talk about the Berliner pneumatic dispatch, the *Rohrpost.*

There was something nightmarish about this to Margaret.

Also making the hair stand up on the back of her neck was the presence of Vitaly. She and he were among the last students to enter the classroom, and so now, in the crunch, he was directly behind her, his body smelling of sea salt and hills. She could not see him, but every breath he took made her feel something.

"Does anyone know how it worked? So far as I understand a dual propellant system was used," Koerfer was saying, warming them up with facts before the theory to come. "The projectiles containing the letters or cards to be transported were pulled in one direction by means of compressed air, then later the same projectile was brought back to its starting point with rarefied air, through suction.

"I'll show you a map." With magnets he put it up on the white board and began to point. "The Berliner system was radial. From the main telegraph office a series of tubes branched to the most important post offices throughout the city. At each of these offices the projectiles were then unpacked and sent on their way again to smaller offices, where they were again unpacked, the cards and letters sorted and carried to the homes of the recipients by telegram couriers. Thus if a letter needed to go from one end of the city to the other, it had first to be sent to the central office, and only from there would it travel on to the other side. The exceptions were the direct lines between the main telegraph office and the Reichstag and eventually the chancellery, and this is where the system became important to the press, who could and did, on certain occasions, tamper with the pneumatic lines. Journalists tunneled underground to dig out the receptacles and read the classified contents. Members of the press weren't the only ones."

Margaret began to imagine journalists tunneling underground like moles, their eyes bleary and dim. She rested her head. This bright, low-ceilinged room did not face out onto a courtyard as most of the others did, but instead onto the empty land beyond the Rostlaube, land that was filled with scotch pines. The pines crowded up against the windows. As the professor talked on, the pines brushed against the glass. The branches lashed, insistent. Margaret pushed the side of her face against the glass, as if to rest it there, and then she could almost feel the skeletal fingers, the whispering smoke of the pine needles against her face. She turned to look out. Deep in the tree closest to her, near the cloistered trunk, she saw, looming in the darkness, a great bird of prey with legs in pants of feathers. The bird did not have any traces of womanliness, and its talons were yellow and orange against the black tree. It cocked an eye at Margaret, a glint of topaz fire. Margaret looked directly at the bird, then turned and looked at Vitaly behind her, to see if he had seen.

Vitaly saw her looking at him and turned his face to the professor, crossing his long haunches. He did not look at her again.

Margaret turned back and there was the bird—she almost had assumed that just as suddenly it would be gone—but in the meantime it seemed to have gotten much larger, now maybe the size of a ten-year-old boy. Through the heavy shadows of the darkening pine needles, Margaret saw the flutter of falling feathers. The bird was losing its mantle. She saw the sheen of gabardine, and before long, Magda's heavy-browed face was grinning at her, grinning and winking, her smile broad. Her teeth looked like old piano keys. Margaret turned her head away quickly and tried not to look out the window again, although she could not help but glance back once or twice, and always the bird was there.

After class, Margaret sat down on a bench outside the classroom to summon her strength. She looked the length of the long hallway. It gently sloped down.

She saw a girl come out of an adjoining corridor and turn south, away from Margaret. Margaret watched the young woman's back. She thought she recognized it. It was Margaret's own long body, with its awkward calves.

Just then, Margaret felt her light blocked and looked up to see Vitaly Velminski standing before her. He leaned in. Her heart stopped. She waited. Finally, she saw that his eyes were not on her. His eyes were on the department's course listings for the coming semester, inside a glass box above her head. Vitaly leaned in further. Margaret's excitement boiled to the point that it was no longer pleasurable, it was only painful, the proximity. The pleasure itself was the pain.

After Vitaly moved away, Margaret wanted to slam her fist into the glass box on the wall. She wanted to break her head against it. She wanted to shatter the glass, and shatter her porcelain self into bits. She hated her invisibility and muteness, she hated the attraction, the stimulation. She would flay and beat and destroy the vestiges of desire. She hated Vitaly for attracting her, and she hated him.

At the library, things only got worse. She was not insane, she told herself, but the frequent bouts of madness were beginning to add up.

When she found the Meissner biography of Magda Goebbels, the one with quotes from Ello Quandt which had made Magda Goebbels appear so sympathetic, Margaret read only three pages before she broke the spine of the book in a rage. She pushed it off the table and onto the floor. She stood up, almost unable to see.

For she had seen enough. The book was a slavering hagiography, Meissner was a sycophant. She had been led by a golden hoop in her nose straight over a precipice. Again and again, there were descriptions of Magda, a woman "of breeding and distinction," "pretty, angelic-looking even, with her pale, gold, silken hair, milk-white complexion and sparkling blue eyes, graceful, dainty and slim," worst of all, as de facto justification for her involvement with Nazis: "mistress of the feminine virtue of adjusting to different mentalities."

Margaret remembered what she had read about Magda's several affairs, the ones she had had to distract herself from Goebbels's womanizing: many were with men who worked in the Propaganda Ministry with Goebbels himself, and wouldn't it not be the most unlikely thing, if the man who decided to write a biography of the dead woman was one of her former lovers?

The most obvious lie in the book was this: Magda Goebbels, who in other biographies was said to have been born to a ladies' maid out of wedlock, was here described as having been "the offspring of a happy marriage."

Margaret was betrayed. The quotations in which she had put so much hope, which had rendered Magda cognizant and remorseful and mercilessly executive in her attempts to avenge herself against herself, *not* simpering, not silly—these were being discredited and crumbling into piles of fakery before her eyes. So Magda had been nothing but a fanatic, nothing but a deranged patriot when she killed her children, and all ideas that she had been a lone Nazi tribunal, turning the principles of inheritance of evil inward on the family of evil itself, were nothing but fantasies. Margaret had been singled out, chosen for tailing by a rapacious falcon, a lunatic, a fanatic, a spy.

The moment fell over her; the burst of a honey bubble. The collapsing that began at Sachsenhausen redoubled.

It was the plainly cheap and inauthentic quality of the available paths into Magda Goebbels's mind. The situation could not be a matter of coincidence. The way Margaret saw it now, the smoke-and-mirrors, mirage-like quality of access to such minds must be intrinsic to the very stuff of such minds. A cephalopod builds its multichambered shell according to the nacreous laws of its species, and so too, this flickering figure of Magda Goebbels, without hardly meaning to, vanished inside layers of narrative artifice—whether by the euphuistic friends she kept, the rhetoric-heavy letters she wrote, the genre-distorted portraits she commissioned, the bombastic films and men she adored—all emanations from her personality which built rightness and naturalism, in layer upon layer, for things that were beyond right or nature. Margaret had thought she would read *Mein Kampf* and enter into communion with Magda Goebbels, but now she saw that without having even planned it for herself, Magda Goebbels would remain an icon on the outside, unreal on the inside, forever and ever.

The characteristic of storytelling that had first become manifest when Margaret was at the doctor's—that the meaning generated through it was not only *one* great falsifier but *the* great falsifying agent at the disposal of the human mind—Margaret saw as the lurking bogey. Stories themselves were the hell that threatened to swallow her up whenever she came into contact with meaning, and meaning was the hell that threatened to swallow her up whenever she heard any story.

Margaret trembled. She left the university in haste.

FIFTEEN · Tales of the Overripe

E rich the *Hausmeister* was having strange days.
He read the diary of the American further. He rubbed his chin, inclined his head, and found that the girl had become obsessed with her older German lover, had even begun to spy on him. She was obsessed in particular with her lover's connection to her parents—the dead father and the estranged mother. It seemed that she had been collecting—nay, stealing—bits of Amadeus's personal papers, and as Erich became more interested, he read these as well.

Margaret had written:

August 15, 2000

Dearest diary,

I looked through Amadeus's file cabinets this afternoon after he went to teach his class; I know he keeps the file cabinet in the second apartment because he doesn't want even his wife to see certain letters. But the main thing is, the best thing is: I found a copy of a letter he sent to my parents and also a few of my mother's she sent to him after my father was sick. So far as I can see, they started writing in November '89. I'm surprised. To hear my father talk, it always seemed like Amadeus was lost forever. But then, my father was not reliable.

Here are the letters (I copied them!):

November 19, 1989

Hello Christoph and Sarah,

It's cold tonight, and I write to you from the Isle of Youth, where the three of us were once together, do you remember? I'm looking out into the widest part of the river, to the Oberbaum Bridge, and your letter from the third is in my pocket.

I know you've heard the news: the world exploded. Ha-ha! The wall opened while I was sleeping. We were all sleeping, and the city cracked. It was overripe, that old melon. Juice and seeds are spilling everywhere now, and we don't have to be strangers to one another any longer. We're wandering across the checkerboard.

I wanted to tell you and Christoph just how it was. I didn't go to the institute on Friday. Do you remember Florian? I walked with him up to Bernauer Strasse. The checkpoint was streaming. Florian thought we should walk over into the West right then. I said no! Ha-ha! The border would close up again while we were gone, that was what I thought. I've survived everything pretty well by never underestimating Honecker and I didn't believe it, even if the man is deposed. I thought if we went through, we'd never get back, and you have to think about something like that. Honestly I kept thinking of trips into Hades, how you're supposed to get stuck there forever. Sure, I'm a coward. They made us all into cowards, cowards and spooks. Although the spooks, they're cowards too.

But anyway, Florian was annoyed with me. He didn't understand, but he wouldn't go alone. He stood next to me for a while on the Eastern side and we watched the other people crossing over, and I smoked for a while and then, I didn't expect it, I hardly noticed it, I was crying like a baby. Everyone who saw my tears stopped and embraced me, that's the kind of day it was, isn't that nice? So you know, we decided to go through after all. I saw the chapped lips on the border guards, overnight they looked like nothing but boys. We walked into Wedding. I swear to God, the air smelled like it has never smelled. People's faces looked different, their expressions changed. We walked between the Western houses, fine, bright, colorful houses. We passed a Turkish grocery and thought we'd go in. I touched the fruit. I thought of Persephone eating four seeds in Hades. (Why did she eat the seeds? Was she hungry? Or just curious? Or was it—and this is my theory—in order to taste something to remember the day by?)

I touched the fruit. I didn't really feel like eating it. I've never had bananas and oranges and I don't lust after them, I'll leave that for the decadents. The fruit was interesting, though, for the sake of the day. I thought I'd eat it. But you know, I didn't have the deutsche marks, the banks weren't giving them out yet. But, ha-ha, you know, Christoph once gave me some deutsche marks. I never used them; I'd never dared. I walked all the way back home and got them out from under the floorboards, this all seems so ridiculous to me now, all these years we've spent under lock and key, it seems like a big joke already.

Florian waited for me the whole time on the other side. We bought almond-stuffed olives, oranges, and Gruyère. I stopped thinking about Persephone. The food was good, Sarah.

I got your letter when I got home. They're still delivering mail!

Well, that's all the news here. I send my greetings to Christoph in particular. I wish him a speedy recovery. Please relay to him, Sarah, whatever of my news in this letter you think might be appropriate. I realize he is sensitive and I leave it to you to decide what is best. Maybe now I'll come and see him. I can go wherever I want now. That would be something.

> Yours,
> Amadeus

January 14, 1990

Dear Amadeus,

I'm sorry we are only writing back to you now. Christoph enjoyed your letter. I know that he, for one, still thinks very fondly of you. He still refers to you as his best friend.

You may have heard from Petra already, the news about him. Two months ago I put him in a hospital. I could have stood it myself, but Margaret and the dog (and I include the dog in this, because Christoph treats Alphonse like a second child) have become very sensitive to the worst of it. The dog—can you imagine a dog that howls every time his master cries?

If you want to reach Christoph, you can write to him at the hospital. I know he would enjoy that. You don't need to be so guarded.

I think I would like to be forthright with you: I have believed for a long time that Christoph was in love with you, and maybe he still is. He was heartbroken you did not let him help you get out. Do you think I'm crazy for imagining that he might never have had as many troubles as he did, if he hadn't lost you? Sometimes I wish that he had stayed in the East.

> Sincerely,
> Sarah

Included was an address for a mental hospital in New Rochelle.

July 2, 1990

Dear Amadeus,

I brought Christoph home yesterday from the hospital. He seems much worse, and it relieves me to have someone to tell.

Well, he had been gone from us for eight months. His eyes are blank, I'm not sure he recognizes me, even after all the visits, and he only speaks in German now, which—I don't know if you are aware—I've still never really mastered. When we got back to the apartment, his performance was pretty typical. He did not look at Margaret, poor little child. She stood behind the coatrack in the hall. She was smiling at him, though, enough to make her face break. He didn't speak to her but when he went by, he put out his hand, as though by accident, and rubbed the top of her head. It looked as though he were looking at a tablet behind his eyes, not out at the world, not at me, and certainly not at Margaret. His lips moved. That's what it's like. That's what it's almost always like with him. I took him to his study, he sat down, he thanked me in German. He picked up one of his legal pads as if he had never been gone, and started writing.

I looked over his shoulder. He had written:

ATT: FBI
I am Christ, the only son of Lucifer.

Why did I bring him home? I bet that's what you're wondering. There were recommendations against it actually. It seems he has managed to make it appear as if he were taking his medication, while at the same time slipping it down the toilet to avoid allowing the CIA to infiltrate his body—with its tiny cameras. The CIA, he tells us, is working with the reconstructed Nazi party, the one that operates out of Argentina and southern Brazil, which is working with the KGB(!!?), and this party wants to kill him. That said, he is very calm, does not get in anyone's way, and oddly, I don't feel afraid of him. Most of the time, except for the German, when I meet him at the hospital, he behaves like a preoccupied professor, the one he was meant to be. It's true he made me get rid of both televisions; "the eyes in the television are unblinking," he told me. But you know, I didn't mind that either, I was glad really. It's just that Margaret, at the loss of the TV, seems to have only become more inarticulate. Sometimes I think she's gotten too much from her father's side. I worry for her, but what can I do? I took her to the child psychiatrist for a while, but she throws fits every time. She hates the doctor, really hates her. And the doctor did say the girl was making progress at our last visit, but the child is so good at putting on a show for her . . . What bothers me the most, really, is that Margaret is such a quiet little thing, so tongue-tied, and I like to talk to her, espe-

THE HISTORY OF HISTORY

cially now that Christoph is gone. Why did I end up with such a quiet child?!

Well, after I left Christoph in his study the other day, I came here into the kitchen and found your letter on the counter.

Amadeus, I'm not playing things as coolly as I would like. I can't tell anyone here about that part of it. It's nonsensical and sadistic or masochistic or maybe a little of both, but sometimes I do things to provoke Christoph deliberately, things I know will set off his paranoia. There was one occasion, for example, when I took Margaret and left for a vacation in Wyoming without telling him. It was only to avoid having to go through weeks of his accusations beforehand. But when I came back, he started looking at me with a sly, mistrustful gaze. You know that gaze of his—he had a similar suspicious expression before he ever got sick, through those thick glasses of his. Later, I read his legal pad (I always read them, or have them translated, just to keep track of his thoughts, but that too, he notices. In fact he thinks it's CIA surveillance).

He wrote: "They have made a new Sarah, almost a perfect facsimile. But the moles on the upper arms of the new Sarah are misplaced, and their constellation bears false witness."

Then there is also the fact that I've been snapping at Margaret, saying cruel things.

But the worst thing, the single worst thing, is that while he was in the hospital I got rid of his dog, his beloved dog. I told him Alphi was dead. Don't you see, Amadeus, with the girl, and now with Christoph's father staying in the back room sometimes when he's not in California (that has really made Christoph worse, I think. How he hates his father!) I just couldn't handle the dog as well. But maybe it was also a matter of vengeance.

We both miss you, Amadeus! If only you could come to us. Are you still thinking of coming? I hope you will think of it.

Yours,
Sarah

PART II

ROPE

The fascination aroused by Hitler and his demands on the nation did not only have to do with sadism but also very much with masochism, with the appetite for submission, behind which stood an impulse toward the desecration of authority that was much farther from the surface of consciousness (one thinks of Luther's tone on the topic of the Pope).

—MARGARETE AND ALEXANDER MITSCHERLICH
THE INABILITY TO MOURN

SIXTEEN • Redemption Beckoning

It all began on the way to the Schöneberg archive. Although Margaret had painted a portrait in oils of the Nazi propaganda minister's wife, photographed it, uploaded it, and retouched it, made shining digital variations, and all of this was done in a spirit of finding beauty in the woman's face, and although she had read *Mein Kampf* as though it were a Bhagavad Gita, writing out many of the dubiously sympathetic passages in a tight hand in her own notebook, in the end, she had still not quite been able to stretch her brain far enough.

And after the Meissner biography was revealed as a sham, a despondency settled over her. The hawk-woman at her window was oppressive—nothing, really, but an instrument of terror, and the terror breathed down her neck day and night, infecting her small pleasures. Nightly dinner had a vague smell of guano.

On that fateful evening when everything changed, Margaret was in fact still trying: she was intending to find Magda Goebbels's birth certificate and prove to herself conclusively that the woman had been born out of wedlock—she was already ninety-five-percent certain—but this was the way it was with her, everything shifted, her mind's promises to itself were never kept. And so she was setting out doggedly, heading for the Schöneberg archive.

Down the Grunewaldstrasse she went, west toward Rathaus Schöneberg and John-F.-Kennedy-Platz.

The sky was a shade of blue that appeared wet, like new paint, and everything in the city, the buildings included, seemed restless.

Already when Margaret turned onto Martin-Luther-Strasse, she saw something in the distance: not a single bird—no—today it was a large swarm. Thousands of birds, and at first, reflexively, she mistook them for a convention of the taloned sparrow hawks of the Magda kind, and with all her soul she wanted to turn back toward home. But only a moment later, before she could swing around, she saw that it was not birds of prey after all, but swallows. Of course, it was only swallows. It was that time of twilight when swallows dive, in the light-filled evening, in the sleep-filled sky, and thousands of them moved in a globe of motion, according to their own complex design, around the spire of the massive city hall at John-F.-Kennedy-Platz, which rose like a fist of flesh in the early dusk.

There was something strange about the birds. Even if they were not the hawks, there was something unsettling. It took Margaret a moment to identify what the irregularity was, but finally she realized: the birds were silent. These birds did not make a single cry. The effect was almost to make her feel as if she were bicycling in a muted digital rendering, or—another thought—as though the birds were in that phase of rage where speech becomes impossible.

Margaret stopped her bicycle on the wide square and watched. The edges of their swarm were camouflaged by the late shadows, and she could not see how far into the distance their numbers spread. In silence, they made slow circles, sweeps, and caesuras, their shapes so dark, they seemed to leave trails of smoke behind them.

And then, almost imperceptibly, there was a change. They began to spiral downward. They were circling toward the open square and the surrounding canyons and depressed rooftops; they were beginning to alight on the ground. And as they did, their black forms broadened and stretched. Each bird was elastic, each bird was lengthening. Each bird grew a face. Each bird stretched into a long, thick, humanoid shadow.

The masses of black shapes, the birds in human shadow form, they moved down out of the sky, floating like dry leaves into the streets, quickly gaining detail: men and women, old and young, all of them withered and tarnished silvery like daguerreotypes. Their garments reeked of mothballs—woolen, worn and ash-smeared. A watch chain on the body of an old man; two grey, moon-shaped faces—sisters— moving at a loping pace arm in arm, their hair curled into small circles ridging their brow; elsewhere a thin baby; a flirtatious pair of platform sandals on the small feet of an adolescent girl. Deeper and deeper into the throngs of shadows Margaret went, rustling with them across the square.

Here they were, Margaret thought. So they had not evacuated. So this kind of ghost was in Berlin too. For a moment, she felt the flushest sort of excitement it is possible to feel. They were coming for her.

She reached in front of her. She took an arm in her hand and looked down to see it. It was encased in plaid wool. She pulled on the sleeve and turned her eyes toward the place where a face should be, her vision patched around on all sides, and saw as though through the wrong end of a telescope, the grey face of a young man, not fully mature, with wavy black locks.

The boy looked away from her in the direction of the spire of the town hall. He pointed to the clock. Then he too looked up at it with a steady gaze. Margaret turned her head. The hands and notched numbers of the clock rushed toward her eyes in a blur of movement. Whether the graphology had physically come free, or whether she had simply lost the ability to tell time, she could not say. The boy, for his part, shook her hand from his sleeve and walked backward into the throng, where he was lost from sight.

Margaret got back on her bicycle and pedaled furiously. She arrived at the archive. The fluorescent lights of the entryway were heavy on her face, and she stood for a moment to catch her breath. She closed her eyes.

There it was. Margaret saw the woman in the dress walking up the oval staircase. Margaret saw her from a blue distance, and then the fist of a thing crashing through the skylight, coming down from the roof above. And it fell, fluttering like ash, through the central shaft of the stair's helix down to the mosaic on the basement floor. Her inner eye's lens darted down now toward the fallen thing and she could see it, she could see what it was: it was a bird. It was just a bird. Light and small, it should not have broken the glass. Why did the bird break the glass?

Margaret went into the visitors' reading carrels. The archivist looked up at her. Margaret was flustered, unkempt, her lips and cheeks were glowing with a distinct pulse of their own.

The archivist quickly disabused her of the idea that she would be granted permission to see Magda Goebbels's birth certificate. It was against data protection laws. But Margaret noticed that the sound of the name, Magda Goebbels, after she had spoken it, was hefty and cumbersome in the room. Her eyes drifted away from the archivist to the windows; suddenly she was full of loathing. Margaret muttered something bitterly, about the archive making nothing, but nothing at all, available to the public, bureaucratically keeping everything, even very old and senseless things, under lock and key. At the end, she even mumbled a phrase that she knew was taking things too far—she said something about the archive "protecting the guilty."

The archivist set her face. For a moment both she and Margaret were quiet. Finally the woman puffed her blouse out and pointed emphatically to the shelf. The museum, she said, with prim emphasis, recently made the collected Schöneberg police logs available to the public—everything up until and including 1966. Margaret was very welcome to look at that.

This was a shameless non sequitur.

But still, Margaret's rage dissipated. She had other worries. The shadows she had seen outside, she felt they were pressing against the window glass, beginning to beg her for something. So now, embarrassed and clumsy, Margaret indeed hoisted down a police logbook; she chose the one from 1943.

At first, Margaret only pawed through it without reading it. She thought she would wait until the archivist was in the other room and then quickly leave. But, despite herself, Margaret became involved. She read through January 1943, and already, something of interest caught her eye. There was a letter of complaint from a middle-aged woman who had walked her cat on a leash in the Kleistpark. She was peacefully making a round in the late afternoon when a a policeman set upon her and beat her with a stick, merely because cats were forbidden in the park. Was it possible, Margaret thought, for everyone in a society to be variously psychotic, all at the same time? She got out her notebook and pen. She copied the letter of complaint in its entirety into her notebook.

She moved into the records of February and March. These were mostly concerned with the police seizure of apartments recently "abandoned" by Jewish families. There were entries concerning the looting of Jewish homes, many reports of calls from neighbors complaining that the loot had not been equally divided. Also many entries concerning Jewish suicides. The suicides coincided with the mass deportations, the period when Berlin was undergoing its "cleansing" by Goebbels.

Then Margaret came to the log of Police Revier 173, and all of a sudden her breath, which had been even, stopped, and her heart, which had been loping, sped up to a trot. The first entry, on page 143, was this:

March 3, 1943, circa 9:00 p.m., the married couple Franz Strauss, born 11/5/06 in Gross-Strenz, and Regina Sara Strauss née Herzberg, born 11/20/09 in Schwedenhöhe, living in Berlin-Schöneberg, Salzburgerstr. 8, committed suicide by natural gas.

They took their three children, Rahel Strauss born 7/5/32 in Berlin, Gerda Strauss born 2/27/39 in Berlin and Beate Strauss born 4/3/42 in Berlin, with them into death.

Margaret froze. She did not think immediately that this entry would bring a revolution to her life, but one of her fingers, which had been winding a strand of hair, went still, and a long, breathless moment passed.

When she came to herself, it was as if she had stepped behind a curtain hitherto hiding the harshest lights in the world. Red spots glowed before her eyes; the lights coming in from the street contained parts of the spectrum that she had never seen before. She felt her chest begin to tighten, and a clever fever, a madness, a vast energy flickered in her.

She stood up. The energy made her almost nauseous. Standing bent over, she read the passage a second time. Her fingers, as if controlled from afar, brushed over the print of the logbook; she had a hallucination that the letters were made of loosely strewn sand; sand that could be swept away with reverent fingers. Something told her, whispered to her, that there would be pictures beneath.

She rubbed. She rubbed harder, feeling split into two persons—one who knew this was madness, and one who believed that there were pictures underneath. The second person would reveal them. She would expose them come what may.

Margaret was out of control. She felt a keening pity for what she had read, and also a terrible pain. At the same time, she was knocked hard by a sense of tyrannical exclusion. She pushed her chair back with a suffocated gesture. She gathered her books and threw them in her bag. At first she thought she would simply run, but then she looked at the police logbook lying there on the table and could not bear the thought of leaving it behind. She quickly searched for change, made a ten-cent Xerox copy, feeling all the while as though she would be sick.

Outside the archive, the headlamps and neon signs cast snakes of light over the Hauptstrasse, striking Margaret's eyes with lasers menacingly futuristic.

The lay of the land here is very important in what happened next. Precisely: the old villa housing the archive was close up against the road. Behind the villa, a modern annex had been built, which held a small branch library. Farther still, behind the library, was a broad and sloping pasture of a city park, opening out toward the north. The park was reached by a wide and graveled path. It was this path that Margaret turned down now, her legs numb, meaning to cut home in the blessed darkness, for she was in a state of extreme light sensitivity now.

As she moved through the twilight, however, she came to the entrance of the branch library, squat under the sunset and, as she looked over at it, her head bounced in surprise—it seemed to be staring at her with a single glassy eye. Above it, the last light of day was a wide yellow stripe on the far horizon. Without knowing why, Margaret pulled the handbrakes of her bicycle, and it skidded. Before she could think, she was lofted into the air.

The back tire's brake had not been properly able to grip since the late summer, and when the front tire stopped so abruptly on the loose gravel of the path, the rear of the bike kept spinning and swung out.

Margaret's limbs pumped the air. She tried to heave herself away from the bicycle and land on her feet, but her legs were numb and disobedient as in a dream, and her head was spinning. She went down sideways, falling heavily on her left shoulder and hip.

And then, an entirely marvelous thing happened. Everything began to tilt. Margaret looked into the night sky, and the stripe of yellow, seeming to grow three-dimensionally above the low roof of the library, blew up rhapsodically with color and warmth.

The pain in Margaret's limbs and the emotion in her heart clasped then, coming together like the teeth of a zipper. Margaret's eyes would not move from that thick, warm stripe of yellow. Now it was beginning to billow like smoke, to represent something terrible and beautiful at once, and she stood up. The hurt in her body, the inflammation, ballooned—she was on fire, and she began to yaw toward the dimensionalizing yellow stripe. Three uncertain, swaying steps toward the giant color that was bleaching now, losing its heat—and Margaret felt convinced that before the yellow light disappeared, it would let her float into the center of it. She put her arms up high and wide—she felt her arms lengthening and strengthening around the entire earth. All the way around, her arms might reach, all the way to the hidden yellow sun. If only the night sky, that bleachworks, would not destroy the yellow king! And then as though possessed—she startled herself terribly—her lower jaw dropped open, and, like water from a tipped bucket, sound came glistening out. Which is to say that she began to yell, and simultaneously she began an almost comical clenching and unclenching of her fingers—she was both surprised and amazed—the grasping had a frightened, unnatural quality to its rhythm, and she gave a series of high and imploring cries.

On the slate staircase leading up to the library's blind eye, she threw herself down, in sudden and total capitulation.

But the new position did not put an end to it. With her eyes closed, the black letters in the police log, telling her of the Family Strauss, came swimming to Margaret. The letters gushed closer, lost some of their darkness, and soon melted into the shape of a strange man, it looked like a monk, a monk dressed in hay-colored robes. Margaret could see him. His hair was like transistors and his earlobes dangled. He too was falling down before the setting sun, and this was all at once vivid: the monk in his hay-colored robes and pendulous earlobes, prostrated before a sun that was as red as an animal's heart, beating and loping.

Here was Margaret in Berlin, where only the last, pale yellow stripe smarted against the bleachworks of the sky, and there was the monk in some world far away—he saw it all burn, he saw it all burn bright as a furnace fire.

And then Margaret knew.

The monk was an ancestor, a visitor come to her bearing tidings, a visitor sitting somewhere along a line that ended in—prostrations before this Family Strauss. They, they and only they—*they* had conquered the setting sun. They were the true conquerors of the disappearing light.

What had they done? Faced with deportation, the Family Strauss had chosen to kill themselves and their children rather than go through the hell served to them. They had chosen to die privately rather than in the chambers in Poland. These people killed themselves and their little daughters on the shoulders of God, to escape soul-destroying torture, the humiliation of death at the hands of dog-men. Nothing could be higher than that, nothing more elect.

Margaret was resolute and sure. She thought of them and believed. The Family Strauss in March 1943 was where innocence was active. Innocence had been in a coma, but now here it was, coming back to life. The idea of active and effective innocence was the bright light behind her eyes; it was the voluminous stripe spreading its cloud further into her mind. This was the hidden, ever-disappearing goodness. This she had yearned for so long. This was the friar's lantern.

Here is how I will go about it, she said to herself. Here is how I will save myself. People—for once, people—who acted cataclysmically in the service of love.

That was how Margaret saw it, and horsemen of joy came riding to her.

She closed her eyes tighter so as to better see, buried her face further into the gravel and pinched at her heaving flanks, trying to see more clearly. The monk slowly dissolved, and another image bore down in its place: already she could see a girl, it must be one of the Strauss children, the oldest girl, ten years old, almost eleven when she died, a child with a face like roses and sandpaper, her head surrounded by light. The girl was wearing yellow cloth, the same color as the almost disappeared sunlight, and she was coming closer. She was filling Margaret's eyes and quenching her ears. The child spoke clearly. This is what she said:

On that day Mother made us come out for a walk in the park. We didn't want to. Not even Father. We are hungry. We think only of sleep. Mother said we would like the snow. The storm was coming all day, and now it was here and the flakes were very large like moths against our cheeks. We went to the Stadtpark by the Rathaus. Mother says it looks like the Jardin du Luxembourg. Once she was there, in Paris. She says it is beautiful. Mother is beautiful. I walked behind with Gerda. Mother carried Beate and walked beside Father. Mother and Father argued about something and the snow was thick, I couldn't hear what they said. Gerda was tired. I let her ride on my back. I became breathless. Up ahead, I saw the golden stag on its pedestal, surrounded by dark snow, bright like a moon in the afternoon that was much more like night. Mother and Father slowed down and I caught up and then I saw Father was crying. Father did not cry when he lost his position at the conservatory and he did not cry when he lost his job at the factory, and when he began to sleep all day or sit looking out the window after he had finished giving me my lessons, he did not cry. He taught me French and mathematics and he taught me the violin.

Mother is beautiful. She has a friend who gave us money when Jews weren't allowed to work. We were hungry. Mother couldn't buy food with the money without ration cards. She decided to use the money to make her hair blond so she would have an easier time finding a private position as a maid in a rich person's house. In the beginning it looked hideous. Very orange. But she went back to the salon every ten days, and soon it was gold blond and yellow. Some people said she should have used the money differently, but Mother always said that now that Jews weren't permitted to emigrate, the best way was camouflage.

I trusted Mother. Mother promised she would never let them take away any of us like they had taken away Berthe and her mother. She didn't care what anybody said and she fixed the collar of my coat so that I could wear it so the star didn't show when I wanted, and we would go to the pictures or look at the fabric in a fancy store. Father always said that nothing bad would happen if we would just learn to follow the new rules, for God's sake! It would blow over. But mother said, it's too late for that now, Franz.

Two weeks before the day it snowed, Mother came home from the Tombanzens'. She said she didn't have to go back the next day. They were kind to Mother, but now Mr. Tombanzen had to go off to war and they would have to do without help. Then Mother couldn't find anyone to give her or Father any work.

Father cried in the park. When we got home, he was very tender to us. Mother was busy around the house, cleaning and putting things in order. She told us we would all sleep on the floor of the kitchen tonight, all together, and wouldn't that be fun? At first we thought it was fun. Then after all the bedclothes were laid down on the floor, we felt strange. Mother closed the door of the kitchen. She used our extra pairs of underwear and some socks to plug the space at the bottom between the base of the door and the threshold and also around the edges of the window behind the blackout shade where it was loose. When Gerda saw her underwear were getting dirty in the window frame she began to cry, so baby Beate started crying too. Mother told us to hush and held us all three very tightly. Father turned his back and I saw his shoulders shaking. Mother said the bad people in the government would never find us. She said she was keeping us safe now, hush.

On the ground in front of the glass branch library, Margaret hid her head in her hands.

She rose. The sky was dark purple; the yellow stripe was gone, and the air around her was thick. People—she said to herself—people who acted cataclysmically in the service of love.

She took lunging steps even as she hobbled with pain, and made it over to her bicycle. She rode back toward the Grunewaldstrasse. With every downward shove of the pedal, each more stabbing than the one before, she came further into a sense of grand-scale homecoming.

Once in her apartment, she moved in a loop from living room to bedroom to hallway and back again.

The child who had spoken to her was with her. Rahel Strauss's young voice lapped at her ears, sweet as milk.

With the voice playing, she saw the painting she had made of Magda Goebbels lying next to her bed. She laughed with a bitter contempt. It was inert, deactivated like a discarded toy. False prophets would no longer tempt her, she said to herself. Some people—at least once—had done something right. She had been blind to that. She had believed that every comprehensible human action was corrupt.

She looped around the apartment, careening. What was Magda Goebbels? What was the hawk-woman? She was nothing but a shadow! The insanity of the last weeks hit her in the chest.

She considered this apartment she had lived in for five years and saw it in every way reborn. The ceilings were very high here, the French doors opened between the rooms, allowing each room to flow gently into the next: an apartment built at the end of the old century for graceful, romantic ways of living; you could hear Dvořák breathing through the floor plan. Margaret saw that it was possible to think of the lives that came and went in this apartment as expressions of a single spirit, her own life separated from the other lives that had passed in it before only along a single axis, an axis of time, which she knew now, she knew for certain now, could be collapsed like a telescope.

She shook with the joy of the mercy-shown.

Only seconds later, however, she went into a mild panic. She smelled the dust and mildew in the apartment. She considered the floors, once sleek parquet, now covered in musty wall-to-wall carpet. The scent of the carpet's peculiar dust filled the nose. A leering sort of sadness took hold of her for a moment. These rooms, built spacious, gracious, and light, had almost nothing in them to remind of the fine old days. The few pieces of furniture Margaret had were picked off the street or bought at the shabbiest of flea markets. The former tenants—their ghosts—would laugh at the shambles, and they would laugh at her, Margaret. Berlin had fallen; Berlin had been destroyed. If Lucifer had once been an angel, he had long since gone down. Was anyone or anything in this city a continuation of what it had been—either for good or evil? Was there any continuity at all?

Then she thought of the Family Strauss, the nobility of their decision, and the idea of nobility in general: its music, its architecture, its moral independence, and she asked herself with atrocious anxiety: Can I possibly follow them? Can I possibly be *like* them? Do I have the character?

Character or not, she would try. She could not stop herself from trying.

And if she could manage it, if she could manage to swim in their wake—Margaret lay her head back on the sofa and closed her eyes, her happiness swooping back in a rash of light. It came to her, chanted as though a triumphant rhyme, washing her with its purple, the lullaby of possibilities.

The swallows would speak. The clock would take back its numbers; the balconies would resume the cradling of their lost, cupped lives. The faces of the living would contort to mirror the faces of the dead, the written words would fly like homebound bees to the spoken. The secret meaning of the city would manifest itself, the house numbers alight from the clouds of the mind to fix themselves to the permanent book written underground. The numbers would correspond to the forgotten names, the shadows to the bodies, the palimpsest ache to the threaded ruins.

Hands were stretching out to Margaret, offering every fine thing, every decipherment. And her breath was full of oxygen.

Just before she went to sleep that night, she thought of the doctor's forest film and its so-called "perfect pregnancy." It wandered into her mind after a long absence. She asked herself then, very seriously, whether the prophecy had not been fulfilled. Everything will be revealed, she thought. And meaning—meaning was not going to be a stranger to her after all.

SEVENTEEN · An Expectation of Mirrors

The next day Margaret was soberer, but still, the first thing she did was think of the Strausses, and she acted immediately.

She went to the apartment building where the family died. She knew the Salzburgerstrasse well: it had been nearby all along: a small, tree-lined street behind the town hall, beyond the cake-like Nordstern building.

She bicycled. Her body was still bruised, and in her joints, the fall of the night before was lurking. This might have brought her into a state of reflection: the pain as she felt it in Schöneberg's dowdy day was so different than the pain as it had been in Schöneberg's riddling night!

But she silenced all uncertainties. The voice of the child had been palpable, as shimmering as shimmering can be. It had filled her with an ecstasy larger than life. And so what was she to do? Once you've met something unimaginable you can never unmeet it again. It will never be disentwined from instinct.

And, all reasoning aside, whether she could justify it or not, she had known from the moment she woke that morning, under the rustling bedsheets, by her excitement and happiness and energy, that she was going to be riding high all day.

In fact, she fantasized for the greater part of the bicycle ride, hatching ideas of gifts she would bring to the Strausses memory and places she would go to find their traces.

She pedaled off west into Jewish Switzerland toward the Nordstern behemoth. She was excited, nervous. Never had she been so exuberant and frightened of rejection at once. Never had she been so preoccupied, and before she left home, she had not even noticed the absence of that incredible lurking bird who was usually outside her window.

Number 8, when she pulled up in front of it, turned out to be a rich building with blushing white skin. Its fleshy balconies squeezed the flanks of the building, like twin rolls of plumpness on a woman's back, giving the place the simple, softhearted, motherly style of the Weimar era. All of it pleased Margaret.

Margaret waited, and after a while a man emerged from Number 8. Behind a tree, lost in fantasy, Margaret almost missed her chance. She dashed to the door and caught it at the last moment before it clicked shut. She moved into the foyer, her sensitivity to everything around her fantastically acute.

Inside, it was quiet, as the homes of the wealthy are always quiet, with thick, grey carpets over blue tiles. It's just as I imagined it, she thought, just precisely as I imagined it.

The walls were decorated with elaborate plaster moldings. Muscled young heroes carrying horns of plenty curled themselves around mirrors. Margaret looked into the first one. She saw herself reflected in the milky glass in a miracle of integration. She felt flattered to be included.

She could hardly move, she was so pleased. And she noticed an extraordinary effect. The mirror changed her face. She was the same in every detail, but the sum total of the details was an expression her face had never carried before, and perhaps never would. An expression of serenity. Margaret's face staring into its own eyes from across the mirror had a gentility and an equanimity to it, like a woman in a Vermeer, both as if she had no passions and as if she could go on living, softly and in the same way, forever. Margaret tilted her head to the side, considering this new, soft person. Maybe this face was caused by the light in the foyer. It was light soft and filtered; it was light like grey velvet.

And then Margaret noticed another effect. The foyer was slightly trapezoidal, and the mirrors were not positioned directly across from one another but at a slight angle, so that not only could Margaret see herself, she could also see herself reflected in copy after copy, extending far into the wall. In each copy she became more haloed by the soft light, more filtered and obscure. As she looked back into the wall at herself, so far away, the mirror corridor curved, and the tiny Margarets eventually went lost from sight. Margaret brushed her hand against her face. The dozens of Margarets in the hothouse of the glass did likewise and the synchrony of it blasted like an orchestra.

Margaret went out the back entrance of the foyer and into the courtyard garden beyond. The sun came through from above and the place was rich with pine. There were juniper, ferns, and rhododendron. She looked up at the side-wings and thought that the Family Strauss must have lived here in the back. They could never have held on to one of the fine apartments in the front all the way through 1943.

In the foliage, she saw a little brick path that led through the bushes. She followed it to a man-made pond, where a little jet of a fountain bubbled and arced in the sunlight. But the sun didn't reach all the way into the pool, and she looked down into the dark waters. The pond was swimming with goldfish, each about the size of a finger, some of a red-orange color, and others orange and white like bridal kimonos. Margaret stood over it, moving her lips.

She went inside again. She went back to the mirror, wishing to look again at that passionless, unpained face.

She gazed.

Something behind her head moved in the mirror. A quick, dark shadow. It passed once, twice. She whirled around. Was it the shadow of a tilting bird? Maybe a starling had flown in from the courtyard. But the room was so still. Margaret's heart beat. In the mirror, she saw the shadow pass again. The skin of her back went tight with goose bumps. She stood very still, her heart at a gallop. "I won't move, and then it will go." She stared straight ahead into the mirror. Her face was framed in the oval—it had turned white, and beneath her sleepless eyes, the crescents darkened.

Then all at once, stepping in from the side, a silent figure came. A woman stood next to her in the mirror. Margaret spun around. But no, there was no one in the room. The woman was only in the mirror. The apparition had a soft, round, worried face, dark eyes, and tired blond hair. She was wearing a dark wool dress with a slightly yellowed, white lace collar.

The woman—Margaret felt sure of it—was Regina Strauss. She stood in the mirror portrait very near Margaret, close next to her, good as a mother or a friend. She opened her mouth, and although no sound came from her pale lips, Margaret could see from the way she held her mouth that she was speaking.

The woman was saying a great deal. With her head held steady, she was telling Margaret a long and lonely story, holding her face expressionless, but Margaret was no lip-reader and could not make out the words. Although there was a sisterly warmth in the proximity of their bodies standing side by side *in* the mirror, there was also a sort of coldness—their faces opposed and their eyes meeting *across* the mirror.

At first, Margaret tried hard. She smiled back at her. She smiled and nodded, encouraging the apparition to speak, trying to follow her lips and divine what it was the woman was telling. But the words she was repeating over and over did not grow clearer.

Margaret strained hard, but she could not make them out.

After a while, Margaret began to feel chilled.

She spent the latter half of the day at the public pool. In the echoing hall, she swam up and down until she was hypnotized and could not think. On the way back home, she looked up at the sky.

She would later call it a spiritual aftershock. She looked up; she saw a complex grid in the sky. A grid of quasicrystals on the ceiling of the world, like the ceiling of the shrine of Darb-i-Imam, only deeper, only ghostlier, etched into the filling night. And at first Margaret was full of fear. She looked up into the quasicrystal heavens and was frightened that *there was a pattern,* there was a design governing behavior on earth. Past and present, a repeating pattern always circular, knowing no progress that does not loop back again. The heavens were a bureaucracy, cycle-bound, administering life on earth—playing fast and loose with Margaret's red lips and tearing heart. And her head went weak.

That night, Margaret slept badly. She woke up several times, wondering when morning would come. Each time, she was afraid of returning to her dreams. At around six o'clock, just as dawn was breaking, she opened her eyes with Regina's lips before her, and now, with a certainty so heavy, she felt as if she were being forced through the bed, she could finally hear the words that Regina had repeated in the mirror: the words that had been moving on her lips—*retten Sie uns.* Save us.

EIGHTEEN • They Played Hearts

Margaret played for the ghost of Regina Strauss, and her passion welled higher and higher. It kept spouting until finally it welled over and spilled the cup.

In the morning she had heard Regina's message, *retten Sie uns,* and in the afternoon the excess began. Margaret decided to go out and buy a deck of cards.

Oh, she would buy a deck of cards. Under the right conditions, going out to buy a deck of cards can be the most exciting journey of your life, assuming you think the cards will bring you communication with a ghost. And in fact, the entire walk to the shop sent quivers down her back: the close, tight streets, dodging what dogs have done, the smell of bakeries and the cool discs of faces bobbing in stride above dark clothing draped over swinging, mortal forms, the angles raying out from the vanishing points of sentinel avenues—those angles cut sharp as scissors, and all of it was promising, and all of it was fine. Margaret went down Akazienstrasse and stopped at a tobacco shop that also sold leather goods; there was a counter made of dark oak that smelled of shoe polish and another bright counter for the sale of lottery tickets and another place for the sale of cigars.

When she got home, Margaret opened the cellophane wrapper at the kitchen table. The table stood at the end of her long, narrow kitchen under a single window, and the cold light fell on the table like a spotlight.

Margaret challenged Regina Strauss, the mother of the three dead girls, she challenged her to a game of Hearts. She was not quite insane—it was not the fever, for it cannot be said she did not know this was an absurdity: trying to make a ghost play cards with her in the kitchen. But she saw herself a scientist conducting a perhaps overly ambitious experiment that was nevertheless not unwarranted by certain suggestive trends in the data. She knew the woman might be a matter of her mind, she knew it. But now she also thought she had been given a glimpse of where the ghost resided—whether physically or psychically, she chose not to try to decide.

Here is what she thought: the woman-as-ghost was present in patterning. It had first occurred to her after seeing the sky the night before, when she looked up and saw the grid of quasicrystals carved in the heavens. The pattern in the sky was a sign of the ghost's recent visit—or at the very least, a sign that Margaret's mind was receptive to such a wonderful illusion. When the royal standards fly over the castle, the monarch is at home. Now, if Margaret wanted to communicate with Regina, all she had to do was concentrate on quasicrystal grids, or on photographs of the ceilings of medieval mosques, or on the gilt edges of fine china where the curlicues go click-clack; the fugues of Bach in which the tonic subject loops and repeats. There was Regina, there was the very idea of a Regina, of a good visitor from the past who infiltrates the present and makes a beating counterpoint there, delivers meaning there, by way of her intricate regularity of personality. Margaret grew sure of this, and various things began to dance and tighten in her mind. The iron grates of balconies, the engraving on the lid of a silver pocket watch, the handles of rococo forks and spoons, the scabrous plaster molding around the upper edge of her bedroom, and now the playing cards and their promise of a game—it all opened up before her, conduits to a better life.

These cards. First there was the fact of their flip-side pattern—a circular snowflake in the center seemed to be exploding with mathematics before Margaret's eyes. Surrounding it were stylized interlocking oak leaves. In both of these, Margaret saw the soul of Regina Strauss sleeping, promising enlightenment, Enlightenment.

And then once she had shuffled and cut the deck, she turned it over and it happened: she found to her joy she had bought a French deck. The queens bore names in Gothic letters: Judith, Argine, Pallas, Rachel. Margaret stared at their brocade robes. The queens had been wearing the same robes for over six hundred years—was there anything more constant in culture? Even religious rites are not so stable as playing cards. Margaret's eyes began to swim.

She dealt out the entire deck between herself and Regina.

Easily one might say it was senseless to play Hearts with only two players—it meant you always knew what your opponent could and would do—if your opponent had any sense. But that was just the idea.

Margaret wanted to play a game of cards with Regina precisely in order to allow the ghost an opportunity to make sense. To give her an opportunity to be rational.

This is how Margaret began to be greedy in her good fortune: she began, despite all intelligent ideas, to suspect that she was one of the lucky ones, one of the chosen who have been allowed contact with the Divine, and now she could not stop herself from testing it, from testing the divine idea, like a deliriously happy yet previously insecure lover demanding ever more extreme displays of romance. Margaret felt nervously triumphant, sure the ghost would jump at this chance, but that did not mean she was not teetering precariously.

Margaret went over what she knew. It happens that in the game of Hearts, the card to be avoided at all costs is the Queen of Spades. It happens that according to Diderot's encyclopedia, the four queens in the deck—Rachel, Judith, Pallas, and Argine (anagram of Regina!)—symbolize the four means of ruling: by beauty, by piety, by wisdom, and by right of birth. It happens that the four suits are a matter of caste: hearts of the clergy, diamonds of the merchants, clubs of the soldiery, and spades of the serfs. It happens that the Queen of Spades is called Pallas, the queen who rules by wisdom. It happens that the four kings, David, Alexander, Caesar, and Charlemagne, are emblems of the four great monarchies: Jewish, Greek, Roman, and German. It happens that the husband of the Queen of Spades, that is, the King of Spades (or is he her husband?) is David, king of the Jews. It happens that the Queen of Spades is sometimes called the Black Maria. It happens that Black Marias were the vehicles used to take away Stalin's victims during the purges. It happens that the Queen of Spades holds a tulip in her hand, a crimson flower, with its bell-like blossom inclining heavily toward her Roman nose. It happens that the Queen of Spades is the only one-eyed queen.

Margaret took her half deck in her hand, and for her Regina, she put the other half in a neat pile across from her. The chair there was a black folding chair. As soon as she put the cards down in front of it, this chair seemed to grow quieter and appeared to be weighed down, with an expression on its chair-face of an interested though uncomprehending dog. Margaret laughed at herself for thinking this, but she was not unserious.

She held her twenty-six cards in her hand. She looked—among them she did not find the Queen of Spades. So Regina must have the

Queen. She looked further through her own cards. She did not find the two of clubs either.

So she wrote in large letters on a slip of paper:

Two of clubs begins the game.

She pushed the paper to the middle of the table, put her own cards in the inner pocket of her jacket, and went out of the room, quivering. She was not so far gone that she did think: What am I doing? Do I really think it is possible to play a hand of cards with Regina Strauss?

Did she?

Her belief in Regina's miraculous power to intervene in her life was strong, but it was not invincible; no, let us not say that it was a perfect faith. It had only taken on a certain hue: her need for the woman was so great that she was going to press her into being, ram her mind to its limits and will a miracle of intervention out of—if necessary— nothing.

It need not be described how, the next morning, Margaret woke up, and how the game of Hearts flew back into her mind, how she crept down the hall toward the kitchen full of expectancy, how she did not enter the kitchen feet-first, but peeked around the corner, leading with her head. There she saw: Regina's half deck still in its place on the edge of the kitchen table, in front of the black metal folding chair. In the middle of the table, however—could it be? A card. Margaret went closer. A card had been played.

The two of clubs.

NINETEEN · Roses for Rahel

And then there was a long period when Margaret was both manic and unwell. Every morning for three weeks she went into the kitchen to find a different card played. Eventually they had broken every suit, and it was dazzling to Margaret, dazzling. Sometimes Regina took the tricks, sometimes Margaret took them, and when Regina took a trick, Margaret placed it, with ecstatic reverence, in a little pile next to the rest of the woman's hand. By and large Regina played intelligently; always by the rules, and Margaret rejoiced.

The one contradictory point was this: a number of times Margaret deliberately, self-sacrificially (for both she and Regina had already acquired hearts and she no longer hoped to shoot the moon), played a card that might have allowed Regina to slip her the Queen of Spades. Yet the Queen of Spades was never slipped. They were almost at the end of the game, and the Queen of Spades had still never been played. Margaret was too devout to peek at the pile of cards in Regina's remaining hand.

It must be noted that a strange thing happened when it came close to the end and it was almost one-hundred-percent certain this card was not going to be played. Despite Margaret's elation over the game, the absence of that card gnawed. It was mysteriously significant. The exact reason why it bothered her so much, she did not know. All she could say was that still something was not right, and it hurt her. Only a minor detail, really, but even one small detail out of alignment, one card not played that logically should have certainly been played by now, meant the ghost was distant, uncommitted, even unreal. Almost precisely because it was a trifle, the sort of thing it would have been easy to ask about if Regina had been alive, nothing awkward, nothing extreme, it made Margaret tremble with agitation.

She had tempted and received a miracle, and now she was paying a certain kind of price—the price of living with its fickle power. Bringing a god down to earth, one must always pay a similar price.

So Margaret saw that it would be necessary after all to return to the territory of the unequivocally real, at least for a while. There had to be some extra element of real-world information with which she could moor the ghost. In the spirit of finding that information, she sent five e-mails to the Centrum Judaicum in the center of the city. They would have information about Jewish families who committed suicide during the war, she thought; they must know something real about the Strausses. But the archivists were not answering her queries, and Margaret grew distraught. She could not wait. She would go to the archive in Mitte herself.

Frau Jablonski from the archive greeted Margaret after Margaret came sweating through the metal detectors of security. The young woman was small, spoke with an effervescent flourish. She led Margaret up a dark staircase and into a little office that at first appeared to be a closet.

"I'm not sure what I can tell you," she said. "You've written us six e-mails over the last three days, but you should know that there's no information about a case like this. Suicides of this type were very common. Hundreds of Jewish families in Berlin committed suicide at exactly that time. What do you want us to tell you?"

Margaret was distracted. "I want photos, or to know what jobs they might have had, whether there was any family that survived, what year they married, if either had any previous marriages, names of siblings, what became of their belongings, whether they had any children other than those who died with them, what synagogue they attended," Margaret said, all in rush.

"Yes, I understand. But none of those questions can be answered— by this archive at least, with the exception, theoretically, of finding the surviving family. But the unfortunate coincidence here is that both the name Strauss and, let me see your e-mail"—she turned to the computer—"yes, and Regina Strauss's maiden name, Herzberg, are very common. There are thousands with those names."

Margaret's eyes flashed back and forth and around the room, desperate.

The woman watched her. Margaret caught her doing it. But the woman was kind to her. She said, as though not caring whether Margaret was insane or not: "There is something I can help you with, though. I can tell you where they are likely buried."

Margaret shot up from her chair.

"Go up to the Jewish Cemetery at Weissensee, and there, in Field D, you'll find the graves of Jews who committed suicide in Berlin to escape deportation. There are over a thousand in that cemetery alone."

"Oh!" said Margaret. "Oh, thank you!" She got out her notebook and wrote in large black letters, *Weissensee Friedhof, Feld D.*

"Why are you so interested in this family in particular?" asked the archivist, looking at her.

"Oh," Margaret said. Her cheeks were hot, her mouth dry and hungry. "Who can answer such a question." She fled toward the door. "Thank you, thank you very much."

Out on the street, it started to rain. The air smelled of earth and damp granite. Forgetting her bike in her excitement, Margaret ran through the rain down the bottleneck sidewalk to Hackescher Markt. She got onto the Number 4 tram just as the doors closed. The yellow centipede went up the Greifswalder Strasse, passed through Prenzlauer Berg. She cursed herself for not having thought to buy flowers—if she were visiting a grave, she should have bought flowers!

On the tram the passengers were dripping with rainwater, and the air soon became humid. The tram climbed onto higher and higher ground, emerged in Weissensee, where the city's density unfurled and dissolved. The sun reappeared, and the part of East Berlin that is still so much as it was before the change—it spread its arms.

The tram stopped in the new sun, and someone stood to get off—a young woman. Margaret could only see her from behind, but something about her figure caught Margaret's eye. The girl was tall, with a narrow back and long hair—the curl of it in the humid weather— Margaret recognized the hair, just as she knew the gait, just as she knew the posture: the way the young woman held one shoulder higher to keep the handles of her bag hooked onto it. It was just like Margaret. Margaret had a sensation of red curtains closing around her head, a sense of light passing through prisms; she felt hopeless and warm at once—the sensation of a story coming to an end, a movie finishing, and she stood up and tried to follow the girl. She wanted to see her face.

But she had recognized her too late. The girl was off the tram and Margaret was still on it as the doors closed. Margaret went all the way to the back of the car and looked out the rear window, and now she could see the girl raise her face into the sun, seeming to float as the tram moved away from her. It was Margaret's face.

Margaret got off the tram in Weissensee and turned into a side street. Her head was still dazed—she was empty and fresh as though she had slept.

Then she had luck: she spied a little flower shop on her way to the cemetery. One of the Vietnamese establishments that only has a couple of bouquets, the rest of the vases empty but for a few bundles of artificial flowers. Margaret found a little potted rosebush. It cost almost nothing. She felt so light; a happiness like sugar-water bubbled in her throat. The pink nubs were small and perfect enough to be mistaken for the flowers painted on china, and she convinced herself that the children of the Family Strauss would be pleased.

Out here in Weissensee, the apartment houses' flesh was old, almost grey. These buildings were set far back from the street, and the gardens in front had high brick walls and arched iron gates. In some places the skin of the flesh seemed to have become dry and fallen away, and the red muscle beneath was exposed, what might have once been the redbrick of inner walls, and it was a ruinous beauty. Margaret made her way to the cemetery over the cobblestones, hurrying along with the potted rosebush. At the end of the road the buildings stopped, there was an open bramble, and the blond, healthy skin of the cemetery's entrance rose over the near horizon. Margaret could hear birds calling, water gurgling in the fountain of a hidden garden. The street was deserted. Margaret drew closer. She noticed the absence of the usual guard for Jewish institutions, and the place seemed enchanted.

She walked through the arch and into the cemetery.

First came the feeling of sudden darkness, not as when the sun is behind a cloud but rather as when it goes flat behind the discus of the moon, and the birds grow dull. The trees grew up higher than the eye could see, in a heavy halo. The impression was of islands of bone, as in a great blond-brown archipelago rising out of the sea. The aisles between these tumbledown graves crept away into the haze, around bends toward a missing horizon, and the darkness of shadowless moss seemed to grow seamlessly into the darkness of decrepit mausoleums.

Margaret moved uncertainly. She saw a sign: Field A. She followed the path, going by graves from the nineteenth century and then, just as soon, graves from only the year before. She curved with the high wall around the inside edge of the cemetery, circling.

At first she thought she was alone in the entire place, but when she passed Field C she heard a regular scraping sound. Shovels and plastic buckets were left askew on the ground. She looked down the long aisle. In the distance, two bright specks twinkled: old women. They were raking gravel.

She came up on Field D, and here the graves were not marked in Hebrew but in German. Margaret began to read the names on the gravestones. In the second row there were stones so tightly grasped by the roots of ivy that names could not be made out. She worried that one of these graves might be that of the Family Strauss and she would miss them.

She walked more slowly. Her only hope was that she would sense the graves if she did not see them. It was in that spirit that she focused on the complex pattern of the cobbles under her feet.

She passed into the fourth row, and there it began: gravestones very small and flat, on each nothing more than a lone family name and an endless repetition of the same years of death: 1943, 1944, 1945. Ivy drew back and exposed names: Stein, Schwarz, Moses, Rosenberg, Benjamin—and on and on, the suicides went.

Under a tall elm, toward the back wall of the cemetery, Margaret pushed back a creeper of heavy ivy. With no warning at all, there they were.

On one side lay Franz, in the middle a single grave with the names of the three little girls, Rahel, Gerda, and Beate, and on the other side Regina. All three short mounds were covered in ivy, puffed and waxy, like feather beds fluffed and tucked at the edges. As soon as Margaret rustled the ivy with her hands, she could see hundreds of red dots— the ivy was rich with bright, red berries.

At this sight, a quotation wove in her mind: *They seemed like sleeping children, struck by fever, for their bodies, arms, and faces were covered in red spots*. A faint spasm ran through Margaret. This is what had been written by a journalist, but not about these children. That was about the Goebbels children.

Margaret sat down heavily on the ground. She felt an enormous fatigue.

The silence of their absent breath. She shifted on the hard ground.

She looked at Regina Strauss's grave and opened her mouth. She wanted to say something. She was not sure how her voice would sound in the open air. She spoke haltingly. "I wanted to find you," she said aloud. "I wanted to ask you what to do."

She took out a handkerchief and rubbed her nose. She looked off down the long aisle. Standing up, she took the rosebush, finally, and nestled it into the ivy near the head of the girls' grave, just under a gnarled little elm. The red lips of the roses brimmed into view, the ivy forming a high collar around the flowers.

Margaret's temples throbbed, and her back ached. She thought: Now I should go. But then she looked at the little rose plant and thought that it would not survive. Wouldn't it be better if she could plant it in the ground? So she reached into the ivy again and looked for a place to dig with her nails. But the roots of the ivy had spread into all parts of the soil, and the earth was as tight as a trampoline. She straightened up and made as if to leave again, but as she walked away, she thought of the plant dying.

She heard a repeated sound, slow and rhythmic in the distance. Far off, the two old women were raking gravel, almost at the vanishing point. Margaret squinted her eyes at them. It occurred to her that they would know what to do about the rosebush. She followed the long aisle. As she got nearer, she saw that they were stooped, fat women in housecoats, their cheeks red. Their hair was tied up in handkerchiefs in the old-fashioned, servile style.

They both stopped raking and looked at Margaret when she neared.

"Excuse me," Margaret began. "I've brought a little bush with me and I'd like to plant it. There's so much ivy on the grave though, I don't know how to get it in," Margaret said. Her American accent became stronger than usual.

The women stared at her.

"What's that you say?" The one woman looked over to the second old woman for help.

The other one nodded. "She's asking us if we know how to plant a flower."

"I don't know," said the first woman.

"We don't know," said the second.

"Oh," said Margaret. There was a long silence.

"Over there is Frau Schmidt. She's the one who does the gardening. She's Frau Schmidt. She does the gardening. Look—there she is." And the two pointed both at once down another aisle that sloped deep into the bowels of the cemetery. Margaret saw, indeed, another their number in the distance.

She went. Even from afar, she could make out that this third woman's back wasn't straight, and she had grown gnarled. Margaret got closer. Under her quilted coat, the woman wore a formless cotton dress with large daisies printed on it. Her hair was dark and her nose tipped up. Beneath this nose, on her upper lip, a downy black mustache grew.

"Excuse me, I'm trying to plant a rosebush," Margaret started, breathlessly, "but I don't know if I can plant it in the ivy."

"What sort of rosebush is it?" said the woman, leaning on a spade.

"I don't know. It's very small."

"I mean—is it a groomer?"

"A groomer?"

"Yeah, a groomer."

"I'm not sure," Margaret said.

"Where is it?"

"I'm sorry, I left it at the grave."

"Oh, let's go see, let's go see."

When they arrived the woman began to cluck.

"It's a groomer all right!"

"Is it?"

"Yes it is. Oh yes." And with a violent motion she grabbed ahold of the plastic pot. It had become wet, sitting in the ivy, and it slipped from her hands and fell onto the path at her feet. The plant tumbled out, its soil molded—this began to fall away in clumps. It came to rest with its roots in the air.

"Oh goodness!" said Frau Schmidt.

"That's okay," Margaret said.

"I'm awfully sorry. I'll tell you what. I'll plant it anyway. We can't plant such a thing in the ivy. But we'll plant it next to the grave." She gestured toward the open space separating the Strauss graves from the neighboring ones.

"All right," said Margaret, looking doubtfully at the broken plant. She stood, biting her lower lip and looking at the graves, the plant, and the powdery white daisies on the blue cotton dress of the gardener.

The woman tilted her head back and looked up at Margaret. Then she picked up the plant and plopped it back into its pot. "I'll do it when I get to it," she said. "I won't be in Field D for a while yet."

"All right," Margaret said. "That sounds good." Margaret took care to again nestle the pot into the ivy.

The woman hustled away at high speed, bobbing up and down.

Margaret turned and walked out of the cemetery. She thought: Better not make any grand gestures again. She felt tired, and foolish. She rubbed her head. I have no place here, she thought. Again she saw the white daisies on the blue dress of the gardener. It represented something to her, something about the broad world with all its salt and pith getting funneled down into the strings that tie a sausage together. At some point, every person must make a pact with futility.

Her bicycle she had forgotten in town, and the heel of her shoe was coming loose as she walked back to the tram stop. It flapped against the cobblestones, flip-*whack*. She walked down the cobblestone road. There were sparrows on the ground by a high chapped-flesh wall, little tan and twig-colored nothings, picking at seeds. Margaret felt her chest hardening with pain.

The same day, Margaret returned to the Schöneberg archive. She thought, at the very least, she could find out what Herr Strauss had done for a living, or where the family lived before they moved into the apartment on Salzburgerstrasse. Her desire to know more felt like a heavy hunger, a longing for milk and oil, and in any case still desperate.

The archivist with her dancer's body silently took down two heavy address directories from 1939 and 1941. Each listed address and occupation of Berlin residents by name, and together they peered at the Gothic script. There were twenty-three Franz Strausses listed in Berlin in 1939, and sixteen in 1941. None of them resided at Salzburgerstrasse 8. Just to be sure, Margaret checked the 1943 directory as well. Nothing.

As Margaret prepared to leave, her heart sinking, she said to the archivist, "The name is so typically German. It hardly seems like a Jewish name at all." The archivist, like most educated Germans scrupulously careful when it came to what sounded and looked Jewish, gave Margaret a glance of feigned incomprehension. After a brief silence, however, she chanced an observation: "It isn't really a Jewish name. What did you say the full name was?"

"Franz Strauss."

"Just listed as Franz? No second given name?"

"None."

"Well then, he most probably wasn't Jewish."

Margaret caught her breath. Her face became hot. She saw what the archivist meant. The police would have recorded him, according to Nazi law, as Franz "Israel" if he were Jewish, just as his wife was listed as Regina "Sara." The family must have been mixed.

Margaret knew she should not be, knew it was nothing more than a detail, but still, she was crushed. When she got home, she looked at her photocopy of the police logbook page where the family's death was registered, and saw confirmation in the margin. A longhand note, so baroque as to be almost illegible, which she had not before even bothered to decipher, read: *"Bericht an Stapo mit dem Hinweis, dass Nachlaß dem A.G. Schb. übergeben wurde, weil der Haushaltungsvorstand Arier war."* So it was even specially noted that the head of house was "Aryan." Margaret had been blind.

In light of this new information, it was unclear why they would have had to die. She had checked already: mixed couples were not rounded up with the others, not in Berlin. Officially, the decision at the Wannsee Conference was to wait until after the war before considering the eventual extermination of the mixed and the mixed-married, a dangerous position for the Strausses, but not deadly, not in 1943.

How was Margaret to understand their decision?

They could have saved the children, she thought. It went through her mind again and again. Wasn't there anywhere they could have sent the children? It was common, she had found in her reading, for the children of mixed families to be sent to non-Jewish relatives, where they were passed off as war orphans, of whom there were in any case so many, particularly after the bombings of cities began.

And then Margaret was reminded of something else. When she was a child, a friend told her at a roller-skating party (this was a friend with eyes like a forest sprite) that she, Margaret, was a "mongrel." When she went home, she told her mother. But her mother did not, would not, tell her what the word meant. But she looked at Margaret and said, "Maybe you are a mongrel."

Her mother was tired and unpredictable. At least, that was how Margaret remembered it.

That night, Margaret was awoken abruptly from a dream.

There was someone in the bedroom.

She could hear the noise of frantic and uncaught breath.

In a ball of fear, she lay quiet.

It took her some time to realize she herself was the one making the sounds. She was lying in bed, breathing hard. Her fingers were rigid, stuck in claw-like shapes, her body curled.

Sometimes, before he had gone to the hospital and stayed to live there, her father had shut himself in his study and would not come out, even if Margaret beat on the door and called to him. His breathing behind the door—he sounded as though he were on the verge of death, and her mother led her away, and explained to her that her father was panicked and afraid.

After a while, such sounds frightened Margaret badly. She felt her own panic creeping when she heard her father's panic, and in her place under the desk in the long apartment on the Upper East Side, she began to try to escape.

At first it had been a picture in a book that was the portal. It was a picture of an old woman riding in a basket in the night sky, sur-rounded by the moon, planets, and creatures with pointed heads. The picture frightened Margaret, but not like life frightened her. Life, when it frightened her, made her feel that all the edges of her body were under attack, a kind of arachnophobia: a sensation of infection and infiltration.

But when the picture frightened her, it was kind. Its terrors had power, and depth, and even scent, yet at the very same time, it all remained far away. And if she looked at it correctly, the picture could be seen to have more than one surface. It was into this picture that Margaret began to disappear, filling in more and more detail of the world beyond the depicted, where the woman hurtled through the night sky—up and up, rising toward the moon, visiting cities made of lapis and alabaster, floating palaces with mile-long hallways and trap-doors. After some practice, Margaret could enter the picture without the book. She closed her eyes and saw the road into the sky. It was very smooth, with a surface like Chinese lacquer. She slid along the colors away from the brown apartment, at first with vague participation but later much more completely, so that when she came back from the reverie, it was as if she had slept.

And so now, Margaret could feel it: she wanted to ride the rainbow again, to again have the sensation of riding through the night in a basket on a band of vivid color.

She knew the story of the Strausses was slowly fading and thinning for her. The mystery was not at work. The mystery should have caused the story to echo and resonate—mystery is the great enhancement of the unknown—but instead, the mystery was quieting them out. And the problem was this: she could have lived with any element of their story remaining unknown but one—whether they were right. If she did know their location in the moral world, then they would disappear from the physical world.

In the next days, the card game at the kitchen table came to a complete halt. Margaret herself was the one who stopped playing. Her mind was tired, and she thought the story was at an end.

TWENTY · The Violence of Nostalgia

The mistake was made: the muscle of her mind had slackened, and all it took was an instant: the beast sidled in. The tent poles fell and the tent too, and there was nothing to block the coming animal.

Restless, uneasy, Margaret often went walking in the next weeks. One night she went east, walked away, out of Schöneberg. She crossed the railway lines that form the border with Kreuzberg. She stood on the bridge over the emptiness between the districts. Alexanderplatz sparkled distantly over in the center of town, and under her, the railway cut grooves ever more deeply into the land, like water over centuries chafing deeper into a riverbed.

On the Kreuzberg side, the apartment buildings were tenement-like, covered in tattoos. On the Schöneberg side, there were gold rings on the chimney-fingers, but also much crumbling bone. Looking off toward town, Margaret felt a wayward love.

Down in the ravine where the train ran, a wan field opened up on the side. A dilapidated *Biergarten,* shut for the winter, rested darkly. A narrow stairway led down from the street above. Up on poles, dark lights were strung around the tables and benches, and the dead wires looked skeletal; light too is a kind of flesh. So here: a skeleton of the summertime.

Margaret was drawn to it. She climbed over a low gate, and went down into the empty *Biergarten.* She sat on a chair and drew her body together for warmth. She closed her eyes.

It was no coincidence, the *Biergarten.* She had known it from before, from her earliest days in Berlin, her first attempts at independent spring living: people with beer mugs in their hands shivering in outdoor cafés, crowding themselves into blotches of kingfisher sunlight in the prickling early spring air. Margaret tightened her eyes. It was the skeleton of the summer, and she was younger then. She remembered her first days.

———

Nineteen years old, a fresh arrival from the new world to the old, her eyes flashing. Her first day, she hoisted her suitcase off the baggage belt at Tegel, and already that same afternoon, an electric pulse in her fingers shocked anyone she touched, so great was her sense of possibility.

She was free, her father dead of cancer after years of frightening mental illness, a terrible quarrel with her mother behind her—and her bag hoisted from the belt and it was as simple as that: she was on her own. That first day in Berlin, her back arching, rising toward the sky, she was greeted by an old man in the subway station, a man she had never seen before, with the words, *"Mein Liebling! Ich liebe dich!"* and then kissed on the neck, on the platform with the train rushing by and the man gone before the train was. People seemed to sense intuitively that any overtures toward her would not only be welcomed but ratcheted up.

Margaret came to Berlin fleeing, but she also came to Berlin running straight into the arms of her dead father. Her father she had loved like some quintessential thing. He had been mentally ill, he had fought his cancer only weakly, but through all this, she had seen him as though he were cradled. Off in the haze, he was miniaturized but not diminished: he was a tiny, perfect figure so small as to be invisible, running back and forth in the palm of her hand.

Now she had come to Germany to study her father's "soul," as she called it. She was interested in everything he had been interested in. His paranoid mind shot like an arrow to the Stasi, to the CIA, to the KGB, to the postwar reconstructed Nazi party in South America, and so Margaret too was interested in these things. She did not put any stock in his paranoid fantasies, but her veneration for him coalesced with her estrangement such that his obsessions seemed dignified and only coincidentally wrongheaded. In fact, such organizations became, to Margaret, a form of evil nebulous and mythical, not terrible at all.

In any case, her first Sunday in Berlin, she was already trying to know him. She set off to meet an old friend of his, and she felt, in anticipation of this meeting, almost as if her father would come along with them, return from the dead out of old friendship. Her father had always spoken of this man with moist-eyed fondness: Amadeus Vilnius, Slavist.

The man on the phone, when Margaret heard his voice, did not disappoint, either: he sounded over the wires like pebbles brightly colored under water.

They agreed to meet in Friedrichshain. From there, they would walk to the Soviet Monument in Treptower Park. This destination, too, was chosen meaningfully: Margaret's father had talked about it once. He spoke of it using both hands, his thickly lensed eyes and hoarse voice becoming emotional with wonder and disgust.

It was on the platform at Ostkreuz, then, that Margaret Taub first saw the man she would always want to see ever after. Later, not a single thing about the moment she first saw him went lost. This was how it was: the station was nothing but a knot of criss-crossing platforms, and on that sunny, first-spring March day, the damp air was filled with coal dust left over from the winter. Crowds moved toward the ring trains on the overpass above and toward the East-West axis trains in the shadows below, and Amadeus got off the train in these shadows. At first, he too was in shadow. But as he drew closer to Margaret, he came into the light—she remembered it so well!—and the world seemed to tilt into alignment. He was dressed like a student, in dust-covered black corduroy guild pants with two gold zippers, a coarse sailor shirt, androgynously shaggy hair, and a rosy face. Everything around him seemed to instantly become a part of him: on the white-washed station walls, letters were stenciled—networks of exposed wires filigreed the sky, grids of windows gave a Bauhaus effect, and the world seemed to be smoking its grandfather's pipe. The station felt as if it were held together with black electrical tape, and Margaret's spirits rose like a baby's hand toward the unfamiliar flame, automated beyond reason.

Not long after she picked him out in the crowd (he told her on the phone what he would wear) she waved at him. Amadeus saw her do it. And already then, something strange occurred. He saw her wave, and he recognized her, but he looked away.

As he came closer to her, too, there was something overcharged. The first thing Margaret thought was: What beautiful eyes he has. And the thought was perhaps too simple and pure for their relationship. A single note had been sounded bell-like and left to vibrate a long time on its own.

She moved her mouth and said hello; he nodded and tilted his head away from her. Yes, it was an awkwardness too much for strangers. She filled the silence—babbled about coming to Berlin to study history, and Amadeus laughed quickly, made a derisive comment about the field attracting "the morbid pedants of the world," although she knew he was himself a history professor and he must know that she knew it, and the second thing she thought about him was, How diffident he is, and how sour, but it did not stop her from following his face with her attention, her body frightfully still.

From Ostkreuz they walked together to Treptower Park. And in some subterranean part of her she began to feel, walking next to him, as though she were attractive and delightful to men. Who knows from what source such feelings well up in some company but not in others.

On that Sunday, the entire population of the Eastern city seemed to have rejoiced at its freedom from the cave of the indoors and taken to the park along the river. They passed *Biergartens* where the old ones in their polyester were dancing to oompah-pah, small children went by on tricycles at astonishing speed, almost knocking down the lumbering flâneurs in their paths, the ducks were back, and when they stopped, Amadeus festively bought two *Currywurst* from a stall, claiming *Currywurst* a great delicacy, and even too, whatever it was between them disappeared for a moment; we should not overstate the initial attraction. A few minutes long, Margaret looked at him and briefly thought him ridiculous; he seemed foreign in a foolish, foppish way.

But finally they came to the Soviet War Memorial, the object of their wanderings, and it was here, beneath the Russian soldier–ogre with German babe in arms, so large that directly beneath it you could not even see it, that everything went irrevocably awry. Specifically, Margaret asked Amadeus to explain the names and platforms of the German political parties, and while he spoke, he looked once into her eyes. It took him a long time to explain, and their eyes met several more times after that as well. Margaret's entire chest began to expand, and a sense of unbelievable suspense and fear and almost painfully sharp anticipation overtook her. It is only illicit love that causes such gargantuan arousal, and that is a great misfortune.

By the time they were climbing through the bushes and over a fence to get into an abandoned amusement park, Amadeus, a bit out of breath but eager to appear fit, had begun to incandesce toward her, with a bright firefly gleam of attention. Breathlessly he declared that she was "very well read," although later he would insinuate that she was just good at fluffing.

And then once as she climbed over a barbed-wire fence partially caved in—they were trying to get back out again—she smiled particularly broadly over at him and he said, "You know, you look very much like your mother when you smile," and Margaret said, "You don't know my mother," and he said "*Doch,* once I met her. Before you were born, your father brought her back with him one summer," and Margaret was surprised at this and shivered. She had not known her mother ever made such a trip; her mother had never mentioned it. But it made Margaret feel all the more of a pounding in her chest, that he was no stranger to her history. He had known both her parents in the time before she was born.

Later that day, the two of them still together although night had come—chapters of time fell by so quickly, it was extraordinary—first in the park and then later a friend of his joined them in a café: a short, bristle-haired man named Florian. Then in another café, then in a restaurant and then in a bar, Amadeus made money quickly appear and fly into the waiters' hands before Margaret could move to pay for herself and like magic, a relationship of dependency sprang up between them. After the comment about her likeness, Amadeus never again mentioned her mother, nor, more strangely, did he ever again mention her father. It became—how can it be explained? It was not even as if he and Margaret had met by chance. At least that would have been spoken of now and then. The reason for their meeting was left so unspoken that it was as if they had met by magic.

Margaret misunderstood this. She took it to mean he was uncomfortable talking about her father's troubles: most people did not know how to talk about mental illness, and Margaret was used to that. Also, she sensed Amadeus was the sort of man who could not address death and other stirring things—exile, separation, and betrayal. He was both too soft and too hard for it. When the heat is too high in the oven, the bread becomes stone-hard on the outside while still almost liquid in the middle, and later when she got to know him better, she found this intuition regarding his character had been correct, and so she left it alone. To her later regret.

That night already it began—the love affair in his freezing, coal-heated second apartment, where Margaret's little envoy of the heart to a world free of advertisements found its perch, in those loose, cool, summery years after the end of Communism and before the beginning of true capital; a society breathing out at the end of state control but not yet fighting toward wealth, light-headed, perhaps slightly flaccid and all-embracing, a slacker student of the new, like Margaret herself.

In those early months, Margaret began spending the night with Amadeus regularly. She remembered in particular how very cold his place was, even in the spring, and how he still needed to feed coal into the oven, which he would often forget to do, so the corner room, with its high balcony over the silent street, at the far eastern end of Friedrichshain, gave off an odor of cold, and of unforgiving, oxblood-painted, dusty wooden floors. She remembered that his bookshelf held *Problems of Dostoyevsky's Poetics* by Bakhtin, and this book fascinated her. It was also in these months that she began to wear a perfume that smelled like freesia flowers, but ritualistically: she only wore it when she knew she was going to meet him. Then to lie in the coal-smelling room with the book, on the sheets which were cold to the touch but clean-smelling, over the mattress on the floor which was even colder against her bare feet, and lined with coal powder mixed with the smell of freesia, and he would speak to her of his other women, and she felt safe and coddled despite that, or maybe because of it—she thought to hear of his other women drew her into a society with them, and all of them were foreign and hidden and preserved outside of time, like flowers pressed into oil. It is terribly seductive to have a style in which to think of oneself.

Once, she remembered, he told her that his favorite novel was Lermontov's *A Hero of Our Time,* and gave her his extra copy. She took it home to her much warmer, more modern apartment, and read it through in one afternoon and evening.

She remembered the night after she finished reading this book; it was very late and she was alone, the light glowing yellow around her like a sickness. A horrible sensation of fear and misgiving crushed her, a certain knowledge that in choosing this man she had chosen wrongly; that any man who loved such a book, where a cavalier draws all his romance and exultation from the bittersweet moment when he leaves his beloved behind, could only be rotten at his soft core—what she knew from her boarding school days Mary McCarthy would have called a "dangerous neurotic."

But what did it mean? What was the ailment? She thought that night for a long time about Amadeus, about his tendency to love her more, chase her with greater consistency and desire when she was running away from him. She had wanted to give it a name, to know

whether she herself was at fault for having dived into the shallows of a
heart such as his.

But at the same time, even after that night—and mark, she never
completely forgot the realization of that night—*her love for him only
grew.* That was the contradiction. The love became a world unto itself.
It was both the liability and the fallback plan; her undoing but also her
reward for bearing up under the undoing, the forest of pain, but also
her comfort as she wandered lost in that forest. The itch of it, the
painful itch of the love that would not cease; the inability to think
of anything else when inside such a circle of longing and incomplete
satisfaction and longing again—none of it was capable of coming to
an end.

Margaret opened her eyes in the closed-up *Biergarten,* now returned
to herself. Several types of pain snaked through her at once. The day in
Treptower Park wavered, the tail of it at least, before her eyes, and
then fled. In its place, her eyes filled with a blackness the color of pressure. She was on a folding chair in the cold night air, in the defunct
Biergarten by the railway tracks.

Slow on her feet, she walked back to Schöneberg, her mind gone
black and old.

She thought: I was wrong to remember. To remember is wrong.
Memories—true or not, enactments of any kind, attempts at experience inside the head, playacting with neurons hidden behind the bones
of the skull, are the enemy of life. It was the doctor who first taught her
that.

On Hauptstrasse, a 148 bus passed by her in the night, and she
looked into its aquarium lights as it passed. In the back of it, she saw a
girl sitting in a black overcoat over a sailor-striped shirt. She and the
girl had the same wide-set eyes, the same long bones, the same skin
dotted with moles. The passenger's veins had the same streaking presence behind the freckles. Margaret saw with absolute clarity and certainty this time: it was Margaret, another Margaret, it was no one but
Margaret herself. She was riding up toward Prenzlauer Berg to visit
her lover, the older man, the friend of her father's. She was still travel-

ing up there! And the bus passed by and the young woman was gone, but Margaret was left on the street shivering and shaken.

Curtains closed around Margaret's eyes, there on the pavement. Through the diaphanous fabric she could see the alternating shadows, the correspondence between prisms. She heard a radio far away in a high window, playing a tin melody she thought she already knew.

There was something else, Margaret thought, something else she was meant to remember.

TWENTY-ONE • Escape from Berlin

The next day Margaret woke up to another changed city. Even before she went outside, chords at the bottom of her mind—and dark they were, dark and in a minor key—suggested that her memories had wrought shadows. Her insanity was slavishly returning.

It was the sky this time, the sky that was rich, the sky that was moving. Specifically, from the heavens, and all over Berlin, dangled rope ladders. Many thousands of rope ladders, and the day was overcast, so these ladders swayed down from the iron-white sky like silken threads of rain, all through the air, over the rooftops, jangling and swinging with life, coming to a ponderous end several meters above the surface of the earth, although some of them dragged against shingles, dipped into chimneys, obstructed the paths of pedestrians.

The rope ladders had an effect on the city's flesh. The long, rainy skeins of rope caressed and flicked the rooftops, and there were spasms and convulsions here and there.

The effect on Margaret: the ladders drew her eye up into the sky. A dangling rope ladder is nothing if not an invitation. Berlin seemed infinitely expanded—its coordinates recast, a new dimension beckoning.

And now shall be told of an adventure of Margaret's mind that had the result of making her fright, which until then had been uncertain and porous, become tight—acting as a sealant, as it were. The rope ladders were an invitation, and Margaret did not turn it down.

She looked and wondered why no one was climbing the rope ladders into the sky—such a natural thing to do! Okhan at the Döner bistro, and the tiny woman with her giant husband who ran the bakery, the Armenian woman hanging out her cobwebbed window, and the bushy blue-eyed dogs at the Internet café—all were going about their business. Except, unlike last time, Margaret saw this, took it in quickly, and did not miss a beat. This is what she had come to expect—she and the world would always diverge.

One ladder near her hung alluringly in front of the art supply store, and she let her eyes drift up, let her head flop back. High up, the ladder was lost in the low clouds.

Margaret had a dizzy feeling when she looked up there. She felt herself reflected as in the endless glass world opened by two mirrors facing each other, a glimpse into the featurelessness of eternity. Margaret took off her felt hat and clapped it over her chest. She wiped her hair away from her face but the wind blew it back into her eyes.

She went upstairs and called her boss at the tour company. Her tours had been irregular lately and with scarce work there was scarce money, but now, despite that, she would cancel her tour that morning. It left her boss in the lurch, he would be put out, but she couldn't help herself. Margaret would accept the challenge. She would climb out of Berlin.

She went back outside. With the new goal in mind, the ladders seemed to go on even longer before they met the clouds. It seemed an awfully long way up. Wouldn't it be easier, she thought, if she started from a point already high in the sky?

But there was only one great hill in the flat city of Berlin. This was the Teufelsberg, the mountain in the Grunewald Forest on the outskirts of the city.

She rode to Nollendorfplatz and took the train to Zoo Station. She carried her bicycle into an S-Bahn car and began the ride out into the Western suburbs. Near the Grunewald, already before she got off the train an unctuous sense of déjà vu laid its fingers on her.

Still on the platform, she knew that below, at the mouth of the station, she would find a small tavern with a gravel garden, outdoor tables, and a black picket fence.

And lo, at the exit to the station, she found a tavern with a graveled terrace, collapsible tables made of wood and iron in obedient rows, and a black picket fence. Just as she had thought of it: the kind of place where you can buy *Wurst* and beer, an old place, a summer resort for the Wilhelmine petite bourgeoisie. Margaret could feel the women of 1910 in their summer cotton dresses and petticoats, the portly men in waistcoats, dancing to a brass band—she felt it as if she had put her hands near a fire and come upon a wall of heat.

And all the while, the rope ladders swayed above.

She took out her city map, unfolded it to its farthest Western grid, and once again, when she saw the scheme of streets, with the pattern of the encroaching woods and lakes, something about the lay of the land struck her as familiar and terrible. Her aim was the Teufelsberg, Devil's Mountain, the highest point in Berlin, but her fear was almost too strong to continue. The map grinned up at her in its yellow and blue cover from the bottom of her bag, with cackling, mocking familiarity.

Margaret made her way through the streets of suburban houses, and the gardens of the homes were small here, the dwellings seemed to shoulder up on her—there was an atmosphere of institutionalized eavesdropping.

Margaret's bad feeling peaked when she neared the end of the road. Here the street quit abruptly and left off for the navy blue of the pine forest. She stopped still. She would not walk forward into the Grunewald Forest. As surely as the seagull with flute-hollow bones cannot fly into the storm, she could not go on.

She decided her bicycle was the way to make an effort at proceeding. It was the only way of having more momentum than fear. She mounted the bike and set off precariously. She rode along the brambled path. Her heart beat but her speed was a salvation. She pedaled, and several times her skinny front tire was bested by one of the branches that lay in her path and it skittered off to the side. She did not end up on her back only because she was gripping the handlebars with such force.

The forest broke and a freshly paved road opened up before her. An elderly pair of men were walking down it.

The men were speaking Russian. They were laughing. They were drinking from a shared flask. Margaret asked if they knew where the Teufelsberg was. One of the men, his craw pink and loose, his German broken, laughed at her and gestured toward the west. After she passed them, she looked back over her shoulder and wondered what these two were doing here. It was her first thought outside of fear in a long time, and with it she noticed her misgivings pass. All of a bright sudden she was thinking with optimism.

She turned a bend and there it was, the Teufelsberg, before her, looming like a skyscraper. Right away she knew that she had never been here before, that her sense of déjà vu, too, had fallen away. She had been expecting a hill sloping gradually out of the landscape, covered in trees. Instead, a soaring, cliff-like structure of land rose before her. It was grand, it suggested the myths of icebergs floating in the night ocean.

Approaching the giant, she saw a zigzagging flight of stairs cut up the side of the vertical wall, and she was sure that her mission to climb out of Berlin was going to succeed, for already beginning to ascend the rough stairs she felt that in some essential way she was escaping, her heart casting off ballast.

She got to the top; she was panting. She had counted sixteen flights.

Up here the land spread around her in a vast plateau, as on the roof of a tower, and this, too, was right and good. As she often recited on her tours, the Teufelsberg, an artificial mountain made of the remains of four hundred thousand bombed-out Berliner buildings, was "the collected works of Adolf Hitler." Now the great mass clambered toward the skies.

And here, too, the rope ladders were swinging in the heavy wind, filling the air in their locust swarm. The nearest ladder she grabbed hold of and, indeed, the grey sky was much nearer to the ground than it was on Grunewaldstrasse.

She began to climb with an energy that amazed her. The ladder was not pinned to anything below, so it was a jaunty, difficult ascent, the rungs twisting and spinning. But the effort of bringing her feet onto them occupied and emptied out her mind. If she looked down, she was hit by vertigo; if she looked to the side, she was distracted by the sight of Berlin laid out around her, and so she did neither.

Finally, she burst through the clouds. She had a sensation of pure happiness. The sun was bright and warm up here, the freezing early spring air somehow left behind. The smell of the open breeze embraced her, chilling the nostrils only slightly—tenderly. She turned her head up in exultation.

She was not fated to enjoy her happiness long. Just as quickly as the first, another whiff of air gusted toward her on the back of the other. A second scent, horrible and familiar. The smell of bird droppings. They were there, in the clouds. There must have been ten or eleven— nestled among billowing vapor—enormous birds of prey, as big as elephants, most of them a dark, silvery grey, cosied up like smoky jewels into the pillows of cold.

Without a second thought, in a steady panic, Margaret began to lower herself back down the rope ladder again. But this was a more difficult and slower operation than going up. Dangerous slowness, really. Before she could get very far, the bird that was nearest to her began to pick its way across the cloud landscape in a slow approach, its head thrusting forward in repetitive jabs. As it came, it began to change. The head shrank, the shoulders narrowed, and the dark, grey-black feathers molted quickly to reveal black gabardine. Gleaming now in the bright, super-stratospheric sun, the grey-blond Marcel water-waves were fire to the eyes. It was the hawk-woman.

"Ah, Margaret!" it screeched, in a megaphone-loud, bird-like voice. "You remember me, don't you? I'm Magda! How delightful we should meet!" There was a whistling sound all around, and these pronunciations, for all their volume, were almost lost to the wind. Margaret didn't say anything, but her foot, which was looking vainly for the rung beneath her, was making the sad-futile gesture of a blind inchworm at the edge of a leaf, casting feelers into nothing.

The woman had trapped her. Margaret had no choice: she gave a nod.

"Going down so soon?" screamed the figure. "But if you don't like it here, you could continue up!"

Margaret was prompted, then, to look *up* the rope ladder, which, stunningly, did in fact continue into the ether. "What's up there?" Margaret asked doubtfully.

"Wouldn't you know it! All the people you have lost," was the gleeful response. Margaret stared up into the bright, endless blue, with the rope ladder tracing into it like a fishing line. "Perhaps you would like to see the one you left behind, Margaret?"

Margaret thought about this. Perhaps she would like to see—but the screeching voice of her interlocutor interrupted her thoughts. "And also there," said the woman, "are all the people *I* have lost."

"The people you have lost?" asked Margaret, dazed. "I'm going down." And again her feet began to jab at the air, looking for a rung down.

"Stay awhile," said the hawk-woman. "We can have a little chat."

"That's all right," said Margaret, and again focused on her footing.

The rope ladder, however, seemed to have shortened in the meantime. Below her it did not extend much more than four or five feet toward the earth, which was far, far away. Margaret's back prickled with electricity, her skin cold. For a brief instant, she thought she would jump. Assuming this was a dream, she'd only have to suffer the suffusion with fear, and then she'd be awake. But she couldn't be sure. And if she was wrong? So she stayed.

"Ah, I see you've decided to have a little chat with me after all!"

screeched the bird-woman. "We have so much in common, you and I. I've been meaning to make your acquaintance simply for ages."

And Margaret was warmed by this, despite herself. "Really?"

"Oh, yes!" the bird-woman said in a quieter, more human-like voice.

"Well—" Margaret paused. "That's nice."

"I think so too! What a lovely little setup you've got there in the Grunewaldstrasse. You and I are going to be the best of friends, I know it already."

Margaret would have shuddered at this, but she found that with the rope ladder gone and her imprisonment in the clouds, the woman's friendly overtures were more winning. She said, "You know, my ladder here, it's shorter than it was. I have no idea how to get down."

"Oh, don't worry about that for a second! *I'll* take you!"

"You?"

"Gladly, my dear. Just hop on my back. I'll fly you." And with that, downy feathers began to sprout from the woman's face and hands, her clothes fell away to reveal the buttressed chest of her bird-self. Her face extended and her nose lengthened and latched into a beak. She fluffed her wings tentatively, and they spread wider and wider, telescoping from some inner resource. The woman's wingspan was as broad as a city street. It seemed safe enough to ride on such a massive bird. As the wings were folded in again, Margaret inclined herself toward the back of the predator, and put out her hand. But with a great screech, the bird hopped away from her and swooped up into the sky. The sparrow hawk flew so high she disappeared from view in the clouds. Margaret craned her neck. But then the bird was plummeting back down toward her, Stuka-fashion, and without even realizing what was happening, Margaret was scooped up onto her back and borne away, traveling at high speed.

They jetted across the mist, they broke through, they swooped and dove, and then they were back below cloud level in bracing Berlin. There was the city laid out below, like a veined butterfly pinned down on the earth. The arteries, capillaries, bundles, clots, and junctures of the city streets interlocked and weaved. It all happened so quickly the eye couldn't keep abreast. Margaret got used to the overstimulation, but by then the hawk had begun to fly lower still. They flew east along the line of Strasse des Siebzehnten Junis and coasted down toward the Brandenburg Gate.

Margaret looked for her favorite monuments. There was the dome of the cathedral, fluorescent in its green copper cloak. Then she looked beyond it, off toward Alexanderplatz, but there, something wasn't right. The TV tower was missing. Where had the TV tower gone?

"The TV tower—" Margaret cried. But she could hardly hear herself—the wind was rushing by her ears.

The giant bird flew to the south now, veering away from Unter den Linden and turning along Charlottenstrasse, and as they moved even farther to the south, the high-rises at the base of Hallesches Tor were missing too. They moved into Kreuzberg; Margaret looked in vain for the Memorial Library. It was gone. She wished the bird would fly even lower so she could see what was on the site instead. But the bird was holding her altitude now. The tracks of the U1 were clearly visible from this height, although there was a portion that seemed to be dented as if a snake had flipped onto its back. The canal ran under it. And yet, where were the housing projects that should have risen up over at Kottbusser Tor? The city seemed so grey.

But Margaret saw now where they were going. Up ahead was moribund Tempelhof Airport. Margaret had never had a chance to fly into this airport before—there were almost no flights through it these days, and Margaret's many pilgrimages to the Nazi-era building had been only by bicycle, just to look around. So her spirits lifted a bit—she was finally going to see the place from above, just as she had long wanted.

In the 1930s, the building had been designed to look from above like a great eagle with wings outstretched. The press had been jubilant when the design was announced in 1936, and the architect, Sagebiel, swept the public off its feet with his much touted "largest building in the world."

The bird began to circle the grassy landing strip, coasting lower with every revolution. Margaret had the sensation of being sucked down a drain. Their speed increased, or maybe it was an illusion the earth was so near. Finally they landed lightly on the grass of the airfield.

As soon as her feet hit the earth, Margaret began to run away from the hawk-woman without a word of thanks or goodbye. But she tripped and fell into the grass, and the hawk woman caught up with her without trouble, in half-human, half-bird form. She came upon Margaret, who was still lying on the grass, and loomed over her.

"Margaret, honey," the bird said.

"What?"

"This has been lovely. But there is something fabulously important that I still need to talk to you about."

"What is it?" Margaret shivered.

"You don't have very much time."

"What?"

"You don't have much time until you have to come with me underground."

"Underground?"

"I hope you'll come at my invitation. We'd love to have you. But if you don't come on your own, I'll fetch you. I'll carry you there, Margaret."

"I don't understand."

"When it's time, I'll carry you."

Margaret turned at these words. She didn't pause. She ran toward the reception hall. It wasn't until she got to the building that she dared turn around again. The thick grass of the airfield was a-flutter, waving in the breeze that must have come up only now. There was no trace of the massive bird. And there was no trace of the woman either.

But all was not mended. Turning back toward the terminal, she saw that the building was dark. Of course, the sun had burst through the clouds again, and maybe it was just a trick of the eye, the washing-out effect of the brightness, but as Margaret got closer to the building, it still seemed dark, and half was encased in scaffolding. Even more strange, the scaffolding was made of wood. The sign Margaret had so often seen from the Ringbahn, the famous lettering that should have impressed the eye from the sky, *Flughafen Tempelhof,* was also missing.

The place was deserted. The empty reception hall glowered at her, the windows dark. Margaret pulled back one section of a fence and entered. Shouldn't there have been more security? Inside, too, everything was wrong. Half of the ceiling she knew so well was missing, and there were nothing but piles of bricks and dusty drop cloths all around, without any airline check-in counters or the usual blue and red logos to be seen. As she walked through the long hall to the other side, her footsteps clattered loudly on the marble floor.

She came out the other end. Over her head came the sound of sawing, and yells between men. She was under a mess of wooden scaffolding. Two construction workers walked the boards above her.

Margaret stood very still. The workers had not noticed her, and she was glad of it. An odd thing: they seemed to be old men, both seventy if a day. Margaret positioned herself where she could see them but remain hidden. She watched. The men moved strangely. Their pants were belted high, and also unusual for German construction workers, they wore no bright colors. The accent of their Berlinerisch, as they yelled to each other, was somehow unfamiliar, overly stylized. The melody seemed rounder and jauntier than what Margaret knew.

She ducked on tiptoe back into the reception hall and walked back to the other end. Her heels clacked. Margaret tried to bend the sound away with a lithe ankle. It was better, she thought, to avoid running into those construction workers again. But she didn't know how to get out. Already she was tired of walking, and her fear was dragging heavily behind her.

She went into a stairwell in hopes of finding an exit from the upstairs, which by some vague recollection she thought was at street level on the other side. It was dark in the stairwell and smelled thickly of fresh plaster. She wound round and round, flight after flight. Finally she came to a landing that had a window to the outside. She dashed to it, overcome by claustrophobia. But the window only looked out on a dank, concrete courtyard. She heard shouts and looked down. A group of construction workers were on the paving stones below. Or were they construction workers? Again, there was something wrong. They were in clothing like pajamas; they spoke to one another, and even from this height, Margaret could hear that their language wasn't German. It sounded Slavic. Margaret's hair was standing up now, and she slumped down against the ground, her back to the wall. But in another instant she rose again and peeked through the window a second time, her fingers shaking as she heaved herself up on the sill. This time her gaze was focused, seeking. Off to the side, in the courtyard, was a truck, and it wasn't a model from Margaret's era. On top of the truck two men lounged, in black uniforms with machine guns slung over their shoulders. And then a thought crossed Margaret's mind: *Organisation Todt.* Other than forced labor, Margaret had almost no associations with Hitler's engineers, and so now she began to be hugely afraid.

The workers spoke a Slavic language. They were from the East. And if they were slaves from the East, then that would explain the condition of the airport—unfinished.

The men in black uniforms frightened her more than the German construction workers. So back down the stairs she went, all the way through the reception hall and main building, and outside to the wooden scaffolding again. Without giving herself time to become afraid, she clacked her heels loudly so the two elderly construction workers, still up on their scaffolding, would be sure to hear her. From the wide drive where the taxi stand should have been, she yelled up at them. "Hallo? Excuse me!"

The construction workers looked down at her in astonishment. There was a long silence. Finally, one of them, the one with the beard, said to her, "What are *you* doing here?"

"I hit my head," Margaret said.

The man looked at his companion. His companion shrugged. He turned back to Margaret. "We don't like the girls from the BDM."

"What?"

"Oh—" He left off. "I was just poking fun," he called out, smiling sheepishly. And his companion gave him a look of despair. Margaret considered—BDM, those were the Hitler girls. The Hitler Youth girls. Feeling so frightened now that she thought she would pass out, she looked down at her feet. She looked down at her shoes. But she was not wearing *her* shoes. Nor *her* pants. Nor *her* shirt. Instead, a dark blue skirt, a white blouse, and a black neckerchief, and over everything, a short jacket with four patch pockets.

Very afraid now, she called up to the two men on the scaffolding, making up a lie: "I've been hit on the head. Can you tell me please, I know it's odd, but what year is it?"

"Why, little ninny *(Dummerchen)*! It's 1942."

And Margaret looked at herself, in her patriotic uniform. She thought, So it's true about me, and she felt so much hurt that when the black started rising she did nothing to stop it. She only felt a bit of the fall; the last thing she remembered was the smacking of the back of her skull against the concrete.

Margaret woke up, she knew not how much later, back in her bed on the Grunewaldstrasse. She was no longer wearing the BDM uniform. But she had a pounding headache and some dried blood in the back of her hair, where the skin broke when she hit her head. She got up, went into the bathroom and looked in the mirror.

She gazed into her face with hatred. The uniform had fit. It looked all too crisp, sharp—stunningly attractive.

The very next day she gave a tour, and when she was at Hitler's bunker, again she saw the bodyguard, Arthur Prell, talking to young people on skateboards in the park adjacent.

TWENTY-TWO · A Taxonomy of Sins

With resolve, and a pounding desperation, Margaret returned to Dr. Gudrun Arabscheilis once again. She went through the muted ivy courtyard and proceeded upward with a firm, clacking step. She would do things differently this time. She would demand a fair hearing no matter what the woman tried on her. In her bag she carried her American passport and two other forms of identification.

But when she arrived at the office, nothing was as it had been before, and her ambitions began to flounder and distort. At first the change was subtle. The stairwell simply had a different smell.

Then as Margaret came in and walked past the coatrack, the place became more unfamiliar still. In the waiting room was an intense heat. Margaret instantly began to sweat in the dryness of it. The room was very dark, and the lights glowed yellow.

At the reception desk, the dour nurse, almost hidden behind an enormous jade plant, was asleep with her mouth open. The lights seemed to give off a vapor.

Through the hot ether, Margaret could hear a sound. A great whooshing, windy assibilation of hot air and beneath it a stuttering, mechanized clack-clack-clack. The sound of a running film projector. Margaret tiptoed down the long hallway. Opening the oak door of the examination room, she was buffeted backward by the heat, the air hot and dry as in a sauna. The curtains were drawn and the room made light-tight against the dusk. It was close and musty in the heat.

On the wall next to the door, a film was being projected. Black and white; the forest scene, a boy in medieval garb with sword in hand rising out of the lake, with great scabs of light burning across it.

A sudden glimmer in the recesses of the darkness—two round Os— perhaps the lenses of the doctor's bifocals. But Margaret felt as if she had trespassed, and she withdrew and closed the door behind her. She walked back down the hall and sat on a chair in the waiting room.

She closed her eyes. The heavy heat was richly soporific, Lulled by the whooshing clack of the film projector's noise, Margaret fell asleep.

When she awoke, the receptionist was still breathing behind the counter with an even, whistling rhythm. Margaret went down the hall a second time. Now the examination chamber was brilliant with light, and Margaret stepped through the door. The old woman's skin glowed with sweat, and an album of black-and-white photographs lay in front of her on the desk. Over it, she held an enormous magnifying glass, and her ruddy, hot face hovered close to the book.

"Ah, Margaret *Täubner*," the doctor said. She did not look up. "Be so kind and give me a moment, will you?"

Margaret tried to say something acquiescent, but only grunted softly, the words sticking in her throat. She pulled at her collar. The doctor moved the magnifying glass toward the top of the oversized page, her massive head moving with it, eyes just a few centimeters from the glass. After three or four slow minutes, she spoke.

"What can I do for you, my dear?"

Margaret breathed out. "Help me."

"With what?" The doctor elongated her vowels.

Margaret was oddly unprepared for the question. She thought for a moment. "Well," she said slowly, "help me—get rid of the past."

It seemed like the sort of large-scale request to which the doctor might be able to respond.

But the doctor only went back to her photographs. She turned a page, peering again through her thick bifocals and the large magnifying glass. The room was silent.

Margaret had imagined, on her way over, that the scene would play very differently. She had seen herself stepping forward and speaking in a loud voice of her ever-increasing terror. Now she found herself cramped by the true. The cue of the room revivified the memory of her last visit, and the doctor's eccentricity rose up against her. How could she have forgotten her mistreatment at the hands of this woman? She began to feel her old anger. She watched the bulbous-headed doctor peering idiotically at the uniformly grey pictures, which, from Margaret's vantage point, looked like little grey fractals: each one randomly, differently the same. Margaret gave two loud, suggestive sighs. The woman looked up again.

"What is the trouble?"

"I told you last time," Margaret said. "My own past isn't coming. I'm drawn to the past before I was born."

"What do you see in it?"

Margaret wondered whether the woman had forgotten everything she had told her. Dr. Arabscheilis spoke much more slowly than she had last time, soberly and detached, and it crossed Margaret's mind that the woman might be addicted to some kind of prescription medication.

"I'm unable to find a place in it," Margaret said, still making an effort. "Don't you remember what I told you?"

"You have no place in the past," the doctor said slowly and without lifting her head.

"But I do."

"You do?" asked the doctor rather absentmindedly. Her face was hovering, a dragonfly of attention, over the pictures.

"Yes, I do." Margaret thought of the night she had knelt before the yellow stripe and worshiped the Family Strauss. She took a breath. "I can do all my living through other people," Margaret began. She stopped. The room was quiet. Margaret felt as though she were hoisted up, floating on the heat.

"What does it mean to you, to live through others?" asked the doctor. Again, without any special interest.

"Well," Margaret said. There was a way in which the woman's cool, slow detachment might be read as encouragement. Detachment prevented the woman from talking very much. Maybe she would listen this time, Margaret thought. She had been longing for the doctor to listen.

Margaret began to formulate what she had been thinking about as she was trying to fall asleep the night before. "Once there were people who suffered horribly," she said. "They suffered so much that all other kinds of suffering must be inside that one great suffering."

"What?" the doctor asked.

"Comprehensive suffering," Margaret said.

"What are you speaking of, my child?"

"Don't you think there must be such a thing?"

"I have no opinion," said the doctor.

"But isn't there something—about innocence?" Margaret asked. As this last word came out of her mouth, she felt ridiculous, buffoonish even.

But she pressed on. She was focused on the graves of the Family Strauss, with their waxy pillow of black ivy and rash of scarlet dots. Margaret looked at the floor, noticing in the corner the movement of falling dust.

"But sometimes," Margaret went on, "I think no matter how much I search for them and think of them, their innocence can't be transferred to me. They are so quiet. And also I wonder, is innocence even a sign of goodness?" Margaret looked at the doctor, waiting for the woman's face to move. But the room was silent.

Then the doctor spoke all at once, and when she did, her harsh voice was decisive and unyielding. Margaret jumped. Dr. Arabscheilis spoke loudly, almost making of her acerbic idea an incantation, and it became apparent she had never been absent from the conversation at all.

"Listen, comrade. I'll tell you something. Death has an aesthetic appeal, but there is no aesthetic appeal to death on a mass scale. All stories in this world are premised on the idea of character as arbiter of destiny. But these people you like to think about, they were killed regardless of their personality. So now you switch it around, you make destiny capable of arbitrating character. You want to make the victims purer by ex post facto decree, by virtue of their deaths alone." The doctor hummed a little tune to herself and looked away, her head was swaying. "But there is no link between these people and what happened to them," she said finally. "No link at all." She hummed again. "You have become sanctimonious in your obsession, comrade."

Margaret was upset. "No, it's not like that," she said. "Let me tell *you* something." She rubbed the flannel wool over her knees in haste. "The thing is—there's something else." She spoke louder, trying to pull together her courage. "It's not just the victims. The killers, too. They shadow me. She—" Margaret corrected herself, "*They* have been shadowing me for a long time, only I didn't want to mention it. They come at me—and they're disgusting, they're desiccated hawks, nauseating. But sometimes they seem intriguing anyway—like—like intelligent, righteous souls." Margaret still couldn't bear to name the name. "They want to carry me away with them. I can feel it. They want to carry me away with them, dress me in their clothes." She scowled, her face, she could feel, was bright, and her eyes were swelling. "If I don't do something, they're going to come for me," Margaret said, beginning to cough. The heat was rising in her face; the room had begun to twirl, and she grabbed onto her chair to keep from falling over.

The doctor was silent. She stared at Margaret. It was as though she thought the longer she trained her blind eyes on her, the better she would see her.

Margaret knew her own head was not right; she knew that today she was going to behave in ways suspect and irrational, but her fear was too strong now; she held on to the chair, racked by vertigo. She whispered—she did not want the nurse outside to hear—"I think I'm attracted to them."

"I'm sorry," the doctor said, overloudly. "To whom? Of whom are we speaking?"

Margaret kept her head down, talking past the doctor, her cheeks hot. Even as her vertigo grew, her only hope was to reveal herself. She must reveal the workings of her mind even if it damned her straight to hell. "To the—to *them*. Sometimes when I read their memoirs and biographies, they seem normal, and often ingenious. I imagine them moved by an emotion something like nobility."

The doctor laughed.

Margaret startled.

"Comrade, we'd all like evil to be simple and obtuse, but it's wieldy and intelligent."

Margaret looked at the doctor for a moment, but she barely saw her. "There's more," she went on instead. "It's almost as if I like them *because* they are killers. I read about them instead of the victims because it seems less painful. Just for having been killers I am hungry for them, and feel soothed by them. For that reason alone, I'm willing to follow them down any path they devise."

The doctor remained silent, her blank eyes fixed now on a spot on the upper wall as if she were waiting for something.

Margaret's voice became louder, ringing in the wide room. She was leaning forward over the doctor's wide desk, supporting herself on her fists. "But I'm lying." Her brow pulled together. I think it's something worse." Her eyes were narrow. "I notice—" she stuttered. "I notice similarities. Similarities between myself and them. I think—they might be my own kind." What would the doctor say to that?

But the doctor only laughed hoarsely. "Come, come," she said. "Is this not a sort of hypochondria?"

Margaret's face was puckered. She paused for a long moment, gathering herself together, and the clock in the room ticked louder than before. She thought: Because I am as passive as their women, and as zealous as their men. Then she wiped her head where the sweat had begun to bead, and she thought, And I am as zealous as their women and as passive as their men.

Fearing the worst, she took the German copy of *Mein Kampf* out of

her backpack. Yes, she had brought *that* with her also. She loathed herself. She began to read to the doctor in a loud, deep voice that had a
brassy quality. She was terribly upset.

"The people in their overwhelming majority are so feminine by nature
and attitude that sober reasoning determines their thoughts and actions far
less than emotion and feeling. And this feeling is not complicated, but very
simple and all of a piece. It does not have multiple shadings; it has a positive
and a negative; love or hate, right or wrong, truth or lie, never half this way
and half that way, never partially."

"Do you know what it means to me," Margaret said, "to have to live
with *those* words having been written by *that* man? What am I supposed to do with it? How am I to go on living? To have been diag-
nosed by him—he was right! This is what I am!" Margaret spoke
quickly, it might even be said: hysterically.

"Comrade. Calm yourself. It sounds like the boilerplate of any armchair political strategist. There's nothing shocking in that. Surely you
can find something more hard-hitting in that book of yours."

"It's not boilerplate *to me*!" Margaret shouted. And then she muttered more quietly: "And even if that's true, wouldn't it be significant
if we discovered his politics were just like everyone else's?"

"Comrade." The doctor knocked her knuckles on the desk impa-
tiently. "There is something you're hiding from me," she spoke in no
more than a whisper, "hiding from me very mean-spiritedly, as is your
wont. You demonstrate a marked tendency to aggravate your illness.
But we'll leave that for the moment. I see clearly, now, why you lost
your memory."

Margaret glanced up at her.

The doctor went on: "It is because you have no system of ethics."

"I'm not sure I follow." Margaret's vertigo redoubled.

"You, my pet, are having an identity crisis that has become moral
despair. It is impossible for the human animal to remember his or her
own life without cleaving a line, a line of some kind, however capri-
ciously zigzag, lazy, narcissistic, arrogant or, on the other hand, self-
blaming and unforgiving, between right and wrong, credit and blame.
Why? Because this is what makes it possible to distinguish between
nostalgia and regret. The border between the two is of pivotal impor-
tance in the formation of continuous memory. Eventually, all of us will
stop thinking back, if we don't know with what attitude of the soul to
do so."

The doctor sat back in her chair and paused, and when she spoke again it was in a louder voice. "There are pure paths that will lead you away from your troubles if you have the—the *talent* to find them. You must handle the historical idea and your own memory of life equally, like a delicate pancake you are trying not to rip."

Margaret looked at the doctor.

"I'll tell you a story," the doctor said, "and then I'm afraid you must go." The old woman with her giant head sank further into the chair. She appeared to be interested in other things this night.

"All right," said Margaret glumly.

TWENTY-THREE • Beautiful Albert

M ore than twenty years ago, my brother died," the doctor said. "But let me start even many years before that, when he was still a very promising young man; this would be in 1938. Young people were in the youth groups they had then. My brother was an unusually talented, bright young man. Very high-spirited. There was nothing he couldn't do, nothing he couldn't do extremely well. He was with the HJ photographic society, and they were in the mountains, what we call Saxon Switzerland. They were taking pictures and making films for the Youth Sports and Games Party Congress Exhibition. My brother was the sort beloved for his iconoclasm. He always could push through a new and startling idea—for a wild stunt, a fabulous show. He was also remarkable for his collectivist spirit, his indifference to danger, and his natural tendency to look out for the younger and the weaker. These were the days of *'Führung der Jugend durch die Jugend'*—in other words he was a natural leader, a lover of excitement and action at the helm of a happy, singing, strapping passel of young men. If he had a fault, it was his carelessness when it came to his personal well-being—his sweaty, relentless physicality. His indifference to pain and discomfort, and the pain and discomfort of others—it was something he simply didn't understand.

"And then there was the little issue of pyromania. He had a sort of arousal, an overweening vivacity that I often observed myself, at the mere thought of watching something go up in flames. And when he and his boys set something on fire they responded, I do not shy away from telling you, by jumping up and down, hitting their own faces with excitement and arousal.

"In any case, my brother had an idea, an elaborate vision that even in the planning phases brought him the most zealous admiration of his compatriots: he wanted to make a film that would depict the legend of a youth rising out of a lake of fire in a ring of flames, the half-human, half-god foundling child of the fire giants, Surtr and Sinmore, come with sword in hand to fight at the helm of the Wehrmacht. He chose a point where there was a craggy, romantic outcropping of rock, and a slightly higher rocky ledge upon which the camera could be perched." The doctor stopped for a moment. "Is this constellation familiar to you, my pet?"

"Yes," said Margaret, darkly.

"Good," the doctor said, beaming. "In any case, he convinced the boys of his group—and they were easily convinced, let me tell you—to trek the distance from Dresden to the mountains rather than ride via omnibus, so that he could appropriate the gasoline they would have used. He meant to set the lake on fire by pouring the petrol over it and dropping a lit match. Then, the next thing was, a boy was meant to walk backward off the ledge into the flaming lake and swim down under the water. The idea, of course, being that later the film would be played back in reverse, and the youth would appear to be rising out of the flaming depths. I myself was invited to come along on the trip," the doctor said, with a little shake of her head, her lips drawn as though she tasted something sour. "I saw all of it—unfortunately." She paused. She moved her tongue.

"The trouble, as it were, was in finding a suitable 'actor' to play the fire child. My brother felt it should be a boy of great physical beauty. Further complicating things, there were not many boys, when the day finally came, willing to walk backward into the fiery lake. My brother had only a few in mind who he felt had features fine enough to come into question, and of these, the first two bowed out."

Margaret listened. The tips of her fingers grew cold.

"There was one boy in the group, a youth of sixteen, who was very beautiful and something of a maverick for those times. He let his hair grow long in black Indian waves, bucking every tenet of his milieu. He was unusually haunting of face and charming of spirit.

"Now it happened that about this boy, my brother had some special information. He knew that his father's mother was Jewish and that his mother's father's mother was a Jewess as well, although up to this point the boy's family had managed to keep it quiet. And taking this boy aside into a glade, on the day filming was meant to go forward, my brother told him—all in the spirit of realizing his creative vision, mind you—that if the boy didn't volunteer for the stunt, my brother would have no choice but to tell the rest of the group about his mixed heritage.

"So the boy—he conformed.

"The tragedy, however, was that walking backward, and deliberately avoiding taking a strong jump away from the cliff, so as not to compromise the look of the thing when reversed, the young man, Albert was his name, did not manage to get far enough away from the edge. As he tumbled downward, because the cliff was not sheer, his neck snapped."

The doctor got up from her desk and took several steps to the side of the room, away from Margaret.

"The story does not end there. After Albert's death the fact of his partially Jewish roots came out, via an anonymous tip to the *Gauleiter*. Where the tip came from, we'll never know, although I have my suspicions; I know my brother too well. In any case, the boy's family quietly prevented an investigation into the incident, so as to prevent further misfortunes.

"As for my brother—the internet never cast a shadow. He became ever more boisterous, more hail-fellow-well-met—more beloved than ever of his peers. Our villa on the Wannsee was the scene of picnics, barbeques, boat races. The basement den smelled of cigar smoke and the meaty sweat of boys. This was where my brother and his friends had their powwows. They played darts or table tennis.

"A year later, my brother volunteered for the Wehrmacht. He was sent first to Riga. I heard some stories about his life on the Eastern Front, or behind the front, as it happened—but let's not make things complicated. The upshot is: after spending several years in Russian captivity, in due course he came home, one of the lucky survivors.

"Back in Germany, he did a bizarre thing. He made a sort of conversion. He had a strange and unexpected relationship with a bohemian, a floozy, a rabid socialist. No one could understand it. What did he want with the Marxist strumpet? Her skirts showed her hairy knees.

But I understood him. She was not so different from my brother. A theater director and "dance poet" she called herself. And in fact they quietly married, had a son together. Soon after, however, the radical woman insisted on moving to East Berlin, where she meant to be part of a new, socialist dawn. She took the child with her. My brother never spoke to her again." The doctor focused her blind eyes on Margaret, with a slightly curling lip.

Margaret felt her fingers grow colder still.

"Well." The doctor sighed, turning her head away. "My brother became a successful film director. In Munich. And although he never remarried, he gradually made a complete return to his old politics. He made a series of successful films through the nineteen-fifties, *Heimat* films, sentimental tripe, mostly, but he made a name for himself and was ultimately invited to Hollywood, where he had a measure of success once again. And then in the early seventies, I don't know what—something in the mood of the times, perhaps, moved him to make the second highly peculiar swerve of his life.

"He was invited to lecture at the film school at the University of California in Los Angeles. I believe the first lecture was there. When he came on the stage, the kids booed him because of the type of thoughtless films he made in Hollywood; he was considered very retrograde—but that's an aside. In any case, my brother, he thought back on his life and what he could show the young people, what he was truly proud of—to teach them about filmmaking. And do you know what he pulled out? The old scraggly footage from the HJ. That is, the one hundred and thirteen seconds of Albert's death.

"The film of this, the ever-so-silent film, my dear"—and she inclined her head toward Margaret—"had survived, of course. My brother saved it carefully, hiding it in a metal box at the back of his closet, with his pornography collection actually, as he told me once, not without some of his old bravado," the doctor said, in a tone of great detachment. "He showed this film, still somehow proud of his creation—with its brazen swarms of light, the fire in the lake and, moving liquidly, in the center, the young Albert himself, floating up out of the lake and across the screen in a black-and-white haze. That's how my brother described it—how it stood in such contrast of purity with the coed bunch in their modern lecture hall. That there was a pristine, Wagnerian horror-beauty to the sight of the boy in his medieval costume, his sword clutched tightly in his long-fingered hand, rising up from the fire below. The flickering of the flames twisting like lightning across the shimmering lake—" The doctor turned her head, holding it steady. She looked at where she could see Margaret as a dark shadow.

"Now finally, at this late date, in the seventies, my brother talked openly about the boy's Jewish background, his strange position in the HJ, that he died instantly when he fell. But of course, he neglected to mention his own part in the boy's death—that he had blackmailed Albert.

"But still, after he gave his introduction, there would come a hush in the hall, an expectancy—a feeling of suspense and concentration. During the screening, the students' faces were flushed and their eyes bright and slightly wet—one could not help but gain the impression that they were, well—that they were achieving release from it—from watching the boy die.

"In the months after these screenings in the U.S. there was a change in my brother. He didn't laugh all the time as he had before; he completely lost touch with his son, who was still in the GDR with his mother. He confessed as much to me on the phone, and oddly enough, he seemed to listen when I spoke, which he had never done before. Or maybe he was merely distracted, so it seemed as if he were listening." The doctor drummed her fingers on the desk, her blank eyes fixed straight ahead.

"Then he moved back to Germany without warning, breaking a film contract. He showed the footage to a German audience, this time at the Freie Universität here in West Berlin, and I attended this one, and I saw the hungry, excited look in the eyes of the young people here too, just as my brother had described it. What I remember most vividly is that he brought his cigarettes into the lecture hall with him. Even then, this was against regulations. He smoked them uninterruptedly during the screening and discussion afterward, dragging long and hard at each contact with the lips, his eyes protruding out of his well-formed skull with intense concentration. As we left the hall he continued to smoke and afterward in the car. He was deeply elated. He told me excitedly he thought the film was possibly the greatest thing he had ever done. He gave a little laugh. Then he added: 'Perhaps it's the greatest thing anyone has ever done.' He continued to show the film all around the country for a few more years, usually under the aegis of 'anti-fascism'—my understanding is that the film was read by the young people as an extraordinary artifact. I believe the idea was that they watched the film with analytical minds, taking apart the symbolism, considering it as a little piece of flotsam in the debate over the links between German romanticism and fascism. Several essays were published about it in very well-regarded journals. But that did not quite explain the strength of the crowds that turned up in the auditoriums where it was shown.

"Over time, my brother became maniacal. We fell out of contact— one year, two, three—I lost count. Then, out of nowhere, I received news that he was dead. He killed himself. It happened while he was abroad, visiting his East German son, who had defected to the States by then—a disastrous visit, obviously. All this, just as his reputation was enjoying a softer chapter.

"He left behind an elliptical, highly out-of-character suicide note, which I have always assumed he pieced together from other people's writings—it was plagiarized, I believe, mostly from the letters he received from the university students, but it was unsettling to me nonetheless. It ran to forty-five pages. He wrote, among other things: 'I can no longer live with my love of the sublime. What are we, what sort of animal is man, that even our elite feeds off the slaughter of the most beautiful among us to satiate its aesthetic needs?'

"He went on to defend himself and his followers, drawing a parallel between Christianity—a religion built around the gruesome crucifixion of the 'lamb of God'—and the religiosity surrounding the Holocaust, which rests on the invocation of the gruesome murder of the innocent."

The doctor put her hands down on the desk. She was quiet.

Margaret could not breathe. The doctor was not going to continue. Margaret colored. Sweat raced down her nose. "But that's ridiculous. There's no connection between the crucifixion and the Holocaust."

The doctor remained silent.

"Your brother, he was jumping on the bandwagon," Margaret said. "Our culture—no—Christianity, the way it's become, it doesn't get a spiritual reward from human sacrifice—not as it's practiced now." Margaret coughed. The lights were spinning. She felt sick. "If there was interest in that movie," she said, making a grab at an authoritative tone, "it was because people crave sensation, and the spectacle of the old Nazis is something morbid that everyone wants to see." She sat up straighter, trying to catch her breath, thinking of her customers wandering around Sachsenhausen and her own loud voice ringing against its walls.

"But you," she went on after a moment. The doctor wasn't responding; she had dropped her head forward. "You—how could you show this movie to me?" Margaret said. "It's nothing but a snuff film. You called it 'the most meaningful thing ever made,' wasn't that it?" Margaret was stretching her neck up, swallowing the lump in her throat. "You were trying to hypnotize me." She left off. Her temples jounced. She found she wanted to take the tiny old woman and shake her by her shoulders until the gigantic head fell off and rolled across the floor.

And then something occurred to her. Why was the doctor casting the whole thing in such an atrocious light? Why was she making Margaret feel such shame? Margaret burst out: "But what about it? What would be the problem if the crucifixion and the Holocaust were understood the same way? Christianity," Margaret stuttered, "is a path of the spirit. Why can't the study of the Holocaust help the world in the same way—a spiritual path—if it can be that. If it can be that, then why not?" Her eyes unexpectedly filled with tears.

But the doctor came back to life and laughed. "You mean, if the sadistic torture and murder of an innocent prophet can lead to cathartic cleansing of guilt through proxy sacrifice in third parties even two thousand years hence, then why can't the more recent murder of six million European Jews have exactly the same effect? Remember what we are talking about, my dear: the death of *Jews* at the hands of those claiming to be redeemed by the crucifixion of a Jew. And now you want the killing of six million more to nourish the spiritual life of future generations, is that it?" The doctor tapped her fingers on the desk.

Margaret pulled her hands over her ears, and her voice, when she spoke, came out in puffs. "You've made this into a terrible thing. I know why you showed me the film. I see what you were driving at all along: you were accusing me. You think I am one of those young people in the university, slavering over the hallucination of the beautiful sacrifice. That's why you showed me the film at the beginning—to expose me as a cannibal," and the lights blinked before her eyes like strobes, and she was certain there were birds in the potted tree at her side.

Dr. Arabscheilis put her hands palm-down on the desk. She turned toward Margaret with her giant, bespectacled, golf-ball eyes.

"My dear, I genuinely had not thought of that," she said. "But perhaps," she went on, taking up a pen from the desk and making a note to herself on a pad of paper, "perhaps you *are* a cannibal. Think of what direction you are headed, comrade. Before his breakdown, when he was making *Heimat* films, my brother's back-thinking, so proud and so corrupt, was largely aimed, like everyone else's, like *yours*, my pet, at aestheticizing unbearable memory. Not *an*esthetizing— *aestheticizing*. The difference is everything." The doctor, with her white eyes, stared in Margaret's direction for several long seconds. "Let's call a spade a spade, shall we? The murder of the Jews of Europe in the twentieth century is *only* interesting to people for whom it is *not* unbearable. Interest in terrible things is always a symptom of detachment."

Margaret's face was pale. She did not speak. Then she said hoarsely, "But, Doctor, I *do* think it's unbearable."

"Precisely! You *think* it's unbearable, and that is important for your uses of it, and yet it is not unbearable to you, else you wouldn't think of it."

The doctor waited for Margaret to reply, but Margaret was silent, twisting in her chair. She coughed painfully.

"You're not well, are you," the doctor said.

"I feel sick."

"I think you've gone a bit off. But this is natural. The remnants of an ethical system are holding you back from adopting your notion of beauty, corrupt as it is. And a sense of beauty, my pet, to each his own, is the weir that staunches the flow of madness."

Margaret was silent. She pulled fitfully at the pills on her violet sweater.

The doctor spoke again. "When you first came here, I thought that moving your own life into the space directly in front of your eyes would just be a matter of brightening up your mind. I did not realize to what degree you've allowed other people's lives to hijack your own."

"But, Doctor, I've been trying to tell you that all along. I said it before. I'd like a reversal. I don't want to—whatever this is—I don't want to do it any longer. Whatever you began in me, I don't want to continue." Margaret raised her voice further. "And I'm not who you think I am. You call me Täubner every single time, but all along I've been someone else." She began to rummage in her bag. "Look, here is my passport"—and Margaret took it out and pushed it across the desk. "Get your magnifying glass and read it," she cried. "Read it! Taub!"

The woman made no move. Her shoulders were slack and her hands still. The passport dropped heavily on the table. "Take your passport? Idiot child!" she yelled. "If only I could get my hands on that jezebel of a mother you have. You're not entirely a Täubner, as we know well."

"What?" Margaret looked at the doctor.

"And I did not show you the film because I thought you were like the youth at the university, nor to make you feel yourself any sort of cannibal. On the contrary, my dear, my reasons were much more prosaic. I knew you had already seen it. I thought it would remind you of our common past."

"Our common past?"

"Yes."

Margaret sat down quickly. She looked at the doctor. She began to feel as though she really would be sick after all. Her mouth watered and her eyes too, then her ears tingled and the tips of her fingers went to sleep and her stomach lifted. She was embarrassed, her hair was cold with sweat.

She was forced to run out of the room, but she only made it into the hall, where an extravagant wave of weakness overcame her.

"Abandon reading!" the doctor yelled. "Go directly to the source. Go and meet the killers! See if they still call to you, when you see them in their stinking flesh!" The doctor's voice was getting hoarse, "And if you can find a way to join the victims without gassing yourself, then go to them too! Go as close as you can!"

Margaret was already in the WC, hanging her head. After a few moments, the nurse receptionist appeared at the open door behind her. She did not enter. She looked at Margaret with wide eyes.

Walking through the waiting room, Margaret was still queasy. It was the heat of the place, she decided. It was the heat of the place that had made her sick.

Stepping out into the cold city, she breathed the pricking air, and her nausea abated at last.

Margaret did not want to think about the doctor's suggestion of a "common past." Indeed, she pushed the Taub-Täubner opposition out of her mind entirely.

What resounded in her beseechingly, however, in the hours after she got home, was the idea that she had no right to her interest. She was a cannibal licking the bones of the past clean of flesh—she told herself this, as if it had not been the doctor's idea, but her own.

TWENTY-FOUR · The Children of Grimm

Margaret still smarted from the blow of the doctor's lurid insinuations the next day. But it cannot be said that the following catastrophe was in any way related to her grief.

She was giving a very early morning tour of the city's main attractions. Not quick to introduce himself, like a sly, lone wolf, running along behind and beside her, was a dedicated type: a young German academic. This was odd for two reasons. The first was that Germans almost never came along on the English-language tours. The second was that this German man knew a great deal more about German history than Margaret did. He was writing a dissertation on nineteenth-century Italian battle paintings: "panoramics," he told her. But walking around Berlin, he slowly exposed the many years of his youth dedicated to German military history, and this included everything to do with both the old Prussian capital and the Third Reich. He had a wide, calf-like face, listened to her with an earnest, energetic ear. He was very tall, with a pronounced version of what some people call *O*-legs, over which he wore high-waisted black jeans. A little kepi from the First World War sat on his head. "Please call me Philipp," he said to her, in excessively enunciated English.

Margaret saw quite soon that this man was one of the perennially shut-out of this world, who are so often the most knowledgeable and the most disciplined, but look unfairly ridiculous when they go out in society because they do not know anything about matters of the heart.

She moved the group down that street in central Berlin that was once called Hermann-Göring-Strasse. She felt ill at ease and exposed. The visit to the doctor had left Margaret's self-esteem in ruins, and now here was this officious man—his face thrumming like a pocket calculator, checking and rechecking the accuracy of her tour.

So today Margaret did not go into any trance at all and even made an effort not to lie.

They came to the large raked-earth building site, where the new Holocaust memorial was under construction.

The monument was almost finished now, and only a few of the concrete slabs had yet to be installed, mostly down at the southern end. The rest, in their thousands, heaved up into the morning light.

Margaret frowned, looking backward into the light from the east. The monument was equal parts Black Forest and English garden maze, cast in shades of ash, slate, and metallic. The highest blocks rose up and caught the light and glowed white like chimneys. Margaret, squinting, caught sight of a little cat sitting on top of one of the concrete monoliths, crouching in wait. But she looked again and it seemed as if it were only the white morning sun cresting a slab. She moved along the flank; the group followed. They came abreast of each long aisle, trapezoids appeared, flattened, and then disappeared as the perspective changed, each long, empty aisle a reminder of emptiness to come. It made for a visual addiction, and Margaret could hardly tear her gaze away.

She directed the group to the observation platform, gave them ten minutes to themselves, and they clambered up, obedient. Margaret stayed below. She walked down the side of the memorial, glancing absently down its aisles, as in the stacks of an outsize library.

Unexpectedly, she detected movement from inside the site. Margaret looked. It was two small children. They walked hand in hand, parallel to Margaret, but far away from her along one of the distant aisles, progressing in small but determined children's steps toward the end of the site to the south, appearing and disappearing as they went behind the blocks and reemerged again, two small people, alone in a labyrinth of towering blocks—a vast warehouse of darkness and light.

In their slow progression, they were dropping behind them a stream of white—it was maybe snow, maybe Styrofoam, maybe the Moscow pollen of poplar trees—Margaret couldn't guess. In any case, the cottony white blanketed the ground behind them as they walked and marked their narrow path. The figures, so brave and so young in their earnest trajectory, were in shadow, disappearing and reappearing behind the pillars.

At first they walked slowly. Then, still hand in hand, they began to run, faster and faster. Soon they lost hold of each other's hands, and in their desperation ran increasingly apart from each other, losing each other in the maze. Margaret, trying to keep up a view, ran along the side, her shoelace untied and her wet pant cuffs flapping. Now it was the taller child coming closer to her as the smaller one got farther away. Margaret could hear—a small, frail voice. As the child neared she could see its hair—it was grey. The child was falling and stumbling now on the rough earth; the other one was vanished. And then Margaret could see—almost, at least, for her view was partly obstructed by one of the stone pillars—as the larger child fell into one of the empty holes.

Margaret cut in to the memorial and ran to the empty grave.

She looked down inside it. The child was not there, and not at the next, and not in the next after that. Margaret, breathing heavily, sat down at the foot of one of the blocks beside a yawning, waiting hole.

She sat several minutes. She could not seem to collect herself.

She went back out, finally. She almost collided with the German student, Philipp. He took hold of her arm. He touched her with an awkward, formal gesture that was at the same time far too intimate. It made Margaret queasy. She wrenched her arm away.

Gathering the customers together, she led them around the corner to the site of Hitler's bunker. She had gathered her wits somewhat, but still the Communist apartment complex in front of her in flesh form looked almost like chanterelle mushrooms.

"The first thing you'll notice here is that there's nothing to notice," Margaret began, looking down at the tarmac. "But directly under our feet, Hitler's bunker is sinking deeper into the earth."

Some people took out their digital cameras.

"Hitler moved into the bunker in the middle of March 1945 and was far from lonely here," Margaret said, still breathing hard. "The twenty-room bunker was occupied by his dog, Blondi, the puppies she gave birth to during this time, his vegetarian cook, his three female secretaries, six bodyguards, his valet, his girlfriend, Eva Braun, come up from Munich, and ultimately the Family Goebbels as well, with their six children, who were between the ages of four and twelve. It was a rowdy life, down in the bunker, in those final days.

"Where you see the orange barrier," Margaret said, turning to gesture behind her at the entrance to the parking lot, "was the center of the bunker."

But at her turn, high up behind her, in one of the windows of the chanterelle block of flats, there she was: the hawk-woman, with her heavy brow and clothes of black gabardine. She beamed down at Margaret—sunnier and brighter than ever before—a smile for professional photographers, a rapacious smile, designed to make Margaret

cower. And then she was calling to Margaret, loudly and clearly—
"Yoo-hoo!"

Margaret pretended not to hear.

Margaret turned back to the group before her and her mouth
worked automatically. She jabbered on about Hitler's dental records.
At some point she could not help herself and looked back at the hawk-
woman in the window again, and she was still there, she with her
gleaming water-waves of blond hair, her rich bun. Magda Goebbels
was still looking down at her indeed—this woman, who was bird of
prey and rich man's wife rolled into one—with the widest and most
welcoming of grins.

"We simply *must* meet again!" the hawk-woman called. "I won't
take no for an answer!" She lifted her hands, these hands, which,
white like seashells lobbed heavenward, caught Margaret's instant
dazed admiration, and she began to wave enthusiastically with both of
them. "Yoo-hoo!" she called again. "Don't you hear me?"

Margaret turned her back. She patched together a final few words
about the bunker and asked if there were any questions. She lived to
regret it. A raised hand. "What happened to the six children?"

"Which?" Margaret asked, knowing full well.

"You said there were six children in the bunker."

"That's right."

"Where did they go?"

"Well, that's a sad story, actually." Margaret looked over her shoulder at the high window again. The cold air was blowing through the
lace curtains. The hawk-woman was gone.

"The children were given poison, apparently by their mother, and
all of them died."

"Oh."

Now Margaret looked north and saw something only a few meters
away.

The rival walking-tour company, Berlin Hikes, had a group of
tourists standing not far off. Picking his way around the back of the
group, peering now over this shoulder, now over that, was a tall, gangly old man. He yelled: *"Ich bin der Prell! Ich war dabei!"* The old bodyguard, the radio operator, Arthur Prell.

"Let's continue, shall we?" Margaret asked. She felt a wind pick up
the back of her coat and move up her spine. And let us admit that
within Margaret now, a powerful hatred was growing—a hatred for

that spry old man. She despised his saucy, challenging way, his horsey face, his reeking polyester suits.

At the end of the tour, Margaret glanced up from her wallet of tour tickets and change. The German student was still standing before her. The man who said his name was Philipp had punched his chest forward, his boyish face, astonishingly, on the verge of tears. He spoke in a low, intense whisper, his syllables clipped and short, straining with injured pride. "Margaret, why do you insist on continuing this charade?" Philipp breathed in and out through his nose, his mouth pinched in self-conscious valiance. He was like a toy soldier.

Margaret turned her head and looked at him strangely. She smiled, however, with an effort at pacification. "I don't know what charade you mean. I'm often tired after a tour. I hope you don't mind—I'll be going home now."

"Margaret. Stop. Just stop." His voice was artificially deep, and he had switched into German.

"Yes, I'll be going," Margaret replied in English.

"Margaret. I'm sorry."

"Sorry for what? Everything is fine. Just go home. It's time to go home now," Margaret said, smiling broadly, although by now her heart was pounding.

"Margaret. It's possible I was wrong—attacking, the way I did." Again, he switched into German. "You were right, what you said about it afterward. I made an ass of myself. It was not right to attack Amadeus."

At the sound of this word, *Amadeus,* everything changed. Margaret looked at him and would have believed anything at all. Even her hardest certainty disbanded into foam. "From where—how do you know that name?" she asked. Now it was Margaret who switched into German.

"Which name?"

"Which name?" she repeated, aghast. "Amadeus!" she whispered.

"Oh, be quiet!" Philipp said. "Are you trying to humiliate me?" His voice was peevish, precisely staccato.

Margaret looked harder. It was true that he had been showing an unnatural familiarity toward her throughout the tour. Margaret looked directly into his face. Do I know this man? She looked him up and down, regarding his small, glittering eyes, his button-down shirt, his black, high-waisted jeans. Philipp remained before her with his eyes cast down, his brows drawn together, his nostrils flaring with pouting rage. Finally Margaret glanced down at his shoes, which were very stylish, of dark green alligator skin with Cuban heels. She looked at them. Her heart sank slowly. These shoes—she recognized. She had chosen them for him herself.

TWENTY-FIVE •
A Lesson for Hussies Everywhere

She looked at the shoes. Her eyes made haste from the shoes, over the belt, along the chest, and back to Philipp's face. Now she saw his tight lips. This was Philipp, her Philipp. If she was not very much mistaken, this man had once loved her.

He had loved her and she had scorned him. Instead of loving him in return, she only played at a life with him, and she felt a perspiration of shame, looking at him now. She had eaten his dinners and borrowed his books, meeting Amadeus all the while. Philipp, who tucked his pajama shirt into his pajama pants at the same angle every night; Philipp, who every day waited to eat his morning egg until he had eaten his morning slice of black bread, because otherwise he might get a protein shock; Philipp, who as a man did everything exactly as he had been taught to do it as a boy—she had never loved him. Although she spent far more time with Philipp than she did with Amadeus up in Prenzlauer Berg, she was so entirely swept up in the chaos and power and irregularity of Amadeus that she never noticed her duplicity. Philipp was something that happened to happen to the shell of her, the unfortunate colonization of an underdeveloped nation.

Even now, looking at Philipp, what she remembered most was her escaping mind, how every minute of sitting near him or listening to his breath, she had dreamt of Amadeus. Even after so long, Amadeus was the siren song. A trance of memory overtook Margaret, as she hunched over her bicycle on the way home, the tall man leaving running after her in the street, his kepi from the First World War fallen into the road, and it was not of Philipp she dreamt, but a memory of the other man, of the delirium.

She could see the arching station of Alexanderplatz. She could see herself flying to meet Amadeus there.

From the station they would go to dinner, or out to a velvet bar; the night would drip, time would slow. The first glimpses of Amadeus, walking toward her on the station platform, were as beautiful later as they were the first day. It was these meetings in public places that were somehow the core of her happiness, happiness unbearably sweet.

Amadeus was always late, and it was always clear by his wet hair and soft cheeks that he had only just showered and shaved. He wore a clean shirt, usually pale—light blue or peach, with an embroidered black insignia, newly ironed. Over the fresh shirt he would wear a dark and dusty suit. The suits were ancient and worn-in, never once washed, permeated with the scent of Gauloises Rouges. He had always thought beforehand to touch himself at the corners with the products that made such an intoxicating perfume to Margaret. He put Wella hairspray in his hair, Nivea deodorant under his arms, and some sort of aftershave on his cheeks, Margaret wasn't sure what, but she recognized it when she smelled it infrequently on other men, and she had the same feeling of weakness and submission, just as the advertisements presumably promised.

Was it the foreign smells that had made her so in love? Or was it being in love that had made her adore the scent of French smoke and German preening?

His face—drove her mad. The high forehead and skin dark and freckled, the bright, bright eyes the color of lake water, ringed with black lashes, the red-grey cheeks—his face looked like Hölderlin's, but attached to the body of a man ready to die. One shoulder was higher than the other and this gave him a romantic gait; his legs were long and powerful, his chin had begun to double. The impression was of a man who had an old, sad story to tell. That was the first point. Not everyone looked to Margaret as if he represented a history of love and death. Secondly, whatever it was he represented was a cryptogram, a grotto shrine dedicated to a religion she did not understand but in which she yearned to believe. When he moved toward her in a crowd, and she saw his head disappearing and reappearing as he came closer to her, it was the ultimate kind of perception—slowed and stately and musical—as if she were the groom standing at the front of a church watching the approach of his bride, his woman of destiny, eyes filling with tears. This kind of perception happens infrequently, but if at all, then usually at the cinema. If it happens outside the cinema, then it is remembered forever. There is beauty everywhere at such times, you could cry when it comes, and the world around you resonates with one whining and perfect harmonic. Nothing can compete with so beautiful a feeling, and Margaret's addiction followed naturally.

One mild, sweet summer evening in 2000, Amadeus called Margaret and suggested that they go to the outdoor cinema in the Volkspark Friedrichshain. It was showing a Russian film. Amadeus was brusque with her. He did not mention outright that his wife was gone to visit her sister on Lake Constance, and so Margaret was uncertain. It was rare that he was willing to go to a public place with her in his own neighborhood.

"But are you sure? Can we really meet there?"

"I just told you, shnooky. I wouldn't have suggested it if we couldn't."

"But I thought—"

"Don't think."

"Aren't you worried that—"

"I'm worried about nothing." He cut her off. "There have been vacations taken by certain people. There. Does that make you happy?"

"Vacations?"

"Yes."

"Great!" Margaret said, as she understood. She began to laugh, overjoyed.

She knew how she was supposed to feel, as the other woman. She was meant to feel conniving, bitter, fiercely competitive. And sometimes, it was true, she did feel that way. But most of the time, her role as the other woman was quite different than anything she might have projected before it all began. She saw herself as completely helpless, so helpless, in fact, that her womanly status was accentuated and forced out like a pink flower blooming too early, with sadness and tragedy. She felt desperately, fatefully female, like a Titian Leda raped by the swan. And sometimes she knew it. Sometimes she would suspect, in very clear terms, that Amadeus's marriage was the single most potent source of her happiness, for it was the strong arm that took all power out of her hands. This powerlessness lent her body femininity, her love fatality.

There are two kinds of passionate love. The first is when lovers collapse into each other. The second is when one lover collapses under the other. In the first instance, two identities flow together. Oh, there are issues of autonomy to be resolved for a while. But later, after everything finds its balance, the slightest glance from the other is an encouragement, an enhancement of self, and both lovers become stronger than they would have been alone.

But this, of course, is not what Margaret knew. She knew the latter kind.

In the second instance, the crusher sucks a bit of strength from every moment in power, and the crushed one becomes crazy with desire and thirst after lost ego. While this latter type is clearly a perversion and a misfortune, it is also somehow—can you understand this?—an ecstatic pleasure for the one who is crushed. There is something about this crushed passion that suspends reality, and elevates an ecstatic trance in its place. It brings the crushed one into contact with a divinity—and the bliss, the *Rausch,* comes in awesome spikes.

The peaks of these spikes were pushed even higher by other aspects of their affair. Amadeus never spent any time with Margaret that wasn't charged with the fullest secrecy and co-conspiracy. There were no sporty walks in the woods, no vacations to peaceful, pressure-releasing locales, only the thunder of city life with its heavy, woolen veil of architecture, its gin tonics and endless subway rides under the fluorescent lights. And at the beginning of the night neither of them ever knew whether they would end up in the same bed—never once—whether the game would yield happiness, and so every single evening was full of suspense—an elaborate game of chess in which his heart was his king—she was trying to knock it over, and her intelligence was her queen that she was using cunningly, and every pawn was a glass of wine that he bought her and watched her drink, making soft contact with her knees. And when it was her king—which was the soft access to the place between her legs—that was eventually knocked down, for that was what he wanted and the point at which he considered himself the victor, she never minded. That was the release, the mysterious prize. Could this subway ticket, bought for a couple of deutsche marks in a sleeve of inebriation, longing, and electricity, be the ticket to bliss?

While she waited for Amadeus the evening of the Russian film, she read Gogol on the platform. But even after all the years of their affair, she was only pretending to read—in part because she would not have missed those first glimpses of him for the world, and in part because her heart still beat too hard. There had been times in the past when she had deliberately made herself late in order to be sure that he, instead of she, would be the one to stand forlorn and searching on the platform, but she had found that although this was a kind of victory, she had been the one to lose. Of course it was so. When she was late, the anticipation of meeting him was soured by worries that he would have already left, or that he would be offended by her extreme tardiness (she had to be very late in order to be later than he was), and most of all, she missed those sweet moments of joy when she first picked him out, as he neared her in the crowd.

Amadeus was not the kind to greet her with more than a pat on the head, a tousle of the hair. He gave her a wink and put his finger under her chin, not as if he would kiss her, but to bring her chin up.

That night they took the streetcar up the hill along Greifswalderstrasse. They sat in the overgrown park, in the Communist-era amphitheater with the giant screen. It was not dark yet, but previews were already coming on. Amadeus got up right away after they sat, having said very little to Margaret since he first met her, and went to the concession kiosk. When he came back he handed her a Czech beer and put something in a gold wrapper on her lap—an ice cream bar. He smiled at her and pulled her earlobe, whistling to himself as he opened his beer. He did not ask her whether she wanted a beer or an ice cream bar, nor had he asked her what kind she would like—almond or vanilla, Czech or German. Indeed, he never asked her such things. He had no idea what she liked. But he knew what he liked, and he knew what he wanted for her, and he knew he was paying. And in point of fact, Margaret looked up at him gratefully when she was presented with these gifts. She thought he was like the tomcat that leaves dead birds on the doorstep.

She was beautiful when she was near him. When she went to meet him she wore the perfume that smelled of freesia blossoms.

Margaret found it impossible to concentrate on the film that night, as she always found it impossible to concentrate when he was near her. All she knew later was that the cinematography had been brown and gold, that the dialogue was slow, and the film almost silent. This was the sort of film they always chose, *he* always chose.

Later they found themselves in one of the nearby beer gardens, where the honeysuckle grew up trellises. They talked for a long time about Walter Benjamin. Amadeus did most of the talking, since Margaret didn't dare say much in German on a topic that meant so much to her. Going around in life using German, which Margaret had learned only a few years before, was like walking around in high heels—although it drove up the aesthetic rush of going out on the town, it was dreadfully uncomfortable after a while, and there were certain places you couldn't go.

Later the conversation shifted to university gossip, and Amadeus said something Margaret didn't like. He said that really, but for the fact that they were so stupid and he wouldn't want them, the girls at the uni were wild about him, looked at him with doe eyes, he could have any one of the young things.

Margaret went silent. Amadeus didn't notice. He kept talking.

"What exactly does your marriage mean to you?" Margaret finally broke out. "Anything at all? Do you hate her? Do you hate Asja?" She spoke the name to hurt him. Amadeus didn't like Margaret to use his wife's name. Never had he used it himself in her presence, referring to his wife only as *"die Mitbewohnerin"* ("the roommate") or simply: "other people." If it hadn't been for a bit of detective work, looking at the last name on the mailbox at their apartment and then a series of Internet searches, Margaret might never have found out Asja's name at all. So Amadeus winced at the question.

"My God." He wiped his head. "How did we get on this topic?"

"You're thinking of getting yourself a mistress at the university, aren't you?"

"Gretchen (he called her that sometimes—always, always, Amadeus preferred the diminutive of any name), don't be silly. You know that's the last thing I want. Your demands are difficult enough, I'm halfway dead trying to keep up with you. Another woman would be suicide."

"Why do you do this to me? It's been more than two years now. I know you love me, no matter what you say." Unexpectedly, for all her happiness, Margaret began to cry. "Why do you do this?"

"Come on, don't cry. I do it because I can."

The tip of Margaret's nose turned to ice. The summer evening had grown cool, and she had only her cotton sweater. "Because you can?"

"It doesn't hurt Asja, and it doesn't hurt you. When you get tired of me you'll grow up and get married yourself. I'm not doing anyone any harm. It's just a matter of good management. Keep little wife number one happy. Keep little unofficial wife number two from getting upset. That's all. Settle down now, unofficial wife of mine."

"I'm going to leave you."

At this, Amadeus was ruffled. He shrugged his shoulders, but she could tell he was hurt. "But you'll always come back, we can't stay away from each other." He gave her a pained and serious look.

"No, I'll never come back," Margaret said, her voice thick.

"You're vicious. How you women torture me. And you Americans are the most terrible. You learn it from the oil barons. You're warmongers."

"Don't talk to me." Margaret said. Amadeus was quiet. Margaret spoke again: "I'll leave you forever someday. And when I do, it will be terrible. Terrible things will happen."

"But not now," and he threw a half a breadstick into her hair, which was curly and could catch things, and then reached to get it, as if he were drawing it out of her ear. "There now, look at that, you've got breadsticks in your ears. Why do you store your breadsticks there?"

He winked at her and laughed uncertainly, catching her eye. At last, Margaret smiled.

On Amadeus's birthday, he threw a party. He invited Margaret, typical of his munificence when it came to sharing his life with both his mistress and his wife.

The day of the party came and Margaret's heart scratched at her throat from the early morning. There was something that had risen in her like an enchanted beanstalk overnight, with a great, muscular hydraulic push out from the ground. It was a burning jealousy. She thought of Amadeus's wife, Asja—nowadays she knew a thing or two about her. The woman was also an academic. Her name had a *von* and her West German family had a large house on Lake Constance. Although Margaret sometimes thought she was as much in love with the idea of Asja as she was in love with the idea of Amadeus, she was not ready to cede him to her; she had been convinced for some time now that it was she, Margaret, that he loved, not his wife. So she planned her day carefully. First, she would go to the shops and buy herself a new dress—so that she would stun all who saw her. She repeated several times to herself, "She shall *not* look better than I." Then, she would go and have a free makeover at the French department store where they were having a promotion, and then she would go up to Alexanderplatz and pick out a gift for Amadeus at the electronics store there, and finally she would stop by a bar and get herself a stiff drink to make the arrival easier.

This was the breed of desperation that flourished throughout the affair.

Margaret did go to the shops, but it took her a very long time to make up her mind about a dress, and she fell behind on time. In the end, she chose a white canvas one that grazed her self-consciously small waist, clutching close around her self-consciously well-shaped breasts. It closed with a red belt. She went home to change into it, and in the end had to race to Alexanderplatz, where once again the shopping took longer than expected. She ended up going down a side street to a junk shop, where she picked out an antique radio in a teak case. The radio was very heavy, and she worried that its grime would get on her white dress, so she carefully wrapped it in her trench coat, and became very cold as she lugged it uphill, north into Prenzlauer Berg. In those days the trip from Alexanderplatz into Prenzlauer Berg was still through unreconstructed factory buildings abandoned like silos, and walking up the empty streets, with their slopes and brown cobblestones, she was alone. She listened to the sound of swallows. She passed leafy residences and the brick water tower that rises into view from behind a gentle hill, and she realized that with the heavy radio in her arms, she could hardly go into a bar or rather, if she did, she would attract too much attention.

So instead, her stomach rising into a collection of hasty insects, she stopped just before she got to Amadeus's fine apartment on the Winsstrasse at a Döner kiosk, where she bought a little flask of vodka from a smiling Turk. He watched her as she drank. Margaret felt very conscious of being a girl in a white form-hugging dress. She quickly finished almost the entire little bottle, right there on the street. When asked, she made up a story: she told the Turk that she was about to see her beloved whom she hadn't seen in many years; she was frightened of what he would think of her after all the time passed. He laughed. He offered her another bottle for free. She accepted, and by the time she arrived at the apartment on Winsstrasse she was quite beyond self-awareness in the conventional sense. In particular, she didn't notice the time—in her rush, she had been too quick, and when Asja opened the door, Margaret found she was the only guest—it was just man and wife at home.

With her dress and her fresh face, Margaret had been successful. She was tall, Grecian-formed. Asja was tiny beside her, blouse old-fashioned; and she wore no bra beneath it. Her breasts were visibly sunken. So Margaret, young, muscled, in her radiant white dress and upturned breasts, had trounced her opponent. But she saw right away that she had beaten her with far too rousing a gesture, as though she had raised a sledgehammer to kill a moth.

Asja, standing indifferently before her, or perhaps with only a slightly sniffy dislike, had not even bothered to put makeup on her face, and her clothes were quiet, aged, poetic, asexual. Asja, Margaret thought, managed to have more class and style than Margaret would ever have.

That was how Margaret saw it. Her yearning for Amadeus had never been divorced from her desire to live like Asja, to be just as Asja was.

The two of them looked at each other, and then all at once began to fuss, in sugar-sweet voices, over the placement of the dirty radio, an item Asja eyed for a long moment once it was put down in the bedroom.

The apartment had very high ceilings, shining parquet floors that buckled ever so slightly. These Amadeus had stripped and refinished himself. They gave off a golden glow now. The moldings around the ceilings were broad and detailed, the balconies large, and filled with hyacinths, climbing roses, dill and basil. Amadeus's study, where the party was to be held, had a large fireplace with a great Parisian mirror above it, bookshelves lining one wall, and a thick white carpet in the center of the room into which the feet sank with gratitude.

The kitchen was down a long corridor all the way at the back of the flat. This is where Amadeus was, when Asja ushered Margaret in. She said he was putting together the salad—he knew how to make a good vinaigrette. Margaret had never known that Amadeus knew how to make a good vinaigrette. She had never seen him cook in all her years as his mistress.

In Margaret's drunken state, her embarrassment was both aggravated and mitigated, depending on how you considered it. Drunkenness only allows for one emotion at a time. The emotional thrust of the drunken mind has the wattage of the sun whose light burns out all other stars. So Margaret was sunk deep inside her excruciation. On the other hand, drunkenness also softens and blurs, so she found this excruciation much easier to tolerate than she might have.

Amadeus came in to see her in the study in the blank instant after Asja left for the kitchen. If he had not been so big, and Asja so small, Margaret would have entertained the possibility that they were the same person, exchanging masks, to fool her. She tried mightily to hide her intoxication. Amadeus was in high spirits. He pretended she was not his mistress of course, saying in casual, avuncular tones, that she looked "like a model." This was colder than any unkind words. But he was quite taken with the radio, his jowls bouncing with a warm smile when she led him to it. He spent a nice amount of time twiddling the dials and pretending he knew how to fix it, as it seemed to be broken in the end, although it made a humming sound and the board lit up when the knob was pushed. After a while, he offered her a drink. He said that so far it was only the red wine that was open.

So she took red wine. Somehow, shortly after, when three or four more guests had arrived, as she was tripping gaily down the long corridor to the kitchen with the wineglass, she managed to spill it all down her white dress, in a long vertical stain the color of a pig's kidney.

She went back into the kitchen, where Asja was working on the last of the dinner preparations. Asja said to Margaret, in a voice that Margaret would never forget, "Oh, you've spilled your wine."

They looked at each other. Margaret wanted to laugh at the clarity. It seemed so keen, the rightness of her red humiliation—the scarlet, organ-shaped stain marking her brand-new dress, the obvious, quiet pride and womanly satisfaction of her hostess. But Margaret too felt satisfaction, though it only lasted a short while—not the pleasure of the masochist, not in this case at least, but rather of the eager gamester, who sees that the gauntlet, thrown down, has been registered, the challenge accepted. The show will go on. Nothing has been canceled, far from it. Asja said in the same flat, slow voice: "You must use salt, otherwise the stain will be permanent." And she handed Margaret, with a slow hand, a box of sea salt.

From then on, Margaret lost all control. She treated the stain on her dress with almost the entire box of salt, most of it ending up on the floor of Asja and Amadeus's bathroom, the little pointillist crystals bouncing merrily away. Margaret began to cry then, drunkenly, with sarcastic self-pity, feeling that her eyes were crossing, or the room was moving up and away, or her sinuses were imploding. She cried easily and without strain or shame, like an actress. She cleaned herself up and headed back toward the study, noticing on the way a handmade calendar with a snapshot of Amadeus in his youth on the month of July. This she tried to rip off for herself and put in her handbag when no one was looking, but found she couldn't detach it from the construction paper without tearing the photograph, so she left it with just the corner pulled loose. She wept to herself: You've just pulled the corner loose, he'll never come free from her handmade calendar.

By midnight she had to be sent home; she was crying openly by then, looking like a little girl, her streaming hair framing her face in tenebrous curtains. She told no one why she was crying of course, but everyone looked at her quizzically, then down into their wineglasses, then back at one another, smiles regarding their own conversations reemerging already on their lips. But Amadeus reached through the door and squeezed her hand as she was leaving. She left the cold thing for a moment in his hot grip—soft and motionless.

It was after that night that Margaret began to go out with another man: the upstanding Philipp. Chivalrous Philipp, who, when he learned of her affair with Amadeus (his love for Margaret having grown obtrusive; he broke into her e-mail account one starry night when she did not come to him), surprised everyone by going up to Prenzlauer Berg to fund Amadeus. When Philipp found him, he beat him. He raised his limp fists and punched him and kicked him several times with his green crocodile boots, until Amadeus had taken to the floor, panting, his arms over his head in a theatrical pose, frightened out of his wits but not actually hurt. For that, Philipp was too much man of his milieu. Afterward, Margaret looked at Philipp and he looked like a gargoyle. From then on she would not meet him, and there were no more breakfasts of black bread and eggs, and Margaret's attachment to Amadeus took on a renewed desperation.

As for Amadeus—troublesome triangulations with women were the stuff of his entire life. So when Philipp beat him, he howled—but resignedly, as if he had *almost* expected this to happen all along.

When Amadeus was a young man in *Gymnasium,* just cutting his teeth with girls, he had a virulent case of macho pride and a mild case of cerebral palsy. The palsy left him weak, and thus also with the sensation that he was entirely at their mercy—the mercy of women: too much man not to be spared their attentions, not enough man to be sure he could satisfy. His homunculus damaged during birth, the palsy left the right side of his body weak, and he compensated by building up the muscles on the left side, hobbling with the force of a beached swordfish that will regain the water after all. He played soccer until he fell into bed exhausted after the afternoons on the field, and he was very good at the game. He had managed that. But he never got rid of his daily physical intimidation. He was afraid of branches falling from trees when he stood under them in the summer, afraid of icicles falling from eaves in the winter, and after the Wall came down, afraid of foreigners, because their males were so often tough.

For their birthdays, he gave both Margaret and Asja escape ladders made out of rope with metal hooks at the top to go over windowsills, in case either were ever caught in a fire. He was afraid of fires. And there was a famous story of how once, late at night, on the subway with Asja, he abandoned her. A group of Russian men boarded the train and began eyeing Asja. Amadeus heard them say rude and lascivious things, thinking their language wasn't understood, and Amadeus, instead of defending her, changed to a seat where he did not appear to be her squire and kept his head forward. When she berated him afterward, he said, "Better you get raped alone, than you get raped while I get beaten." And then he laughed and laughed, until Asja laughed as well.

But all the world's dangers aside, women were frightening on their own. They had always seemed to Amadeus a prize too heavy to carry. They wanted everything, and they would suck out his hard-won strength, force him to procreate when all he wanted was to escape the tightening noose of life. When he didn't call, they cried, and then what was he to do? It was unbearable, and then when he felt like crying himself, it was unbearable, he thought he would collapse. So, early on, he had discovered that he must take control of women in order to keep women from taking control of him. The extraordinary thing was that they seemed to like it that way, at least the ones who came back, and there were several of that kind.

He had gotten into the habit already at eighteen or nineteen of having a stormy relationship with a strong and severe woman on one side, while at the same time sleeping with one or two soft and pliant women on the other. This was a habit he never broke.

Amadeus sometimes felt sorry about the situation with Margaret. But then again, who was the victim? She wasn't so weak. It was precisely her youthful strength that had first attracted him. She was very tall and long-limbed, her femurs looked like the kind of things one could use to defend oneself in time of war, solid as cricket bats, and that was what Americans were for, weren't they? Ha-ha.

Of course, it had then been a sort of surprise to discover how very fragile Margaret actually was, the young thing. And now, after the birthday party, she was fighting like an animal cornered, but again, was that Amadeus's fault? Really she was crazy, she was a *completely* insane person, and sometimes he thought that that alone was a reason to keep his distance from her.

On the other hand, from the beginning, he had never met a woman who *wasn't* insane. It was the price of sex. They seemed to be strong, women, but then all you needed to do was to begin to withdraw intimacy, and they went mad. Amadeus always did pull back—it was a double satisfaction: allowing him to avoid an appearance of weakness, and at the same time making their desire shoot through the roof, destroying their strong exterior. He liked to see them like that. *But she breaks just like a little girl.* He thought of the song. It had become an act of his personality.

His wife, Asja—he met her while he was getting a second Ph.D., a *Western* one this time, unassailable. He married her because she was the only woman he ever met who could unwrap a birthday gift and dismiss it in a single gesture, with the same haughty grace with which his mother had been able to do it, the sort of cruelty that only enhances beauty. Asja was the last child of her family, born late—in 1965—the very same year that her father was indicted for war crimes. After this father disappeared to a haven of which only certain other veterans of the Waffen SS knew the location, Asja grew up with only her mother and siblings, the mother having various peculiarities. She made the children peel the skin off their grapes before eating them and would not speak a word to them until they were done. It was things like this that made the children wary of their mother.

After Amadeus and Asja were married, they locked themselves into a strategy game of humor and ice. They were both very funny, and they were both very cold. It didn't matter that she grew up on one side of the Wall and he on the other, those cultural differences were only fuel for their loving hatred of each other. One day he would pretend he didn't hear her when she came home from work—even if she perhaps yelled to him some news, that she had been awarded, say, a coveted grant. He would pretend to be deep in his work, only greet her over an hour later. From Asja there was no exasperated "can't you even say *hello* to me?" Instead, she simply put the fresh mozzarella and tomato salad he had made for their dinner down the drain, insisting even under duress that she had never seen such a salad—her face unimaginably blank. Later they would make fun of the neighbors together and the sex would be fantastic.

But once he did not help her to the hospital when she had an attack of asthma. In retaliation, she secretly erased the article he had been writing diligently for weeks, both the copy on the hard drive and the one on the back-up disk. Then months went by without sex of any kind, or even any acknowledgment of the other's existence.

But as long as Asja was home, that was the main thing Amadeus cared about. He trusted that with her devotion to the church, she would never be unfaithful to him.

Margaret Taub, on the other hand, not a religious girl, had never once lashed out or been unkind, never done a harsh thing, never even ribbed him. Her love for him had disarmed her, she said. This was gratifying to Amadeus, made him feel the conqueror, but also made Margaret a bit unexciting. Submissiveness had its uses, but she was certainly no "true love" as Asja was. When Margaret finally did begin to turn vindictive, her claws emerging, he found his passion for her growing for the first time.

Amadeus knew that he was dependent on the lock-dance with women—deep down he believed he loved women more than life itself. What he couldn't stand, couldn't bear to even think about, was the prospect of losing any woman he had ever had. He made a point of trying to seduce each of his ex-lovers regularly, with even more dedication, not less, after his marriage. He became peeved if an ex-girlfriend left the country, or even left Berlin.

There was one night when Margaret was going to Paris on vacation, threatening never to come back to Berlin, when he completely broke down. He invited her over, exceptionally, to the apartment on Winsstrasse (Asja was away visiting "family"), and he was unable to keep his eyes off her all through dinner and kept his hands on her knees under the table, and then afterward, in the bedroom, he drank vermouth straight from the bottle and sang "I Saw Her Standing There" in such a way that it was meant for Margaret and Margaret alone, and then he started crying and was not able to stop, and then he started drinking schnapps, and pretty soon he was sobbing. He got slaphappy, insisted that he wanted to sleep with her even though he was clearly too drunk—he danced naked to the Smiths and put his head under her skirt, and then undressed her and kissed her breasts but as he was kissing them, he started crying again, his tears running the length of these upturned slopes.

Margaret was in transports.

He kept saying: "I rejected you so many times, I don't know why I did," until Margaret began to cry too.

But then the next day he wouldn't go with her to the airport even though Asja was out of town and it was a Saturday, and Margaret's face hardened and she took off the bracelet he had given her and threw it on the pavement in front of the café where they ate breakfast. Amadeus admitted to her that all the emotions he gave her were self-serving and cowardly, but he said it in proud defense. He said it was right of him—it was all he had ever meant to give to her. At least he was consistent.

TWENTY-SIX · Erich

Erich the *Hausmeister* stood across the street from the apartment house on the Grunewaldstrasse. He was hidden in the shadow of Number 54. From here he was leaning back on his heels, regarding Number 88 cannily. It huddled between two buildings more ornate than itself, but still it was apparent that Number 88 had once been a grand place to live, as Erich estimated with a certain paternal pride, although, precisely because his pride was of the paternal kind, not entirely approvingly. Number 88 was his adopted child—he would have told anyone that. The façade was covered in red brick; there were white balconies and crumbling white plaster moldings in the classical style. It was Erich who had made sure the moldings were restored after the old pattern, and he who had organized the repair of the balconies.

Now Erich regarded the building cannily. He already knew who was at home and who wasn't, but still he surveyed the windows for any sign of life. He had a grocery cart in front of him, borrowed from the nearby Lidl, and he was massaging clumps of almost dried pigeon excrement into fibrous balls. When he was sure no one was coming in any direction, and that the shadow falling on him was heavy, he lofted one of these clumps of droppings up and across the street in a tall arc, his sinewy arms surprisingly powerful, but unsurprisingly accurate. His thin, ropey arms, they *looked* as if they would be accurate. The first ball dropped down onto the lowest balcony. Erich couldn't be sure, but he thought he heard the *plop* of the ball doing what it was meant to do—that is, upon impact, splitting up into the many clumps of droppings it was composed of, so that the floor of the balcony would be strewn with the solidified excrement.

It wasn't that Erich had any ill will toward the tenants. They were nice people, always cordial when they passed Erich on the stairs. However, the Croatian couple had been resisting the installation of anti-pigeon spikes along the wide stucco railings of their balcony. They preferred to use the ledge as a sort of breakfast table for their coffee tray in the summers and as a place to air musty carpets in the winter. They also claimed that no pigeons roosted here, they had never seen a single one. Erich knew better. He was finding ways to convince them gently, rather than picking a fight. He felt it was important that he do this while it was still early in the spring, when they wouldn't yet think of eating outside.

After he had gone into his garden house and washed his hands, he set to work digging up the hard ground and putting flower bulbs in the courtyard. He was only putting in one bulb per meter—a minimalist look that he had seen in a gardening magazine once. It struck him as very economical.

As for the American, Erich had seen her on the subway earlier that same day. Erich almost never took the subway, preferring his mountain bike, but this had been a special trip to see his lawyer—he had had good enough reasons to hire one. Not suing anyone, not exactly at least.

He had seen Margaret right away, but she had not seen him. Typical of her. She was sitting with her head thrown back; her eyebrows drawn up in a peak of amusement; her gaze on something off to the side; her mouth in a knowing half grin. Even at a glance from the other end of the car he had recognized her—she was identifiable by the adolescent's bravely pathetic habit of believing herself to be masking best her insecurities precisely at those moments when she most revealed them with painful inanities of gesture. Look at her legs, side by side in that simpering, pinup-girl position. He had thought his own mother was a generation too late for such stylization. Margaret's body was tall, thin, and limbs gangly—it wasn't right for her to make those coy moves! She kept her shoulders hunched up so high that the blades cut sharply out of her skin. It looked like she would keel over with eagerness to please. When she got out of the train at Rüdesheimer Platz, she wobbled her head. Margaret always walked in a way that made it look as if she knew she were being watched, her arms swinging, her head bobbing up and down, winningly cheerful, like an ingénue or a nymphet.

The problem with the show, Erich thought—what made it ridiculous, *some* would say—was that Margaret's face didn't fit the part, when she was motionless she didn't look at all like a puppy or nymphet of any kind. She had a very high forehead and a pointed, knowledgeable chin. Her dark eyes, on those rare occasions when she revealed them completely, were sensitive. She should have been reasonable. Erich would not have minded being her friend.

Erich was on his way home when he ran into Margaret on the subway. At just that moment, he had nowhere he needed to be. So he followed Margaret off the train. It wouldn't do any harm to see what she was up to.

Margaret walked by the Justizkammer and Erich followed. Margaret walked and walked, and Erich followed and followed. Finally they were almost at Nollendorfplatz, and lo, Margaret went into the St. Matthias Church. Erich ducked inside as well, almost catching up as he caught the heavy door before it closed behind her.

The church was empty. Margaret, in the still, moist, cold air, knelt in one of the back pews. Erich was surprised. And then surprised to see her face in an expression broad with the laxness of despair, the way of looking when there is finally no one left to look at.

Erich thought of one of her diary entries, one he had read a trifle too absentmindedly, not really taking care to decipher it; it seemed like more of the same gushing nonsense that filled the rest of the journal, albeit a trifle more overwrought, with slightly more self-satisfied, mysterious references. In retrospect, these were easy enough to decode. He had simply lived a long time outside the society of women. In any case, he grasped its meaning now in the church, and he began to think of the large men's coats Margaret had begun to wear.

More than two years ago, Erich found what appeared to be the entire contents of Margaret's wardrobe in the trash—girlish, coquettish clothes. And once, too, he saw Margaret throw something yellow-gold out of the window and into the chaos of the neighboring courtyard. (Over there, they had no *Hausmeister*.) Later, Erich went and rummaged through the wet dead leaves and rusted coat hangers and garbage lids. In amongst, he found a simple brass key, single-toothed, as though for a piece of furniture. It had been in the autumn.

Now that he was beginning to understand, he felt sorry for her.

February 3, 2002

Oh, dear God forgive me, but I have the most wonderful, most wonderful news! Amadeus was not careful with me, and to be entirely frank, I was not careful with myself and now things have gone all the way. Oh gracious, sweet God! Let it work out and be good for both of us. I must tell you and only you, silent journal, that this was unplanned for Amadeus but not really unplanned for me. For months now I've been trying to make things happen accidentally. I don't think Amadeus suspected anything, and the second two weeks of this month have been a time of perpetual suspense. Looking out my window I've seen so many women with round bodies walking by, as if taunting me. This morning I almost killed myself biking over to the drugstore to buy a test, I didn't pay attention to the traffic at all, and a woman called out to me: *Junge Frau, sind Sie lebensmüde?* And that's the one thing I'm not, see, I'm not tired of life! But sometimes life is so alluring that in rushing toward it you rush over the edge of it, and so when I changed lanes directly in front of the car coming up behind me, it was one of those moments where I was gripping so firmly at the quick of life that I couldn't even consider the possibility that it could come to an end.

Oh, let Amadeus leave Asja, and come to us!

I'm so happy. I wonder if it will give my life meaning. I imagine it will. How nice to have something to work for. I am so good with things that don't demand that I divide my attention—I love activities that allow me to stay at home and focus on what I can see clearly in front of me. Which is such a good description of what this will be like! I'm teetering on the verge of the most perfect happiness.

TWENTY-SEVEN · The Lake of Fire

Margaret awoke the day after she encountered Philipp on the tour. Philipp in his green alligator boots, Philipp with his toy soldier's gaze—and she was sick with memory.

She did not want to think.

With exhaustion, she heaved herself back toward Regina and the Family Strauss, knowing full well what she was doing. She was finding a way to think about herself that did not involve herself and, what's more, involved finer, more gracious people.

She became something like a detective; it was an Indian summer. She looked a second time at the date of the Strauss family's suicide. She opened a clean notebook, turned to a white page. March 5, 1943, she wrote down in block letters at the top. She double-checked—the date coincided with the so-called *Fabrikaktion*—the factory action—at the beginning of March 1945, when the Gestapo rounded up Berliner Jews from the factories where they were enslaved. They were forced into cattle cars bound East, the point after which Goebbels declared Berlin *judenrein.* So the suicide must have indeed been an evasion of deportation, as Margaret had first believed.

She turned to the biographies and journals of Jewish women living in Berlin with non-Jewish husbands.

She suspended her tours and read under the feather bed at home, leaving the house only to buy cans of kidney beans and frozen spinach.

She learned a great deal.

Although officially exempted from deportation, mixed families, who were deprived of all chances of work, were on the verge of starvation in 1943. Jews were denied the papers that would allow them not only to work but also to travel, that would allow rations for meat, dairy, and vegetables. If the non-Jewish spouse did not divorce his spouse, he was in a terrible position. He was called a *Rassenschänder*—

race defiler—usually denied work, denied food, marginalized and iso-
lated as much as, or in some cases even more than, Jews themselves,
mobs sometimes being even more enraged by their own kind "gone
astray." Denunciations to the Gestapo were a daily occurrence. Mixed
families were hounded by continual visits from the police and random,
inexplicable deportations of entire families. Although the non-Jewish
half of the couple could easily divorce his spouse, the consequence was
grave—the Jewish half would be starved to death or slaughtered. In
Berlin at least, this consequence was known full well. So despite the
official exemption of mixed families, Margaret began to see very well
how the Strausses might have been driven to kill themselves.

But still the question of the children. Why, at least, wasn't there anywhere to send them? Weren't there non-Jewish relatives' homes where
the children could be sent, passed off as war orphans, camouflaged?
The question would not leave her mind.

Margaret reread her copy of the entry in the police log yet again.
This time she focused on the places of birth. *Fritz Strauss, born 11/5/06
in Gross-Strenz, and Regina Sara Strauss née Herzberg, born 11/20/09 in
Schwedenhöhe.*

She began to search. She took out her atlas of Germany. And oddly,
neither city was in the index.

She looked at the names again. Perhaps she had misspelled or mis-
remembered. But no. She went to the computer. She put Gross-Strenz
into Google and found only one reference—on a genealogical page
tracing an American family's origins—to Poland.

All was given away. Both places must be in the eastern realms lost to
Germany during the war. Margaret took out a world atlas from 1938
and turned to the pages showing the old Germany. She found Gross-
Strenz near Wohlau, a tiny place in lost Silesia, not so far from Breslau,
in today's Poland.

Then she looked for Schwedenhöhe. Today, it seemed, the place
was called Szwederowo, in what was once Posen. But in the 1938 atlas,
even after looking at Posen until her eyes ached, she found no trace.

She sat back in her desk chair. Half of today's Poland was once German. This family that with such cunning laid itself into a mute and
message-less grave to escape the Nazis—not only were they wiped
away without a trace, but both husband and wife came from towns
that no longer exist.

From the suicide note of a Jewish wife and mother married to a non-Jewish husband in 1943, Margaret copied the following into her notebook.

> Please try to understand me. I am desperate, crushed, without hope. I can't continue to breathe. I am afraid of the prison walls which await me . . . Forgive me that I leave you like this. I am powerless . . . my heart is tearing apart. I am perspiring with fright day and night.

Margaret read this. Her eyes flicked back and forth.

She would return to the Salzburgerstrasse, she decided. If there were a secret door that might crack open and let her approach them, then it would be there.

At the Salzburgerstrasse, she would look for the ghost of Regina Strauss one more time.

Having made up her mind to go, Margaret longed to already be there.

That afternoon, on her way out of the flat, she pushed her hand into the cabinet by the front door, looking for the second key to her bicycle lock. The old one's shaft had broken off, that cheaply made thing.

So this was how it happened.

As she pushed her hands about in the drawer, she found a little perfume bottle, marked on one side with the word *freesia*. Margaret's face darkened. She hoped it would not be raining outside. Where was her umbrella? The days were so dark, with all the clouds.

Over Western Schöneberg a heavy fog was floating. Margaret waited for someone to come out of the outer door at Salzburgerstrasse 8. She sat on the stoop. Her back curved with fatigue, her head she held down, her hands she tucked under her thighs. After a while there was a rain so light that although she could not feel it against her cheeks, the earth around her began to crumble with it.

The time of her life that had belonged to Amadeus was present beside her, coiled like a snake. It flushed her with a certain smell of hopelessness, a piece of moss stuck to a shoe tramped indoors—impropriety and shame. The trouble was this: she felt that the young woman who had loved Amadeus was not she—it was someone else. Or no, not someone else! But it was a character in a play for which she had only memorized the lines, nothing more than a dramatic idea she had had—an idea that she had given power over her tongue for one long, endless summer that went on for years. But it had never been more than an idea. She had been high on love, how could it have been woven into life? The sense of disjunction dragged at her, pulled her under the ground.

Finally an old woman came out of the house and Margaret caught the door. She stepped into the foyer. The light in the foyer—the soft, rich foyer—was milkier than last time. It was almost melting in the rain. Margaret looked for a long time into the mirrors at her gently doubled and tripled reflections. She looked for the ghost, she looked for Regina Strauss. But there was no motion in the mirror. The silence was strong; it hurt her ears. She moved her hands to break the stillness. The silence crept.

She went out the back door of the foyer and into the courtyard. She followed the little path that led farther into the greenery. She emerged in the back garden where the goldfish pond nestled in the high grasses, surrounded by tall juniper. All the plants whispered, rustling, given voice by the rain. She looked into the pool and saw the goldfish under the *plink-plank* of the drops; they were of the darkest orange, like strips of fire.

The rain slowed to a drizzle, and then stopped. The pond was dark, but even with the grey light of the day, here too was a reflection, and Margaret saw a bit of herself shaking in the ripples. And then for a moment, she thought she saw herself, but underneath the fish—deep underneath the fish.

A movement caught her eye. Under the water, there was a white and moving face. Pale, silken hair, and dark, pooling eyes.

The black reflection of the tree branches cut into the woman and seemed to bind her at the bottom of the pond. The flame-like fish swam above her eyes.

Margaret put out her arms and reached down in the water, deep down. She touched the woman's shoulders. She could feel the collarbone under the cold. Under the skin, the bone was seashell; it cut upward, and the woman's elastic skin contracted.

Regina Strauss turned her face up to Margaret, her neck dripping back. Her dark pupils widened into rabbit-hole mirrors. Margaret felt the understanding gaze.

Margaret leaned forward toward the little pond. When she found Regina's wet arms under the water, she was moved by instinct: she dragged them out into the air, and laid them, dripping, over her own head. She assumed the posture of a supplicant: she knelt and pushed her forehead against the muddy bank.

She bowed down to the water.

She bowed down to Regina.

She prayed to Regina, to the woman who was near.

And then she began to hear a sound, rising out of the water. She put her ear toward it. She heard a moan; she heard the woman's voice crying out three-dimensionally. She could hear the voice, thick with bubbles, and she submerged her ear to listen as it gradually became intelligible. Regina was speaking quickly.

TWENTY-EIGHT · Dreams During Illness

Listen, Margaret, listen. When it first started I began to say to Franz, lying beside him at night, "We're pressed so! If we were made of carbon, we'd already be squeezed into diamonds"—making light of it, you see. And he would kiss my hand, call me "my diamond." Now that it's all over, here we are, it's come to pass: We've flown up. We've come and gone. We're diamonds of the night sky.

I came from Posen. I came from Posen to the big city. I came to my husband, we were married, we had a child, and when the government changed, I took refuge in a new church, the church that would save me but did not.

Where to start the story of how things went wrong? It began much earlier, but I'll start in the summer of 1939, as that is when, for me at least, our death began seeping in.

Nineteen thirty-nine we got a canary for Rahel's birthday. She was turning seven years old, old enough to care for the bird herself, we thought, a precocious little girl. Gerda had been born that winter, I was often tired, the baby didn't sleep through the night. Rahel could use a little amusement at home. Many of her friends had left Germany already. She was at the school with the gentiles, but they knew she was of mixed birth, and did not play with her. She was a lonely, quiet child. Our apartment was often as silent as if we had never had any children.

We went to a place. You could buy birds there, on the corner of Fuggerstrasse and Motzstrasse, in a fine, stylish apartment house. The bird seller lived all the way at the top, under the roof, in a sort of garret with a winter garden built out of glass. Being on the corner and up under the roof, the place was struck with sunlight, and it was dreadfully hot, with large, blazing windows. It smelled wretched. A Jewish man by the name of Apfelbein who had been run out of business by the Nazis was trying to make a living in secret; he was thin. Officially he merely had a lot of birds that he cared for, and sometimes he gave them to his friends who wanted them as pets. If we made him a gift of some money in return, then no one had to be the wiser. In the old days before

'38 he had had a large pet shop on the Kurfürstendamm that even sold fancy-breed ponies in the courtyard behind.

We asked for Herr Apfelbein's advice, but he did not speak to us in reply, he spoke to Rahel directly, told her about birds in a way she could understand. Rahel was a shy child. There weren't many who could draw her into conversation, but he seemed to have a way with children, and soon she was speaking freely with him. He pointed out several birds in the row of cages, and she became excited. She was already quite overstimulated—it being her birthday. She liked two of the canaries. You could see why she chose them. They stood out—one was a vibrant yellow and the other a bright white. In the spirit of the occasion, her father and I told her she could choose whichever one she liked. She went back and forth between the two, talking to each bird in a soft, singsong voice, asking, "Would you like to come home with me, little bird?" She even went so far as to name them both—the white Sarto and the yellow Ferdinand. But she made no move to choose. After half an hour, we felt embarrassed—Gerda was starting to cry in my arms—and Herr Apfelbein began to look at us with interest to see what we would do.

We thought maybe, since the birds were not expensive (Herr Apfelbein was ready to give them to us for almost any price), we would buy both. Franz was still working at the time. Rahel smiled at the idea and looked at us triumphantly. I remember she had most of her milk teeth still, being a little behind for her age. But Herr Apfelbein shook his head.

"Don't get two birds, young lady," he said, addressing Rahel, "unless you have a lot of space for two cages. If you have both in one cage, one of the birds will die. Not right away, but after one year, maybe two years—one of them will die."

We looked down at Rahel, who showed no reaction to this news. She stuck her finger through the bars at the white bird and cooed at it softly.

All of a sudden, with the strict, schoolmarmish air I knew meant she was only happy, Rahel spoke. "Which one?" she said.

"You mean which one dies?" he asked her.

Rahel caught her breath and looked at me, all at once panicked by shyness.

But the shopkeeper went on good-naturedly. "That's a funny thing. You'd think it would be the smaller one that would die, wouldn't you? But it's not always the smaller one. Sometimes it's the healthier, larger bird that dies, the one with the most beautiful song, and the funny-looking runt with the short legs that lives. It's a simple thing only: the dominant bird lives."

"The dominant bird lives," Rahel repeated, breathing in and out. She was quiet for a while, and then just as suddenly as before, she spoke up. "How do you know which it is?"—this still shrilly, as if she were testing a pupil.

"You *don't* know," Herr Apfelbein replied. "That's the thing. There's not a dominant bird or any other kind of bird at the beginning. But then, when the moment is ripe, there's a fight. And whichever bird wins the fight—he's the one who *becomes* the dominant bird."

Rahel paused, thinking about this painstakingly, I could see. In the end she asked, "And what about the second fight?"

"That's precisely it: there's never a second fight."

"Why not?" the child asked.

"The bird who loses at the beginning thinks everything will be better for him if he lies low. Better he gets used to things how they are. Then he won't involve himself in any more nasty situations, lose an eye, or tear a wing. In fact, the second bird knows that the dominant bird doesn't really have a better life. They both can live well, you see. The new order is just an order like any other order. Each one has his place. An orderly birdland."

"But if you say the second bird dies, I suppose he does get hurt," said Rahel.

"Well, that's true, young Fräulein, you have a point. But like I say, you're not supposed to keep these birds in cages together. I'm referring to the ideal conditions in the wild that the birds were first used to; the conditions that taught them how to live."

"But how will it die then? Will the other bird kill it?"

"No, no killings!" He raised his voice. "I'll tell you. These birds are territorial. Do you know what that means? That means each bird needs his own living space." Herr Apfelbein caught my eye.

"And he kills the other bird in his space!" Rahel said excitedly, with a certain gusto.

"No!" the man cried out, "I told you, no killings!"

"What then?"

"Well, it's a slow process." Herr Apfelbein became pensive. "The dominant bird feels like he has to oversee the other bird—not hurt him, you understand—just oversee him. Nudge him. Peck at him while he's eating. The other bird can still eat, but probably not his fill.

The dominant bird screeches at him, sings louder songs, and sings more songs, and sings more often. Not so bad really. But the other bird—he won't be able to move about the way he wants, drink water when he wants. The strain on his nerves—that's what will kill the other bird."

"It'll break his heart," Rahel said sadly, quick to understand.

"That's right, it'll break his little bird heart."

Rahel didn't say anything more.

Franz, for his part, hadn't been listening. He was carrying Gerda around the shop and was now at the end of his rope. And can I tell you? He insisted on buying both birds after all, thinking that Rahel would be pleased with him in the end, but also eager to get out of the bad-smelling shop. Herr Apfelbein caught my eye again. He shrugged.

As you may be able to guess, I was not insensitive to the allegory, and neither, I am certain, was Herr Apfelbein. I was even interested in having both birds, as a test. It stayed with me, in any case, became a marker in my mind. There is nothing like fear to make one begin to see oneself mirrored in animal life.

The problem came with the woman upstairs, Frau Schivelbusch. She lived in the apartment on the top floor of the house, and back then we lived in the apartment beneath hers. She thought the canaries were too loud. And it was true, the canaries were unusually eager to sing, in competitive spirit with each other.

Frau Schivelbusch had been our friend for several years. Not the closest friend, but Frau Schivelbusch had an amiable face. Her eyes were wide-set and merry, her smile broad. She was a good woman. At first, the summer we got the canaries, everything was all right. She even let Rahel lead her to see the birds in the back bedroom shortly after we got them, while Rahel was still so excited. But then September came and the war began, and her son, Karl, who worked in the typewriter shop at Viktoria-Luise-Platz, signed up as a soldier right away. And while everything was going so well, Karl fell, in May of 1940 during the invasion of France. He got a posthumous Iron Cross, and she was proud; it was sent to her in a red velvet box, which she showed me, weeping. She added a lock of his hair to the box, that she had cut off while he slept when he was just a babe, and then she kept the whole thing open on the sideboard, in the dining room where she no longer entertained. The dead son had been her only child, and his father was a fallen hero of the Great War, so Frau Schivelbusch was left very much alone.

Even then it was still not so bad with the birds and Frau Schivelbusch. It really only got bad with the first air alarms, when we started having to go into the cellar together. Frau Schivelbusch had taken in a war orphan by then, a young boy of twelve. His parents had given him the Nordic name of Björn. Frau Schivelbusch must have felt pity for the child because his mother had been killed in the early bombings, before really there were any significant fatalities. So they had this in common—both their losses were early losses, out of synch with the nation, which was just then on the cusp of glory. Squeezed by the public's happy delirium, they both had no choice but to shut up—I saw that distinctly, how their Nazi friends made them hide their tears.

But Frau Schivelbusch changed after she took in the boy. She became a model of what was then called "good citizenship." I saw the lonely widow carefully sewing a giant Nazi flag as big as a bedsheet, actually partially made from a bedsheet. And Frau Schivelbusch left off talking with us, and she cupped her hand on the side of Björn's eyes as she and he walked past us in the stairwell, like blinders around the eyes of a horse. And so what could I do, I grabbed the girls' hands and pulled them out of her path. But it was a betrayal; yes, it was a betrayal.

A year passed. The birds, Sarto and Ferdinand, sang uninterrupted, in a fight to the death. In July of 1941 I discovered I was to give birth again, and I was not glad. But what could I do? Franz was so unhappy in those days, and suddenly he was happy about my pregnancy, naïve, still convinced no one could harbor ill will toward an expectant mother. And Franz also, I think, still hoped we would be granted a son. Of course, Frau Schivelbusch did not congratulate me—by the time my condition was obvious, the ordinance against friendly relations with Jews had already passed, and she, with her eagle eye, made sure that the other women in the building followed it to the letter. That winter, Franz was not allowed to perform concerts or give lessons at the conservatory any longer, and his brother, sister, and father cut off contact with him, thinking that in this way they would encourage us to divorce, not destroy his promising career. Only his mother still spoke to us, and then by post. At this time, Franz was becoming sicker with the melancholia that had plagued him since 1935.

At around the same time, I saw that the white bird, Sarto, was flourishing, while the yellow bird, Ferdinand, was losing his gloss, looking smudged, the feathers of his breast spiky as if wet. By this time the shop at the top of the apartment house on the Motzstrasse had closed, and in any case Herr Apfelbein had disappeared.

So now I often said a prayer for the bird Ferdinand at the same time I was praying for my family.

When I was already quite large with the baby in January, the Nazis made an ordinance that Jews had to give up all clothing made of wool or fur—it was all the warm clothing I had. Franz and I discussed it and we decided that since I did not have to wear the yellow star, being privileged through my marriage, I should simply ignore this ordinance. That was really the best thing—just pretend as if I hadn't heard about the rule.

But Frau Schivelbusch began to eye me, and I could see she was estimating my fur coat. It wasn't long before she had given the tip to the Gestapo—I knew it was her by her eyes. They came banging on the door. Franz went to answer with Gerda in his arms. My little girl was two years old then.

When they left, they had my fur coat and all the wool sweaters with them. The sweaters I had knitted myself.

I became sick with influenza the next month, most surely because I was always so cold, rubbing my red hands together. My ears when I came home from work every night were pink like the flower they call the bleeding heart, as Franz said, always his way to see the beauty in things. Perhaps that was what caused his terrible melancholia.

During my illness I had a very high fever, my lungs were so full of fluid I couldn't sleep, and my cough was painful like a blunt knife scraping my lungs.

In my sickbed I became more and more deeply removed from myself. My head was spinning, my soul was floating. After the days without sleep, I was somewhere far away. Thinking back on that time, I have memories, very vivid memories. For days on end, I left my body and went to some place of hallucination.

In my sickened state, my thoughts about my belly, now round with eight months of child, completely changed. I dreamt this roundness was a unit of earth burying me under the ground—the weight of it, that is. As I lay sweating and feverish on my back, I dreamt I was already buried. Or, more precisely I should say: I dreamt my body was already buried. My soul, for its part, flew straight off. As it happened, straight into the Alps of Switzerland.

As a girl, my father used to take me with him when he went on business to Paris, and afterward we would travel to Switzerland to see an old friend of his, a certain Oswald in Basel. My father was a hobby botanist. He used to say that you didn't know what it was to love a plant or flower until you had loved it in the pure sunlight and sweet clover scent of a mountainside in Switzerland, where the colors are brighter, and life a more virtuous adventure. Myself, I don't remember the scent of clover so well as I remember the mountain reek of cow dung, fresh milk, and the cheese of Gruyère, but these memories of smells are happy ones.

So in these days of sickness in February of 1942 I remember my soul floating into the Alps and coming to rest next to a waterfall on the mountainside, in heavy sunlight. I was weightless, carefree, as if all things in the dark world were very far away. I sat by the water, the sun warmed me just enough, and the rushing water exhaled a cool windiness that refreshed me, also just enough. The grass blazed green, the sky blazed blue, and the mountaintops stretched off and off into the far azure. I released my feet from my pinching winter shoes as if I had been bound in the leather for a hundred years, and my toes spread at last. I dangled my feet in the water, as I had as a girl. I breathed deeply, filled with the soaking joy that only a dream can bring.

After a while, on the bough of a fir tree standing just a few paces away from me, a canary of a bright yellow color alighted, like a dab of ochre paint.

"Ferdinand," I said in surprise.

The bird cocked his head

"Ah, Ferdinand," I said, my mood drawn down by this reminder of home.

The bird fluttered to the ground, and hopped onto one of the stones not far from me. He cocked his head at such a jaunty angle, and then he spoke to me.

"What is it you're doing here?" he asked.

"I don't know what you mean, birdie."

"You die, lady. You leave your children who are living."

I was very surprised at this suggestion that I was dead or dying. Up until that moment I had not really thought of it in those terms—I don't know how to explain. It was true I had a strong sense that my body had been buried. And yet, I did not think of myself as dead. So I went over this news of my death. I tried to examine my emotions. I found to my surprise that I felt no unhappiness, only relief. And I knew I should feel both more and less than relief, and yet I couldn't seem to gather the necessary passion.

And so I had a moment of revelation. I was extremely pleased at the discovery of the worst not having brought me any unhappiness or pain.

Realizing I was happy, I turned to Ferdinand and said, "You know, I don't mind to die."

"But you leave your children who are living," the bird said.

It struck me that Ferdinand seemed to be suggesting I had some choice in the matter. Gracious me! I thought, if I'm dead, then the influenza has taken me. What can I do?

But then it occurred to me that perhaps I was not fully dead, and there was still some element of choice after all. Now this struck me with its heavy light. In the mountain sunlight, I was silent for a long time.

The odd part was that although I felt tender and loving—not cold at all—I still felt very removed from the idea that my life need last forever, even that my life need *be,* ideas that before I had always grasped with fervor. Instead I thought: Life is not enough. Life is not enough on its own. One must also have a goodness, a place, a time, a happiness, a purity of life. Really, not having these, it is not so bad to die.

And so I said to the bird, "To die is not such a bad thing."

"But lady," repeated the bird stubbornly, "you will leave everyone behind."

Finally, with this third reminder, the bird's words struck my heart. A heavy pain fell over me; I didn't know if I would ever see my Rahel again, or my Gerda again, and a sudden ache in my breasts came for the baby I would never know. And how would the children get along without me? So I was split in two. On the one hand, I thought: I would like to be finished now with living. On the other: If only there were a way to bring the children with me.

And that is just what I said to Ferdinand.

He replied, "Go then, go and bring them all. Take them away, up into the mountains. Together, forget Schöneberg."

I considered his suggestion, quite taken aback. "All come together?"

"Yes."

"Won't they condemn me?"

"No one will condemn you."

I went over this. My mind quickly sketched out the edges of a plan. But still something held me back.

"I would do it," I said, "but I'm afraid I would never be able to recognize the moment. What if we died too early, and I stole from my children days of life, or too late, and I took from them the possibility of a soft death? I would never forgive myself."

To this the bird replied, "Just as every day is a good day to be born, so too, every day is a good day to die."

And then it was as if the reel caught on fire. The scene vanished in a half second of hot whooshing. I opened my eyes, my fever broken and my hair slick with sweat. The sounds of Sarto's twitters and songs seeped into my sick chamber from the adjoining room. Heavy curtains were drawn across the doorway. A dark light filtered through the blackout shades, meant for times of air raid, which Franz must have drawn so I could sleep. I didn't remember. But my headache was gone. The air in the room was close and motionless, smelling of dust and sour sweat.

I told myself then: Regina, you will get back into the habit of living, in order to cultivate, with cheer and strength, the habit of death.

After my recovery from the illness, the dream I had of the Alps and the bird faded from my mind, and I lost this idea that I would take my own life, bringing the children with me. I regarded the notion as a passing madness, an excess of illness's despair, and it never crossed my mind that I would go through with such a plan. However, there was a change in me. Having once been introduced to the idea that it would not be so terrible to die, I was never again intimidated by the fear of death in quite the same way. I was like the tame bear who has discovered he is stronger than his master.

As I neared the end of my pregnancy, I reached a point of near perfect inner stillness. At night I read to Rahel and Gerda until they fell asleep, looking out the window for long, empty minutes, taking aimless walks. I remember that I began to recognize patterns with greater alacrity than I had ever been able to before. Once we had rain followed by a cold snap. Afterward the trees were encased in sleeves of ice, so that the skeleton of wood glowed with an inner fire.

I saw Jewish friends and acquaintances infrequently now. Most were spending all day in faraway factories where they had been called to do forced labor. They rose before the sun and came home exhausted long after dark. I was released from this by my condition, but Franz expected a call from the Gestapo any day. He had managed to convince them, so far, that he was too ill and had too many influential friends, but this sham could only deceive so long. During the day he sat by the living room window.

I continued my work as a maid at the Tombanzens'. I should have worried over what would happen when I finally had to give birth and could no longer work there. But instead I told my baby, "Stay down below just as long as you can, little submarine of mine," and I think I remember believing that if I communicated passionately enough, the baby might shrink back down in size, stay in hiding, in my body, for-ever. These sorts of thoughts also released me from the impatience that usually accompanies the end of pregnancy.

Strangely enough, through all this, Ferdinand the bird stayed alive. It was as Herr Apfelbein had said it would be, at least in part: the bird did not thrive and he ceased to sing. But perhaps thanks to Rahel, who took such care of the birds, little Ferdinand clung to life.

At night I read to the children stories of the mountains, of the oceans, of faraway cities. After little Gerda fell asleep, I told Rahel about the cafés and boulevards of Paris, about what I could remember of the silks the ladies wore there. My girls had never been to the sea, never been to the mountains. They had never been anywhere but the sandy plains of Berlin. I read to them about Wally of the Vultures in the Alps of Tyrol, and about Heidi of the Swiss Alps, and Winnetou on the American plains. I reminded Rahel of the time before the war she hardly remembered. I always fell asleep instantly as soon as Rahel's eyes closed, so exhausted I was. But never did I consider letting go of these nightly readings, as they held my dreams gentle. Often Franz would come and sit in the chair by the bed where Rahel and Gerda and I lay together, facing away from us and looking out the window, but inclining his head to hear the story, and sometimes turning his face to meet my eyes. We exchanged a look of pride when Rahel asked one of her questions at once naïve and wonderfully precocious.

I got a letter from my sister, then still living in Schwedenhöhe, saying that she was to be resettled with her family further to the East.
Then came no more letters.

One night at Eastertime I slept poorly and woke up to the air-raid
siren. Again we would have to go down to the cellar. I noticed that the
bedclothes around me were wet, and it wasn't long before I realized I
was in labor.

Our midwife from my last births was gone from Germany—she left
already in 1939. Franz telephoned Dr. Epstein, but there was no
answer—of course in the middle of an air-raid there was no answer;
Franz rang up my sister-in-law, who hadn't spoken to us in so long,
again no answer. We went down into the cellar with the neighbors and
for a while I tried to disguise my contractions, shutting my eyes. But it
wasn't long before it was impossible for me to hide my pain, and the
contractions were closer together. Franz's face became whiter and
whiter.

We waited together for half an hour, and then another half hour.
My contractions continued. But a little later I began to realize that the
all-clear would not come before the baby. So I sent Franz upstairs
again, to again try Dr. Epstein, but the switchboard operator told him
something ghastly: the doctor was deceased. Franz called over to Sveta
Grigoriev. She said: Didn't you hear? Epstein took his own life with
veronal.

Well, the gas in our building had been turned off, but unbeknownst
to anyone, Franz went into the front cellar and turned it on again.
Then he boiled my sewing scissors, and boiled more water and
brought it back down in a washbasin with the scissors. He got newspaper for the floor. His face was so white. During my previous deliver-
ies he had always waited in the parlor. Now he held my hand. I began
to scream. The intensity of the pain was more than it had been during
my other labors and I felt sure there was some sort of terrible compli-
cation. Still no one in the room moved. The neighbors were silent,
their faces, as Franz told me later, white as snow. Frau Schivelbusch
held Björn's head against her chest, although the boy kept twisting
backward to see.

Ah, and Franz, poor Franz. Always one never to set foot in a gro-
cer's shop for it was a woman's place and not a man's, who stayed clear
of the kitchen, was uncomfortable with the sick—such a man was he.
And now here he was, with his sleeves rolled up before the cold eyes of
his neighbors, forced to deliver our child like a midwife, his heart beat-

ing, his eyes full of fear. I was so proud of him. I don't remember much of this, but after a time, in a fog of pain and sweat, I began to push the baby. What I do remember is that I was, in those last moments before her birth, happy at last to think that I would see this child. For months I had been willing her to stay inside me forever. She came out, and I cried. Franz washed the baby at my direction on the floor of the cellar, and then he put her to my breast. The child was yellow with jaundice, her skull cone-shaped from the squeezing. I put her face to my face and kissed her, and when the afterbirth came out, we improvised the cutting of the cord, neither of us knowing if we were right. We felt terribly uncertain. I thought my child would die.

In the next weeks, however, the baby thrived against all expectations. And although I never would have expected it, I too survived the birth. We named the baby Beate, a Catholic name, not wanting her to suffer as Rahel had.

To my relief Franz got a letter from the labor department soon after, and started having to go to Fromm in Köpenick. There was a factory there. It took him so long to travel, and he was not paid, we got only the ration cards. But now I felt at least some assurance that he would not be on one of the lists. He spent all day in a room with two massive ovens and a terrible heat, and from morning to night he had to shove a two-ton metal frame in and out of the oven, ruining his fine violinist's hands. Despite my protests, he shared his meat, fruit, and vegetable rations with me, as I only got Jewish rations, which did not include these things. The result was that he became increasingly thin. But otherwise, he said, how was I to nurse our child? I think it was now becoming clear to Franz that he and I would not survive the war. But he always thought our children would.

Shortly after little Beate's birth, the Nazis passed an ordinance that Jews could not have household pets, and this included dogs, cats, and canary birds. I was so tired now, I think it was because of that—I "forgot" this ordinance. Ferdinand and Sarto continued to sit in their cage in the living room, cared for with loving constancy by Rahel, who was growing up so quickly.

But Sarto was nothing if not a powerful singer, audible in those early spring months with a trill that blew like dark smoke out our windows. It wasn't long before I found a note under our front door from Frau Schivelbusch, saying in pinched phrases that it would be better for us if we were to "cease and desist to harbor beasts and fowl reserved for Aryans," as if we were keeping a zoo! I did not think I could stand another visit from the Gestapo, but I should not have busied my head. The Gestapo came anyway.

Let us simply say: they came and after they left both canaries were gone, the robust Sarto and the ailing Ferdinand. Rahel cried and cried.

What happened in the next days is interesting to me still. For a while the unaccustomed silence reigned oppressively. But! Then I began to hear birdsong again. And not only the song of Sarto, but also the song of Ferdinand.

I did not speak of this to anyone.

As I washed our ever-regenerating piles of dirty linen, I could hear it—I was still bleeding since the birth, the baby's diapers, little Gerda's wet nights—I listened to the singing birds. Sometimes it is so clear one is going crazy. I remember hearing the bird twitter when Franz told me of the first large deportations. I heard the birdsong while I listened to Rahel recite her square roots and European capitals. I heard the birdsong and I thought of my home in Posen, now burnt down in war. I heard the birdsong and thought about what could and could not be. With the sleeplessness of the baby and the ever-returning air-raid siren, waking up, shaking Rahel awake, carrying Gerda and little Bibi, as I called my Beate, downstairs with our always-ready suitcases of diapers and toys and blankets, nights spent in the basement, and then the worry, always the worry. I hardly had any sleep, and it didn't surprise me that I should be in a world outside worlds, a funny, dizzy, drunken place, a place in which birds carried off by the Gestapo return to sing inside the walls, and in the stairwell, in hidden places in the courtyard, and in the garden.

The birdsong was so fragile, so difficult to hear. One day as I was washing the dishes, Rahel said to me, "Mother, why is it I still hear Sarto and Ferdinand singing?"

I gave her the broadest smile—and looking down at her I wiped from my face soap bubbles that had floated up and stuck to my skin. I dropped to my knees and said, "My darling." And then we both stopped and stood very still and listened, and sure enough, in a moment we both realized that we could hear it distinctly outside of our mind's ear, with a sudden clarity of sensation.

And so, almost giddy with the feeling of not being crazy, I led Rahel down and out into the courtyard, and we stood at attention with our heads tilted up toward the house around us, which was in a U-shape, the two wings cradling the garden. Now it was clear enough that the sound was coming from our wing. And we both looked at each other and gave a sort of laugh because we thought the sound was coming from our own apartment. It was beautiful to see Rahel's face change with the perception. She looked up to our open kitchen window and looking back at me with her eyebrows raised. It was beautiful because I could see in her face that the world affected her the same as it did me. Even if she was only a child.

It sounded like the bird was in our flat but we knew the bird was not in our flat. We went back up the stairwell of our wing. We stood near the doors of the apartments as we went further up into the house. Finally we had passed our own floor and had come to the top, and of course it was from behind the door of Frau Schivelbusch's apartment that the sound of canaries trickled.

So Frau Schivelbusch had the canaries.

It was very difficult to calm Rahel once we realized what had happened. The little girl was beside herself. She wanted to go up to Frau Schivelbusch at once and kick in her door. I reasoned with her, explaining that we were unlucky to live in these times, that we had to do our best to hold on to our dignity, and didn't she want to grow up to be a dignified lady? But even I was not convinced. I wondered if I was not destroying her.

As for me. There came a time when the choir I sang with at the cathedral protested my presence, even if I stood in the back, although my conversion to Catholicism was many years past. Father Loewe asked me to leave, and then, after that, I ask you, what more could I do to preserve my faith? What of my hope for the future?

There were some days during the months when I was planning our death when I didn't suffer at all. That's a funny thing: you domesticate fear. I only cried in anticipation of the worst, but somehow during the worst itself, I only thought about this or that part of now. It was through a series of very soft, gradual changes that I became accustomed to a new trajectory for my life and the lives of my children.

When I was young I had thought I would live with a family, a community, someday likely have grandchildren. Now I did not have these ambitions any longer. Instead I thought, Perhaps tomorrow I'll make a doll out of the red velvet of the sofa cushions for Gerda. We don't need the sofa cushions anymore. And these small things rather than the large things kept me in the habit of moving forward. And on some lighthearted days I even thought that the ambitions could be halved forevermore without a change in my moment-to-moment happiness, like the mathematical paradox of a man crossing half a room, and then half the remaining length, and so forth, and thus never reaching the other end of the room. The idea of a changed period of time for my life, once it was established, filled me with neither fear nor intense loathing—fear is rooted in uncertainty, and unlike Franz, I had no uncertainty.

I don't mean to say that's the way I look back on my life now from up here. In the nightmares I sometimes have while sleeping in eternity, I know horror, disgust, and hatred over what was done to us—and these feelings are truer because they see the tragedy in its entirety. It is with these feelings, too, that you should remember what happened.

But I will still insist that often in my daily life at the end, every change in our circumstances took on that muted quality that gently colors the life of any sane person, for good or ill. No matter how misshapen or how terrible true life becomes, it is always calmer, less emotionally vibrant than in those vivid dreams that prepared me for our death.

As for why we killed ourselves the way we did: we thought better to die like the canary than to die like the hunted. Every day is a good day to be born, every day is a good day to die.

From those years, what I remember most is our picture book, *Du Mein Tirol,* with the photographs of the fresh alpine air, and the thickness of the grass on the mountainside. The sound of the waterfall, the smell of cow dung.

When Margaret woke, she was lying on the ground next to the goldfish pond at Salzburgerstrasse 8. The hair on her head was matted and wet.

She had been so deeply concentrated for so many hours, her body had gone lost. The fatigue, the limpness, that comes of such concentration broke over her. She sat up very slowly. Her face was ashen. She felt as though there was less oxygen in the air than there had been before, and her throat was full of lumps.

After she got home, she went around for a while as if nothing had happened. She was terribly hungry. She opened a can of kidney beans and another of peeled tomatoes and dropped them into a pot. The apartment around her smelled of old musty carpets; the smell reached her sharply. She chopped onions and fried them. She browned a fist of hamburger. She glanced under the toaster as she searched for the wooden spoon. She saw the crumbs there. She added the meat to the pot. Looking down into it, she felt a nausea.

She left the food simmering and went into the bedroom.

She searched through the titles on the bookshelf, Yes, there was a book called *Du Mein Tirol* in her own shelf. It was part of a series of travel picture books from the 1930s. She had bought them at the flea market for pennies. She fingered the yellowed, fraying pages.

What she had just heard in the Salzburgerstrasse, was it a communication from beyond the grave?

Or had she dreamt the whole thing herself?

She desperately wanted it to be a real communication.

She looked more closely at *Du Mein Tirol*. For the first time, she noticed that on the frontispiece of the book, the name "Karla" was written in a script both childish and old-fashioned. She looked through all the books in the series and saw that Karla had signed her name in each one. The signature was a little different in each book, and in different colors of ink, as though Karla had written each signature at a different time. The variation seemed to breathe life into the name: a rag on a clothesline animated by a breeze, the variation of the script whispered "Karla."

Margaret put the books back into the shelf. She looked out the window. She sat down on the bed. She got up and thought through the story she had heard from the beginning to the end, from the canaries, to the birth, to the grass on the mountainside.

The window to her bedroom was open, and the white cotton curtains moved slowly, swaying to their own dirge. Something about the movement of the curtains made her think of her life with the hawkwoman, Magda Goebbels. A very slight shudder ran through her. Regina Strauss's voice—how could she be sure of the sound of it? Had it really been her? She could not help but recognize the presence in that story of a book she owned. It made the entire thing suspicious. Perhaps it had all been her own madness. Now, in her mind, the sound of the woman's voice was filled with a crackling, obstructing static. The static obstruction that was Margaret's life.

And there had been more than one such trace of her own life.

But Margaret wanted it to be a real communication from beyond the grave. The desire rose in her, very hard and very strong, steam-rolling her consciousness. She put her head on the desk and strained to remember one last detail of the story, the detail that could not possibly be invented, the detail that would be both the proof and the borrowed rib to make them breathe.

Instead, all at once and without warning, she began to cry. She cried and cried. Margaret cried because she could not remember any such detail. She cried because their lives had been stolen then and forever. She cried for what had happened in her own night's yard, for the dep-rivation. She cried because their lives had been thrown away sense-lessly and they had no memory except this moribund memory she had lent to them herself.

She cried. She had water coming out her mouth and nose. The sobs began to rack her as though she were being shaken by a foreign body—a three-hundred-pound angel come to beat her into submis-sion. The effort of holding her body upright at the desk, her white fin-gers gripping the polished wood, took all her strength.

There was a vacancy like hunger in her chest—the desire to give herself to them by believing. Isn't that all that's left to give the dead? What a slight gift. But no, she thought, it's not slight. (This was a wail, heartbroken rage.) Anybody on the street—if you ask: Would you like to be remembered after you die?—the answer will always be yes. Immortality is desired more than food and air. It is not so terrible to assume no one wants to die. The Strausses should be real, she thought, and they should have a mind wrapped uncritically around them in an embrace, a mind that doesn't panic—so they won't have to scrounge or connive in lust or anger—someone giving their lives the floating, crys-talline perfection of angels riding on white horses above the waves of this worldly storm—someone to catch them in a net!, her heart screamed. I will catch them in a net, and even if the thing in the net is nothing but a cipher, the net will be real, and the net will be beautiful.

How she longed to hear the voice of Regina Strauss again, if only for a moment. This was her longing now. The voice was the meaning, the voice was the ghost.

Margaret recognized a ghost for what it was: a ghost is the resonance of a life. A ghost is the intense and prolonged sympathetic vibration for the dead in the world of the living. A ghost is something in which everyone can and must believe.

Margaret drank a glass of water. She breathed in and out. She looked at the blue glass in her hand. There were many tiny air bubbles caught in the glass. The water, too, was full of points of light. The movement of water from the blue glass to the muddy pink flesh of Margaret's throat occurred to her as something significant and great, and in a wave of happiness, she ate some thick bread with pieces of carrot in it; she cut up a tomato and ate that too, and then she drank more water. Her head was clearing at the pace of a tide, at the pace of the sun moving across the sky.

She felt clean—the tears still wet on her face were made of the salt and water of her body, a body that was—finally—not entirely bad, a body that was full of concern and full of care.

I love them, she thought, and she realized right away that she had loved the Family Strauss for a long time. She had never allowed herself the identification, but she now recognized that it didn't matter whether she was worthy of it, it was still there—this love that made her eyes again fill with tears.

The stew had burned in the meantime; it didn't matter. Margaret was full of joy, full of recognition. And tonight she went so far as to think that perhaps she did not deserve to die.

PART III

TUNNEL

The addiction to a center, above all to the human center, usually ends in the four-hundred-year-old cell between witness and perpetrator. You sacrifice yourself again in the figure of a black reflector. And then they have you just where they wanted you. You are the center.

—SASCHA ANDERSON

TWENTY-NINE • Iron Waves

His eyes—blue, blue, the color of lake water, ringed with black lashes. His skin: brown and pink with dark moles.

She had told Amadeus she was expecting a child.

It was late spring of 2002, and they were sitting on a bench in an overgrown corner of the Volkspark that runs along Weinbergsweg, where the earth smells of worms and poison ivy and broken beer bottles. They had just had sex in the dark, on a bench. Margaret had not allowed him to get her drunk and Amadeus could never relax when a woman was not drunk, and he had dropped all semblance of courtship. Revelers were coming out of the bars on the hill and their voices were loud, but they couldn't see Margaret and Amadeus through the thick of the bushes.

Amadeus suspected instantly that this was the thrust of a well-planned dagger. How could it have been accidental, when he had been so careful? At least, almost always he had been so careful. *Maybe* it was an accident. But he had seen the witch, the vixen, the succubus, with her hand covered in ejaculate, and he shuddered at where she put her fingers. He knew. He knew what this was, despite her play of guilelessness.

He offered her two thousand euros, an abortion, and a one-way ticket to New York City.

He was angry, this man who had never before wanted a lover to leave his neighborhood. It was not merely because Margaret was such a ruthless shrew in her destruction of his marriage. His marriage was brittle, and its existence, at this point, arbitrary. Nor was his anger because of her duplicity. What would have been the crucial point for most men, the thing that would have destroyed all hope of happiness—that she had tricked him into having a child—was not what most bothered Amadeus. He expected this kind of thing from women. No, what made him livid, turned him against her with the full force of his personality, was that she was trying to make out of their love affair a small human being.

Amadeus had *never* wanted a child, never under any circumstances, not with his wife, and not with anyone else.

There was a story one could tell, a story of a family, the mother's birth in the Ukraine followed ten years later by the grandfather's deportation to Siberia. One could tell of how the grandfather was never heard from again—or at least not until fifty-five years later when one found out he was remarried and living in Vladivostok. You could tell of how the grandmother, with three children at the time of her husband's disappearance, made her way alone to Brandenburg overland on foot with the children in wartime, how she had turned hard, when she didn't have enough to feed them. Of how since then she had not once been back to Volhynia, where she was born, where she bore her children, where her family had worked the land for five generations. Of how her oldest daughter married a certain Heinrich whose father was killed outside Leningrad; Heinrich, who fled from Königsberg to Leipzig in 1945, and never once went home. Of how at Amadeus's birth, father and mother did not react to the child. One could tell of how Heinrich stopped looking Amadeus in the face when he was nine years old, the same age Heinrich was when his father was killed outside Leningrad. One could tell of how Heinrich hanged himself in the garage—one fine day—and Amadeus found him after school.

One could tell a story of an uninsulated family. One could say that Amadeus had no desire for children because non-disappearance of people and continuity of home were lacking in the family's blood, and these are the things that make children welcome: home and non-disappearance of people.

One could ask what happens to people who never go back.

One could ask what becomes of the children of people who never went home. One could say the family had been in a lock-dance with the twin forces of death and not-coming-home for as long as anyone could remember, a dance whose steps were of the same pattern as Amadeus's relationship with women—beckon and retreat, beckon and retreat. His was the life that doesn't entirely want to live, the desire that never finds its ease, the thirst for a milk that you are poisoning even as you drink. That a family that never looks back creates a son like Amadeus—a man who looks back always, but on things painless and far away, insulates himself from knowing how close to the surface of the skin his blood runs.

Yes, one could say all of that, or one could drop the topic and say instead that Amadeus simply didn't like children and never had.

And whatever story one chose to tell, the fact was that Amadeus desperately did not want whatever was growing inside Margaret's young, non-European body.

She had caught him off guard.

When she told him about the pregnancy, Amadeus slapped her across the face. He was a little drunk.

When he hit her, Margaret looked as if she had swallowed a silver dollar; it was caught in her esophagus.

Then he offered her money. He might have wasted time doubting the child was his, but he knew about Margaret and her self-sacrificial gambits. She was too careful to accidentally get pregnant by the wrong man. He zipped up his pants and went home. He transferred the money into her account, and he made sure he never saw her again.

Margaret fell behind at the university. She stayed up late thinking of the baby and wondering what kind it would be.

She was still in love with Amadeus.

She was married to her body now. Part of him was in it. She should have thought of how to care for herself, but instead she was still staring at Amadeus in her mind, wondering when he would come back to her. For the life of her, she could not leave the city where he was.

At some point during the pregnancy, she received a letter from him. The letter told a story of her own mother and father. It was more than a lock-dance with death and not-coming-home, she thought then. It was more than a fear of children. He had never loved her, he had never even seen her. At least, this was how she understood it. Her world unlaced.

He wrote:

Dear Margaret,
    I'm not willing to meet you. Do you hear? Don't come by here like that.

I want you to listen to me. I'm going to tell you something that will make you flinch, but you deserve it. Maybe it will make you understand. You have forced me to the wall. It's something to do with your mother and father.

In 1979, your parents spent the summer in West Berlin. Your father was doing research, and sometimes they came over to the East to see his mother. It must have been five or six times. When they did, I used to go and meet them. I'd wait outside of the checkpoint at Friedrichstrasse, cool my heels on the other side of the river, trying to be a bit discreet. (Even being seen with them—Westerners, and your father a dissident— it was a liability for me. That was back when I was trying to get into the Party.) So I waited on the Northern side, under the big old copper birch trees that stand on the chalk banks there. I could see the station, and the border patrol on the other side of the river through the leaves, and the S-Bahn trains would curve in from the West. I could make them out through the trees.

I'm just trying to paint a picture for you, so you understand.

I'd sit and smoke, and at some point they'd turn up. Out of the Tränenpalast they'd be coming, looking rumpled and triumphant. Sometimes they would have been waiting in line to get through and sometimes it would have taken quite a long time.

Their clothes always looked so nice to me though, that's something I'll tell you. You could peg Western clothes from at least half a kilometer away. What a fine duet they were, your mom and dad! Sarah always with high color in her cheeks, and Christoph next to her was just as tall and skeletal and morose as ever, but a fine-looking man, distinguished, a bit of the medieval knight about him. And me, I'd feel silly—that summer we had nothing but rainy weather and I'd have wet hair, water dripping from the leaves of this damn tree I'd sit under, and my glasses would fog up as soon as we went inside. (God I love contact lenses! No more of that sort of thing now.)

Anyway, they'd come up to me, smiling, I'd get up from my bench. First I'd put out my cigarette, then I'd shake Christoph's hand. Christoph was like a brother to me, I loved him, but that summer it wasn't very good. I could tell from the first time they came over that it wasn't going to be any good. He didn't even feel like a friend—there was just a ringing sound in my ears when I tried to talk to him.

Well, but I'm exaggerating. We had a good time. He'd been gone for seven years, mind you, and seven years is a long time. That was the bulk of the problem. We were only nineteen when he got out, the lucky bastard, traded out after his imprisonment. The Stasi used to make those sorts of trades. I guess you must know this. I can't say I ever found out how he ended up in New Jersey, though, or why he went to Princeton like that. Can't say I cared very much, although now he's dead and I wish I knew.

Oh, but who cares. It's *Wurst* to me now. Better to forget.

The thing is, we were both studying Russian history, and that commonality, if you will, was pleasant at the time. By the time we'd get into my car (my dad's actually), we'd be filling up the silences by, you know, joshing each other about Karamzin, making jokes about Lermontov. Your father fancied himself a great hero of his time. We both sort of thought of ourselves that way. I'd say something like: "You should have stayed here, Christoph, if you wanted to study Russians. We have plenty here." He'd nod his head and frown in a serious way, wouldn't show any recognition that my testicles were on the chopping block. He didn't seem to take any of it in. This was the summer after the Wolf Biermann affair, and I wasn't doing so well.

I will say this: maybe we didn't pay enough attention to Sarah. Sometimes I think that was why things turned out the way they did. Women will go at your throat if you don't give them attention. The thing was, she didn't study Russian, and so she couldn't catch the jokes. There was no help for it. Come to think of it, her German was a floperoo as well.

You know what else? I think Christoph was embarrassed of your mother, of all things. What a pretty woman she was! And so young. I remember in particular that she always wore these gold-rimmed earrings. There is a certain kind of man who's embarrassed by having a pretty wife. Your father was that kind. These earrings, anyway, they had cameos of Lola Montes in them. Your father had given them to her. I really liked them on her.

I don't care what Christoph thought—as far as I was concerned, your mother was fantastic. No, she was more than fantastic. She was Christoph's prize. What he got for breaking free. Here I was, doing stinking work, slogging through theories of materialism I didn't believe in one wit, making compromises with the university administration, and there was even this man from the Stasi whom they were making me have these meetings with from time to time; I was giving him some info here and there. I was trying hard to get into the Party, as I mentioned, although I never did get in, damn them. Ha-ha. It's all so funny in retrospect. And maybe it was these ridiculous meetings with your parents that got in my way. I don't know. I'm not going to read my file. To tell the truth, Margaret, I was more cynical when I was twenty-five than at any time afterward. The wound was freshest. I already mentioned Biermann. I took the whole thing very hard.

And you know what—the fact that your mother was Jewish, or her mother was Jewish, or whatever it was—*that* was really something. The love of a Jewish woman! A damn interesting thing for a German man of my generation. A Jewish woman—never touched, never tampered with, family intact—there's only one way to look at it: it's a sort of exoneration from the inheritance. I mean, that's how personally we took things. And with fathers like ours, well especially Christoph's— why not personally? Oh, that Venus of a mother of yours, that Sarah, was the light flooding into the backseat of the Trabi after the rain. I was shy with women back then, but I kept glancing over my shoulder at her, and she would smile at me, although God, I admit it, Christoph and I were both kind of snubbing her; what can you do, she didn't know German, and she didn't know Russian.

Christoph, to hell with him, he'd reach into his bag and pull out such riches—poststructuralists, deconstructionists, all these big names. Books I could have sold a kidney and not managed to rustle up for myself in the GDR, not at that time. And then we'd be at a stoplight and he'd do that thing of his—he'd turn his face away but put out his hand, and he'd be pushing deutsche marks at me. It was great, he was a grand soul, but there was this part of me that wanted to bash his head in. How the deuce did he get the upper hand? When we were in school, I was the one with friends. My grades were even better. So how did he have the power of the gift? Who appointed him?

Oh, your mother was lovely. The thing about me is: I've never been entirely indifferent to the wives of my friends. There's something delicious about them. Women I find on my own can't possibly be as alluring. You might say there is no cathexis there.

I'm talking in circles around the hot broth. Here's what you need to know: for a few weeks that summer, while Christoph was busy with his big, important research at the Stabi, I waited outside the checkpoint at Friedrichstrasse for your mother alone. I drove her in my father's car to the apartment in Friedrichshain. Part of me would pretend she wasn't Christoph's wife. I never quite understood her English, for example. Man, she could talk to let the sow out! But at the same time, secretly, I liked her precisely because she was no stranger at all; she was like a sister to me, she was the wife of my brother-friend, Christoph (which, to be entirely honest, is part of why I got started with you too.)

As for your mother—I don't know why she did it. She said something once—about Christoph. Since the wedding night, apparently, he had been lying in bed with his back to her. Wouldn't even turn around. He said he was tired. Christoph was not thriving in New Jersey, for obscure reasons, but maybe precisely because so obscure, all-powerful. That's my sense at least. Later she told me that Christoph was in love with *me,* things like that. I don't know. Better let sleeping dogs lie. Let dead dogs lie. Ha-ha.

What this means for you, Margaret, I can't say. I realize I should never have gotten involved with you. What's done is done, and there are some pretty ticklish issues here, although—no—I am not your father, not unless your mother carried you for fifteen months. But still, I hope you'll stay away from me, and from my wife, for that matter, and handle the matter of the pregnancy as you know you must.

Friendly greetings,
Amadeus

THIRTY · The Return of the Tundra

There was a time that followed Margaret's communion with Regina Strauss. It was a time in which she knew only two things: One, she had once loved a man named Amadeus. Two, the redemption she felt in loving the Family Strauss was a relief.

She continued to give tours under flowering spring trees, and at first it was a warm time. Then, as if riding the waves of her love for the Strausses and her forgiveness of herself, memories began to come at an accelerated rate. Margaret remembered short, bright films, dreams from the missing time.

Vodka, subway rides, waking in strange beds, doctors' appointments, clothing she had once owned, and vodka again.

She began to sink deeper; she began to remember the sorts of things that are too small to be endured—the sheerest grains of sand, they fall through the cracks of any defense. She remembered the bracelet Amadeus had given her—she broke it on the sidewalk the same day; the smell between his shoulder and his neck. And her life split into two films, two films that had nothing to do with each other. She longed to let water flow over the newly remembered second film, ruin the celluloid. She was having dreams of chickens trapped in burning yards, dreams of houses built on sand washing into the sea, dreams of cruelty from strangers.

Until finally, one night, she had a dream that was worse than the chickens.

It was the worst thing of all. She had a dream of the Salzburgerstrasse—the Strauss family's last home.

In the dream, it was raining outside. The foyer of Number 14 was hushed, and the foliage pressed against the glass from the mossy courtyard, leaves and branches thick as tongues, soaked in rain. Already, everything was suffused with what was coming.

Outside, a few shrubberies and one or two puny saplings loomed lushly, deliriously so: a wall of pity-green flowers, drawing their tongues along the panes of glass in the aluminum wind.

Margaret went out to the courtyard, in search of the speaking pool, full of anticipation. She put her ear into the pool as she had done once before. All was murky. The goldfish were gone.

Beneath the water, only silence had its home. Margaret gave up at last. Her ear was cold. She went back inside, shaking droplets from her hair. She walked through the grey velvet interior to the mirror, to the place where she had first seen Regina.

The room smelled of dust. She went to the oval of the mirror and brought her eyes up.

Suddenly, the room was darker than it had been a moment before.

Margaret touched the frame and saw her fingers were shaking. She could hear a fluttering.

Oh, the shadow-woman appeared almost right away. Glowing, it moved in beside her, glowing, the woman in her faded hair and brittle, many-times-washed, starched lace collar. There was Regina, there she was, looking out at Margaret.

Regina was as Margaret remembered, only far more so. Her eyes were large and round and pooling and her glance was sweet and soft and reproachful. She was silent, and for a fraction of a second, Margaret felt herself begin to catapult on waves of the old ecstasy.

Almost right away however, the life inverted. First, it was the smell of mildew. Margaret saw something in the woman's face. There was a glint of blood. A glint of blood in her cheeks—something grasping—hope or hatred or fear, Margaret could not tell, but it was the manifestation of a quickened heart.

Margaret spoke first. "I wanted to know about—our game of Hearts." Her voice rasped in the silent room.

Regina looked to the side. She sighed. She looked around, but not at Margaret, and she flushed. Margaret repeated herself more desperately now. "Won't you play?"

Regina sighed again, strangely, cryptically. She pulled at her hair, then she shrugged, and her eyes flashed in a way that spoke of some hidden passion. She looked at Margaret and seemed to muster her.

Margaret saw something bad in that look. In a rush, as if in a reflexive gesture of self-defense, Margaret brought her arms up toward those narrow shoulders beyond the glass, and her movement was two-sided: both meant to hold Regina back from her, but also the beginning of an embrace.

Before her fingertips could touch the glass, Regina spoke, and her voice shattered the room. "I was lying, Margaret. *Ich habe gelogen.*"

In the foyer a smell of tundra rose, and then a smell like sweet grasses beginning to rot at the end of summer. The smell of herd animals and manure, and then the smell of wet, overripe clover. The room began to change; the streetlights' bulbs, aloft in their cast-iron trees, came on outside; the glass at the front of the foyer and also at the back pressed toward Margaret; the walls of green flowers floated nearer. Each cupping blossom began to spin, cups of water glinting in the light, and the water carried the scent of tundra, the scent of an old and tired buffalo lying ready to die near the water, the scent of fish on sparkling northern riverbanks that are eaten and later shat out. *Despite everything, I believe in the good of humanity,* came a whisper.

"You lied?" Margaret asked.

Regina nodded.

"About what?" asked Margaret.

"About almost everything."

And then Regina began to tell a story. A different story. At first Margaret could not hear her; she had an auditory hallucination like a loud report. She thought: Everyone is full of danger, but this one person must not be changeable, this one person is my life. Regina's white earlobes caught the light and Margaret could see little earrings on her lobes, what had once been pearls, although the globes of them had been crushed in some long-since-extinguished fury.

She had been enraged, Regina said. She had been panicked, eager, hopeless and blistering. She might have taken the children to her husband's family in the country—yes, for a time, there had been that choice.

But when she still had the chance, she and her husband were quarreling. After her neighbors betrayed her, she could no longer make out the snowy peaks and icy brooks of the Alps—no, that had been a lie, and there was no thought of reading to the children. They had barely enough to eat. And he, her husband, was vile; his mother, too—she did not send them food packages though in the country she had more for one person than they had for five, and once even, several years before—it burned Regina's mind, oh how it burned—she had flung one of Regina's dishes to the ground for its pattern of roses, a pattern that did not match the dishes she had given them. The unmatched dish "injured her eyes," the mother-in-law said. ("It was my dish," Regina said. "It was my own dish.")

Given the chance, Regina dragged her feet. She suggested first of all to her husband that perhaps she would *not* take the children to his mother's after all. Just to see what he would say. And to her surprise he did not reply. He walked meekly to the park. Later that same day he came back. He said simply: I want a divorce. He said he would take the children with him.

That night, when she sat partially undressed—she was bathing the children in a tub it had taken her much labor to fill with hot water—Franz looked at a mole on her back and he remarked on it.

And in that instant she felt under his eyes like an old and ugly and dirtied woman and a flickering came before her and her head twisted. Regina's mind threw itself against the bars of its cage with all its weight then. Outwardly she set her mouth and spoke to Franz all at once, in a strange voice she did not recognize, about how they would have coconut cakes after the war.

And her husband might have noticed her humiliation.

So when the children were breathing evenly, after her husband was laid to bed on corduroy cushions by the kitchen window where he had exiled himself—*his white face, his open mouth, the children too sweet for this world*—the branches of the naked trees tapped at the frozen glass. Regina was frightened and grasping. She was stubborn and feverish and her other chest—where was her true chest, where was her true heart?—her other chest was plugged with the thirst for vengeance, not only against her husband but against this mad and ugly world. His eyes fluttered as he slept and his cheeks were deep rose. What happened as they died, here in this house, was something like the spinning claws of a cornered bear—if you take them with you, *no one shall live.*

So together, they died.

All the gentleness in Regina's face was dissolved. As she spoke to Margaret now, all the broad wisdom was revoked.

It broke Margaret's heart.

"I barely lied." Regina breathed heavily. "I only lied about how I felt. About how I wish we had been. About the feeling within the family, about our psychic life. I did not lie about what happened. If you recall, I never claimed Franz took any part in it."

Margaret struggled to clear her mind. In fact she made an effort to correlate the details of this story with the other one. She saw this was true, perhaps not exactly, but more or less—the main difference was indeed the feeling, the emotional shades.

"But," said Margaret, her voice weak. She thought of how this new story might be taken apart; about how the variations, the fabrications, might continue in layer upon layer forever. "But can you tell me . . ." and now Margaret spoke haltingly, hoping to catch Regina out. "The gas was in the kitchen, you say?"

"I already told you. I didn't move him. For weeks Franz had been sleeping in the kitchen anyway, on a bed he made up for himself by the window. We did not get along. As for the children—they slept with me in the bedroom, but children are easy to carry without waking, once they sleep."

"I see," Margaret faltered. "What about the birds?" She shuddered. "Was that true?"

"That was true, every word," Regina said. She smiled. The way her eyes moved, it seemed she was drugged—her pupils were unnaturally large. "With one difference. After they went to Frau Schivelbusch, I did something. I broke into her apartment when she was at church, and I killed them both—strong Sarto and weak Ferdinand. And Frau Schivelbusch—*I would have killed her too.*" Regina paused. "We were not weak," she said. "We were not the kind of birds—who don't give a second fight."

Margaret cast her eyes down.

Something was happening inside her. Something that was directed not at Regina but at herself.

She felt the chills that accompany a fever. She wrapped her arms around her chest but still she was terribly cold. An involuntary refrain rose in her: *Despite everything, I believe in the good of humanity.* It was a cold, cold refrain. She thought—and now the coldness, the causticity of her thoughts grew further still—of Walter Benjamin, living just a few blocks from this apartment house, as he wrote: *"Kitsch is nothing more than art that has absolute, one-hundred-percent, immediate use-value."* She shivered horribly. To herself, she said: My love has been greedy. My love has had use-value. Her face froze in shame. The Family Strauss—she had latched onto them and used them. She had made them into the perfect sacrifice, just as—her thoughts blackened, swirling in mud—a needy world used Anne Frank, that sweet and self-complete girl, as precisely the sacrifice it needed. To have sacrificed the best, Margaret thought—that was what was craved. Old man history never gets away without surrendering up his prize roses—his hostages of myth and time.

The doctor's pronouncements had planted the seeds, and now they were pushing up. *If we find a lamb,* Margaret was telling herself spittingly, a suitable lamb, and look at it very hard, and agree as a people, as a civilization, that we have, during one long and terrible night of the soul, given up the finest thing to the devil—rendered up the dearest, most gracious, most openhearted thing to the devil, then all human rivalry will be dissolved at its acme; all guilt paid for in one stroke. The finest thing *dissolved before it can be owned.*

Margaret felt this horribly, and in her bitterness the entire thing struck her as defiled and unforgivable, as a crime of the living against the dead. And it was not even because, as she saw it now, this was why people being murdered now, in other parts of the world, are not rescued—because no one knows yet whether they are the kinds of victims that are needed: the pure, the innocent, and the humble, and so we will wait with our hands steepled, and let them go it alone, only calling them up for service after their throats are slit.

No, it was not even this that crushed her.

It was the symbolic itself. Abruptly, Margaret rebelled against—for she could not bear it any longer—innocence by proxy. She could not stand atonement through metaphor.

She looked back into the mirror at Regina standing next to her own reflected face.

"You lied to me," she said.

"I could not have lied," Regina said quickly, and in a new, deeper voice, almost a growl: "I could not even speak." Her words were slurred.

"You murdered your children," Margaret said.

There was a hissing sound. Words rose as though sizzling in fat:

"I would have cut out their hearts."

Margaret drew back. Shivers ran up and down her and up and down her sweat-drenched face. She wanted to flee—to flee for the rest of her life. It is impossible to describe how searingly Regina's words burnt her mind.

Margaret raised her arm to shield her face, but she could see the woman was changing. She was darkening, broadening, and seemed covered in fat and fur. A pelt had grown on her. And more than anything now, it was the smell of grasses. A smell of grasses in the body of a fine and splendidly muscled animal. She was taller than Margaret now, far taller—she was filling out into the most dangerously mothering animal of all—she was a brown-black member of the ursine family, a rearing bear, with paws like hands, eyes like pinecones, and mouth sweet and dandy and deadly.

Margaret covered her face.

She heard a low moan. It may have been her own.

Regina's usual delicate body—all at once it reappeared. Her face was gentle and serene, her presence next to Margaret's image in the mirror was warm and grave, a Solomon, a bearded patriarch.

"Don't cry," Regina said.

Margaret looked up at her.

"It was only a test."

But if it was only a test—Margaret blinked. And then she thought: No. It did not matter what Regina said, the wise and gentle woman was gone, and the bear had come for good. The bear was truer. The bear, if it were ever encapsulated, would not be the sugar pill.

Margaret looked in the mirror and saw a bear on all fours on the floor of the foyer, beginning to rise up again, opening its darling and terrible mouth—an ursine clown, hungry—on top of its hoisting thighs, for Margaret's life.

THIRTY-ONE • The Isolation of the Fanatic

Of course, it was only a dream.

But some dreams will not easily die. In the weeks afterward, a leftover chirring, a fly in the room, an intermittent itch on Margaret's cheek—it remained. The fly's legs chafed her consciousness like the wires of a bugging device that can be discovered but not removed.

Margaret had to find her way back to the old Regina.

A long, long time, she had occupied herself with pageants—she saw that now. Her alliances and identifications were the pseudo-involvement of the sleeping dog that moves its paws as it lies, dreaming of the hunt.

But she had to take sides now. And not take sides quixotically, but by loving the right Regina actively, committing herself through some irrevocable sign. And like so many people whose rage has too long been impotent, Margaret Taub was vulnerable to fantasies of vengeance.

One of the unstillable horrors of the Holocaust is that there is no vengeance to be had. Millions killed by millions more—there is no justice there. There will be no restitution. The victims are too many; the perpetrators are legion. The perpetrators are in every yard, in every government that provided police support, in every town that cast Jews out of knitting circles and marching bands out of guilds and pensions, starving neighbors out to the cattle cars all across Europe. Before and after it was a political policy, the Holocaust was a social movement. Not civilian cooperation but civilian enthusiasm was the sine qua non of the Shoah. A wave of genocidal anti-Semitism washed the Western world during the first twitches of modernity, and the Nazis rode the crest of it as it crashed; gave it forever a German face. But the dagger of revenge lies unused in the drawer. There is no body into which to plunge it. Margaret had been flailing against the stone-cold wall of vengeancelessness—she had been flailing against that nonsense-truth for a long time.

The dream of the bear. To herself, Margaret said it had "broken her heart." But in the days afterward, she thought she had dreamed the dream for this reason: she wished for such a Regina. She wished for a Regina who fought to kill. Not because she loved heroes, not because it would mean justice, but because she did not know how to live in a world where there was no second fight. In such a universe, she did not even know how to think.

Now—mark what happened next. In the following weeks, the dice were loaded. Margaret was stuffed to the bursting point with a heavy desire for vengeance. And if it could not be on a grand scale, then it should be on a small one. And so there came a blind spin of fortune's wheel, and when it came to a stop, the arrow rested on the only person it could have rested on. The only man who was still alive. Hitler's bodyguard, the old man in his potpourri house, Arthur Prell.

Are you surprised? But it could have rested on no other!

This is how it went. The first days after Margaret's dream, they passed slowly, tediously. It was as though, in her fascination with vengeance, Margaret was waiting for the arrival of hordes, an army gathering in the east, and she could not fight her ferocious fight until they arrived. She bided her time.

And then, slowly, she began to think of him. She remembered how, when she had seen him near the bunker talking to skateboarding kids, she had remained still, even when she had wanted to flee or destroy him. And she remembered how, behind the veil of paralysis, she had felt forced to betray her own kin.

She remembered bringing him chocolates, and this was the worst memory of all.

And then at some precise moment, it struck her that Arthur Prell was the only place, in her own life, where the past was still alive. Could he be called a chink in the armor of vengeancelessness, could he be called a hole in the shield of lost opportunity and vanished time?

One night in late April, when the evening outside wore a black and yellow cloak, Margaret looked out into the shadows. The streetlights were yellow fireballs in these days of fog, the trees were black stalagmites of wet dust. Elysian life hovered far above human eyes, and the primrose secondary maze—it was hidden. But somewhere in the darkness out there, that man was living.

She did not know what it was she was meant to do. She was only sure of one thing: the beauty of the early Regina, the one she had first imagined, the unspeakable softness of her sweet story—like the spot on the crown of the head of a newborn baby where the bones have yet to knit together—was only something she could endure thinking of if there were some vengeance to be had in this life.

Even if it was logically impossible, Margaret must have vengeance. She must mark the end of her stupefied, soap-statue innocence.

She told herself: the end of such an innocence will be something hard and terrible. It cannot be otherwise. Because if restitution were made in some more usual way, by embarking, say, upon a life of devotion or altruistic acts, she would only appear to be reformed, while in reality never bending her character, never taking a scalpel to her personality's infection, the infection whose name is passivity.

Margaret looked out the window. The air knit tight together and the fog pressed forth a drizzle. A man on the Grunewaldstrasse—in the smeary ball of light under the streetlamp, he seemed to be dressed all in brown leather. Something about his posture reminded her of Arthur Prell.

Margaret opened the window wide and put her head out into the moist night.

The horselike face of the tall bodyguard, Arthur Prell, bore down on her mind's eye, but when the man turned it was a stranger's face that called its little dachshund after it.

Arthur Prell deserved to be punished, Margaret thought. And she—she deserved to be guilty. What if Prell paid by becoming a victim, and what if she, Margaret, paid by becoming a perpetrator? Her heart beat harder. The man in brown leather disappeared down the street, gulped into the fog.

Margaret drew her head in. She turned her bright eyes on the flat around her. She had a heat in her skull. And on that night, Margaret walked around the center of the living room in a slow circle, as though she would trace a spell, or consecrate a marriage.

The night wore on and she could not concentrate, could not drink, could not stop moving her legs. The time of waiting was almost at an end now—she sensed it. She looped. Her mind worked.

She had to go back to see Prell again. And she was terrified of the visit and of what would happen there.

But it must be.

She circled. She did not begin to move straight until the next morning, when the first thing she did was this: she went back to see the good Dr. Arabscheilis.

At the doctor's office, padded walls of adrenaline buttressed Margaret. She was allowed to go directly through to the back room. She was light; she walked on water.

The doctor was in her old place behind the heavy desk.

The woman caressed the open pages of a book.

"You once offered me mentorship," Margaret began loudly. The room seemed to shudder under the blow of her voice.

Too, the doctor's head wobbled. The woman's gaze remained fixed, startled by the volume. "Who is there?"

"It's me, Margaret. Margaret Taub."

"Ah, my dear Margaret Täubner." The doctor breathed in her rasping, rhythmic way—an aural representation of honeycomb lungs.

"Doctor, I want your advice."

"By all means, comrade. Please. Sit down."

"I want to kill a man," Margaret said. "A bad person, a person whose existence is a travesty."

"My child, what are you saying?"

"I want to kill a bad man."

"Do you mean there is a dangerous sort of person on the loose? Perhaps you should call in the law, comrade."

"No, no," Margaret said. She had not foreseen this. "You don't understand. Anyone would agree that the man should die, but—I would not say he's a danger. Except as a corruption to morals. And he doesn't happen to be at the mercy of any law." Margaret was breathing hard, very much in her own mind. "But I would like you, as a doctor, as a citizen, to give me your blessing."

The doctor grimaced. "*You* sound like the danger, young Margaret. What are we talking about? A parricide? A vaticide?"

Margaret blew out through her nostrils.

"He's an old Nazi," she said. "He lives out in Rudow. He was with the SS."

"Ah," the doctor said, very slowly.

A moment passed.

Then the doctor said, "There are many SS men still living today.

There are many more that are dead already, and many others that are dying as we speak, all without your help. They don't need you to bring them to an early death. They don't do anyone any harm anymore, Margaret." The doctor looked at her. "Is this one particularly bad?"

"He's not particularly bad," Margaret conceded, although only outwardly. "But he's the one I know."

"Is he to be a token murder, or is he the first in a series?" the doctor asked. She touched her finger to her tongue and caught a page of her large, white book with it. The sound of the rustling page loaded the room.

"A token murder," Margaret said.

The doctor, as always, was ruining everything.

"For the crime of having been a member of the SS, a crime of association? Or did he commit particular atrocities?" the doctor asked.

"He was not directly involved in any killing. And if you must know, he has already spent ten years in a Soviet prison." Margaret pulled her opal ring on and off. It had been her mother's. "He was tortured."

"So you would agree with me that this man is not dangerous?"

"I would not say so. Not in particular."

"I see. And he himself never committed any particular . . . atrocities?"

Margaret punched her head forward toward the doctor. "His existence is a crime. He may not be guilty, but"— Margaret spoke in a low voice—"it's a gift, Doctor. I see it as a gift. That a killer is still alive for me to kill. There are still opportunities to carry out justice." Her eyes glowed.

The doctor did not respond immediately. Margaret breathed and waited. She looked eagerly at the doctor. The woman's eyes were half closed.

"It's a gift that I only got by the skin of my teeth," Margaret went on. "I may have been born late, but I was not born *too* late." Margaret was almost shy in her excitement. "Everyone looks but no one acts," she said. "I have been given a great blessing: an opportunity."

There was a long silence. Had the doctor fallen asleep? Her eyes were closed and her chest moved strangely. But all at once the woman spoke.

"Margaret," she said. "Has it never occurred to you, as you've sat with me in this office, that I was once a Nazi myself?"

Margaret looked at her. The walls were very close around her. To the front and back of her, time was contracting.

"You didn't suspect?" asked the doctor.

Margaret was alone now. "I was naïve," she said.

"There are two types of naïfs—the one who is naïve because of lack of attention, seeing only what bounces naturally into his basket of personal greeds, and the one who notices everything but instead of weaving the hints into meaning, lets them lie in shards. Which are you?"

"I'll be going," Margaret said. She stood up violently. Her chair fell over behind her.

"Wait," the doctor said. "I'll tell you my story."

And despite herself, Margaret stayed. She picked up her chair. She had always liked a story.

THIRTY-TWO • The Doctors of Charité

You already know what became of my brother, your nominal"—
the doctor coughed—"your nominal grandfather." Margaret
cried out, but the doctor cut her off with a sharp wave of her
hand.

"Now, my brother—it has probably occurred to you that I was
nothing like him. He was a talented man," the doctor said, "but I was
the true intellect of the family." She smiled tightly. "Forgive my self-
flattery. Although you probably know that in those days, especially
under the Nazis, women were encouraged to stick to the three Ks—
Kinder, Küche, Kirche. It wouldn't surprise me if you also knew that
there were many exceptions to this, none more well-known than the
great Leni Riefenstahl herself, although how she managed to make
her films in that man's world, I'll never know.

"My parents valued achievement, even in women, and when it
became apparent, as I say, that while my brother had charisma, I was
the brains, it was not looked upon askance that I should go to university. And so I traveled every day from our villa on the Wannsee to the
University of Berlin, traveling through the bustle and bustle of
Alexanderplatz and the Scheunenviertel, where immigrants, crooks,
and scalawags had their paradise—it was a different world than the
one I knew.

"I began at the university the same year as my brother's incident in
the Saxon woods, that is to say, in 1938. (My brother was only a year
younger than I.) And I began to study medicine right away. Do you
know who also did that? Hitler's young niece, down in Munich back
in 1931, although it seems she never went to a day of classes."

"The activities of Hitler's niece do not interest me," said Margaret.

"Is that so?" The doctor showed a particular type of contempt at
this, but let it drop. "All right then," she said. "Well, I was a precocious
student. My temperament is naturally scientific. Already in 1941, I
received my diploma with a thesis on endoscopic abdominal surgery.

This thesis put forth various proposals detailing how the practice of endoscopic surgery could be expanded to include many more types of gynecological surgeries than were performed in this way at the time. Endoscopy—the use of an instrument to see the inside of the human body without cutting it open, or making only a tiny incision. Also the mechanical alteration of the interior of the body through the use of such a device. Imagine, then, this idea that you could, for example, take out the appendix of a woman by going in through her vaginal canal and uterus, no major incisions necessary! Incisions can lead to infection, take a great deal of time for the surgeon, who must stop the flow of blood to the area, and are higher risk for the patient as well, who is usually, especially in that era, under general anesthesia.

"But how does one conduct endoscopic surgery—perform a highly precise task, without being able to *see*? These days, they introduce tiny video cameras into the body at the end of tubes, which project everything onto a screen. But in my day we didn't have video, much less exquisite little versions of same.

"This is where an invention of *mine* came in. It was a device I dubbed, rather fancifully I now think, the Inner Eye. Think of the submarine periscope, which uses a system of lenses, prisms, and mirrors to see what is not in the direct line of vision. Now think of that on a very small scale and with hundreds more prisms and mirrors, all much closer to one another. Think of them jointed to one another with dozens of tiny joints, like a snake's vertebrae, so that unlike the submarine's periscope, which is rigid and only sees that which is directly perpendicular, the Inner Eye can bend, twist, curve, following the lines of the body's canals whither they shall lead.

"The only trouble is light. Can you understand that? How will it all be illuminated?"

Margaret shook her head.

"I hit upon it!" The doctor banged her fist on the desk. "Cyalume!" she cried out, old pride billowing from her voice. "Phenyl oxalate ester, the liquid ester which is used in a glow stick."

"I see," Margaret said.

"Once the ring around the head of the Inner Eye was made to glow, there was enough visibility to conduct simple operations.

"My thesis, and this invention of mine, received a great deal of attention, and I was invited to work toward a doctorate. But there was something else that came of it. You see, I mentioned in passing at a conference the great possibilities of using my method in laparoscopic hysterectomies.

"The man who became my advisor was a certain Professor Dr. Hermann Stieve, a well-respected anatomist and gynecological researcher. And he happened to be working, quite openly, actually, with the Gestapo, and had ties to the RSHA. It just so happened that both of these offices were very interested in how women might be sterilized more quickly and cheaply—how hysterectomies could be performed *en masse*. So I was recruited by Stieve to develop new and rapid methods of performing hysterectomies.

"You must understand, these enormous feelings of enthusiasm around my work—" the doctor paused, "affected me greatly." She sighed. "And at first it was pride that moved my heart toward cooperation.

"But I do not think I would have gone along. Even *I* was not so callous. I would not have been so quick to conform if it had not been for something else. Before all this governmental interest began, I had a terrible experience. I was given the opportunity, you see, to try out this invention of mine, my lovely Inner Eye, in a civilian setting early on; it had nothing to do with the RSHA at all. It was the hysterectomy of a woman who had only one kidney and had almost died during the birth of her fourth child. A hysterectomy which was entirely called for and should have been an easy procedure." The doctor spoke slowly.

"It should have been easy. But unfortunately, I made a cut that was a few millimeters to the left. There was massive hemorrhaging. And I lost the patient." The doctor's eyes glowed remotely, blindly. She sat still for a moment.

Then she said, "Comrade, I wonder if you know that there are two types of disappointment: disappointment in oneself and disappointment in God. In other words: self-hatred and alienation."

Margaret didn't say anything. The doctor sighed, and then went on in a grey voice.

"So. Although I had made a strong start, I must say—I gave in. I abandoned my own work and became an assistant to Stieve almost full-time." The doctor sighed again.

"Stieve was interested in psychosomatic illness as it relates to fertility. In particular he was interested in the effects of environmental factors, psychological factors that is, on the female menstrual cycle."

Her voice changed yet again. It became very deep, uninflected. She stretched her words down to an ever lower pitch. "In our research, we were dependent on women who had come to death suddenly. Only in these women could the ovaries and uterus be removed instantly, almost the moment of death itself. The tissue was examined and correlated with the psychological circumstances surrounding the woman's passing. Luckily for our research, there was a glut of women being executed by the Gestapo at just that moment in time, at the Berlin Plötzensee Internment Facility. In large part, 'traitors to the Reich,' political prisoners, mostly Communists.

"At first Stieve merely made postmortem studies of the reproductive organs of these women and compared them with those of women who had died under natural circumstances. Later, however, he began to take a more active role in determining the 'psychological circumstances' that would surround these convicts' deaths. For example, he would decide at which point before the execution date the victim should learn of her fate. We would tell them ourselves, and immediately begin recording menstrual patterns."

The doctor stopped and put both hands on the desk, with the palms, very soft and white, turned up toward the ceiling. What Margaret noticed were the veins of her narrow wrists, wrists that appeared naked and childlike.

"My dear," began the doctor, "you can't imagine how losing my patient in that first hysterectomy affected me. It is a terrible thing, this responsibility for life, and her death convinced me I did not want to stand alone and carry it. Not as a scientist, not as a human, and not as a woman with reproductive capacity herself. Nor did I have a great faith in a higher power, else why should this have been allowed to happen? My wonderful Inner Eye, such a brilliant invention it was! I was disappointed both in myself and in the durability of the soul, which is another word for God. So from then on, I did not think it wise to work as an individual. Frankly speaking, comrade, I enjoyed this work with Stieve, I wanted this work in fact, for the simple reason that it removed the gamble with death: there was no mystery in our patients' survival or failure to survive.

"Do you know when you are greatly frightened, the color leaves your cheeks?"

Margaret started at the direct question. "Yes," she answered, although somewhat uncertainly.

But the doctor took her answer warmly. "Precisely, my child. I know it too. I saw it many times even in this very office. Well, that's what I observed in these women when they were told the date of their execution. It's because the capillaries draw together—nervous vaso-constriction. But this is only part of a much larger response—all of the body's systems which are not active in the fight-or-flight response shut down—the digestive tract, the skin, and the reproductive organs lose as much blood as can be spared. A third of the blood in the abdomen will be removed by the vasoconstrictors and sent to where it is most needed by a body in crisis: the brain and the skeletal muscles.

"This research, then, was central in demonstrating that a woman living in the shadow of massive fears becomes infertile, and that men-struation has a strongly psychosomatic mechanism," the doctor said, her voice ringing out. "No one had known that before," she added plaintively, almost begging.

Margaret's own face turned a deep red, up through her cheeks and under her eyes. She could feel it. She was hot. "Why are you telling me this?"

"My child. We did excellent work. We made an important contri-bution. Today, however, I dare not tell anyone about these studies. They would say what we did was unethical. Today it is so easy not to see that regardless of whether or not we had been there, broadening the circle of medical understanding, these women would have died anyway. That's what has always comforted me. That's what comforted me even then. These women were shielded from the doctor, because they were already dead."

Margaret's face seemed to creak, so stiff was it. "When I first came here," Margaret said, "you tried to give me a medical exam although you were blind—"

"I know this must seem repugnant to you, but at the time it appeared a great good. To make something fine and enduring out of senseless death—"

Margaret stood up. The doctor must have heard Margaret's chair as it scraped away the shine of the wooden floor, because her face rearranged itself suddenly into an expression of panic, and even Mar-garet was surprised. "Wait!" the doctor cried, her voice cracking. She was unexpectedly earnest. "Wait, don't you see! Margaret, you are too quick to judge! Nazism—listen to me—it signified then, and it will always signify, whether you want it to or not, much more and much less than what it has come to casually mean—which is death, and only death! But listen, my pet, it was an inversion of death. It spiritualized everything in its vicinity. God was bankrupt, it was the only alternative some of us thought we had. And it was not the Nazis who bankrupted God, no, that was done already long before. Even now the world is convulsing! And the Nazis offered one asylum." The doctor's hands, as she lifted them in the air, had the most powerful tremor. Her voice rang out, "Do we not yearn to be dissolved into a higher good? 'Your god lies shattered in the dust and serpents dwell among his ruins and now you love even the serpents for his sake.' Have you heard that, Margaret? Joining the Nazis was loving the serpents, yes, but for the sake of *what* did we love them?"

Margaret stood. "You are a witch," she said. Her stomach jumped straight up into her throat, and the nurse-receptionist popped her head in the door to see what was the matter. The doctor, hearing the door opening, thought Margaret was on her way out, and she became more agitated still. She began to feel her way around the desk with both hands.

"It's a higher history! Margaret! Do we not yearn to belong to this higher, more scientific world, you and I? In which mistakes are not failures of God, nor failures of mine nor of yours, but instead of nations running without consciousness on a wheel of fire! Would you not like your life to become art? You have said as much to me before!" The doctor was almost crying.

Margaret, in anticipation of the doctor's physical touch, began to panic, her eyes misting. "I'm leaving," Margaret whispered, as loud as she could.

"Do not leave!" the doctor yelled. "Wait! There is something to be said for dynamism, for courage, for self-sacrifice, for the cult of beauty! Listen!"

"I'm leaving now," Margaret said again.

"But wait! I am not trying to convince you of anything. These are not my views. I was only playing devil's advocate. I too have repented! Listen! Don't you want to know where I got my name? I told you, Arabscheilis is not my family name, nor my husband's. Comrade! My girl, Margaret darling, comrade," the doctor cried out, "just take a look at this, will you look at this?" And with amazing speed she moved back around and opened the bottom drawer of her desk and pulled out a mimeographed sheet, which she shoved toward Margaret. "You told me once that you go up there for your job. You'll have sympathy for this, my dear. You'll know it when you see it."

The paper was yellowed, and the words had been typed, to all appearances, very long ago. It read:

After many years I came upon a report of a comrade about Sachsenhausen, a comrade who unfortunately is only known by his prisoner's number. It's the number 12983. Here is his report: A tablemate of mine, a Polish customs official from the area around Bromberg, was taken by the police president for interrogation. In the night after his return he died a horrible death from asphyxiation. He knew that they had poisoned him. I stayed by him throughout the night until he died in the morning hours. He made me promise to bring messages to his wife and children, and also made me promise to take revenge on his cruel murderers. His death inspired the greatest hatred in me against the Gestapo. His name was Arabscheilis.

"I don't understand," said Margaret.

"But don't you see? I found this many years ago. You think I did not react to Albert's death. But I reacted with every cell in my body. Do you think it meant nothing to me? That's why I changed my name, in honor of the lost people, in honor of the unknown man, this Arabscheilis. Do you think I could love my brother? Don't you think I noticed what he was? You—you and your kind—you think nothing has any meaning to people like me, who have failed ourselves morally, but we are the most sentimental people in the world!"

Margaret turned a cold ear. She even kicked over her chair in protest.

"Comrade, my dear! Don't leave me! I am with you. I—" the doctor stuttered. "I could have betrayed you to your mother! How many times did she contact me, looking for you? But I never did."

"What are you saying?" Margaret turned her face back around.

"Your phone number, it went out of service two years ago, did it not? And you didn't answer e-mails, did you? She called me! And I, an exhausted old woman, went on foot looking for you on her behalf. You were willing to meet your great-aunt then, give her obstetrician's eyes a view of your shame—my vision was going, but I could see enough. But you, you got angry, you spit at me like a snake, just like now. All because I suggested you should contact that trollop of a mother you have!"

Margaret stared at the woman. "But—" Her cheeks were aflame. "Why do you call my mother a trollop?"

"Madness has its reasons which reason cannot know. I'll give you that, my dear. But the man we call your father, poor Christoph, may he rest in peace—was never the same, not after he found out. It destroyed him, even if he did have, have a—well, a touch of the Greek about him! There are men for whom the unquestioned fidelity of a wife is the vertebrae of all independence!"

"But—" Margaret said. She could not catch her breath. "But you're wrong. My father—that's not how it was." Margaret still could not catch her breath. "Why do you pretend to think our name is Täubner?"

"In good faith! So far as I know, my pet, your name *is* Täubner. If your name is no longer Täubner, I cannot say why. In any case you were certainly born Margaret Täubner. Just as I was born Gudrun Täubner. Your mother, may she never reenter Germany, did not explain this American turpitude in any of our correspondence. She gave me your address only, and I wonder if it wasn't a deliberate evasion."

"But why didn't you tell me this at the beginning, instead of wasting all this time?" Margaret was coughing and could not catch her breath.

"Do you take me for a fool?" the doctor asked.

"What—?"

"Deranged! Deranged is what you have been, my shining pet, and the first principle in the treatment of the shell-shocked is this: no sudden moves. You were not ready, perhaps you are not ready still."

Margaret ran out the door and did not look behind her. As she went down the hallway, she heard the doctor's echoing voice.

"You'll be back, my dear. You'll be back to see me. I am not the worst mentor for a girl in your position."

Margaret ran into the courtyard, her chest caving in.

THIRTY-THREE · The U7

On the U7 line to Rudow, the trains are nearly empty. The unemployed, the weary, the angry, and the immigrants sit only sparsely. It was here, only three days later on this subway line to nowhere, where Margaret rode, bound for the home of the aging Herr Prell.

The minutes on the train dragged like years. Hermannplatz went by, a yellow station. A woman got off the train with difficulty, using a walker. Margaret looked on, from under the brim of her slouch hat. She had pulled it very low over her eyes.

Why did no one help the woman? Margaret did not rise to help her either. She didn't want to call attention to herself. She was reckless, careless, vengeful, but she knew she must remain inconspicuous.

Since the visit to the doctor, Margaret had become an accordion of ill humor, unfolding, wheezing with heavy, distempered sounds. Now, as the woman stumbled her way out of the train on her own, Margaret wondered darkly whether she would not be reborn after the death of Prell. It seemed doubtful, but then, she had nothing to lose.

Rathaus Neukölln came and went, the ceilings hung low and royal blue. The seconds dragged.

Karl-Marx-Strasse station drew close. The train halted and a man made ready to get off. Before he did, he emptied his pockets—they were full of shreds of paper—and the white and yellow bits fluttered to the floor. How could he throw his trash on the ground so flagrantly? If only she were a man, Margaret thought, she might challenge him physically. For a moment, she riffled through all the ideas of who she might be, if only she were someone else.

Neukölln station followed in its bright yellow tiles. It occurred to Margaret that there was no rebirth, no changing of character, only momentary evasions—and that was never enough.

Grenzallee trickled by, smelling of mold. It was painted a stale green color like algae, and Margaret thought she could smell the algae.

She was desperate, her head was hot, she could not go on as she had been going. As for the doctor: she wanted never again to think of her.

And then came Blaschkoallee, and it was horrible, the worst of all. On the wall was the graffiti: "The woman maintains the house and the mood of her man." The station itself was grey, the lights painful to the eyes.

Margaret was in a mood of rage, then, by the time she arrived. She was worked into a lather. She rang the bell at Prell's house. When he came to the door, he did not recognize her, but Margaret said she had come for a follow-up interview, and he smiled sheepishly, proudly. He let her in.

His house was stuffier than it had been before. It smelled powerfully of old age. On the wall in the hallway was a wooden crucifix. Right away, already then, in that very first twenty seconds, Margaret thought of her grandfather, who had made films, who had taken pride in the film of a boy's death. When he came to stay with them in New York, he slept through the daytime. Her mother fixed up the back bedroom for him, and he, in the wide guest bed, kept the venetian blinds almost opaque, the sounds of ambulance sirens circling up to the twelfth floor. On the wall across from the bed, he hung an oak crucifix like Prell's, with a Christ figure carved out of the same dark wood as the cross, spine bucking away from the vertical.

And the old man, he slept under an image of unbelievable suffering, breathing regularly.

Margaret had been small, skulking about. She had found his pictures of naked ladies in a metal box he kept in the closet. She found his reels of black celluloid tape.

Now Margaret looked at Prell's crucifix.

The icon of the man collapses him into the instrument used for his torture, the means of his death becomes the symbol of his life; the sacrifice is snapped into the flesh. And then Margaret thought, in a wave of hopelessness, that crime was more powerful than tenderness, that death was more memorable than life. She felt a rage rising. She thought of this man who stood next to her now, as he had once stood goat-like outside a room while children were killed.

Prell invited her into the living room. She sat down by a little side table that was dressed in a white linen cloth. He bustled into the kitchen, came back to her, and stooped to serve tea from a pot.

But Margaret caught him by surprise. She raised her arms and took the old man's face in her hands, her fingers becoming spider's legs, squeezing vise-like. The loose skin on either side of his face doubled.

"How could you?" Margaret gasped at him, losing control of her voice.

Prell's giant, horse-like body lurched back; his neck extended and Margaret, holding on to him, was jerked forward. She reared up from her chair. Prell tried to prevent the tray in his arms from falling, and this confounded his self-defense.

But soon the tray smashed to the ground. He fumbled and caught the cream pitcher, but the teapot broke on the ground and the hot water splashed over Margaret's feet, scalding her ankles. It must have scalded Prell as well, for he cried out in pain and pulled away from Margaret's iron grip forcefully. With one heavy arm, he swiped at her shoulder.

But Margaret held his face ever more tightly on either side with her thumbs and forefingers, and her ears rang. She pushed hard into his jowls and temples. Her fury surged to a peak, and for some reason, Prell finally went limp under her hands.

"How could you?" Margaret let out again.

"How could I what?" Prell breathed hard.

A sound came out of Margaret's mouth. And then another. "How could you have lost faith?" she stammered at last.

"Let me go," he said.

But she held his face longer, and the power was in her and had gone out of him, as a rabbit freezes at the end of its life. He was doubled over, cradling his cream pitcher, his body at right angles.

But then at last he turned his face up, and Margaret looked into his eyes, eyes that darted and flicked about, the navy-blue orbs revolving, and she felt a ripping in her chest. She saw, buried far beneath the reflective sheen of his pupils, in the embers of the rods and cones there, the eyes of the infant she had lost.

The moment collapsed. Prell let go of the pitcher and punched at her stomach with his fist, and although he did not hit hard, her stomach made as though to burst in pain.

She released him. He lumbered heavily upstairs to the toilet, roaring threats of litigation. Margaret felt she was burning into black strips; she did not know what she had done, where to put her shame. She had read—it was Jung who had written—that the more evil is contemplated, the more it enters you, and she wondered under what circumstances she could ever learn how to live, she who had betrayed, or had been betrayed by, every hope and every idea and every icon of redemption, she whose very understanding of these things was in rubble.

THIRTY-FOUR · Reconciliation with Vitaly

T
he morning that followed was very still. Margaret gave a tour. All the while, she quivered. She reached and touched the hands of the customers who came along, and they felt the beseeching tremor in her fingers. They looked Margaret in the face and saw the enormous question there. She was reading their features with her eyebrows peaked like gables, as if she wanted to know the hour and minute they were born. When she had a moment to herself, she tried to soothe her uncertain heart. She thought: I did not kill him yesterday, and I will not kill him today.

In the afternoon, she went to the university.

She would not kill him, she told herself. Not now, and not tomorrow. In a heat of feeling, she spoke with devil-may-care directness to Vitaly Velminski, protégé of Meitler. She managed to convince the smooth and pretty young man, with whom she was not even acquainted, to take a coffee with her in the cafeteria, under the wide modern skylights, under the reaching, new-green trees.

They spoke of humanism. They spoke of capitalism. These were the wires that were fashionably live at the time.

At some point it was a question of whether a free-market society is more attracted to sacrificial lambs than a socialist one. Margaret's idea, which she outlined to Vitaly chokingly, with embarrassed excitement, was this: Older societies, she said, are still religious and altruism is ritualized, and socialist societies redistribute the burden of excess riches through taxation! But other societies, neither religious nor socialist, have hardly any idea what to do with the sleeping guilt that laces the fringes of wealth-amassing hearts, and so the more a little child, a perfect lamb, will be needed for the nailing, for the rendering up to the pedophiles—for the various slaughters, and the people will vaunt their communal obsession with the sacrifices, and find absolution there.

Vitaly, his usual cool and unflappable self, inclined his head in response. He mentioned many interesting names, thinkers who had combed the beach of such a theme for all its many shells.

Margaret spoke hotly, her eyes ablaze, looking often into Vitaly's seagreen gaze. After several hours had passed—more coffee fetched, professors evaluated, eviscerated, and even a long period spent in heavy-breathed silence—Vitaly, in his tweed suit, his penny-green oxford shirt, misinterpreted Margaret's intensity. He opened the palm of his hand. He touched the side of her face.

Margaret flinched sharply.

There might have been a time, very long ago, when, at such a touch, Margaret would have dropped her eyes so that her long lashes spread fanlike over her upper facial bones. She would have made herself into a picture.

There might have been a time more recently, when her flinch, so disengaged, would have extended into a reflexive uppercut to his jaw.

Today, however, she only put out two quavering fingers and slid them under his reliable chin. She turned his face some sixty degrees to the side. She did not know exactly what she was after. She thirsted to see his face from a previously unseen angle, in a previously unseen light, according to a previously unconsidered code of ethics. It was hers, the power of description. She would do the telling.

She looked a long time, and Vitaly laughed a little at first, but then regarded her and went still. Margaret breathed in and out.

Soon after, she stood up and left the cafeteria.

When Margaret was gone, Vitaly sat for a little while longer on his own. A radicalized person, he thought she was. There was a woman, he told himself, who had gone through some kind of education.

Under the fir trees outside the Rostlaube, on the pebbled path between the cafeteria and the U-Bahn station, Margaret came upon a woman with a narrow white scarf pushing a pram.

In the pram, a large, fat, sleeping baby lay on its back with its face to the side. The baby had gone sheet-white, as some children go white during sleep. Its translucent eyebrows were raised, pockmark of a mouth closed. Because it was inert, it seemed to Margaret both less living and also younger than it likely was, for even more than size, it is animation that betrays age.

It was terrible for Margaret to see. For a moment there was a knife turning in her heart, like the pitting of a cherry.

However, as Margaret drew abreast of mother and child, light rain began to fall. Margaret was later amazed at the serendipity of it, for if it had not rained at just that instant, she might have missed the essential gesture. The woman in the white scarf leaned over the pram and drew the flannel of the infant's blanket over its face, so the rain would not wake it.

In that movement, the fabric's edge drew a line across the small white face, and Margaret felt the world spin, and a sensation of radiance.

When she had first begun to remember, when she first knew that her old life was beginning to return, she began to think in vague and later less vague terms that she could not bear it. She could not forgive herself, and if she also would not be allowed to drench herself in forgetting, then she could not go on, and a wild and decisive kind of self-annihilation was the only choice.

But today she developed a thought—it had the following heart to it, although it was wordless: Even if you cannot forgive yourself, and by some poor luck you cannot forgive anyone else either, and there is no vengeance to be had in this baneful world that is slowly suffocating on its own past, there might still be a paradox of goodness.

In the movement of the woman's hand, the line of flannel rising, Margaret's head revolved, and it was an ugly thing that the gesture brought her to remember, but still, the radiance of the coming completeness stole her breath away.

THIRTY-FIVE • The Glow

The next day, the day everything came into its own, was a
sunny day. The sky over Berlin pulsed clear as an unmolested
snow globe, with the same magnifying fisheye. All was calm.
In the Kleistpark, on her way to buy a liter of milk, Margaret saw a
large animal, what may have been a Newfoundland dog.

The buildings around her—it was not clear any longer of what they
were made. Sometimes Margaret looked at them and they seemed to
shudder slightly as they had in the old days, even blush, and then one
or the other might heave a sigh. This seldom happened, however. The
architecture of Berlin was more convincingly of stone and stucco and
steel than it had been in a very long time.

Had her bicycle chain not fallen off the back gear, Margaret might
even have thought that all was coming back into order. She was forced
to get down to pull the chain back on, however, and the sun shone
hotly on her back. She crouched on the sidewalk, her hands smudging
with the dried-out grease, her face twitching, and it was then the thing
came.

She nudged the chain around the back gear and there it was. A long,
dark, barreling shadow flashed under the ground. The earth was
translucent—a two-way mirror. Shadows moved underneath it and
Margaret could see through it.

This is the nature of guilt—foreboding emanates from all things.
Everything inexplicable will be understood as a promise of looming
punishment. Guilt will change every last aspect of behavior, if you
let it.

The chain took to the back gear at last, and Margaret began to
ride toward home, but again as she crossed Martin-Luther-Strasse, the
shadow passed under the earth from west to east at high speed, and
Margaret could see down through the asphalt to the dark thing below.

Even as her heart raced, she was reminded of something. What did
this remind her of?

Then at once, she knew. The way the black shadow revealed the transparency of the earth was the way a mouse running under the ice at Sachsenhausen reveals the transparency of the snow. What might today's shadow be if not a displacement of time? For a moment, Margaret had a feeling of profluence.

The shape underground was many times larger than a mouse. Margaret considered what it could be. Of course, it should have occurred to her at the start: it was the subway train. The U7 line runs east-west under the Grunewaldstrasse, so it was the train, like the dark mouse, that betrayed the earth's translucence.

Margaret studied the earth for a while, and then she looked up. When she did, something caught her attention as it moved along the sidewalk in the distance. An enormous form. It came from down along Barbarossastrasse, near the dark, shaded fountain that runs in the middle of the roundabout, so sibilant under the sycamores. The thing was slow on its feet, picking along with head lurching rhythmically forward and back, like a great avian camel.

It held Margaret's gaze. She recognized it. As it came nearer, all was confirmed: it was that enormous bird of prey, none other than the aquiline Magda Goebbels herself.

The hawk-woman was approaching.

Margaret would have had the time to remount her bike and quickly pedal away if she had chosen. But she froze, she froze. She knew she must stay. If she did not face the bird now, the bird would stay with her all her life.

There was the hawk-woman, large and ugly, picking its way down the street, and there was Margaret, ready for her. And now, just as before, the bird began to shrink and molt as it got close to her, leaving a trail of sooty feathers in its wake. By the time Margaret was standing face-to-face with the being, it had become the woman in her moldy, old-fashioned clothes, the long-dead Magda Goebbels.

"Margaret!" the woman screamed in her bird-voice, "You ninny! Have you been avoiding me?"

"No," Margaret said. "You know I haven't."

"What is it then? Are we pals?" Before Margaret could answer, the hawk-woman answered for herself. "Of course we are. We're thick as thieves. I've got somewhere fantastic to take you now. Somewhere I know you'll like."

"Well—" Margaret began.

But already the woman was growing and expanding, ballooning

back into her bird shape—and next thing Margaret knew, the bird was pushing her giant head into the space between Margaret's legs. She had come at her from behind—so Margaret was somersaulted onto her wide back, and by the time Margaret was righted, they were rising above the city.

The air struck Margaret's face not unpleasantly, but the journey did not last long. They came down already on Möckernstrasse, in the weed-strewn vacant lot just behind the Nazi-era post office.

"Home again, home again, jiggedy-jig!" the bird screeched. She dropped Margaret to the ground in the back, by the muddy pool of water—the bomb-crater pond. The side entryway to the building was gaping.

The figure—half bird, half woman now—beckoned to Margaret. It seemed they would enter the ruinous post office through a gaping, windy hole where there had once been a door. Margaret stepped over the high threshold.

Through rotting floorboards, weeds were growing. Slips of light came in the smoked windows. The hawk-woman led Margaret to a large round hole in the floor—it was the beginning of a spiral staircase that was hidden in the twilight. The stairs circled down into the ground.

At first Margaret resisted, but the hawk-woman came up behind her in the gloom and pushed insistently, until finally Margaret went, the hawk-woman close behind. Deeper and deeper they twisted into the underground.

Low and even light came from the walls of the stairwell. These glowed with a soft, green luminescence. Margaret put out her hand and touched the wall to steady herself. She lifted it to her face and saw the hand was covered in dissolved powder—a shimmering green.

Margaret felt weak, unsteady. The farther down the spiral staircase they went, the less clearly she could think. Her thoughts became muddier and muddier, and shortened, too. The underground, it seemed, was the place where long thoughts came to die.

The spiral went on. Margaret's mind waned. Her feet fell against the stone steps, and she had no prospect or expectation. Something went lax within her.

The stairs opened on a passageway and Margaret's powers of observation dimmed even as the lights grew brighter. Along the corridor, there were candles in holders that made the green walls shine tacitly, like emeralds in the rough. Margaret was now behind the hawk-woman and followed her through corridor after corridor, turning many times.

At last, the hawk-woman turned into a doorway.

Margaret peeked in. It was a hot, blazing chamber that she saw over the threshold, a small room filled with many burning candles. And not only candles. Floor to ceiling, stacked, were thousands of tin cans. They were piled in giant cubes and pyramids like houses of cards, cans with labels marking sardines, marking green beans, marking coconut milk and olives, and cans of paint too, and bicycle oil, and gesso—and cans without any labels at all. Some cans had labels in styles of ages long past, others were modern, all preserving hermetically everything that can possibly be preserved. On top of the cans sat candles, flames flickering, each one dancing to its private tune. The candles dripped wax liberally—and made a cheaply chemical, floral perfume.

In the very center of the room, there was a railing made of tin cans welded together. Inside was a dais, also built of cans. And finally, on top of this dais was an enormous chair, high-backed and imposing like a throne.

The hawk-woman climbed up and sat down in it.

Perched up there, affectedly, her knees drawn tightly together and toes pointed mincingly side by side, the hawk-woman took a golden cigarette etui out of her alligator-skin pocketbook and also a fine lighter of the same metal. With her manicured hands, she put a cigarette to her lips, struck the lighter's cap, inhaled, and let out a puff of smoke, the hanging, left side of her face shivering with the effort. She turned her head. Her heavy brow hung low over her eyes. Her grey suit was of a fine moiré (gone was the gabardine), and the waving water patterns of the moiré shook Margaret's eyes.

The hawk-woman spoke.

"Margaret darling, *you pretty little thing.*" She inhaled sharply. "You're to stay with us here now. Congratulations. This is quite the club."

The cans, the light, the wax—they ate the oxygen in the room, and Margaret thought perhaps this was the reason she could not breathe or think.

Through the cotton of her muffled mind, fear took hold of her.

The hawk-woman pulled out a pair of pince-nez, put them over her half-slack face. She looked up at Margaret. "You're such an obstinate little gnat. You insist on repressing your merry little life." She reached into a short cabinet that stood next to her tall chair. "But I'll help you, Margaret, I'll help you to be mindful of who you are." On her crenellated tongue, Margaret's given name corrupted the air like a curse.

Already now, Margaret began to draw her neck away from the hawk-woman, but the creature's hands were moving, she was pulling out a glass cylinder of the type used inside of pneumatic tubes. She was checking a long label down its spine; first she rejected one glass tube, and then another, holding each one up to the light. Finally she let out a sharp breath of air.

The woman's hands lifted the glass tube in triumph, and her veins, in the heat of the room, were popping out of her skin. They were emerald green veins like the walls in the underground corridor.

The image of the woman's hands was too much for Margaret. It crossed another image—a ghost image in her mind. In that moment, a gentle minor chord sounded. Two negatives were projected onto the same piece of silver nitrate. The two images crossed, matched, glowed, sang.

"I don't want it," Margaret began. "I don't want to see anything." But her eyes misted over as if to become one with her misted inner eye and her clouded mind. She could hear the hawk-woman's voice, but fading now—"Then don't read it, little ninny, you needn't read anything you don't want," she was saying, but her voice was growing fainter and fainter. The woman's hands were dancing still in Margaret's mind, losing all but their lacings of emerald veins. Skeletons they were, skeletons made of arterial vessels carrying blood back to the heart.

And so they carried blood back to the heart of Margaret. They reminded her—a memory floated toward her as though a ship doubling in size astonishingly on the far horizon, growing into a nocturnal glacier before her eyes—they reminded her of a letter from her mother. She had read a letter two years ago, when she, Margaret, was enormous, ready to give birth, and she had been so staggered by the thing, she had linked it with the undesired child. She had never wanted to see anyone in her family again after that letter, including, even including, the child—her nearest kin. The letter from her mother—Margaret's head swam. She remembered, as though it had always been burnt on her retina, the letter of October 2002, when she had been told that she had not always been Margaret Taub.

An envelope, postmarked New York City:

Dear Margaret,

I haven't heard from you in a long time. I know you're hurt. I've done my best. I've really done everything. But you have hurt me too, you know. You can't imagine what it does to me, that you insist on living in that city.

I found the enclosed letter in his things. I'm sorry I only found it now—perhaps it would have been a consolation to you to have it earlier, but after the funeral I couldn't bear to go through his papers for a long time, and before that, well you know how he was when he came home from the hospital. Actually, I don't think I ever told you the worst of it.

Please get in touch. It's horrible for me that you won't get in touch.

Love,
Mother

Another sheet of paper, folded into a small, tight triangle at the bottom of the envelope, was recognizable by Margaret's father's usual habit. Across the triangle, MAGGIE was written in block script.

Hi there Girl!

Summer's winding up. How's camp been treating you? Your mom says you like it there.

Gas prices are sky-high. I happen to be very familiar with the topic of rising gas prices. Your mother took me on a vacation. Two weeks outside the hospital! Back now from 1½ weeks in Vermont. Great trip. Alphonse is reputedly dead (he was an old dog), not there with us in the flesh, but regardless of that arguable supposition, we routinely get Alphi's point of view on most everything during the trip. He slept a lot less than usual (as we hear from him at the hospital as well). Some say I shouldn't tell anyone. But we really *experience* Alphi with us daily everywhere we are, because he's *really* there. But then, you *are* family, and so I'm sure you understand. Alphi doesn't really care that gas prices are so high just so long as we get up and go someplace "good." "Good" he defines as where there's swimming. He likes to play in the shallows.

Anyway, there I go running off at the mouth, forgetting the subject at hand. Unpardonable given the gravity. I want to tell you about my old dad . . . your Opa. I found the paperwork. . . . They had him on trial during the war. They let him go free. But here's what they wrote about him before they did. This is what the Nazis wrote up about him, just so you know. . . . Even the Nazis knew what he was . . . and this is just a sample . . . although my bad translation.

In Riga the SS-Sturmmann Wüstholz ordered the Jews to beat each other to death, at which time it was promised that the survivors would not be shot. The Jews did knock each other down, but not to death. The defendant [my old dad] got in the fray and beat the Jews and also hit Jewish women in the face with a whip. When a break was taken, he played on the harmonica the song "Du Bist Verrückt, mein Kind!" [You Are Crazy, My Child].

He used to play that song to *me*, Margaret. That's how I got singing it to you, before I knew any of this. Before I had done "research." Anyway, this is why your mom and I changed the last name. That asswipe can rot in hell, and I won't hear his screams. Otherwise, with my special hearing, you know I hear very well. Sometimes I *hear* the real pine needles in the forest, and the pins and needles as they go into my old dad's sides. I always hear him screaming down there. Even the devil feels the heat of the fires they've got down there, and when it's your own dad especially, you can hear him scratching and clawing and just trying to get out of the lakes of fires they've got down there. But I won't hear the screams, I haven't heard them since we changed the name. It was a simple thing. When you were four years old, I guess you were too little to notice, a few days after your birthday, we did it. Just from Täubner to Taub, but doesn't it fit? We became the *Taub* family. (You know what Taub means, right? *Deaf.*) I know it's hard for you to understand. I thought I was helping you if I didn't explain. If I didn't tell Maggie what kind of an old Opa she had, she wouldn't hear the screams like her dad did. Little Maggie, you were a good girl. We used to have another name but maybe you can accept that and love the new one as I do. Your mom is the one who told me to tell you. She said you were old enough now. Don't give your mom any trouble okay?

Well, nice talking to you . . .

Good luck with your life,

Love you . . .

Your Dad

P.S. Any misspelled words are stickly (see, I typed strickly . . .) typos. And grammatical styling is for purposes of camouflage.

Margaret remembered her father's letter. But the hawk-woman on her throne was still murmuring and hissing. The woman made sentences, spinning the chubby glass cylinder around in her emerald fingers like a baton, laughing raucously, although Margaret could barely hear her for the pain.

Margaret closed her eyes. Fear and pain both know how to paralyze. Still and hard, the body careens to a stop; the rabbit's heart slows its pound. When Margaret opened her eyes again, the white ink of the light in the room pooled around Magda Goebbels on her throne, her mouth flickering. She prattled on, and still that raucous little laugh was tinkling out of her. The light rose up, and her avian eyes were gemstones sitting in wax.

All at once, she leaned in. Margaret's breath stopped; she felt the hawk-woman nearing. Fear paralyzed her, but she was paralyzed too by what she had remembered—of her father, the spinning cyclone, and her grandfather, the harmonica-player, and of herself—she had carried a little child, and she could not bear it, she could not bear it.

The sensation of the hawk-woman coming closer burnt Margaret's skin. She had a sense of grand-scale entrapment.

And now shall be told of something else. Now shall be told of how Margaret's eyes were plucked entirely away from memories of her own kin and flesh, for the sake of the hawk-woman.

It began when the monster spoke a single sentence, a sentence that caused the collapse of an essential support beam. At first, Margaret was sure she had misheard it.

It sounded like the woman said: "Look at you, Margaret—you're so *thin*," in a tone of vain and humbug envy.

Margaret looked up at her. She looked at Magda Goebbels through a veil of despair, but, still, something in this phrase was too familiar.

Magda Goebbels's antiquated pianola style had thrown Margaret off the scent. But abruptly, Margaret thought she knew her *kind*.

It was a kind Margaret had run into many times. Always Margaret had associated it with chewing gum, flatulence jokes, and America.

You meet her in every cafeteria, in every extended family, and beside every swimming pool. The woman is jazzy, and probably she's rich. She makes a show of asking you about your sex life when she first meets you. She pulls you onto her lipstick team further by insinuating half-truths sotto voce about women of mutual acquaintance. Before she knows you, she says, "You and I have more in common than blood relatives, babe," and if Margaret gropes for the right word, she interrupts to say, in a diction far younger than her years, "Wait, oh my God, are you one of those wicked smart people? You look like one of those."

But always with this type, soon the good feeling turns. It seems at first coincidental, but it is not: she has a husband. And although this viciously tennis-playing woman might speak irreverently of him to begin with, telling you something hilarious about, most likely, his penis, it invariably turns out she has a pedantic, mulish, pharisaical sense of submission to him. A prim and stiff-necked blackout in her sense of humor slams shut whenever there is discussion of his views. And if the marriage has gone sour, then the devotion will jump seats: to her political candidate, her pastor, maybe her thesis advisor. Whatever his title, tears will spring into her eyes when she speaks of "what he has done for me."

Always he has done a great deal. Because for herself, such a woman has no hope. In her own mind, she is as helpless today as she was at her birth. She has pinned her shadow to the wall of him, like a side of ham hung up to dry in a smokehouse.

Yes, Margaret knew this kind very well, it is nothing at all, and the hawk-woman, as Margaret saw her now in a fine mist of bubblegum scent, no longer had the slightest riddle or sharpness or even spook to her venal, bawdy, sanctimonious grasp, and Margaret thought for a blistering instant: I am done with her.

Some things have no meaning at all. The bright flames crested the sardine cans and danced. Margaret looked at the hawk-woman up on her dais. But now, recognized, she was for a moment not frightening at all, and a new energy filled Margaret. The cloud of ink light puddled and pooled, erasing the edges of the woman's moiré dress. She sat huddled on her throne, crestfallen and poor. Margaret stepped sideways and moved back toward the door. She looked at the chamber and the rout of gleaming, dripping candles, and the still, waxy being—half woman, half hawk; half dead, half alive; half wax, half stone.

Margaret heard a shuffling: a trembling of wings. And then the figure on the throne gave a whimpering sigh, and all at once she was made of stone. She froze into soapstone, and the lower half of her—it began to turn to powder and stream away like sand flowing through the waist of an hourglass.

Margaret's heart lunged. She was released. She took three heavy steps backward, scraping hard on the stone floor of the cellar, and then she turned on her heels and ran. She ran, hard and fast.

Out of the chamber and down the long hallway she ran. And although the hawk-woman just a moment before had grown shabby and disintegrated, now the figure had a final gasp of power over Margaret's mind. The hawk-woman might transform herself again and come flying at the back of her, ready to fall on her and take her down from behind, hold her pinned to the ground in her domain. Margaret ran hard; she did not know how to get out, but she took a turn to the west whenever she sensed there was such a turn to take, thinking that in this way she would eventually reach home, through the catacombs reach Schöneberg, although it occurred to her—something—oh so terrible, made her shake: the basement of the old Nazi post office had been built with a tunnel connecting it to Hitler's New Chancellery and, from there, the tunnel went on and led to the underground bunker underneath Gertrud-Kolmar-Strasse where Hitler spent his last days and where he died with Eva Braun, with his dog, and with his dog's puppies. Although now the chancellery, thank God, was destroyed by the Soviets, Margaret thought that without knowing it she could run the wrong way, run underneath Anhalter Station and finally find herself in the collapsed bunker, and there perhaps take a false step and trigger a terrible and complete collapse of the remains, and nothing—nothing could be more terrible than to be buried alive in Hitler's bunker, suffocating in the old Nazi mess, and she, Magda Goebbels, the hawk-woman, with her manicured talons, would welcome Margaret into the shadow life.

Margaret went up and down short flights of rusted stairs, forced her way over loose rubble, peered into crannies, saw toilet bowls that had overflowed many decades ago.

She ran through other chambers and recognized the walls from photographs—high murals there, depicting prick-legged SS officers with arms in deltoid shields draped like fangs to the ground, standing over voluptuous maids: reclining nudes, amateur renderings of the *Venus of Urbino*.

Margaret's spirit was a March river as she ran, and the surface was floating with ice floes, thick as pontoons. Broken apart in a grid the ice was; waters churning and boiling under it; the great, bulky sheets slammed into one another with miraculous antagonism, with a natural hatred—*wham, wham* and again, and Margaret was afraid and kept running.

Her heart thumped, the waters churned, the ice floes slammed. Finally, Margaret found herself in a basement that was neither the waterworks nor the catacombs, and at long last she saw a staircase going up.

She came out in a crypt—a church basement. She came up even farther and saw where she was—it was the church of St. Matthias, at Winterfeldtplatz, and the nave was a cool breath over her head, a billowing arc. Margaret was panting hard and the stitch in her side had grown iron teeth.

All she knew was this: she wanted to climb up into the cool air, away from the underground. She found the wooden door to the bell tower. It was locked, but Margaret threw her shoulder against it, her lungs burning. Again and again, she slammed herself into it; she was hurt, the pain in her shoulder was terrible, but the lock broke after all and the door flew open, and Margaret fell inward with it. She righted herself and began another long ascent, but this time into the soft sky—up into the tower and the clouds, and already she could smell a fresh wind.

As she climbed the stairs, she looked up.

It is remarkably easy to conflate one kind of guilt with another. Guilt is a quicksilver that loves its brothers; it flows naturally according to its own code of gravity, eager to rejoin its own, and in the final reservoir, there are no distinctions. But Margaret, ferocious now, would not let any hawk draw her into an alliance. If her father's father had been that sort of man, then it was all the more crucial that she should not be that sort of woman, for strength of identity is the only protection against clannishness, nationalism, and other forms of incest.

Margaret climbed and her mind cleared. And then, as if out from the rising movement in her legs, came the memory of another staircase, to test her newfound strength. The oval staircase. She remembered climbing that one as well.

She was going to see Amadeus, her body not large yet, although already she could feel the child moving. His terrible letter had still not come, but would soon, after this event.

On this day, she had looked up above her and seen him smoking at the top of the stairs, leaning over the banister. His wife did not allow him to smoke in the apartment, and he was not meant to smoke in the stairwell either, but sometimes he did. Margaret could smell his Gauloises Rouges, and the red flax runners, and see the ash fluttering down. She called up to him. He did not answer.

Margaret was almost at the top, and she called to him again. He heard, but the door slammed. He heard her and he was gone.

She was spurned.

The slam of the door. Nothing would ever be the same.

Just when her spleen was most suffocating—when the death of hope was purest—a bird flew into the convex skylight lifting plump out of the roof. The glass shattered and fell in drops of light, oh the solidified rain!, and the bird—it must have died at the moment of impact—it landed all the way on the basement level, coming down softly like crêpe. Margaret saw it fall down to the tiles, defeated at last. She saw it fall all the way down, from high above.

The falling bird marked her mind.

Soon after, Amadeus's letter came. A green-white mold began in her. Whether or not she was her lover's child—an affair within the family, that had happened. Ecstasy, submission to a homeland messiah, a pollination between flowers of the same plant, a country slimy with the *Heimat* semen of its father, rejecting outsiders violently for the sake of a love affair with its own blood—that had happened. It was as unbearable as anything in memory.

So Margaret did not think about Amadeus. She wiped him from her head. His letter about the affair with Sarah, her mother—she threw it out, she washed it out.

But the eradication brought a disease. The more Margaret did not think of it, the more she thought of other things—the bird, for one—breaking the glass. Each time she did, her throat went tight. She choked. The birds of Berlin began to twitter in poison-tipped chorus then, truncheoning her, and when she pressed away all memory once and for all, it was the birds that flew into the holes left behind. The pigeons stoppered the pocks on the faces of the houses; the birds of Berlin did not cease their chatter.

Margaret braced herself against the graduated walls of the church stairwell. Yes, the birds had marked her mind, moved in where memories should have been, and holding on to the railing to prevent her dizziness from toppling her, Margaret posited a new idea. "A sleeve of time" she called it, a carousel of amnesia, in which all moments are fixed for eternity as soon as, and precisely because, they are forgotten. Fixed eternally and so eventually, when they do return, as return they always must, swallows from Africa, they will be reincarnated as exotics—flies and trees and monsters and trams.

If meaning cannot be assigned to the things of the heart—the things from which meaning springs and to which it belongs, then it will come unmoored and swim unspecifically. And if it swims unspecifically, it is not only the flies and trams and birds and architecture of Berlin that will be impregnated. The entire general world will become heavy with the structure of the private mind. The ghost enters the inanimate and the inanimate enters the ghost. The doctor had said it long before Margaret had ever wanted to hear it.

What the doctor had not described, but which gripped Margaret now, was the consequence. When nothing is assigned a specific hook on which to hang itself, nothing is outstripped—the sleeve turns itself inside-out then rolls rightside again, only to go inside-out once more: a merry-go-round world, a world of hyper-meaning, a world of eternal return at once heartbreaking and estranged: a history of ever-returning history.

Margaret ran her hands along the sloped brick walls of the throttling spiral of the church stairwell, narrow and full of dust, its walls leaning toward her as though a traveling and slanting vortex, and felt her dizziness pass. Margaret's mind opened like a night flower.

She reached the top of the belfry and came out into the air. The day on which her bicycle chain fell from the back gear had not yet died, although she felt as if she had been underground for years. She leaned against the railing and the afternoon sun leaned with her, at an acute angle to the city. In the sharp light, she could see the three-dimensionality of things. She looked down at the palace courthouse in the Kleist-park, looming in shades of bright and dark, and at the high-windowed *Gymnasium* standing next to it, and the hulking bunker from the Second World War that stood behind them both. She saw the fresh green of the leaves catching fire on the orange light.

Again she thought of the sleeve of time. She had been still, and the city, rich unto itself, had moved inside-out.

She blinked, and it came upon her that now she might have the strength to find out the twist of things. She could begin to discriminate what was horror and what was romance, what was myth and what was life; which were signs of despair and which were signs that the city, polyphonic and great, had become a single, monotonous expression of her yearning for things elusive and lost.

With her gaze draped over the roofs below her, Margaret felt a hidden door, tangled in her mind's ivy, come free and crack wide. All around her, the city was dancing for her one last time.

Across the quiet, humanity-scrawled land, the steep auburn roofs of the Martin-Gropius-Bau reared up; the Landwehr Canal, winter swans in the crooks of its banks, turned and shifted its course. For Margaret's inner eye, the swinging afternoon sunlight in the empty upstairs ballroom at Clärchen's Ballhaus glowed upon something hidden: a parallel life behind mirrors. The faces of the dead rose into the bark of the sycamores along Puschkinallee, and Georg Elser, shot to death in the weedy prison yard of Sachsenhausen, moved gently in the sleep of the grave—as if to tell Margaret he knew it all; the houses on Grosse Hamburger Strasse grew steeper and taller out of their chrysanthemums, and the iron eagle on the Weidendammer Bridge rustled its wings; the Wall fell and fell eternally, the crowds surging through the carnival night; the small, broad body of Rosa Luxemburg landed in the canal with a *platsch;* and although Margaret could not see him, she could hear him: the Brazilian man who had come to Berlin just to see the Stadtpark where his mother once played under the golden stag as a girl—as he opened his mouth—to sing tra-la-la.

Warm curtains closed and opened around her mind. Through the fabric Margaret could see alternating shadows, a correspondence between prisms.

She blinked. The sun was down. Now, only the dusty wooden floor of the belfry porch hissed underfoot in the dark.

But in that moment, a feeling of beauty took hold of Margaret—a feeling so rich it dwarfed death. The door in her mind opened and the narrow glimpse turned a magnet key in her eye; she felt light seeping out from the base of her skull. A heavy stone shifted, and the warm curtains billowed no more than by the breath of an insect, but exposed for a brief instant, in the heart of the city before her: a red jewel with a flame inside it, red at its core, arching corridors raying in every direction, toward every fine thing, every decipherment.

Margaret breathed and was flooded. When she would have to die, it would be remembering this:

The sleeve of amnesia holds a mystery—a shadow, an innuendo—that is a weaponry of beauty; it makes of the mind an arboretum, the inkling of lost and hidden things a wind shaking down all the tears left unshed, like fruit from a storm-rustled tree. For good or ill, whether it be necessary to outgrow it or not, the mystery inside the ever-inverting sleeve is an engine to power the task of living, or conversely, a form of deathlessness.

And a ghost, a ghost is the leftover resonance of a style of being, the intense and prolonged sympathetic vibration, in this world, of a life in the next. Once, caught in the sleeve of time, Margaret split herself in two and released a ghost of herself. The ghost went lost and wandering. But now here it was, coming home again.

THIRTY-SIX • Margaret

Margaret lay her head back. She could see.

In the early hours of an already darkening evening, she could see how a young woman had walked down the slope of a cobblestone street in Prenzlauer Berg.

The young woman was carrying a sleeping baby, the child that had emerged from her body in the most recent days. She carried it in a car seat they had given to her at the hospital—a donation for low-income single mothers. She was dressed in heavy clothing made for a man: an overcoat, a slouch hat, and wool trousers, although underneath, a pair of high-heeled boots. The autumn night was mild. Her long, fine hair was unbrushed and matted. Under her eyes, her transparent face was dark, and the child's miniature face too had the papery lacing of acne some babies' faces are born with. From both of them came an odor of sour milk, and from Margaret, sleeplessness. Nearing Number 60, from her vantage point on the other side of the street, she looked up at a set of two balconies belonging to the apartment on the fifth story, and she was crushed at the sight of unlit, lifeless windows. She crossed over and sat down on the stoop of the next house.

She would wait.

She glanced at the child in the carrier. She felt a blooming. There was a tug of pain on either side of her chest as her milk let down. The sensation was blocked out quickly by rebuke, however. She blinked, looked about, erased her mind, really a welcome alternative to despair, and closed her eyes. She tried not to fall asleep.

She sat for a half hour, until finally two boys emerged from Number 60, and she jumped up to catch the heavy door before it closed. She came into the stairwell. The thick oak banister was carved into a shining lion's head at its curving base. The animal's face was scowling and haughty. The stairs curved in an oval around a great shaft of light, lit from a multipaned skylight above. Margaret made her way up laboriously. She almost tripped on the red flaxen runner. Around and around she went.

She strained to keep the carrier from swinging into the railing although its burden was so light—so weak were her arms. On the landing of the top floor she stopped before the apartment on the left side and put the baby down next to the door. She knew when to expect them home, for she had long since been in the habit of tracking Asja's comings and goings—anonymously calling her university office, in order that she—Margaret—might call Amadeus only when his wife was not at home. It was Thursday. Asja would come home at eight o'clock on the dot, less than an hour from now, and Amadeus, if he was not out drinking with his friends, must come home soon as well. She reached into her coat pocket and took out a letter in an envelope. It was labeled "Amadeus." She tucked it next to the miniature body.

Dear Amadeus,

Perhaps you never loved me because I am twenty-five years your junior. Or perhaps it is because I come from the "superficial" new world and you have devoted your life to the archives of the old. You are a reverse Humbert Humbert, who cannot love his devoted Lolita, you neurotic, with your fear of airplanes, men, and tree branches—or why can't you love the recipient of your craven choice of passion? (I can almost hear you insist: for a Lolita I am old, overeducated, that my skin is always white. Not the gold of the new world.) You insist that we cannot be together because of your attachment to your wife. But I ask you, if you were so attached to her, how could you visit me like you did, how could you dominate both my time and heart? I suspect you of misogyny or misanthropy or both.

I have never had any trouble loving you, you have always been easy for me to forgive. But there is one thing I cannot forgive. Why did you slam the door when I most needed you?

When you receive this letter, you will have our child in your arms, your arms which I know can be the most tender and compassionate in the world. And should you balk at your task, you won't find me. I am leaving Berlin and won't come back. I've found a job abroad. My plane leaves before you can find me.

I do not want him. He only came into this world as a bid for your love and he and I failed in that regard so dramatically that now he only reminds me of what a fool I have been. I would be ashamed to offer myself to him as a mother.

Sincerely,
Margaret

P.S. He doesn't have a name.
P.P.S. Please don't show him this letter when he's older.

Margaret took a last look at the sleeping child. She put a drugstore-bought bottle and packages of formula beside him, and then made her way down the stairs.

She crossed the city, returning to Schöneberg, where she began to clean her apartment, a place of grime and filth. Of course she did not have a plane to catch, that part of the letter was a fabrication, but some weeks before she had already had her telephone number changed. She put a new last name on the letterbox. Schmidt.

She held out for two and a half days. On Sunday morning she hurried back to Number 60 Winsstrasse as soon as the subways opened at 4:30 a.m.; she had not slept the night. She had to go through an empty lot in the Marienburgerstrasse and climb over a fence (excruciatingly painful for her stitches) to get into the back courtyard of Number 60, but when she got up the stairs and reached the landing of the top floor, she found the baby was still in the car seat next to the door. The little infant was lifeless. She raised it to her chest. A heartbreaking silence slumped around her. She rang the bell of the apartment, over and over again. Had no one ever come home?

She never found out whether her little baby had cried, if so, why no one had come, or whether the cause of death was something that crept up more quietly than dehydration. All that occurred to her was this: to take the body in the car seat on the S-Bahn with her across the city. She pulled the blankets up around it so no one would see. She borrowed a spade from a suburban garden. She buried the child in the still soft earth of the Grunewald forest. She buried her letter with the child. Around a tree, she latched a bungee cord, to mark the grave.

She had meant to go back home then, but sadness leached into her muscles and undid them, and she sat down against a tree. Her head fell forward.

THIRTY-SEVEN · Erich Again

Something was burning in Margaret's apartment on the Grune-waldstrasse. From the courtyard of Number 88, Erich the *Haus-meister* could see smoke puffing out of the upper panel of Margaret's kitchen window. The window was open, and the smoke flushed out of it, black and sturdy.

He knew that the American was out. He had seen her unlocking her racing bike. He knew that when she was bicycling in the neighborhood she did not wear a helmet, but when she was going a long distance, she did. Today, she had worn a helmet.

So now Erich climbed up the drainpipe next to the recyclables and hoisted himself onto the ledge. His agile body thin as a long-legged spider, he shimmied along the copper overhang that ran above the windows of the *Döner* shop. Margaret always left the window of her bathroom open, and now he went through it.

He fell into the room with a soft bounce and a ripple of popping bones, light as a ballerina. For a split second, Erich eyed a cabinet at the end of the long, lion-footed bathtub. Then he made his quick way into the kitchen.

It was only one burner that was on, and all the smoke billowed from a single pot—it was unclear what it had once been—the charred remains were perhaps lentils by the black outline.

The stove turned off, the pot under cold water, Erich began to look around the flat. Disarray, books, disarray, and more books. It was good he had come when he had. The whole place might have gone up like birch bark.

He returned to the bathroom. It happened that once he had seen Margaret leaning out the window of this bathroom, and believing herself unobserved, she had thrown something yellowy-gold out of it. Later, Erich found the brass key among dry leaves—it had been in the autumn—and it was *ding-dong* in his mind: here is Margaret's secret.

As though he was meant for it, the first piece of furniture he tried—yes, yes, he brought the key with him, for it was always on his heavy ring—opened under the key's ministrations as though charmed. Of course a key opening a lock is not a matter of charm, but still the ease of it had a magic quality, Erich thought.

Inside the drawer of the cabinet was very little. Just a few documents, mostly health insurance forms. And then—a birth certificate.

Erich stood for a long time with his chin in his hand. He thought of Margaret; he thought of her face.

It made him sorry.

But none of this would do. None of it would do at all.

The first thing Erich did the next day: he checked the birth registry at the city hall, for confirmation.

A boy, born September 5, 2002. Christoph Amadeus Taub.

THIRTY-EIGHT • Arrival of the Valkyries

It was a lightning storm outside—the summer had come. The buzzer of the door went off. A clap of thunder fell like the knock of a hammer, the thunder clapped, the hammer fell, the door buzzed, and then there was another knock, and deep voices. It was the accent of Berlin that sent the alarm through Margaret, the deep and angry voice of Berlin at her door. Margaret sat on the floor in the bedroom and listened to the yelling. They were the police, they said, and they knew she was inside. The *Hausmeister* had told them. If the racing bicycle was in the courtyard then Margaret was upstairs, and Margaret closed her eyes and thought of the summer nights in the outdoor theater with Amadeus. She felt the sepia tint of one Russian film they had seen. It hovered on the outside of her eyes. She opened them and looked out at the purple sky. The rains were coming. She did not resist, she went to the door and opened it, but without releasing the chain at first, and through the crack, there were the police officers, a man and a woman in camouflage green were looming above her; they were enormous and blond, the woman, turned in profile on the landing and speaking into a radio, had long golden hair that fell in an elastic band to her waist, her thighs proud and broad. The man too stood on wide-set legs broad as Berliner chimneys. Margaret looked up into their eyes—the light in them glinted, like water winking and shuddering at the mossy bottom of a well. So the police were the Valkyrie, she thought: the choosers of the slain. She opened the door to its widest. She lifted her wrists.

They ignored her wrists. She was wanted for questioning, they said, for questioning in connection with a disappearance. Margaret murmured "Arabscheilis." But it was not that. Someone in the apartment complex had given the tip, they said, had suggested she be charged with the abduction or possibly the murder of a child whose birth had been registered at Charité but had never been seen in any register after that; a child that, even now, the state was trying to find.

They were in the police car on the way to the station. They drove past Kleistpark. Margaret looked out the window and into the Königs-Kolonnaden. Oh colonnade! How beautiful it was. The colonnade, archway upon archway, was detailed, gentle, ordered, moderate. She looked down its length in one quick movement of her eyes and saw everything at once: how it was like doorway after doorway of a long hallway, down which she could move toward the one she had always waited for, whom she had always loved. The sky was purple and the rain was beginning to fall warm, as though from a dog's tongue. She thought of rain, and of fabric drawn over a face. She felt something of the old radiance; she felt something of Regina Strauss.

In her mind, the day became bright and sunny; the birch trees strained down from above and touched the colonnade with silver fingers. Margaret closed her eyes.

Around her—she sat on the tweed seat of the police car—Berlin spread in every direction, and it was nothing but Berlin.

Would it tax the imagination to propose that Margaret was both happy and sane? In her mind the day was bright, and music from far away drifted under her ears. The arrest was a sign, a long-awaited sign, of an orderly universe. The apocalypse had come, and the apocalypse had gone. At the police station she would tell them everything: that she had not meant to hurt anyone; that she had not foreseen the consequences of what she had done, nor the consequences of how she had lived; but she would also admit that she had been a part of something hideous. She would say that she had gone far outside the fold and lived there for a long and looping stretch of time. The significance would be in the telling, in the return to the ranks—to the brave asylum—of those who tell, without distortion, stories of their shame.

Margaret rode in the police car, but she was also floating wraithlike down the stone colonnade in the Kleistpark. A passion spun upon her mood; her eyes jumped over and past the rigorous face of things known. She lay back her head and pushed her cheek against the glass of the car's window. The green of the trees in the park beckoned, just before it disappeared from view—the overture of a new century.

ACKNOWLEDGMENTS

TK

ACKNOWLEDGMENTS

A NOTE ABOUT THE AUTHOR

Ida Hattemer-Higgins was born in Cincinnati, Ohio, and grew up in Boston, Massachusetts. She left the United States in 2001, living first in Tokyo, then in Bombay, later in Stockholm, and for the past seven years as a student of literature in Berlin, Germany, where she has also worked as a walking-tour guide and translator. She now divides her time between Berlin and Moscow. This is her first novel.